THE UNFORGIVING STONE

THE UNFORGIVING STONE

Map drawing by the author
Cover photograph by Adrianna Calvo
Typesetting and cover design by Formatting Experts

ISBN 978-1-8382227-0-3
Published by Volker-Larwin Publishing

THE UNFORGIVING STONE

A NICK FISHER NOVEL

ALEX DUNLEVY

NAMED CHARACTERS

iv

Magda . . . . Polish girl, drunk at Moondance
Manólis Alexandrákis . . . . Owner of Moondance beach bar, Síva
María . . . . B&B host in Anógia
Martin McConnell . . Retired dentist from Northern Ireland living in Néa Roúmata
Martina . . . . Attendant at The Temple of Akesó
Matthias . . . . German hippy at Síva
Michael Martin . . . . Sam's father
Michális Kasotákis (Mikey) . . Young Greek from Thessaloníki staying in Síva
Nick Fisher . . . . Former DCI in The Met now living in Saktoúria
Níkos . . . . Constable from Palaióchora
Panagiótis . . . . Provider of grapes for the kazáni in Saktoúria
Pandelís . . . . Constable from Chaniá
Paul Fisher . . . . Nick's late father
Peter Weston . . . . Joint-owner of Villa Erató and husband of Linda
Samantha Martin (Sam) . . . . Fiancée of Jason Buckingham
Sandy . . . . B&B host in Panórmos and grandmother of Chris
Sean . . . . Irishman on holiday in Síva with Siobhan
Sergeant Jansons . . . . Latvian policeman
Shirley Fisher . . . . Nick's mother
Siobhan . . . . Irish woman on holiday in Síva with Sean
Sofía . . . . Nick's housekeeper/cleaner
Spíros Tavouláris . . . . Greek partner of Kristīne and assistant at Moondance
Stávros . . . . Garage owner in Langós
Stefan . . . . Swedish dopehead at Moondance
Stélios . . . . Owner of Sorókos Café in Síva
Stephen Buckingham . . . . Jen's husband (after Nick)
Sylvie Deschamps . . . . French camper at Síva
Tásos . . . . Foolish constable from Paleóchora
Thanásis Konstantópoulos (Thaní) . . Investigations Sergeant with the Cretan police
Uldis . . . . Kristīne's former partner
Ulrich . . . . German hippy at Síva
Valádis . . . . Constable from Chaniá
Vangélis . . . . Constable from Chaniá
Vassily . . . . Russian guy with French girlfriend at Moondance
Xará . . . . Kósti's teenage daughter in Saktoúria
Yiórgos . . . . Fisherman/philosopher in Saktoúria
Zoë . . . . Nick and Jenny's former babysitter in England

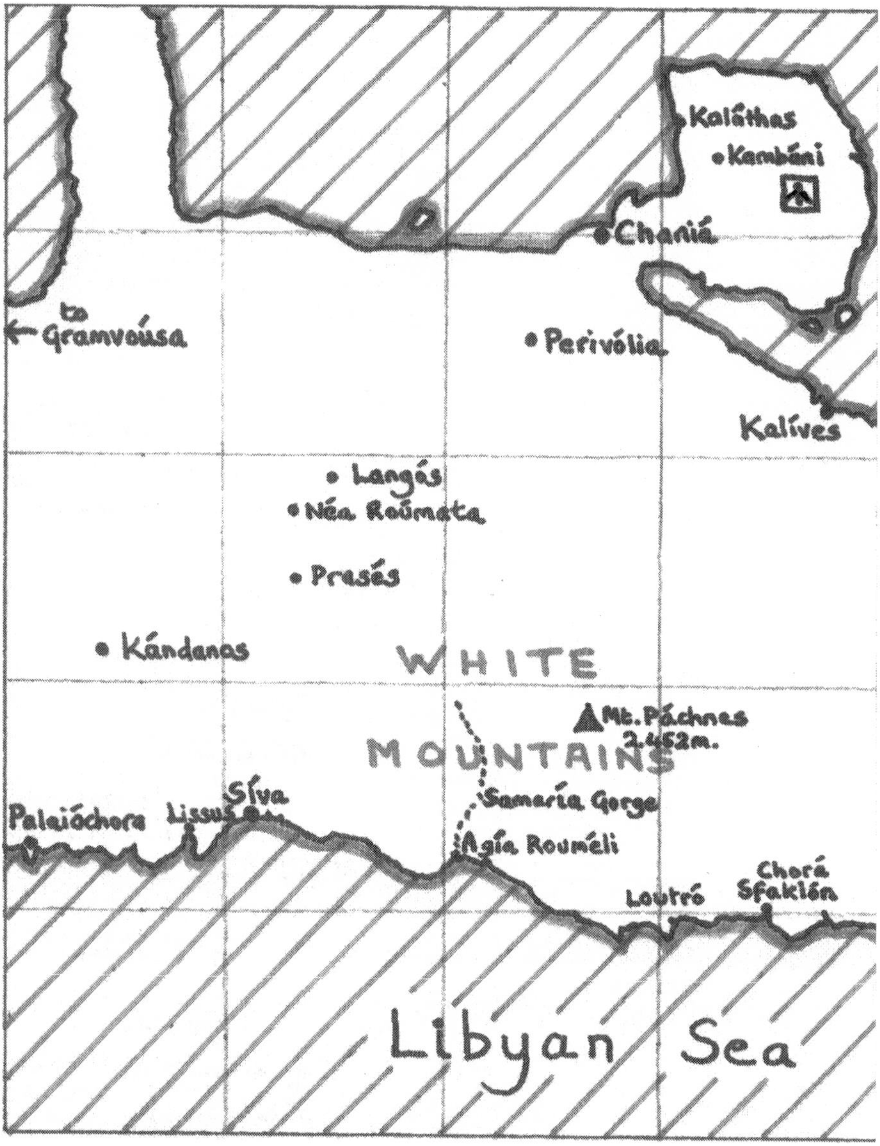
Kalâthas
Kambáni
Chaniá
to Gramvoúsa
Perivólia
Kalíves
Langós
Néa Roûmata
Presés
Kándanos
WHITE MOUNTAINS
Mt. Páchnes 2,452m.
Samaría Gorge
Palaióchora
Lissus
Síva
Agía Rouméli
Loutró
Chorá Sfakíon
Libyan Sea

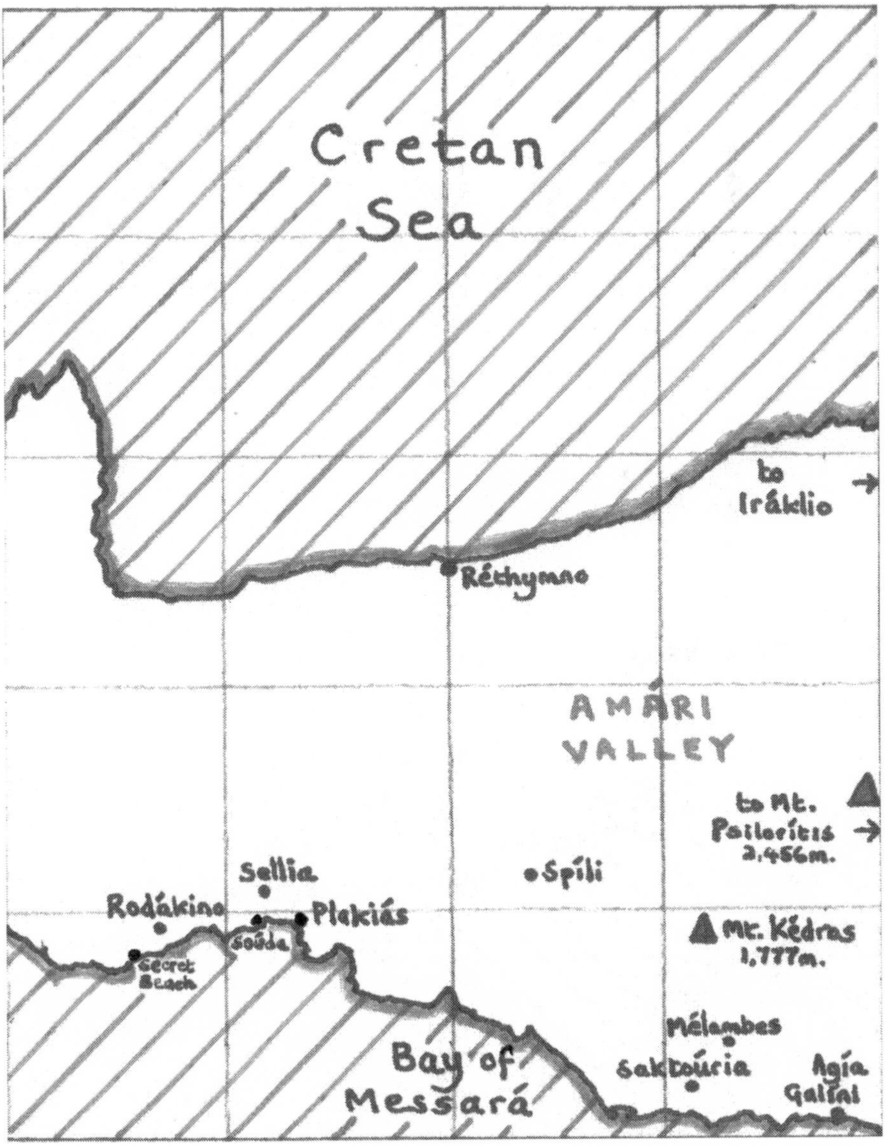
Cretan Sea
to Iráklio
Réthymno
AMÁRI VALLEY
to Mt. Psilorítis 2,456m.
Spíli
Mt. Kédras 1,777m.
Sellia
Rodákino
Plakiás
Soúda
Secret Beach
Mélambes
Saktoúria
Agía Galíni
Bay of Messará

CHAPTER 1
NICK IS WOKEN

Nick Fisher emerged from under the pillow and jettisoned the sweaty sheet. One by one his eyes unglued themselves, only to recoil from the blaze of light. He explored his mouth and, unsurprised, found an alien, leathery creature floundering in a sandpaper cave. The room no longer yawed, at least. He was thanking the gods for that when a pulse like a steam hammer kicked in at the back of his head.

He was in no condition, he concluded. Not yet. Instead, he lay simmering, brooding. What *dared* tear him from those healing arms of Morpheus?

Was it that relentless sun? Even now, in mid-September, it pierced the curtains like a halogen searchlight, blinding its way across his face.

Was it the village wildlife? The blasted cockerel was always a contender. But so were the damned dogs with their tiresome yapping. Sofía's donkey was a less likely culprit. True, its bray was monstrous, but it was seldom heard. Mostly it spent its time standing. Sad-eyed. Waiting. For work. Or food. Or maybe for love …

Was it simply one of the noisier Greeks, perhaps that lugubrious fishmonger? Nick could hear the man's van, graunching its way up the narrow streets, sinister growls of "Psária frésca" coming from the crackly, roof-mounted speakers, alternating with blasts of tragic lyra music. *Sounds like he wants us to bring out our dead rather than buy fresh fish,* he mused, as he drifted back to sleep.

Moments later, Nick's subconscious was struggling to fit the mobile phone's ringtone into his medieval plague nightmare. As a passing-bell, it failed to convince and Nick came awake in a rush and lunged for the bedside table, knocking over his water glass.

"Shit! Oh, *bugger* it! Hello?"

"Are you all right, Dad?"

"More or less."

1

"Only I've been ringing the landline for ages. Didn't you hear? You're not still in bed, are you?"

"Might be."

"It must be well after ten there. Are you ill?"

"I'm fine. Just a drop too much rakí at the kafenío, perhaps."

"A-ha."

He sat up, rubbed his face with a wet hand for a moment.

"So, Hun Bun. How are things with you?"

"Oh, the usual stuff. Working hard, going to the gym, trying to get on with my boring flatmates."

"Playing hard too, no doubt."

"Who, me? I'm in bed by eleven with a good book."

"Not *the* Good Book?"

"No. I wouldn't go *that* far."

"Seen your Mum at all?"

"I was there last night, for dinner. The Creep was there too, unfortunately, but Mum was looking good."

The Creep was her polite name for her stepfather. There were many less charitable. A trained psychotherapist, Stephen Buckingham was an intelligent, caring man in his late forties. He was always Stephen, never Steve, and had absolutely no sense of humour that Nick had been able to detect.

"That's why I called, Dad. While I was there, Mum told me that Jason's in Crete. Right now. I had no idea."

"He is? Well, well. He didn't tell me either. I'm just his Dad who lives here."

"He's there with Sam until the twenty-fifth and I know where they're staying."

Her words hung in the ether. Nick could see where this was going.

"Look, Lauren, I know you mean well ..."

"Dad – they're camping at Síva, right now. That's just along the coast from you, isn't it?"

Lauren always thought of Crete as a tiny island, he noticed.

"It would be two and a half hours' drive away, probably. You can't

2

just go straight across from here. There are mountains in the way; bloody big ones."

"Well, that's not so far, is it? What else have you got to do, Dad? And don't you think it's high time you two patched things up? You haven't got to know Sam at all and it's only six months till the wedding."

"I won't be invited to their wedding, Lauren. He's travelled seventeen hundred miles to *my* island and hasn't bothered to mention it. Doesn't that tell you something?"

"It tells me that you're both pig-headed, stubborn idiots."

"Don't be so damned cheeky. And your brother is not an idiot. He just hasn't forgiven me. And he has a point."

"So, *tell* him how sorry you are. At least *try* to heal the wounds, Dad. Or what? Are you going to let this go on for the rest of our lives? This might be a last chance to sort things out. They won't be in Síva for long."

"What's she like, Sam?"

"Don't you remember her?"

"We've never met."

"You have, actually. Just the once, at Andrew's wedding, way before they were engaged or anything."

Andrew was Jen's brother's boy and Nick remembered that awful wedding. Jenny was diagnosed just a few days before and she had decided they must keep it to themselves. It was no surprise he had forgotten about meeting Sam. He did remember drinking far too much cheap champagne and feeling crushed by the weight of their terrible secret.

"I don't remember," he said.

"Well, you must have seen pictures, Dad. She's a gorgeous, little blonde. You're bound to like her. I'm sure all men do."

"Miaow! But what's she like *as a person*, I meant?"

"I can't say I know her well. We only met a couple of times. Enough to see that Jason's besotted."

"And Sam?"

"I hope so, Dad."

3

"Look, it's a beautiful idea, Lauren, and it's sweet of you to call, but it isn't going to work. I think it's better if I stay here quietly. He knows where to find me."

"Oh, *Da*-ad …"

"I'm sorry, darling, but Jason will let me know if and when he wants to work things out between us."

"You'd let him marry someone you've barely met?"

"He's a sensible lad. I'm sure he's chosen well."

"Oh, for God's sake, Dad …"

"I need to go now, Lauren. My housekeeper's here."

There were sounds of heavy banging on the front door, which was then opened. Nick placed the phone on a dry part of the bedside table and stared at it for a long moment.

"Yeiá sou, Níko. Kalá eísai?"

It was the usual conversational shriek from Sofía, and right away she started clattering around the kitchen, talking to herself and admonishing him with squeals of Greek for the mess in which he lived. Nick stood up too quickly and his head swam but he managed to grasp the doorknob. After a quick shower, he threw on shorts and a tee-shirt and made his way downstairs. Sofía was attacking the wine-stained table-top with vigour.

"I bring froúta," she said, jerking her head towards the sideboard and grinning. Nick saw grapes, plums and peaches in a cracked, yellow bowl. "For me."

"*From* you, you mean, from your garden? How kind you are, Sofía. Will you have some coffee?"

She pulled a face. "Ness? Óchi!"

"Ah yes, you prefer that Greek sludge of yours. Sorry. Signómi!"

Sofía shot him a fierce, wide-eyed look before the infectious smile re-surfaced. Nick chuckled and took his mug of strong, filter coffee out on to the terrace with a bowl of sheep's yoghurt, then came back for the fruit.

"These peaches look great," he said, holding one up and smiling. "Thank you. Efcharistó polí." She beamed as she always did when he attempted some Greek.

4

It was already quite hot, the sky cloudless. The sleepy, turquoise sea darkened about fifty metres off the beach. In the tiny harbour, men were hosing down brightly coloured fishing boats. Away to the west, the shingle beach was backed by cliffs and, in the far distance, the White Mountains glowed dusty pink in the morning sun.

*

The water was always refreshing here but today it felt like holy water. Miraculous. An instant hangover cure. Nick ducked his head under and struck out with a vigorous crawl until he was two hundred metres out. Then it was breaststroke, parallel to the beach and looking down through water so deep and clear that he had to shrug off a touch of vertigo. Sea bass flashed silver from one of the larger rocks. He rolled onto his back and felt the healing warmth of the sun. His head was clear now, eyes washed bright.

As he made his way back to the shore, he spotted a red and yellow bobble hat capping a laughing, bearded face.

"Yeiá sou, Óchi Psári. Ti káneis?" Yiórgos called.

Nick waved. *Óchi Psári* or *No Fish* was a standing joke now. On Nick's first fishing trip, he caught nothing. Zilch. He was persuaded that it was just bad luck. Maybe the fish were not biting that day. Or the bait was wrong. He went out again, just a few days later, determined to do better. But again, he caught nothing at all, though the others landed almost twenty fish between them.

In the bar that night they teased him: "Nick *Fisher*? You no fisher-man, Níko. You No Fish!" Then they started calling him Óchi Psári, falling about laughing, holding their sides. And then, seeing his sad clown face, laughing louder still, slapping and kissing him exuberantly on both cheeks. After that, Nick excused himself from fishing trips, but the name stuck.

He stood in the shallows, took a few tentative steps onto the shingle beach.

"Phewee, that was wonderful," he said, grabbing the towel. Then he grasped the gnarled, bear paw that Yiórgos proffered.

5

"Good to see you, Yiórgo. How were the fish today?"

"Lucky."

"Lucky?"

"Yes, I don't find them."

"Ah. That's tough for you, then."

"It happens sometimes, Níko. Don't worry. Tomorrow they will be back, and they will be a little more big."

"And they need to be, don't they, if we're honest?"

Yiórgos gave him a glum stare, then raised his eyebrows and tilted his head by way of confirmation. Catches were smaller now; the Libyan Sea almost fished out.

A strengthening breeze swept a chilly gust down the mountain.

"What say I nip home to change and then buy you a beer at Kostís's?"

The smile lit up his bearded face like the sun escaping from a cloud.

"What say … yes, my friend!"

The wind was ruffling the surface of the sea. Some cloud had gathered around the summit of Mount Kédros, but there should be plenty of good weather yet. Nick jumped into his old US Army Jeep. There were dents and scrapes on the dusty, olive paintwork, the seat leather was torn and only the frame of the hood remained, but Nick would have nothing else for these rock-strewn roads and precipitous tracks. The engine roared into life, the gears crunched, and he sped up the steep and pitted road, tooting a Greek farewell and leaving a dust cloud to swirl in the wind.

*

Later, in the kafenío, they had the place to themselves apart from an older couple, lunching on the terrace.

"Oríste!" Kóstas brought two bottles of the local brew, Fix, a bowl of peanuts and some iced coffee for himself. He lit a cigarette.

"It's okay. They are from Oslo," he said in a sotto voce growl. Nick understood; they were not Germans. Even now, the older villagers bore wartime wounds that refused to heal.

"So, Níko, you have fur of dog? You feel better today?"

"That would be *hair* of *the* dog," corrected Nick.

"That depends how many you have!" teased Yiórgos.

"Haha. As it happens, I do feel surprisingly good, thanks. A nice breakfast, a revitalising swim and I'm ready for anything."

"You bit sad last night, on your own?" asked Kóstas, in his avuncular voice.

"Not really, Kostí. And how could I be when I have all this," he extended his arms to encompass the sea and the mountains, "and my wonderful, Cretan friends?" He inclined his head, raised his glass and grinned: "Yeiá mas!"

"Yeiá mas," they chorused in return.

Later, over the second beer, he told them about the call from Lauren and immediately regretted it.

"You *must* go, Níko!"

"Of course, you must. What are you waiting for, Níko? This is your boy. Family. Flesh and blood. You must go, make everything okay. And then you will go to the grand wedding."

"If only it were that simple, Kostí."

"With family it *is* simple, Níko. You meet. You fight. Maybe you cry a little. But then you all have big hugs because deep down you love each other, no? And then, life not so bad. Believe me. I know this. You will see."

CHAPTER 2
SÍVA

Second Lieutenant Leonídas Christodoulákis was with the Chaniá Prefecture which polices the whole of Western Crete. He received the call just as he sat down to Sunday breakfast with his wife.

"Good news, Leo. You get a nice trip to the seaside today."

Leo pulled a wry face and rolled his eyes. He saw his wife's mouth tighten. Then he reached for a cigarette.

"That sounds ominous, Captain."

"I need you to get down to Síva. A body has been found on the beach. Young, female, a tourist I should think. A couple of jokers from the Palaióchora station are securing the scene, supposedly. I need you to take charge of the investigation into her death. Make sure everything's done right, find out what the hell happened. Okay?"

"All right boss. I'll take Thaní with me, if that's okay? I'll check in later when I have some news."

He called Investigations Sergeant Thanásis Konstantópoulos at home.

"Hey, Thaní. You're a guy that needs overtime, right? Good news, then. I need you right now for two or three days, I should think."

"Okay, boss. Glad to escape, to be honest. Ioánna is teething. We didn't get much sleep."

"So, meet me at Giánni's place in Perivólia. Soon as you can. We can drive down together. You know how I love to save money for the Prefecture. I'll brief you on the way."

Thaní knew this meant a hair-raising drive, overtaking on blind bends in a car filled with Leo's cigarette smoke, but that came with the territory.

"I can be there in twenty-five minutes. Where are we going, boss?"

"Make it twenty. We have a body – in Síva."

8

*

Everything seemed normal. Tourists were breakfasting on piles of fruit and yoghurt at the tavernas behind the beach. Campers were already swimming and sunbathing. It was a beautiful, clear day, already hot at ten forty-five with a good, strong breeze from the sea. Thaní hoped it would blow the smoke out of his clothes.

They saw that thirty or forty people were gathered by rocks at the end of the beach. It took Leo and Thaní almost ten minutes to get there, stomping through the shingle, working their way around sunbathers. Some reached for clothing at the sight of them, but Leo was not interested in the naked or semi-naked bodies. At the end of the beach, a constable explained that they would have to wade round to the second part of the beach where the body lay.

"I'm sorry, sir. There's no other way."

"Don't you have a boat with you, for God's sake?"

"No, we drove here; it's quicker, sir."

"What a bloody circus," cursed Leo, as he and Thaní started to take off their boots. At the other side, on the second beach, they unrolled their sodden trousers and cursed again as the shingle hurt their bare feet.

"Look at these idiots, Thaní!" grumbled Leo, gesturing at the constables from Palaióchora. "They've cordoned off only *part* of the beach, they've let half the crowd on to this end and they haven't even covered the body. It's pathetic."

As they came closer, they could hear the uniformed constables remonstrating with the crowd. Some seemed shocked and subdued at seeing the body, others angry at being unable to use the beach. Judging from the idiotic questions, still more seemed alarmed or confused. This was just the sort of chaos Leo expected. He nodded to the constables, stood in front of the yellow tape, and faced the crowd. He clapped his hands three times and then spoke in English:

"All right, everyone. I am Christodoulákis, police lieutenant from Chaniá. As you can see, we have a death to investigate. We have no

9

choice but to close this part of the beach for a forensic investigation.

"You must understand that. For today at least, you need to find somewhere else to enjoy. It's a big beach; there are many nice places.

"Now, if it was you who found the body or if you think you knew this girl, please stay behind as Sergeant Konstantópoulos here would like to talk to you. Otherwise, please. Let's go. There is nothing more to see here."

He turned to the young constables.

"Right, I need you to move this tape forward twenty-five metres and extend it over the water, out to that big rock. I don't want people swimming or wading round to this part of the beach at all. Those that are here already, move them out.

"And you? – go find a large tent to put around the body. I don't want this poor girl to be part of the tourist entertainment. Now let's get moving."

Leo clapped his hands again, the crowd started to disperse, and the constables set about their business. Just three people stayed behind.

"Which of you found the body?" asked Thaní and two people said, "We did," in unison.

"Okay, and you?" He turned to the third person.

"I think I met her yesterday. If it *is* her, then I was at the same place until maybe two in the morning."

"You will wait, please."

Leo saw that Thaní could handle the questioning alone, so he slipped on his forensic gloves and turned his attention to the body.

The girl was lying face-down on the shingle, wearing patterned, red bikini bottoms. The water lapped the lower half of her body. Her blonde hair was matted and bedraggled. Her left arm was close by her side, awkward-looking, the hand underwater and palm-up, while her right arm was thrown forward, the hand palm-down on the shingle as if she had made one last, desperate grab for the shore. There was a tattoo of a pale blue butterfly above her right shoulder-blade. The left foot looked odd, somehow, so he lifted it clear of the water and saw that it was bruised and lacerated, the leg already stiffened by rigor mortis. There was also a wound to the back of her head, he noticed. The base of the hairline made it difficult to see but there was some coagulated blood in the hair, and he could feel damage consistent with quite a severe injury.

Leo stood up and stretched. She would have been a young girl, perhaps seventeen to twenty years old. He stripped off the gloves and lit a cigarette, sucking the acrid smoke deep into his lungs as if in self-mortification. His own daughter would have been a similar age, had she lived.

What a terrible bloody waste, he thought bitterly.

"Sir?"

Thaní was calling him over.

"I have taken details of the Swiss couple who found the body, boss. They were out for an early swim at around eight fifteen. Something didn't look right, her lying like that, half in the water, so they thought they'd better check. Knew not to move anything, touch anything. One of them stayed with the body while the other went back to their tent and called us."

"They did well. Must have been a shock for them."

"Yes, sir. They'd never seen a body before. They're staying in Síva for several more days, so I've let them go, for now."

"And this young man?"

"I am Michális, but they call me Mikey."

"You are Greek?"

"Yes. I am from Thessaloníki, but I have been here all summer."

"And you knew this girl?"

"Not really. But I'm wondering if it's the girl from the beach bar."

"Go on."

"I was there late last night. Moondance, it's called. There was this English girl with long blonde hair, attractive. She was a little drunk, I think."

"And you recognise her?"

"The hair is the same. She's young – I would say late teens or early twenties. I was dancing near her and I remember seeing a tattoo."

11

"A tattoo where?"

"At the top of her back, on the right. Was it a little bird?"

"What colour bird, Mikey?"

"Er … blue. Definitely blue. Pale, not dark."

"Could it have been a butterfly?"

"It could … yeah, I think that's right. Sorry."

"That's okay. You're being helpful. Tell me, why did you think she was drunk?"

"She was drinking rakí in shots, getting loud, flirty. Then she had a row with her boyfriend. He looked really pissed off with her. I think she was embarrassing him."

"When did you last see her?"

"I was there when it closed, around two. I didn't see the boyfriend then, but she went off up the beach with the German guys and some other woman."

"Can you give us any more on these people and where they were going?"

"The Germans have been here a couple of weeks. There are three guys, usually together. One of them might be called Rick? Cool, quiet guys. The girl is very friendly. I don't know her name, but she speaks English to them, not German."

"Is she English too, then?"

Michális shrugged.

"And where do you think they were going?"

"They set off up the beach, towards where we are now. That's all I know."

"And the dead girl, do you know her name?"

"Sorry, no."

Leo took Thaní aside and asked him to go through things again with Michális, take a formal statement from him. He asked him to try and get more detail on the people, especially the boyfriend, and whoever else was at the beach bar that night. After that, Leo spent a couple of minutes berating the constables for their sorry efforts and ordering them to make a thorough search of the beach. Then he decided it was time to call in.

"Captain? Christodoulákis here."

He ran through what he had discovered, keeping it short.

"So, where do we go from here, Leo?"

"Well, sir, in all likelihood it's a simple drowning, but ..."

"Do you know Síva, Leo? On a balmy, moonlit night in September, I think it's hard to drown there."

"Perhaps, sir, but this girl was drinking a lot earlier, may have taken something else as well, I suspect. It was late, and she'd have been tired. Perhaps the row with the boyfriend upset her?

"And I've checked the local forecast; the wind was strengthening during the early part of the night, waves cresting. All these things could have a bearing. If her judgment were affected, she could have taken on too much and found herself in difficulties."

"I hear you, Leo, but I'm sensing that you don't buy that."

"I just don't know at this stage, sir. I'd like to be reassured that the injuries to her body and the condition of her lungs are consistent with drowning and I'd like to talk to the boyfriend. Until then I reserve judgment."

"All right, Leo. That sounds sensible. I'll get the Medical Examiner down to you as soon as I can, and I'll call the Forensic Science Division. It may not be a crime scene, as such, but the FSD may want to send someone from Athína, nevertheless. You need to focus on finding out who the victim was and who the boyfriend is – and if he's still there."

"Yes, of course, sir. I'd appreciate some more troops here. There are a lot of people and I'm going to need foot soldiers to go around with photos and questions before all the tourists and hippies move on. It's that or shut the place down for several days and keep everyone here."

"No, Leo. You can't do that. Media attention that could damage tourism is the last thing we need. God knows they're having a tough enough time already. I can let you have two of our lads for two or three days and I'll arrange for you to keep the constables from Palaióchora for the time being."

It wasn't enough, but Leo knew it was all he was going to get.

"Thank you, Captain. As soon as possible, please."

"They'll be with you in three hours. I'll come back to you on the ME."

Leo was going to thank him again, but the line was dead.

CHAPTER 3
FROM HOPE TO DREAD

By the time he turned south, through the orange groves, Nick was feeling a surge of optimism. The sight of the White Mountains always lifted his spirits, put things in perspective. And, as he drove, he was remembering his early days as a father; the way Jason used to cling to his leg, stare up at him in awe. The times when he carried Jason on his shoulders while little Lauren swung, giggling from their hands. When Jen was well and happy and the future was full of promise.

Jason grew into a geeky, solitary boy. He would be found playing computer games in his bedroom rather than plastered in mud on a rugby pitch or having wild adventures in the woods. And Nick found that hard to accept, at first. This was not the son he had expected. His lack of physicality was a disappointment. But Nick made an effort, got to know the boy, and grew to appreciate his quiet intelligence and sensitivity. They were hugely different animals but there was a calmness about Jason that signalled inner strength, resilience. Nick liked that.

They might have become good friends later. Nick could have taken him for a beer or a round of golf like other Dads. If his golf were not so bloody hopeless, that is. And if they had not fallen out quite so badly. *And, if my grandmother had wheels, she would be a bicycle*, he chuckled to himself, recalling the barmy old saw from the north-east that Jen used sometimes. In his heart, Nick knew that easy camaraderie was not going to happen now, but surely there was enough from the past to rebuild some kind of relationship? Surely, they could find some shreds of love, some mutual respect? Maybe this girl of his would be the key to unlocking that …

*

Nick did not know Síva well, but he had stayed there briefly several years before. The camping was behind the beach, he remembered, to the east of the small town. He pottered down the main street, turned left

15

in front of the beach, then passed a couple of tavernas and guest houses and parked on a corner, facing east. A wide, shingle beach stretched out before him, leading to a rocky outcrop some six hundred metres away. There were no facilities other than basic beach showers about fifty metres to his right. Swimmers and sunbathers were scattered in small groups along a strip, five to twenty metres back from the sea, right the way down the beach but, at the far end, it looked more crowded. A dried-up riverbed split the beach and led back to a gathering of fifty or sixty tents and several dusty camper vans, some of which looked like they had been there for months or were perhaps abandoned. Washing lines with fluttering beachwear stretched between the vehicles and the tamarisk trees. White ash blew from barbecue grills. To the north, the land climbed steadily back to the barren mountains.

He had made good time. It was eleven forty. At a café overlooking the beach, he ordered coffee and a spanakópita, filo pastry baked in a coil packed with buttery spinach and salty feta cheese. After that, he felt good. He warmed to the atmosphere of the place. It seemed very international, very relaxed. There was a hippy feel to it. People looked interested in each other, intelligent and kind. Oddly, a French group at a nearby table seemed agitated and tearful, though. They were talking rapidly and kept glancing over at the far part of the beach. He had no idea why.

Nick tried not to get his hopes up. At best this would be an ice-breaker. Three years was a long time in the life of a twenty-one-year-old. He would find the tent, ask them to join him for a relaxed lunch and take it from there. He could always book a room locally for a day or two if things went well and they wanted him to stay on.

*

It took only a few minutes to find the tent. The dull, tan colouring was distinctive, and it looked old-fashioned against the Day-Glo fabrics of its more modern neighbours. But it was a good, sound tent, Nick remembered. In the family for well over twenty years. He hesitated for a moment but then he spotted the tiny Union Flag that Jen had sewn on all those years ago, the first time they went camping abroad.

The flap was loose, and Nick sensed right away that they were not there. He called out:

"Hello-oh. Anyone home? … Jason? Jason, are you in there?"

Nothing. He looked around at the nearby tents. The neighbouring tent was all zipped up, like they were gone for the day. And he could not see anyone close enough to be sure they would know Jason and Sam. He lifted the flap and swung himself inside.

His first impression, when his eyes adjusted to the shade, was that there was not much there. Apart from a Lilo and a sleeping bag with a pillow, there was just the one backpack, a separate wash bag and a large, black plastic bag. He started with that but found it was just dirty clothes, predominantly those of a young woman. The washbag seemed to be exclusively female. There was nothing a man could shave with, though Jason might have grown a beard, he supposed.

As he turned his attention to the backpack, he heard someone close by, speaking Greek. He had better be quick. He saw a purse and a soft toy that might have been an elephant but went straight for the red passport. A pretty, blonde girl stared out from the photograph and he read the name Martin and, underneath, Samantha Claire. He dropped it like a hot coal, back into the pack, and hurried out of the tent.

A couple of guys were talking, about fifteen metres away, but they did not seem to notice him. The taller guy was not dressed for the beach, though. *He could be a cop in plain clothes*, Nick thought, so he took a wide berth, circling round to the front of the campsite, nearest the town. Two young men were standing by a hammock, talking in accented English. He decided to take a flier.

"Hey, guys, may I speak English with you?"

"Sure. I am Austrian and he is from Spain, so we are speaking English already."

"What's that cop looking for, do you know – is it drugs?"

"No man, relax. It's not a bust."

"What then?"

"He's trying to identify the chick that drowned this morning."

17

Nick felt the sudden coldness of dread, clutching his heart.

"The what?"

"Sorry, man. Didn't you know? It's all over town."

"I just arrived. What chick?"

"The cop thinks she's English. Young, blonde hair, quite pretty, he said."

"Did he have a picture?"

"He didn't show us one."

"And he doesn't know who she is?"

"He says not. He's asking around. Soon he'll find someone who recognises her from the description, I guess. It's a small community here."

"I'm sure he will. God, what a terrible thing."

"It's awful man. The whole town is shaken up. People are asking how it can have happened. I don't think anyone ever drowned here, at least not in summer."

"Do you know where it happened?"

The Spanish guy pointed east, to the farthest part of the beach.

"There's another beach beyond those rocks. The body's there, if they haven't taken it away."

"You saw the body?"

"A lot of us went to see when the news broke, around nine, nine thirty. She was just lying there. They hadn't covered her up or anything. But it's all cordoned off now."

"What did you see?"

"She was face-down, half-naked. Her legs were in the water. There was blood in her hair, I think."

"How old was she, would you say?"

"She was young, man. Real young. I'd guess twenty, tops."

"Are there many English girls here?"

"There are a few but they tend to be older. Most of the younger girls here are students from Greece, Italy, Germany, Scandinavia."

Nick thanked them and moved away. His heart was pounding now. The scant description sounded like Sam. *Please God, let it not be. And where the hell was Jason? Why was none of his stuff in their tent?*

18

*

Nick hurried across the beach from the campsite to the rocks. He joined a small crowd pressed up against the tape, but there was nothing to see.

"It's on the other beach, around the rocks, mate," someone told him.

The tape stretched right across the water to a massive rock, where it was tethered. Nick stripped off and waded in. He swam out twenty-five metres and from there he could see most of the other, smaller beach. There was an orange tent at the water's edge. Presumably, the body was in there. He saw two uniformed policemen and one in plain clothes. As he watched, the uniforms seemed to be scouring the beach while the other guy was talking on his mobile phone and striding around, head down, the hand with the cigarette gesticulating between drags.

He thought about breaking the cordon and talking to this guy. If the body was Sam's, then Nick was her future father-in-law. He could demand to be told what they knew and, with his background, maybe they would tell him, even let him see her. Maybe. Then, if he recognised the body from that passport photograph, he could take them straight to the tent – and the passport. Maybe. On the other hand, they could ask him things about Sam that he would be unable to answer, having barely met the girl. They might not believe him. Or they would want to know why he was there and where his son was. His gut told him that speaking to them at this stage would surrender any small advantage he might have and could lead to trouble.

Instead, he went back to the beach crowd. He listened intently but the conversations were in languages he did not understand. He found a few who spoke English, but they knew no more than him. No-one could put a name to the body.

It was time to change tack. He was dry already, so he dressed quickly and headed back to the town. As he walked, he scanned the photos on his phone until he found one Jen had sent last year. No beard then, but it was a good likeness of Jason. He decided to work on the dreadful assumption that the body *was* Sam's and that his son might be unaware of what had happened or worse, somehow involved. Either way, he would need help. And, soon after the police found someone who could identify the body, they would learn that Sam was engaged to be married and they would start searching for the fiancé. It did not sound good. Nick needed to find Jason first.

CHAPTER 4

THE MEDICAL EXAMINER

The Medical Examiner arrived at three thirty in the afternoon. A woman in her early fifties with dyed black hair scraped back into a tight bun, she looked cold and haughty. Her face, once beautiful, had the sunken, rheumy eyes and hollow cheeks of a heavy smoker. This was confirmed by her unnaturally low, gravelly voice:

"So, we meet again, Kýrie Christodouláki."

"Yes. Hello, Doctor Pánagou."

"What delights do you have for me today?" she smirked, grimly.

Leo explained the finding of the body and his perfunctory examination as they made their way to the front of the beach.

"So, I will take a look here, but the body will have to come back to Chaniá for a full post-mortem if there's any possibility that drowning was not the cause of death."

"I understand that, Doctor."

"And apparently, I am to do the crime scene work as well, in case it was a crime. Athína has no-one to spare, they tell me. So, I will take all the photographs and measurements and bag up any evidence I can find, in and around the body."

"I have constables searching the area. I'll let you have anything they turn up."

Leo helped her into the rigid inflatable boat that the police had commandeered, then the constable gunned the twin, sixty-five-horsepower outboards for the six hundred metre trip down the beach and around the big rock, as the area to the left of it was now cordoned off. Leo helped the doctor out of the boat, getting wet feet again as he did so. They entered the orange tent that was now surrounding the body.

"My God, it's hot in here. What idiot put a tent around her? Now I must work quickly before putrefaction sets in."

"Sorry, Doctor. That was my idea. The tourists were gawping. It was all rather unseemly."

"Dead bodies *are* unseemly. People need to see this. Death is part of life, no?"

"Of course, but not a welcome part. Especially if you're on holiday with your family."

She grunted, which Leo took as despair at the pointless niceties of an overly protective world.

"So, who is she?"

"We don't know, yet. But she's thought to be an English girl. And we know that she was alive around three am when she went for a swim on her own, apparently. We're looking for people who can help us identify her."

"All right, Lieutenant. You can leave me to my work now – and tie that flap back please, before I pass out."

Leo was glad to escape into the sea breeze. He took the opportunity to call Thaní.

"Any developments?"

"Yes, boss. I hooked up with the constables from Chaniá and they're looking for people that recognise the dead girl from her description. A photograph would be a great help."

"We have to wait until the ME has finished."

"Okay. I took the statement from Mikey – Michális Kasotákis – but he didn't add anything useful."

"Nothing more on the boyfriend?"

"Not from him, no, but I was able to find the three Germans. I don't know which one Mikey thought was Rick. There's an Ulrich and an Erik so it's one of them, I suppose. And, through them, I found the third one, Matthias. He calls himself Matt and he's with a girl called Andie. She's the one Mikey saw them with at the beach bar."

"So, this is all of the group that left the beach bar with the dead girl?"

"It is, sir."

"Good work, Sergeant."

"Thank you, sir. I'll interview them now and let you know what I find."

22

*

Thaní decided to interview them separately to double-check their stories. He started with the girl:

"Okay. Your full name, please."

"I'm Andie Fessler. Andrea."

"Andrea Fessler. German?"

"Nope. I'm from the US of A."

"You are what?"

"American?"

"And you knew the dead girl?"

"Barely. We met last night."

"How would you describe her?"

"Cute, petite, tipsy. I remember blonde hair and red bikini bottoms. She was wearing a skimpy top, kinda fuchsia-coloured and a pareo."

"What?"

"A pink top and a wrap." She tugged at her top and then mimed wrapping her body to get the message home.

"We will search for these. Do you remember a tattoo as well?"

"You know what? I think I do – was it a butterfly?"

"Where?"

"At the top of her back somewhere?"

"You are an observant woman, Ms Fessler. Do you know her name and nationality by any chance?"

"We called her Sam. I guess that was short for Samantha. I'm sure she was English."

"And you met how?"

"There were five of us dancing together at the beach bar: her, me and the German guys over there. Then the bar closed at two and we all went for a swim. She wanted to swim around the big rock which I thought was crazy. It was dark, it was late, and we'd all had a lot to drink. It wasn't a great idea. And anyway, by the time she came back, we were ready to leave. Erik and I just wanted to get it on."

"Get what on?"

"You know. Get *it* on. Get together. Have sex."

"I see. And you said, *came back*. Where had she been?"

"Oh yeah. There was this boyfriend. Or they might have been engaged. Anyway, she was trying to ditch the guy. He pulled her off the dance floor earlier and then he turned up while we were swimming and they argued some more. They fought briefly. In the end, he went off."

"They fought?"

"They sure did. It was hard to see, but she slapped him hard and then started pummelling his chest. He threw her down. There was a lot of shouting and swearing."

"Did you get his name?"

"Never heard it."

"Was he English, too?"

"Can't say for sure."

"And why did you think they might have been engaged?"

"I can't be certain, but I saw her massaging her ring finger when she came back, like she was trying to revive the skin, you know?"

"And did you see a ring there earlier?"

"Maybe. I'm not sure. Sorry."

"So, going back to the swim, you didn't want to do it?"

"Oh, *I* wasn't gonna do it anyway. No, we just made our excuses and left her to it. I think we were all relieved."

"You left her alone, at three in the morning, so you could *get it on* with Erik."

"I guess it doesn't sound good, does it, but she was being a real pain in the butt by then, quite abusive."

Thaní gave her a steady, impassive stare.

*

At four forty pm, Thaní called Leo. He went through the detail of the interview with Andie and then added:

"I've also spoken to the three Germans, as a group. They were planning to leave today but I've required them to stay in town for the moment. They confirm Andie's story but with a little more colour."

"Go on."

"The break-up with the boyfriend was described as vicious and unpleasant at the end. They were twenty or thirty metres away, but they're all certain there was physical contact and they all heard her slap him, but they couldn't agree on whether he then pushed her to the ground or hit her in the face. Two of them said the boy seemed badly shocked when he eventually left."

"It was dark, wasn't it? How would they know?"

"Just from tone of voice and body shape, they said."

"Body shape? What the hell does that mean?"

"One of them – Matt I think it was – said he looked defeated, slumped, kind of, as he walked away."

"It's three am and he's making judgments about the body shape of someone he doesn't know – in silhouette? I don't think so, Thani. That's what we call a creative witness. A decent attorney would tear him to shreds."

"Yes, boss."

"What else?"

"They all thought she was being unpleasant and aggressive and put it down to too much alcohol, although none of them knew her before that evening."

"Drugs?"

"They were all cagey about that, but when I said we weren't interested in drug offences, they did admit that marijuana and ecstasy were readily available among the beach bar crowd. They wouldn't be surprised if she took something."

"I guess the post-mortem will tell us. Did you speak to the bar owner?"

"Manólis Alexandrákis, yes. He remembers that she was quite drunk and flirtatious. 'She was a typical English girl,' he said. 'They come to my bar dressed like whores, they parade themselves in front of the men, they drink till they throw up. She was like all the rest.'"

"Not impressed, then."

"Hardly, but I guess he sees the worst of them."

"Anything more on the late-night swim?"

"They walked up to the end of the beach so they could swim naked, apparently, but our girl kept her bikini bottoms on."

"A modest whore, then."

"She told Andie it was her period."

"And this thing about swimming around the rock?"

"Yes. Ulrich said she seemed determined to do it and he feels bad now that he didn't stay with her. Blames himself. He thought it was foolhardy after the evening's excesses, but she seemed like quite a strong swimmer and it's not that big a deal."

"No, it's not. I'm looking at it right now. Might be five hundred metres, perhaps a little more."

"But at night, after drink, maybe drugs?"

"Indeed. Maybe she threw up as she swam, and choked? Okay, Thaní. Excellent work. The ME is still here. For your boys' search, we'll have to use a photo of the dead girl's face, in the absence of anything else. I'll email you that and you can get some prints made at the hotel.

"Get the boys asking around the tavernas, bars, campsite and rent rooms places. Find out who she was, where she stayed. There must be a passport somewhere in this town.

"Also, try to get a handle on the boyfriend. What does he look like, what's his name, where's he from and is he still here in Síva? You know the drill. And we need to move fast. The population of this town is always on the move. We already lost a ferry load."

"Shouldn't we just close the place down, boss?"

"For a drowning? I think that'd be an overreaction, don't you? Anyway, let's see how you and the boys get on this evening. You have several hours. Get organised. I'll have these lads come and join you as soon as they're done here."

"Sir."

Leo lit a cigarette and stared out at the rock. The sea looked so calm and inviting. Although the breeze was quite strong, the sea was almost unruffled. Further along the beach, people were in the water swimming, snorkelling, or floating on Lilos. There were even a couple of pedaloes. He tried to picture it at night, transformed into a sinister place of danger and death, where a supposedly good swimmer could be dashed against a rock or choke on her vomit. He was not convinced. It would have been a moonlit night, too. *Either this girl had been very foolish or very unlucky, or there was more to this than met the eye,* he mused.

Pánagou came out of the tent and stretched.

"Let me have one of those, please," she said, nodding at his cigarette. "I'm giving up, so I don't have any with me."

She lit the cigarette and inhaled deeply, then sent a long plume of smoke up into the breeze.

"Thank you. So, there is not much I can tell you yet. She was young, perhaps eighteen to twenty-two years old. She's been dead ten, maybe fifteen hours, so the time of death was between three and seven am, since you said she was alive at three. I'll need to confirm that in the laboratory.

"Her body is unmarked apart from the tattoo, of course, some indentations to the face and two recent impacts. The left foot is cut and bruised, maybe from contact with a sharp rock, and there is an injury to the base of the skull, just above the hairline. This could also have been caused by a rock, but the impact is rounder, not jagged. This would have been a powerful impact."

"I noticed that the rocks nearer the beach are different, more rounded."

"Yes, this is so."

"But?"

"Let's think about what happened, Lieutenant. She is either alive and swimming into the shore or she's already dead and being washed in. Maybe she choked or had a heart attack or something. I don't think so, but I could be wrong. Okay?"

"Yes. Go on."

"If she is alive, she can resist the force of the waves, to some extent. It's hard to imagine her hitting a rock hard enough to cause this impact. But even more difficult is *where* the impact is. You'd think she'd have hit the top of her head, not the base of the skull."

"Supposing she was out of control in the water?"

"So close to the shore? Why? There'd have to be a freak wave or something."

"And if she were dead already?"

"Then one could imagine a harder impact, for sure, but the position of the wound is still problematic. Also, there is blood coagulated around the wound and in the hair. This suggests that the injury was *not* post-mortem."

"So, what are you saying, Doctor?"

She ground her cigarette-end into the shingle and looked up.

"You are the detective, Christodouláki, not me. I will say that I must take the body back to the laboratory before I can make my report and that these indications may change. What I will say now is that the head injury *seems* to be inconsistent with colliding with a rock whilst swimming."

"Do you think *that* was the impact that killed her?"

"Very likely yes, unless I'm wrong and she was dead already."

"So, someone could have hit her with a rock?"

"A rounded rock or some other blunt instrument, yes. It cannot be ruled out."

"So, this is a murder inquiry."

"It may become so, Lieutenant. Now I will organise the removal of the body to Chaniá and I will let you have my full report as soon as possible."

"When might that be, Doctor?"

"It will be as soon as possible, as I said. I have a life, unlike this poor girl, but I will do my best for you."

"Thank you, Doctor Pánagou."

"You are welcome."

Leo went back into the tent and used his phone to photograph the dead girl's mottled but oddly beatific face and, as an afterthought, the blue butterfly tattoo, and then emailed them to Thaní. When he came out, the ME was berating someone on her mobile phone:

"I don't give a damn. Get him here now! The sooner he gets here, the sooner he can get back to the damned wedding."

28

Leo raised an eyebrow as she ended the call:

"Not *his* wedding, I hope?"

"I didn't ask."

CHAPTER 5
WHERE'S MY SON?

Nick knew the dead girl was young, English, and blonde. He could not be certain it was Sam, but there were not many English girls of her age here, they said. And she was absent from the tent. And Jason did not seem to be living in the tent at all. It was more than enough to be concerned. But it could still amount to nothing. A quick call could resolve everything. Perhaps they were together nearby, and all would be well. They might even invite him for a drink. Lord knows, he could do with one.

He felt a stab of pain as he looked at his contacts list. Was it even the right number for Jason? He should have checked with Lauren. Damn. He tapped the keys anyway and found himself directed to voicemail.

But what did being directed to voicemail mean? Nick was not sure. Was Jason on the phone to someone else? Was the phone switched off? Had the batteries run down? Could he have blocked all calls from his Dad?

"Hi. This is Jason Buckingham. I'm not here right now so please, leave me a message at the prompt and I'll get back to you."

So, it *was* still his number. Immediately, the phone beeped and Nick responded:

"Hello, Jason. It's Dad. Listen, I came to Síva, but I can't find you. And something's happened here which is making me worried for you. Please call or text me when you get this – even if you don't want to see me. I just need to know that you're okay. As soon as you can, son, please. This is important."

He spent the next few hours walking around the town, looking in every bar and taverna, in case he could see them. Then he walked the length of the beach. Nothing. By six thirty, most people were newly showered and looking for a drink before dinner. He returned to the town and started asking the younger people if they recognised Jason from the photo on his phone, but no-one did. By mid-evening, he was more worried than ever, tired and thirsty. He decided to grab something to eat at a taverna where a folk singer was playing and walked his photo around the audience first, without success. Then he went to the bar and ordered a beer. As it happened, this was the start of the singer's break. He saw her put down the guitar and stroll over, smiling a little.

"Why does the music always stop when I arrive?" he asked.

"It does? Sorry about that. Nothing personal, I assure you. Stick around and you can catch my second set."

"Can I get you a drink?"

"Why not? I'll have some of Giánni's red wine, please."

The guy behind the bar nodded and went to get it.

"You're a long way from home."

"Yep. But that's just fine. Here is cool."

"The States?"

She pulled a face.

"Sorry, Canada?"

"Right."

The wine arrived and they clinked their glasses together.

"Nick Fisher."

"I'm Beth."

"May I ask you something, Beth?"

Nick retrieved his phone and put it on the bar.

"This is my son. He's been staying in Síva. Do you recognise him by any chance?"

Beth tucked her hair behind her ears and leaned forward. Nick smelled cheap perfume and a touch of perspiration.

"You know, I think I do, Nick. I've seen him somewhere. Gimme a minute ..."

CHAPTER 6
SEARCHING THE BEACH

Leo left the doctor to organise the removal of the body and turned his attention to the beach search. He saw that *both* constables were snorkelling and called them into the shore with a loud whistle.

"Why are you *both* in the water? One of you should be searching the beach."

"We already searched the beach together, sir, so that we could snorkel together. Tásos can't dive to retrieve things."

Tásos looked sheepish and Leo gave him his best, unimpressed stare.

"So, what have you found so far?"

"It's all over there, sir." Níkos was pointing to two small piles next to a rock.

"Okay, I see them. Get back to work."

"We've almost finished, sir."

"Have you checked the other side of the big rock?"

"Yes, sir. There was nothing there. Just a few fish."

"All right. Carry on."

Leo saw that the pile on the left was dry. Amongst the discarded plastic water bottles, a purple snorkel tube and a couple of red and white cigarette packets, there was a pair of boy's white underpants and a dark pink girl's top with lace edging around the neckline. The other pile was wet, so they had thought not to mix the two, Leo noted, thankful for small mercies. He put to one side the gashed Lilo in the shape of a yellow and green crocodile. There was not much else: a child's plastic bucket, a camouflage-style, elasticated bandana and a maroon woollen hat. Leo picked up the hat and laid it out on the shingle. He saw that it was a beret with a badge on the front. Leo recognised the iconic image of Che Guevara. The shiny, metal badge was not corroded, he noticed.

Níkos crunched up, dripping.

"This too, sir, but I think that's it."

He dropped what appeared to be a sodden silk scarf onto the right-hand pile.

"Are you sure?"

"Pretty sure, sir."

"Then do one last circuit until you're certain but, before you go, where did you find this?"

He was pointing to the dark pink top.

"That was on the shingle just by the second rock, sir. The one with the orange lichen quite close to the water."

"And the scarf thing?"

"I think it's called a pareo, sir. Just in the shallows, no more than eight metres into the water."

"Near the orangey rock?"

"Not far off, sir."

"Could these items have been together before the scarf was washed off the beach?"

Níkos sensed that his career would be over if he said *pareo* again.

"The scarf is very light so yes – perhaps the wind took it, sir."

"Good. And this?"

He was holding the bandana.

"Oh, that was way to the right of the big rock, sir. I'd say about a hundred and fifty metres out. It was quite a dive to get that."

"You're a hero, Constable," he said, drily. "And this?"

He held up the beret.

"Tásos found that, sir."

Leo called Tásos over. "Where was this found, Constable?"

"Um. I don't quite remember, sir."

"Think man, for God's sake!"

"It wasn't deep because I didn't have to ask Níko to dive for me. I can do up to three metres or so."

"All right. Get back in the water."

When Tásos was treading water at what he reckoned was a three-metre depth, Leo saw that he was about fifteen metres out.

"Now do you remember where?" he yelled.

Tásos was pointing to his right.

"I think there, sir."

Tásos was pointing at a spot in line with the orangey rock but farther out.

"All right. Good. Now do one more circuit to make certain you haven't missed anything and then put these four items in evidence bags and give them to the ME. You can dispose of the rest."

"Back in the water, sir?"

"No, not back in the water, you idiot – this is a beauty spot! In a rubbish bin. Call me if you find anything else. Otherwise head into town when you've finished here and find Sergeant Konstantópoulos. He has some real police work for you."

*

God help us, he thought as he left the constable with the boat for the doctor and made his soggy way back down the beach as a spectacular sunset was starting. When he was two-thirds of the way back, Thaní came running out of the campsite behind the beach.

"We've got her, sir." He was waving what looked like a British passport.

"Oh, well done, Thaní!"

"I guessed they might have been campers, so we tried there first, and before too long we found a French woman who recognised her: a Sylvie Deschamps. She was in a tent quite near theirs and they got talking, here and there. She was able to show me their tent. According to the passport, her name is Samantha Claire Martin. Sylvie said everybody called her Sam."

"Sam was sharing with the boyfriend?"

"Yes – fiancé. She says they were going back to England to get married in March, on Sam's twenty-first birthday."

"What news of him?"

"She was able to give us a description of him and a first name: Jason."

"Where is he?"

"She's not sure, but she thinks he may have left in the middle of the night."

"Terrific."

"She also thinks she saw Sam coming back to the tent a couple of hours after that."

"That's odd. Did they speak?"

"No. Sylvie was half-asleep. She was a bit vague, boss."

"What did you find in the tent?"

"A sleeping bag, a pillow, a Lilo, Sam's backpack, a washbag and a plastic bag full of dirty clothes. The backpack was empty apart from the passport, a few ticket stubs, a purse containing thirty-five euros, a debit card and a credit card, a blue elephant toy and a map of Crete in the side pocket."

"No air ticket home?"

"No, but they do all that online now, don't they sir? Just download it to their phones and use a scanner."

"But you didn't find a phone."

"No. Maybe Jason has the only phone?"

"A young girl without a mobile phone, Thaní? Does that seem likely to you?"

"No, I guess not."

"Then we need to find it. And we need to find Jason. The ME has unanswered questions and I don't want him leaving the island. Give me the passport and I'll alert the British Vice Consulate about Sam and get the ports and airports briefed, but we'll need a photo and full details for him as soon as possible. And I'll also sort out somewhere for us all to eat and sleep tonight. We're not going anywhere for a day or two. You get your team focused on tracing Jason."

*

Leo walked into town and ordered a beer to wash down his cigarette. He thought about calling the captain but decided to wait. He would make the other calls first. He opened the passport and stared at the pretty, young face. It was all confidence and hope. In a moment, he would make the call, and then her mother and father would be told of Sam's lonely death in the dark, so many miles from home.

He remembered receiving a call like that: the stunned disbelief; the sudden deafness to an everyday life rendered meaningless; silence and darkness, punctuated by moments of heart-stopping, juddering shock; an aching void in the pit of the stomach and then the onrush of guilt and regret that never went away.

He ground his cigarette-butt into the ashtray, took a swig of ice-cold beer and started punching phone keys.

*

The next morning, the six policemen were finishing an early breakfast of hard-boiled eggs and sourdough toast with thick, Greek coffee. Then all but Thaní lit cigarettes. Leo brought the small talk to an end by getting to his feet.

"All right, gentlemen. We know each other quite well enough after all that rakí last night."

He gave a rueful look and received a chuckle or two in exchange.

"Now let's get to grips with where we are. Exit points have been primed to stop anyone matching Jason's description from leaving the island. I've alerted the British Vice Consulate about Samantha Martin and they will have informed her parents last night. I'll chase up the ME this morning and see when we can get her report."

"Couldn't we get a full ID on Jason from the Brits, sir?" asked Demétrios, one of the constables from Chaniá. "If they were engaged to be married, you'd think Sam's parents would be able to provide details. They'd know *his* family, surely?"

"That's a good thought, Demí. Families in England aren't always close like ours, but they should know something. I'll follow that up. How did last night's questioning go?"

Thaní answered: "Not great, boss. Without a photograph, it was hard to find anyone who could identify Jason from Sylvie's description. A guy called Jake thought someone like him was looking for a ride out of town quite late, but he didn't know whether he found one."

"So, we have no idea where he is."

"No, sir."

"Then we'll have to go on asking people this morning. I'll try to get a photo out of the Brits. We need to bag up the tent and Sam's things, take formal written statements from the Swiss couple, this Sylvie, Andie, the German boys, Mikey, Manólis and anyone else you've found. Make sure you get all their contact details, then we can let them move on, if they commit to keeping us informed of their whereabouts."

"Can we open up the beach again, sir?"

"Not just yet, Níko. I'd like to hear back from the ME first and check with the captain, so hang on in there. Keep the bathers sweet."

"You can interview those naked Dutch girls again, Níko," said Tásos.

"All right, everyone," said Leo, raising an eyebrow in distaste but otherwise ignoring Tásos, "Let's get back to business."

He called the Vice Consulate right away.

"I think we can help you, Lieutenant," said the British official. "We informed Miss Martin's parents of her death last night and later they asked about Jason Buckingham. They gave us contact details and we then informed *his* parents about Miss Martin, too. Turns out Stephen Buckingham is his *step*father, though. And this may surprise you ..."

"What?"

"...His real father lives in Crete, name of Nicholas Fisher."

"Where in Crete?"

"Saktoúria? It's on the south coast, near ..."

"I know where it is," Leo cut in. "Did they get together here, then?"

"Maybe not. They don't speak. Haven't for years."

"And now the boy calls himself Buckingham, not Fisher. Interesting. Better send me all you have on these characters, if you would."

"We can do that. And we have a passport photograph of Jason you can use. Is the young man still missing?"

"We think he's still on the island. If you can forward that information, tracing him will be much easier."

"We'll do that. And you should know that the parents are friends.

37

All four will come to Crete very soon, probably tomorrow. They're distraught, of course, and desperate to know how this happened."

"I understand. Please send me their details too. Thank you."

Almost as soon as he had ended the call, the phone rang. It was Pánagou.

"I work hard for you, Christodouláki. My report is done."

"That's great news, Doctor. Thank you."

"I will send as an email attachment, but I can tell you the main points. Blood/alcohol levels were high but not incapacitating. Her judgment would've been impaired, but she'd have *appeared* to function normally, more or less. There were also traces of marijuana but not a huge amount.

"Looking at her injuries, there was no residue in the foot wound, unfortunately. No great surprise. She may have kicked a sharp rock underwater and then blood and the sea washed out the damaged tissue. The head injury, on the other hand, showed traces of common beach grit and ascospores from the fungus Xanthoria Parietina."

"Ascospores?"

"These are the sexual spores of the fungus. They help it reproduce and grow."

"What sort of fungus are we talking about?"

"It's a lichen; yellowy-orange. Often found on rocks exposed to saltwater."

"The orangey rocks."

"Indeed. So, the girl's head came into powerful contact with some lichen-covered rock. That's certain, in my opinion. And, given the location of the wound at the base of the skull, my report will say it's probable that someone hit her with a rounded, lichen-covered rock. I think she was murdered, Lieutenant."

Leo felt his pulse quicken.

"Another thing that persuades me," the doctor went on, "is that I found very little saltwater in her lungs. Not enough to be consistent with drowning. Also, there was no indication of earlier choking or heart failure.

"And finally: the indentations to the face. These did not concern me at first because she was found face down on the shingle but, on further examination and from the depth of the marks, I must conclude that her face was pushed down into the shingle and held there for some time."

"But she didn't drown."

"No, she didn't. I guess that her killer was making sure. First, he hits her on the head, hard, then he pushes her face into the shingle to make sure. But the girl is already dead."

"I assume you also tested for sperm, doctor?"

"We took oral, vaginal and anal swabs and tested the bikini bottoms but found no sperm traces."

"Meaning this was not a sex attack."

"Meaning no evidence was found of recent, penetrative sex which led to a male ejaculation."

"Isn't that the same thing?"

"You tell me, Christodouláki. I am just a doctor, remember?"

Leo paused and looked out over the sea, nodding slightly. When he turned back, his face was taut, and his eyes gleamed with a new intensity.

"It seems clear then, Doctor."

"Go find your murderer, Detective."

After Pánagou ended the call, Leo checked his email and found that the full report had come in twenty minutes earlier. He saw that it had been copied to the captain. He paused only to light a cigarette.

"Sir? It's Leo again."

"Hello, Leo. I've read the ME's report."

"Yes, I thought you needed to see that, sir."

"A tourist murdered, here in Crete; not what we needed, Leo."

"No, sir."

"Let's try to keep this under wraps for now. There's no need for the press to be told, for the moment. The drowning story can run for a while yet. We have an obvious suspect and we need to find him and interrogate him. That's your number one priority."

"Indeed, sir."

"And then there's the father, Fisher. It seems odd that the boy chose to visit Crete if it's home to his estranged father – unless he planned to meet him, that is. We need to find the father, too. Make sure he's not involved. Or hiding the son."

"Sir."

"So, I want you to finish up there this morning, tidy up any loose ends, make sure all the evidence is bagged up and labelled, that we have all the signed statements we need and all the contact details for any potential witnesses. Once you have that, I don't see any need to hold anyone in Síva. Let them get on and enjoy their holidays."

"Okay, sir, and I guess I can open up that part of the beach again?"

"It's been thoroughly searched, you told me, so why not, Leo? Let's get back to normal as quickly as we can now."

"Yes, Captain."

"And I want you and Thaní back in Chaniá by lunchtime. Let our constables finish up there. Send the others back to Palaióchora."

"Sir."

CHAPTER 7

IN GIÁNNI'S BAR

Nick watched anxiously as Beth drummed her fingers on the bar. At last, she slammed her hand on the counter and spun around:

"Got it. *Jesus*, what took so long? It's like I have to wait for my brain cells to join hands, these days. I guess it's the wine. Sorry. Your boy was in the beach bar just last night. He's Sam's boyfriend, isn't he?"

"You know Sam?"

"Just getting to know her. She's fun."

"And you know Jason."

"No. But I remember him from last night, on account of the row."

"Row?"

"Well, I think that's what it was. Sam was well-oiled, shall we say, and a little wild. He lost patience in the end and dragged her off the dance floor. They went down the beach *for a little chat* and then she came back alone."

"What time was that?"

"It must have been late because the bar closed soon after."

"Did you see where she went when it closed?"

"No. I went back to my tent. I'd had a few too, to be honest."

"But you're sure about what you saw, about the row?"

"Oh yes. We were laughing about it, in the bar."

The thought of the whole beach bar crowd laughing as this drunken girl teased his son was not amusing Nick. He was wondering what it might have done to Jason, too, when a long-haired, young man burst into the bar. He looked ashen.

"Have you heard?"

"Heard what, Jake?"

"The girl who drowned? Get this: it was *Sam*."

"Oh, no! Oh, God! What a tragedy. How do you know?"

"The cops. They've been asking around all afternoon. But they've started using a different photo and a full name now: Samantha Martin."

Nick felt a gentle hand on his arm.

"I'm so sorry, Nick. Your poor son."

"You're *Jason's* father?" asked Jake.

Nick nodded.

"Oh, wow. Sorry for your loss, man."

"Thank you. I never met Sam, sadly. But now I think my son needs me. Do you have any idea where I can find him?"

"I might be able to help there, Nick."

Jake went on to explain that he had spoken with Jason late the previous night when he was looking for a lift out of town.

"Did he get one?"

"I think he did, in the end. I saw him talking with a couple of Greek guys. They have an old pick-up. They'd have looked after him, I think."

"Why do you say that? Did he need looking after?"

"He seemed a bit tearful, panicky. Like he'd taken the wrong kind of pills? Something like that."

"Where can I find these guys?"

"They live out of town, I think. Hang on, Giánnis might know. He knows pretty much everything that goes on around here."

Jake moved along the bar and started an animated conversation in Greek with the taverna owner. It was a longer conversation than Nick expected. Finally, he was back:

"He wants to know that you're not the police."

"I'm not," said Nick, raising his hands, adopting what he hoped was an innocent expression and shaking his head. Watching the charade without expression, Giánnis kept his eyes on Nick, then tilted his head at Jake in surly acquiescence.

"Okay, then I can tell you. Giánnis knew their father. He is dead now. The boys come to Síva quite often, but they don't live here. He says they have a small farm near Kándanos."

"Where is that?"

"If you have a car, it's about half an hour. I can show you."

While Jake sketched a map, Beth drained her wine glass.

"You're not going *now*, surely, Nick?"

Nick checked his watch. To his astonishment, it was ten twenty-two pm.

"Wouldn't it be better to go early tomorrow?" she went on. "At least you'll be able to see where you're going then, and the farmers will be up. Right now – Sunday night in rural Crete – they're all in bed.

"Giánnis will have something in a pot for you and you can try some of this excellent wine. He also has rooms if you need one. I must go back to work now, Nick. Will you be okay?"

He nodded and gave her a faint but grateful smile. It was sound advice. Jason might already have left this place but, if he were there now, he would still be there in the morning. It was a tough call not to be with him if he was suffering, but blundering about late at night on these mountain roads could make matters worse still.

He called Jason's number, but it went straight to voicemail again. He left a second message:

"Jason, it's Dad again. Listen, I've found out some things and I'm worried you might be in trouble. Please call me urgently, son. We've had our issues, but you need to know that I love you and I'll do everything I can to help, whatever's happened. Just call me, right now."

A few minutes later, Nick was enjoying the music and guiltily tucking into a bowl of stifádo with a small carafe of red wine and a basket of surprisingly fresh bread. After the meal, he stepped outside to call Jen, but her phone went to voicemail too. The recorded greeting was from Stephen. Nick hesitated, then disconnected. He thought about trying Lauren, but did he really want to tell her that there would be no wedding now, that her future sister-in-law was dead and her brother missing? He thought better of it for now and went back in.

As he sat down, Jake came over.

"There you go, Nick. That'll get you to Kándanos. You'll have to get directions from there but it's not far. You're looking for the Manousákis farm."

Nick studied the careful drawing, borrowed Jake's pen, and wrote the family name on the map.

"That's very kind of you, Jake. Why don't you pull up a glass?"

"I won't, thanks, Nick. I need to sleep now."

"So, what will you tell the cops when they come calling?"

"Same as usual, man. Zippo. We don't do those bastards any favours."

Nick chuckled inside, then they shook hands and Jake waved to Beth on his way out. Nick poured the last of the wine into his glass and tried to let the music flow over him. But he could not settle. His heart was aching for Jason, but he was also scared for him. What the hell had happened here?

CHAPTER 8
JASON

The truck was battered and the exhaust shot. Jason was sandwiched between two brothers as they roared through the night towards Kándanos. It felt surreal, leaving Síva on his own with these strangers, nice guys though they seemed to be. The driver claimed he had no English, but his brother was prepared to try:

"You okay, man?" he asked in a kindly voice.

Jason shook his head. He was white and shaking. Later, he managed to tell them that he'd broken with his girl and had nowhere to stay, except maybe the church.

"No sleep church. Is not possible. Priest get mad. You sleep *our* house."

*

The room was basic, not all that clean and the bed was rock hard, but Jason was beyond caring. It was almost four in the morning and he was in a state of nervous exhaustion. He shared a large glass of rakí gratefully with the lads. One of them gave him a sad smile and said:

"Tomorrow better. You see."

Then they gave him bear hugs and left him to fall into a fitful, nervous sleep.

*

He woke at nine, wondering where he was. In the dream, Sam reached out to him, smiling openly in that sexy way of hers, but, when he went to hug her, the mirage faded. Then he heard cruel laughter as she reappeared, looking back at him vindictively. She was in the arms of another man and Jason started groping towards them in a bewildered rage, but his legs were sunk in deep shingle, like quicksand.

In that first, waking moment he felt a surge of relief from realising

45

it was just a dream, but then the reality of what had happened kicked in and his heart gave way.

His body felt old and weary and every bone ached, but he forced himself out of bed and into his clothes. In the kitchen, a well-rounded little woman introduced herself in Greek as the boys' mother and made him sit at the kitchen table while she cooked him a solid but tasty omelette containing potato, mixed peppers and feta. Faced with a choice of Greek coffee or tea, he opted for the tea which she made very strong in a cracked, blue mug. As she placed it in front of him, she smiled and said:

"My son, he come."

Sure enough, just as he was finishing breakfast and looking to escape the mother's third cigarette, the son arrived:

"Hello. My muddah cook for you. Om-let, okay?"

"Omelette good, thank you."

"When you ready, I take you to bus – okay?"

"Please don't worry, I'm sure I can walk."

"You no walk. I take."

*

It was a short drive to Kándanos, a town dominated by a large, sunlit church which seemed to reach for the heavens in glorious defiance. It replaced the one burned down in 1941, Jason remembered. The Nazis made an example of the town to deter partisan raids. They razed it to the ground, killing one hundred and eighty local people.

It was a bit late to ask the boy's name, Jason thought, but he thanked him profusely for his hospitality before leaving the truck and entering the church. Maybe some divine guidance would tell him where to go now? As he gazed at the naïve paintings and ornate decorations of the Orthodox Greek Church, he agonised for several minutes. Candles were burning and the smell of incense was overpowering. The faces on the walls looked kind but they offered no answers. In the end, he decided to take a day or two to gather his thoughts and get in better shape to make the next move. He would take the bus into the city and then head out to Gramvoúsa, a famous beach in the north-west where he was planning to take Sam. He could get a room there and stare at the sea for a while before committing himself further. He hoisted his backpack and left the church to join the little queue for the Chaniá bus.

*

The next morning, in the little rent rooms place near the beach, Jason woke knowing right away that there was no point in remaining. Somehow, he must have worked it out in his sleep, because now he knew this with a certainty that was deep-down and fundamental. He needed to get out of this damned country if he could. He needed to tell his mother everything. He needed the big hugs only she could give.

*

After hitching into the city, the terminus was the usual Greek chaos but eventually he found the bus for the half-hour trip to the airport, and it was air-conditioned, thank God. There would be flights to London Gatwick leaving at two fifty and four forty pm and he hoped he could make it onto one of those. If not, there were several more to various British destinations later in the day. He would just have to sweat it out. He would buy a ticket, get checked in, go through security, and then make the dreaded call to his parents. But first, he would have to charge his mobile phone which was stone dead after a week in the back of beyond. He thought he could do that in the airport lounge.

There were several British people on the bus, and he found solace in hearing English spoken again, but he was still shaky and tearful and dared not talk to anybody. When they drew up in front of the modern, glass building, Jason headed inside, looking for Airport Information.

"Most tourist flights are full," he was told. "But let me see what I can do. You might have to go later, via Athína. Please to give me your passport, then take a seat over there. I will come and tell you what can be done."

47

Jason did as he was told and waited. Other people kept the information desk busy and he was not sure if this woman was doing anything to help him or not. At one point she gave him a reassuring glance, but he was not reassured. After twenty minutes, he was about to return to the desk when a man in airport security uniform approached him.

"Mr Jason? Please come."

The woman on the information desk held out his passport with that reassuring smile of hers and he grabbed it and hurried after the disappearing figure. He caught up with the man and asked what the hell was going on, but he did not speak English or maybe he just did not want to answer. They were now in a corridor in the bowels of the terminal and stopped at an unmarked side door. It was opened by a tall, thin man in his early sixties. Jason sensed that he was English. Behind him sat an intense-looking, darker-skinned man in his early forties who looked Greek.

"Efcharistó," the older man said to the guard, who nodded and left.

"Jason? Hello. Please come in. Have a seat. If I might just take a look at your passport? Thank you."

"Is there something wrong with it?"

"No, no. Just needed to confirm your identity. Thank you. My name is Jonathan Beeson and this gentleman is a policeman. I am from the British Vice Consulate here in Crete and I'm afraid I have some very bad news for you."

CHAPTER 9
ONE STEP BEHIND

Finding the farm took quite a while. The Greeks were always keen to help with directions, but they tended to speak with great certainty even when they were not sure of the way. That, and Nick's poor Greek, led to a couple of detours. When he finally got there, the Manousákis family were kind. The widow gave him coffee and a custard pie while they waited in companionable silence for her boys to come in from the fields. They, in turn, confirmed that Jason stayed with them and that he had broken with his girl and was in a bit of a state. One of them had driven him to the bus stop in Kándanos the previous morning.

"Which bus did he take?" Nick asked.

"Last I see, he go church. No bus."

That sounded worrying. Theirs was not a religious family. What moved Jason to enter a church?

"But he was going to take the bus, later?"

"I think yes, but the bus go many places: Chaniá, Palaióchora, Síva but also many, many other places. Sorry, mister." The boy extended his arms and shrugged.

"And you're quite sure that he didn't say where he was going?"

"He say nothing. I ask him nothing."

"But you'd tell me if you knew, wouldn't you?"

Nick was staring hard into the boy's eyes but found only amenable ignorance there, now touched by indignation.

"I *don't* know, mister. I tell you truth."

*

Nick got out of the Jeep and stared at the signpost. He realised that he did not have a clue where Jason had gone next. The trail had gone cold, twenty-six hours ago. And, after a tortured night and an early start, he was getting tired. Only his fear for his son kept him going.

Then something vibrated in his pocket and the ringtone sounded. He glimpsed the +44 prefix:

"Jason, is that you?"

A pause.

"It's Jen, Nicky. I have some very sad news, I'm afraid."

He had always loved the way she spoke. So clear and confident, rather posh, and with that hint of a tease or a shared secret. But not today. Today she was deadly serious and there was a waver in her voice; she had been crying.

"I know about Sam, if that's what you mean."

"You do? Was it on the news there?"

"I arrived in Síva soon after she was found."

"So, you went after all."

"I did – and now I'm looking for our son."

"We've been trying to call him, but his phone seems to be dead."

"Me too. I left messages. And I looked around and asked around in Síva. Seems he left town in the middle of the night with a couple of young, Greek guys. I've just come from their farm. Jason slept the rest of that night at their place and then took a bus somewhere yesterday morning."

"Why would he leave without Sam?"

"They had a row."

"Oh, dear. It all sounds rather scary, doesn't it?"

"Are you coming over?"

"We're trying to arrange flights to Chaniá for later today. Poor Helen and Mike are coming, of course, and we wanted to be there for them anyhow but now, with Jason vanishing, we *have* to come."

"Okay. Well, I've no idea which bus he took but I guess I'll head into Chaniá and try to trace him there. At least I'll be nearby when you arrive."

"Okay. It's going to be late, though, so I'll call you tomorrow."

*

The traffic and parking in Chaniá were a nightmare and Nick was feeling frustration and mounting panic. Something inside told him time was running out. He was on a one-man mission to trace his son at the bus station or the port. Failing that, he would drive out to the airport. He knew his chances of success were close to zero; a needle in a haystack might be easier. It was already gone three by the time he found the bus station.

There were some offices and shops, but it looked to be a mostly residential area. It was close to the city centre and much bigger than he had expected. ANEK Lines and Ktel buses were littering the sprawl of tarmac in front of the single-storey office and customer reception area. Nick thought it unlikely that Chaniá city was Jason's final destination. If he came here at all, he almost certainly bought another ticket, for the airport or some other place. He would start at the ticket office.

CHAPTER 10

PRIME SUSPECT

Beeson studied Jason with pained sympathy in his eyes while the Greek policeman stared, chewing on his thumb.

"I'm sorry Jason but there's no easy way to say this. Early Sunday morning, the body of a young woman was found on the beach at Síva. She was later identified as Samantha Martin."

Their eyes were searching Jason's face. The colour drained from it as if a plug had been pulled. His voice, when it came, was a hoarse whisper:

"Sam? NO! It can't be. Oh, God … Are you sure? How?"

"We're quite sure it's Sam, I'm afraid. The police are completing their investigations, but she appears to have drowned."

"Drowned? Sam?"

"People do drown on Crete, I'm afraid."

"But Sam's a strong swimmer. She was runner-up in a big schools' competition in England. How could she drown?"

"Well, as I say, Jason, the police are completing their investigations."

Beeson laid a hand on Jason's shoulder.

"I'm so very sorry."

The small act of kindness brought finality and, with it, grief. After the initial confusion, Jason could only think of Sam now, dying so young, so far from home. Three days ago, she was going to be his wife in six months. Now he would never see her again. The tears, when they came, were in floods, accompanied by great wrenching, shuddering sobs. Beeson placed a well-sweetened cup of tea and a box of tissues beside him.

After a few minutes, the sobs lessened and he regained a semblance of composure, though tears still dribbled down his tear-stained face as he gripped a sodden ball of tissues. His eyes looked bleak and frightened. Beeson was speaking:

"I understand you were trying to buy a ticket home?"

Jason nodded.

"That won't be necessary. Your parents and Sam's are flying to Chaniá. All four should be here late tonight. Your stepfather's been trying to call you."

"My phone's dead."

"Just the battery? We can get that sorted out for you."

Jason dug his phone out of the side pocket of the backpack and handed it to Beeson with the charging cable.

"Now, in the meantime, but only if you're feeling up to it, this gentleman would like to ask you some questions, just to help fill in the gaps in his knowledge of the events. Would that be all right?"

Jason looked bewildered but mumbled that he supposed it would be okay.

"Well, then. Here's my card, Jason. Please call me if there's anything I can do for you. Use this desk phone. I'll arrange for some food to be sent in and I'll direct your parents here when they arrive. They were trying to get on a flight due in at twenty-two forty, last I heard."

Jason looked at his watch. More than ten hours from now.

"So, I'll leave you with Lieutenant Christodoulákis, if that's all right?"

Beeson laid his hand on Jason's shoulder once again and then he was gone. Another Greek man entered the room.

"This is my colleague, Investigations Sergeant Konstantópoulos," said the older man. "I must have someone else with me when I ask you questions. It is the law."

"And I will use this, if you don't mind," said the new guy, setting a small recording device on the table.

"Am I being questioned officially, then?"

"Everything we do is *official*," said the lieutenant, sounding bored. "There must be two of us, we must read you your rights, we must record you, we must write reports. Ya-di-ya-di-ya. You understand? It is the law. It is not (how you say?) to make you frightened."

"Intimidate?"

"What? Yes. It is not to intimidate you. Thank you. We are just having a chat, but you are entitled to have a lawyer present if you wish and an interpreter, if necessary, but we will speak only in English, so I think this is okay."

"*Should* I have a lawyer here?"

"That is up to you."

Jason wasn't sure what to do but it was clear that the lieutenant wanted to get on with it and Jason didn't want to appear guilty of anything, so he said:

"I'll answer your questions but, if I feel at any time that I should have a lawyer present, then I reserve the right to stop."

"All right. Good. We appreciate that."

Jason was feeling apprehensive. The younger policeman started the recorder while the older one lit a cigarette and started prowling around the room.

"Interview timed at twelve fifty-two pm. Present in the room are Jason Buckingham, a British citizen, with Lieutenant Christodoulákis and Sergeant Konstantópoulos of the police, Chaniá prefecture."

The sergeant turned to Jason.

"For the recorder, please state your name."

"Jason Buckingham."

"And please read out your passport number."

Jason did so.

"And tell us please, what was your relationship with the deceased, Samantha Martin?"

It was a shock hearing Sam referred to as the deceased and Jason felt tears welling up again. He used the ball of tissues to stem the flow.

"I'm sorry. She was my fiancée."

"We are interested in the events of the fifteenth and sixteenth of September, from nine pm on Saturday until seven am on Sunday morning. Will you please take us through everything you remember?"

The next time Jason looked at his watch, it was three fifteen. Sandwiches were brought in, but these guys showed no interest in stopping. They seemed to live on strong coffees in plastic cups with lids. They drank them through thick, plastic straws and the older one was smoking most of the time. *No wonder they're wired*, he thought.

"Shouldn't we eat something?" he asked, eventually.

The lieutenant threw his hands in the air as if surrendering to some greater force.

"Why not? Why not? But then we must go over it all again."

Around four pm, the tone seemed to change, and the lieutenant led a harsher line of questioning:

"You and Miss Martin were going to be married, yes?"

"We were getting married in March."

"And yet she was not wearing a ring."

"No. As I said, we argued. She took it off. Gave it back to me."

"So, were you engaged or not?"

"We had been. I guess we weren't after that."

"You guess?" The lieutenant was leaning over him, staring at him, breathing stale tobacco smoke. "We don't want your guesses, Mr Buckingham, we want the facts. Just the facts."

"I mean I *expect* we were no longer engaged."

"You expect? What – you are not sure? You have two arguments, one of them violent, she ends the relationship, she gives you back the ring and you are not sure what this means?"

"Of course, I knew what it meant, but it might have been a temporary thing, you know?"

"What? You thought she would call you?"

"Perhaps."

"You hope for this."

"Yes, I hoped."

"But you were hoping for an impossibility, surely? Now, I'm not an expert in electronic communications, Mr Buckingham, but even I know that you won't receive a call on a phone with dead batteries. You hoped. And yet you didn't even bother to charge your phone. You have many opportunities, yet when you arrive here, two days later, the batteries are still flat. The truth is that you knew she wouldn't call because you knew she was dead, and you wanted to remain out of contact with everyone until you escaped. Isn't that so?"

"No. I didn't realise the batteries were flat at first. Then I thought I could charge them here at the airport."

"So, let me see if I have this right. Your strategy for winning back your fiancée is to remain uncontactable and to leave Síva and head for the airport. Am I missing something? Is this the famous British sang-froid? In my country, Mr Buckingham, it would be usual to stay and talk to a lady if you want to win back her affections, or at least to keep your phone charged in case she might call."

"I guess I was confused."

"You are guessing again."

"I mean I *was* confused. I was upset. I didn't think I could patch things up in Síva. She told me there was another man. I felt I needed to get away."

"Another man? Who did she say that was?"

"She didn't."

"Who do you think it is?"

"I have no idea. Maybe she made him up to get rid of me."

"Made him up?"

"Invented him. Imagined him."

"You don't believe that, Mr Buckingham."

"No, I suppose I don't, deep down."

"So, who could it be?"

"I don't know. I never saw her with anyone else."

"And yet you were seen dragging her away from dancing with three German boys; the same boys who were naked in the water with her later that evening."

"I don't understand. Are you accusing me of something now?"

"I think you were incensed at being treated with contempt and then rejected by your fiancée for another man. You were seen pleading with her on two occasions. Then you hit her.

"When she rejects you once and for all and gives you back the ring, you appear to leave but you don't go far. You sit and wait for your opportunity.

"When the others leave, you see her swim off around the big rock and you creep into the shallows and wait for her and then you hit her as hard as you can with a rock. If you couldn't have her, nor would anyone else. That's how it was, Mr Buckingham, was it not?"

"No! Of course, not. I wouldn't hurt her. I loved her. And I didn't hit her. She was hitting me, on the chest. I just pushed her away and she fell over. And you said she drowned. What are you saying now – that she was murdered?"

"I am sure her killer would like us to think that she drowned but that was not the case."

"But I said I didn't think she *could* have drowned."

"This was quite clever of you."

"What? Jesus! You're twisting my words."

"You killed her and then you left in the middle of the night."

"If I'm so clever, why do I just show up at the airport, then?"

"You have to get off the island somehow. Perhaps you think we are too slow and stupid here to have worked out by then just who you are and what you've done."

"But I could have come here yesterday. Instead I went off to Gramvoúsa."

"You were confused. You'd just killed someone. You didn't know what the hell you were doing."

"I just can't win with you guys, can I?"

"It is not about winning or losing, Mr Buckingham. It's about finding the truth. And the truth is that you killed Samantha. You are a man and she treated you with scorn. She throws the ring back at you, laughs in your face and then gets back into the water with her naked men, one or all of whom could be her new lovers. It's all too much for you. It would be too much for any hot-blooded man."

"It wasn't like that, and I didn't kill her."

"Who else had a strong motive, Mr Buckingham? Who else had an opportunity? Who else fled the scene of the crime?"

"I'd like to talk to Mr Beeson."

"You can talk to him in a minute. Right now, Jason Buckingham, I have a warrant from the investigating judge, and I am arresting you for the murder of Samantha Martin. Interview terminated at five ten pm."

The younger policeman then read him his rights and got him to sign a form to say that he had done so. He switched off the recorder and stood up. The lieutenant continued:

"You may speak with Beeson. You may also call a family member or someone close to you if you wish. Then you must come with us to the police station in Chaniá for further questioning."

"But I am innocent. You've got this all wrong."

"If that proves to be the case, you will be freed in due course, Mr Buckingham. We are not savages here. But for now, you will remain in custody pending further investigations."

Leo left the room in a swirl of cigarette smoke, leaving Thaní to guard the prisoner.

*

"Christodoulákis has explained the situation, Jason. I'm so sorry this has happened."

"I'm completely innocent, Mr Beeson."

"The evidence does seem circumstantial, Jason, but in the absence of any other suspects, you are *it* and you *are* in a very tricky situation. They may have arrested you just to make sure you don't leave the country. The first thing is to get you a Greek lawyer. Do you know anyone, or would you be happy for me to appoint someone on your behalf and have them come to the police station?"

"Know anyone? Of course, I don't know anyone, Mr Beeson."

"All right, try to keep calm, Jason."

"Look, just find someone for me, please."

"I'm happy to do that. And I'll explain what's happened to your parents when they arrive."

"Oh God, Michael will kill me."

"We'd better keep you and the Martins apart."

"And my Mum will go to pieces."

"Yes, I'm afraid she might. But keep your chin up, lad. We at the Vice Consulate, your lawyer and your family will be doing all we can to get this situation resolved."

CHAPTER 11
PARENTS

Beeson was irritated to see that the plane was delayed. He was tired and he wanted to get home. Finally, at eleven thirty pm, three of them arrived at the room he had used earlier. They looked pink-eyed, exhausted and shell-shocked.

"Stephen's just sorting out the luggage," mumbled a woman who must have been Jennifer Buckingham.

"Righto. Well, I'd prefer separate meetings anyhow so, if you wouldn't mind waiting outside for a few minutes, Mrs Buckingham, I'll start with The Martins."

Jen looked a little put out but allowed the airport security guard to guide her to a row of seats just down the corridor. Beeson closed the door.

"It's Helen and Michael, isn't it? I'm Jonathan Beeson from the Vice Consulate. We spoke yesterday. I'd like to offer my sincere condolences to you both." He extended a bony hand which they shook in turn. "Please sit down. You've had a dreadful shock and an awfully long day already."

"Is there any doubt, Mr Beeson? Any doubt at all?"

"I'm sorry, Michael. The body's been formally identified, and it is Sam. No question."

The faint light in his eyes went out and his mouth tightened. "Where is she now?"

"She's here in Chaniá, in the custody of the Medical Examiner."

"Can we see her?"

"That should be possible in due course, but you need to know that there's already been a post-mortem."

"What?" they chorused, in horror.

"For a drowning?"

"And without our consent?"

Beeson held up his hands. "Let me explain. Everything moves very quickly here when someone dies. Under Greek law, the ME is entitled to proceed with a post-mortem without seeking the consent of the family if there are any suspicious circumstances."

"Suspicious ... how?" asked Michael.

"Sam appeared to have drowned, at first, but the medical examination raised questions. There were injuries to Sam's body that were found to be inconsistent with drowning and I am told she was a strong swimmer, too?"

They both nodded.

"The Greeks have now opened a murder enquiry and I'm sorry to say that her former fiancé, Jason Buckingham, was arrested just a few hours ago."

"Jason?"

"Yes. He's being held at Chaniá police station."

"You said, *former* fiancé?"

"Yes. It seems Sam broke off the engagement in the early hours of Sunday morning."

"Just before she died?"

"Not long before, certainly."

"And you think *Jason* did it?"

"I don't know what to think, Helen. There's a fair amount of circumstantial evidence and the police have no other suspect right now."

"How was she killed, Mr Beeson?"

"A single blow to the head with a blunt instrument or a rock. I'm so sorry."

Helen's composure dissolved as she pictured her beautiful baby, head smashed, face down and alone in some God-forsaken place, miles from home, family and everything she knew.

"That little bastard," growled Michael.

"Now try not to jump to conclusions, Michael. Jason claims to be innocent."

"He would, wouldn't he? The little shit."

After a few minutes, Beeson took the precaution of leading the Martins out of the other door and asking them to wait in a nearby office.

Returning to the corridor, he saw a man who had to be Stephen with an airport trolley, three suitcases and a large bag. He was waiting with Jen.

"I'm so sorry to make you wait, Mr and Mrs Buckingham. Please come in."

Beeson made the introductions.

"Why not see us all together, may I ask?" said Stephen.

"It's a delicate situation, I'm afraid. Sam appeared to have drowned, but then the Medical Examiner uncovered certain things which now point to murder."

"Oh, dear God!"

"It appears that Sam broke the engagement early Sunday morning. Jason was with her a little before three am and seen to be upset. There was some violence between them. The police say the rejection gave him a strong motive, he was at or near the scene of the crime at the time of her death and then he fled in the middle of the night. I'm sorry to tell you that your son has been charged with Sam's murder."

"What the hell?"

"He told me he is blameless, Stephen. Innocent."

"Well, of course, he is! That boy wouldn't hurt a fly, much less someone he loved."

"She may have treated him rather shabbily."

"He'd be hurt by that, of course, but there's no way he'd turn violent. Never. Not our son. We taught him to turn the other cheek and to forgive. We're not saints or anything – not even religious – but we've instilled strong principles of decency in our children, Mr Beeson. I don't believe he did this – not for a second."

"Well, Jennifer, I hope you're right. Now, if you'll excuse me for one minute."

Beeson slipped out of the office and found the Martins. He suggested they grab their luggage and head off to the hotel.

"It's all rather awkward, isn't it?" he said.

"Rather more than that, Mr Beeson. We booked adjacent rooms."

"You might want to reconsider that," he said as they parted company. "I'll be in touch in the morning."

He went back into the office: "Sorry about that."

"Are Michael and Helen aware of all this?"

"They are, Stephen. I informed them just now."

"And they knew straight away that it wasn't Jason – right?"

"Er … let's just say they're in shock, shall we?"

"What? They think he did it? You've *got* to be kidding me."

"The police have no-one else in the frame and Jason's been arrested and charged. Put yourself in their shoes."

"Jesus Christ. So, they were happy to let their daughter marry someone they thought capable of murder, were they?"

"We need to keep our emotions under control, Stephen, and see what we can do to help Jason. The Martins might be best avoided for now."

"They're supposed to be our friends," said Jen.

"Well, they're not now. That's for sure," said Stephen.

"They've just lost their only daughter in the most distressing of circumstances, Stephen. I think we need to cut them a little slack, as the Americans say."

"So where is Jason? Can we see him?"

"As I said, he's at Chaniá police station. You won't be able to see him just yet. They're still questioning him. At his request, I've found him a Greek lawyer. Her name is Eléni Makrydáki and she speaks perfect English.

"Here's her card. I've arranged for you to meet at her offices in the city centre at ten am tomorrow morning. Her address is on the card. Any taxi driver will know where that is. Now, it's after midnight so I suggest you go to your hotel and try to get some rest. There's nothing more we can do tonight."

"Can we at least get a message to him?"

"You can send something to his phone, assuming it's charged now, but I can't say for sure that he'll have access to it."

"That's it?"

"He knows you're here. Perhaps you'll be able to see him tomorrow."

*

Beeson appeared just as the Martins were finishing a pointless breakfast.

"Good morning, Helen, Michael. I understand that the Buckinghams moved to a different hotel last night."

"They did? Okay."

"I think it's for the best until this mess is resolved. Jennifer left a letter for you at reception which they asked me to give you."

Beeson handed Helen the letter and she read:

> *Dear Helen and Michael,*
>
> *In the circumstances, we felt it best to move to a different hotel. As your friends, we wanted so much to support you through your terrible loss, but the news of Jason's arrest has made that impossible for all of us. We want you to know that we are both extremely sad and angry that Sam has been taken from you. She was a lovely girl and we would have loved to have her as our daughter-in-law. At the same time, neither of us believes for a moment that Jason is guilty, and we will be doing everything in our power to prove his innocence. When we are successful in this, perhaps, in time, we can become friends again. We sincerely hope so.*

Helen dabbed her eyes and passed the letter to her husband.

"We just want to take her home now, Mr Beeson."

"Of course, you do, Helen. I've been in touch with the ME's office this morning. If you decide to repatriate, they'll be able to release Sam to you in six- or seven-days' time."

"What? Why so long?"

"As with everything in Greece, there are formalities to be dealt with, documents to be obtained, but also the body must be embalmed and then placed in a lead-lined coffin for the journey back to England. That's the law here."

"Don't we have any say in that?"

"You don't have any say here, I'm afraid. These things are strictly controlled in Greece. And you'll have to pay for it as well – about three thousand, eight hundred euros, I believe."

"What? We weren't expecting any of this!"

"Well, I'm afraid the Greeks won't release the body without payment in full and Foreign Office policy is *not* to provide financial assistance for the repatriation of loved ones, except *in extremis*."

"Meaning?"

"Meaning the government will only pay if you can prove that you are unable to do so – that you have neither the cash nor any assets that could be sold to raise it."

"Oh, we can find the money, Mr Beeson. It's just a bit of a bloody shock, on top of everything."

"Well, you could decide *not* to repatriate, in which case Sam would be buried here in Crete. They don't cremate here. It used to be against the law. Nowadays, the EU has made it legal but there are just no facilities. The Greeks don't do it, so no-one has built a crematorium, to be blunt. Also, the burial option is for a limited period – I think it might be twenty years – and then the bones of the deceased must be moved to a family vault or a communal ossuary."

Helen shivered. "We're taking her home, Mr Beeson. No question. We'll pay whatever it costs, and we'll wait right here until we can take her back with us."

"Yes, I rather thought you'd say that."

Beeson stood up to leave.

"One last thing, Mr Beeson," said Michael. "We were thinking last night. We might have a second post-mortem done in the UK, just to satisfy ourselves about what happened."

"I'm afraid you'd be wasting your money."

"How's that?"

"The embalming process makes subsequent post-mortems problematic."

"And there's no way of avoiding the embalming?"

"I can ask, but I've been refused before; it's the law here, you see."

Michael and Helen exchanged a worried glance.

"We'd like you to ask anyway, please. Maybe they'll take a more flexible view with her being a murder victim?"

"I'm happy to ask," said Beeson. "I'll let you know."

"And when can we see her?"

"Not for a few days yet, I'm afraid. They will let you see her before the coffin is sealed. The ME's office will let us know."

The Martins looked sad and defeated and Beeson found himself once again apologising as he shook their hands and left.

*

The lawyer's office was in a large, faded Venetian building in Archondáki, just up from the market hall in Chaniá. On the dot of ten, Jen and Stephen were shown in. Eléni Makrydáki got up from behind her desk and joined them at a table with a large pot plant overhanging it. She was an overweight woman in her mid-forties wearing glasses with fashionable, dark green frames. She looked nervous and Stephen noticed that her hands shook a little and she was perspiring despite the air-conditioning.

"Welcome, Mr and Mrs Bucking-ham," she said, separating the last two syllables. "I am Eléni. How may I help you?"

"Our son's been arrested and is in the police station at Chaniá, we understand."

"I know this. How may I help?"

"Our son's completely innocent, Eléni. We want to see him, we want to get him out of there, we want the charges dropped and we want to take him home."

"I see, Mr Bucking-ham."

"Please call me Stephen, and this is Jen."

"Yes, Stephen. I have spoken with the police and what you ask is not easy."

"Go on."

"We cannot see him until the police finish questioning him. They've not yet finished but will inform me when they have."

"Can't we be there when he's being questioned."

"No. He is not a minor."

"How long can they keep him before we get to see him."

"As long as they need for the questioning, but within a maximum of five days the case must be reviewed by the *anakrítis*. This is the investigating judge. If he or she believes that there is a case for Jason to answer and the public prosecutor concurs, then the case must go forward for trial."

"Will we be able to make our case to the investigating judge?"

"That's up to him. They have a very wide brief. He may well interview you as part of his investigation. These days, though, the judges are busy. There have been cutbacks. In practice, he may scan the file and then let the police get on with it."

"That can't be right."

"In Greece, the police are very powerful, Stephen." She spread her hands on the desk and looked at them with her lips pursed.

"Can we at least meet with the police or get a statement of some sort from them so that we know more about the case against Jason?"

"Again, this is not possible. They will make their case in court. We have to make our case as to why Jason did not do this."

"How?"

"We'll be able to speak to him, of course, when they've finished – in just a few days – and then you may need to do some investigations of your own in support of the case."

"And when will the trial be, if there is one?"

"It can be as much as twelve to eighteen months from being charged, I'm afraid. There are backlogs in the system. The ongoing detention of the suspect is reviewed by The Judicial Council every six months."

"But we could get him out on bail, right?"

"We can make an application for bail but, given the seriousness of the crime and the flight risk the courts attach to foreigners, I think we'd be wasting your money at this stage."

"So, he could be banged up for a year and a half."

"In the absence of fresh evidence that proves he didn't do it, then yes, that could well be the case."

"And it's up to us."

"Yes. *You*, and anyone else who can help you; *I* have no investigative powers. The investigating judge is not your enemy, though. If you have new information, I'd expect him to listen and take that into account."

*

The sun was beating down as they left Eléni's office, so they found a shady square nearby and ordered coffee and iced water.

"It's pretty scary, isn't it?" said Jen. "We were all part of the EU not so long ago and yet it seems so different here. It feels like a police state, almost."

"Yes. I'm scared, honey. I'm scared for Jason. He might only be my stepson, but I love him like a son, and I know he didn't do this, but I don't know how to go about trying to prove that."

"Me neither. We need help."

"We do, but, apart from dear old Beeson, I don't know where to turn, frankly."

"I have an idea, but it's a long shot and you're not going to like it."

CHAPTER 12
A VISIT FROM THE POLICE

The sergeant steered into the narrow turning, past billboards fluttering with shreds of old concert posters. The road snaked upwards across the side of a huge, rocky hill. To their left, they could see for perhaps fifty kilometres, straight down a wide, fertile valley with massive, barren mountains to the left, smaller mountains to the right and beyond, the blue Mediterranean glittering in the sunshine. Now they were coming over the brow of an enormous hill and the road ribboned down in alarming hairpins to the sea far below. About one-third of the way down was a white-washed stone village in two parts, clinging to the side of the hill.

"Beautiful, isn't it, Constable?" he said to his passenger.

"Yes, but it's a bit scary, Sergeant. How do people live here?"

"You get used to it; I suppose."

They inched their way down the steep hill and into the village and parked in front of the kafenío.

*

Inside, a large, brown-eyed man with thinning hair was reading a newspaper behind the counter while a girl of about twelve was mopping the floor. Looking up and seeing the uniforms, the man stood and adopted an effusive manner:

"A visit from the Spíli police. We are honoured, gentlemen. I am Kóstas. Will you take a rakí with me, or perhaps some coffee?"

"Thank you, my friend, but we are on official business. We are looking for the Englishman."

"Nicholas Fisher," added the constable.

"Ah, Níkos. He is in trouble?"

"Have you seen him?"

"Yes, but not for a couple of days, Sergeant."

"Have you seen him in the company of a young man, also English?"

"No. I would remember that."

"And is Fisher in the village now?"

"I don't know."

"Do you know which is his house?"

"Of course. My daughter can show you if you wish."

The sergeant jerked his head at the constable.

"Go with the girl. If he's home, bring him here."

She put down her mop and turned her brown eyes on the young constable.

"I am Xará. Come."

She led the way to the side of the building and her motorbike. She jumped on and kickstarted it, then jerked a thumb at the pillion seat.

"Come. I show you."

"Where is your crash helmet?"

Xará gave him the big eyes and a little pout.

"It's the law, you know."

"We are going, like, a hundred and fifty metres. Just get on."

As they watched the motorbike putter up the steep village street, Kóstas placed a carafe of clear liquid and two small glasses on the table.

"This is the first of the year from my kazáni. You must taste it with me, Sergeant. I insist."

"Ah. Well, I hear that you, at least, have paid for a licence, Kostí so I think it would be rude not to. And, while we drink, you can tell me what you know about this man Fisher."

*

Nobody was answering the door. The constable peered through the window.

"Do you have a key, Xará?"

"No. But Níkos is not here, anyway. The Jeep is gone. He parks it here, always."

She was pointing to an alley to the side of the small, stone house.

The constable walked around the house to the alley to see for

70

himself, then took some stone steps up to a roof terrace. He saw that some building work had been going on. An amateur attempt at a wall looked half-finished. Concrete blocks were stacked to one side. From the roof, he spotted a neighbour working on his artichoke patch.

"Excuse me, sir. Have you seen the Englishman?" he called in Greek.

The man pulled his body straight, rubbed the small of his back, then shrugged.

"He comes, he goes. I have not seen him today."

"What about yesterday?"

Another shrug. The constable turned to Xará.

"We're wasting our time here."

"I think so, too."

The constable hopped back on and they pottered back down the steep, little street together past the yapping, close-tied dogs, past the stone garage where a toothless, wizened old woman, dressed all in black, was knitting while two chickens pecked the ground at her feet and past the travelling greengrocer selling vegetables to a small gaggle of gossiping village women who sniggered behind their hands at the sight of the uniformed constable on the back of Xará's little motorbike, before chorusing "Yeiá sas" as they passed.

"The Englishman is not here," the constable duly reported.

"No. He's in Síva, it seems," said the sergeant, looking exasperated as he used a handkerchief to wipe fresh perspiration from his face.

CHAPTER 13
AN UNCOMFORTABLE ALLIANCE

Nick woke in a room somewhere in the back streets of Chaniá, surprised to have enjoyed such a huge sleep. True, he had been exhausted after the fruitless searches at the bus station and then the port, but he had expected to be worrying about Jason all night, rather than sleeping. He quickly dismissed any guilt about that. He would be no use to his son if he did not get the rest he needed.

It was an old house of character, owned by a sea captain's daughter. He lifted the bar and threw open the polished, wooden shutters, letting in the light and sounds of the street. The air was clean with a smell of baking. In the kitchen, he was touched to find a breakfast carefully set out for him.

An hour later, at the airport, he joined a small queue at the information desk. After a few moments, a woman with a friendly and reassuring smile asked how she could help. She looked at the photo for a little longer than was usual, then handed the phone back:

"I'm sorry, sir. I can't help you."

"Are you quite sure? Only you seemed to recognise him."

"Did I? No. He looks a little like someone I know. That's all. Sorry."

And the smile was there again as she turned to the next person in the queue.

As Nick turned away, he noticed a man in his fifties dressed as an airport security guard staring at him for a long moment. Then the man moved his head to indicate that Nick should follow him. After about fifty metres through the main concourse, he stopped under a flight of stairs.

"Please to show me your picture."

Nick passed the phone over.

"And you are?"

"I am his father. I've been looking for him for two days."

"This woman won't help you. She scared of police."

"What have the police got to do with it?"

"They have your son, I think. He was here yesterday."

"Jason was here? Was he all right? Why do the police have him?"

"I don't know, mister. I just see him with them, late in the afternoon. I'm a father like you so I think you should know."

"You're not afraid of the police, then?"

"I know these guys. I was a policeman, before this."

He waved dismissively at his security guard's uniform.

"Where do you think they took him?"

"Who knows? But he was with Christodoulákis, so I'd guess Chaniá police headquarters."

"Where do I find that?"

"It's on Giamboudáki or maybe they have him with the Tourist Police on Irákliou."

Nick was fumbling for a notepad and a pen when his phone started ringing. The man was backing away, smiling and nodding. Nick held up his hand to get him to wait but he seemed to take it as a wave and left.

"Hello?"

"Have you heard?"

"Have I heard what, Jen?"

"She didn't drown, Nick. Now they're saying she was murdered."

"Oh, shit."

"It gets worse."

"Go on."

"They arrested Jason at the airport yesterday."

"Oh, fuck. No!"

He heard a muffled sob. "He's been charged with her murder, Nicky."

"Christ. Could he have done that?"

"Do *you* think he could?"

"God, I hope not, Jen. I hope no son of ours could ever do that."

"She dumped him. Just like that. Gave him back the ring. Not long before."

73

"Did she? I heard she was tipsy, taunting him maybe. Then the row. And we know he left town late that night."

"Did he leave before or after she was killed?"

"That's the big question, isn't it? But time of death is an approximate range, as a rule. Without a witness, it might be tough to prove either way."

"Yes, I see."

"Have you told Lauren about all this?"

"Yes, of course. She's a bit stunned by it all, as you'd expect. You might give her a call when you can."

"Are you here now?"

"Yes. I'm in Chaniá with Stephen. Helen and Michael are here, too."

"That must be awkward."

"Big understatement. We're keeping well out of their way."

"And have you seen Jason?"

"They won't let us. Not yet. We've seen the man from the Vice Consulate and some lawyer. They're no help, Nicky. I'm not sure they even believe he's innocent. And the police think they've got their man. Case closed. We just arrived and we're already hitting a brick wall. I don't know where to turn, how to help him."

"Where are you staying?"

"We're at the Hotel Ideon now. It's just west of the harbour, about half a mile from the fortress, I think. Do you want to come over?"

"I'm on my way."

*

"I'm not happy about this, Jen."

"What choice do we have?"

"He's a loose cannon. He could make things worse."

"What could be worse than this, Stephen?"

"He could interfere, turn the police against us."

"They're already against us."

"He could go blundering about in a drunken stupor, ballsing everything up. Like before."

"Nick is many things, but he's not a drunk. That time before we broke up, he *was* drinking far too much but he was stressed out. And he didn't balls everything up. One time he went too far, and a witness died. It wasn't all his fault."

"How come he got pensioned off, then?"

"His face didn't fit anymore. That's all. Politics."

"He ballsed everything up with you."

She slapped her hand on the table.

"This is not about me, Stephen."

There was a pause, then she looked up and her tone was softer.

"Anyway, if we *didn't* ask him for help now, what then? Do you think he *could* stay out of it? Nick Fisher stay at home tending his garden while his only son is banged up for murder? If you think that, you don't know the man at all. He's *going* to get involved, so isn't it better if we know what he's up to, and help where we can?"

Stephen looked at her for several seconds, then the tightness left his face and he crossed the room and put his arms around her.

"Sorry, Jen. You're right. I just worry about what all this will do to Jason – and us. As a family. Nick's been out of our lives for three years. Jason's shown no signs of wanting to let him back in. And I know the man still holds a candle for you."

"We were married for eighteen years, Stephen. We still care for each other's well-being. It's only natural. But it's no more than that. I chose *you*, remember? As for Jason, even after all their problems, I'm sure he'd give his Dad a hug if he could get him out of this terrible, bloody mess."

*

They met in the hotel bar at seven. Stephen bought drinks including, to his astonishment, an iced coffee at Nick's request, and then they found a quiet corner.

"Jen and I have been talking," said Stephen. "We need your help, Nick."

"You mean Jason needs my help."

"We all do," said Jen, quickly.

"Well, of course, I'm going to do everything I can to help him. He's still my son and I don't believe he did this, no matter what circumstantial evidence suggests. But I'm not a DCI in The Met anymore. I resigned. I retired. I left all that behind me in England. I have a new life here. I have *zero* connection with the Greek police and I'm sure they work in very different ways here. It's not my country and I have no right to interfere. None whatsoever. I don't even speak Greek, for God's sake."

Jen was dabbing her eyes; Stephen was staring at his knees.

"Last week, I was trying to build a wall around my roof terrace. I might plant a bougainvillea, go for a swim, talk with my new friends, maybe even write my fucking memoirs. That's my life now. It's a lot different from plunging into someone else's murder investigation in a foreign country." He paused to let that sink in. "You need to understand that I might mess things up for him, make matters a whole lot worse."

"Couldn't you just go down to Síva, mooch around for a bit, ask a few questions and see if you can turn anything up?" asked Jen. "We'll pay your expenses, won't we, Stephen?"

"At the very least," he confirmed.

"That's exactly what I'm going to do, Jen. I just want you to understand that I'm not a bloody magician. I could get nowhere. Or it could all go dreadfully wrong."

"We have nowhere else to turn and we have to try, Nick. For Jason."

"You think I won't do my damnedest? You *know* I will, Jen. You know I *must*. I won't rest – I *can't* rest – until our son is shown to be innocent and we can get him free of this bloody nightmare."

*

Nick drove straight from the hotel to the main police station. At the front desk, he demanded to see his son.

"This is not possible, Mr Fisher," said the sergeant. "While the police are questioning him, you may not see him. It will be one or two days, I think. Not more."

Nick raised his voice.

"But I'm his father. He needs me *now* and I *demand* to see him."

The sergeant stared at him and raised his chin a little.

"Buckingham has been charged with a serious crime. It is not possible."

"Let me speak to a more senior officer." Nick unearthed a dog-eared business card and laid it on the counter as if raising the stakes on a full house. "I'm a senior police officer in England and you guys need to do me a favour on this. Cop to cop."

But the man was paying scant attention to the card.

"No senior officer is available at present, Mr Fisher, and, anyway, they would say the same thing to you. I know this."

"Now look, Sergeant, I'm asking for your help, man-to-man. I just need ten minutes with my son. What harm can that do? I'm worried the boy might harm himself." But the sergeant's expression did not change one iota. "Is there something I can do for you, perhaps?" Nick started tapping his wallet on the counter.

"You need to stop right there, Mr Fisher, before I arrest you for trying to bribe a police officer. You will leave now and you will not come back until we have given a green light to the boy's lawyer, you have presented documents which satisfy us that Buckingham *is* your son and the boy himself has told us that he's willing to see you. Then, and only then, will you be permitted to see him. Is that clear?"

The sergeant had raised his voice too, and an uncomfortable silence followed. Nick tapped the wallet a few more times, then threw him a twisted grin and walked out.

*

Outside, he felt his heart pounding with rage and indignation. It was not unusual for him to lose his cool with petty bureaucracy. It made him furious to be dealt the impotency card by some jumped-up desk clerk following unimportant rules to the letter. But there was nothing he could do; not here, not now. Even though Jason was somewhere in this building, perhaps less than fifty metres away, no doubt desperate, grief-stricken and terrified. He tried to calm himself a little. He looked at his watch. It was nine twenty-five pm. Two hours earlier in England. At least he could call Lauren:

"Are you all right, hun?"

"Hi, Dad. Still can't believe it."

"I know."

"One minute I'm wondering what to wear for the wedding, the next I find out she's been killed, and my brother's been arrested. It's awful. Just awful. Poor Sam."

"I met with your Mum earlier and we're joining forces on this. I'm going to do everything I can to help."

"You don't think he did it, then?"

"No, I don't, but that's a long way from proving that he didn't."

"Have you seen him?"

"No. The police are refusing access for now."

"God. How must he be feeling?"

"I know. It's cracking me up, but the best thing for me is to get on with it. See what I can find out. Your Mum will see him as soon as they let us in or maybe she'll be able to phone or text soon, at least."

"Let me know what's happening, Dad. I feel out of it here. I could come over."

"No. Don't do that, Lauren. You're just starting a new year. Stay there, try to get on with your work. We'll keep you posted."

After ending the call, he made a pragmatic decision to drive home to Saktoúria. He needed a shower and to sleep in his own bed. Tomorrow he was starting a new job. The job of saving his son. And, if Jason did not kill Sam, that meant finding out who the hell did.

CHAPTER 14
ON THE CASE

It was Wednesday and he set off early. To avoid another long drive, he took the road along the coast to Chóra Sfakíon and then drove the Jeep onto the ferries heading west. By late afternoon, Nick was back on the beach at Síva, staring at the big rock. Three and a half days before, a beautiful twenty-year-old girl called Sam had been bludgeoned to death on this very spot. Less than three hours before that, without warning, she dumped the guy she was due to marry in six months, the guy she had been with for more than three years; his son, Jason.

Two things don't sit right, Nick thought, right off the bat. *Firstly, why would she choose to finish it there and then? That would leave her on her own, a long way from home, having to find her way back. No matter how bad it was, you'd think she'd hang on until the end of the holiday and give him the bad news when she was home safe. Okay, she was tipsy, and sometimes these things just well up and something is said from which there's no going back. Unless ... unless. Yes, maybe that was it. Perhaps she would not be on her own. Perhaps someone else had supplanted Jason in her affections. Someone quite different. Someone who made Jason seem inadequate. Someone she wanted to be with – and Jason was in the way. That would explain her actions and, if this guy existed, that would provide another murder suspect. Perhaps a stronger suspect than Jason. Because, and this was the second thing, he just couldn't imagine the Jason he knew lifting that rock. Surely no son of his could. He'd have been deeply hurt by Sam, for sure, but the lad he knew would turn that inwards. He'd trawl back through his failings, things he could and should have done better. He'd be angry as hell, no question, but he'd be angry with himself. People change to some extent and when he was able to catch up with Jason, three years on, he might be surprised. But the amateur psychologist in him doubted it. And the father in him was ready to rule it out altogether.*

Jen and Stephen should get to see Jason in the next day or two. If they could get some information from him, that would give Nick something to get his teeth into.

"I'm going to need a list of everyone Jason and Sam met in Síva," he said on the call that evening, "a detailed holiday itinerary – where they went, who they met, where they stayed, including Jason's movements between leaving Síva and being arrested at the airport.

"Ask him to be precise about the time he last saw Sam and the time he left Síva. Then I'll need details of all photos, calls, emails and texts from *both* mobile phones and any laptops, tablets or cameras, any records of their activities – I'm thinking notes, ticket stubs, journals, diaries and the like. And any photos *taken by others* in which they might have appeared."

Jen promised to do her best. In the meantime, he needed to talk to those people who were still here. He decided to start with the bars and cafés behind the beach.

*

On the same Wednesday morning, Leo was called into the captain's office, first thing.

"So, we've detained the English boy for around forty-four hours, Leo. How's it going?"

"We've questioned him three times, sir, but so far he hasn't changed his story."

"He still maintains that he's innocent?"

"He does."

"You've applied pressure?"

"To the limit of the law, sir. The boy is tired and stressed – and depressed, I would say."

"That doesn't surprise me. No physical damage though, I hope?"

"No, sir. We came close, once or twice, but no."

"But you still believe he's guilty?"

"As you know, sir, there's circumstantial evidence and a strong motive and he did leave the scene of the crime …"

"But a confession would be helpful, to say the least, in the absence of any physical evidence."

"It would, sir. We're not going to find an eye-witness or a blood-stained rock with his DNA all over it."

"Well, I'm getting pressure from two sources, Leo. Athína is trying to wrest the case from us – the Serious Crimes unit – but I've prevailed upon them to give us a further week. The fact that they know you and have respect for your work in the past helped a lot."

"That's good to know, sir. We'll try hard to wrap it up in a week."

"If we can show that we're making real progress, I might be able to get a little more time than that. You know how it goes."

"Yes, sir."

"The other pressure is from the British Vice Consulate who are demanding access for the boy's parents and his lawyer. They've been waiting a day and a half already and I'm inclined to let them in tomorrow morning. You can have another go at the boy in the meantime."

"I can't object to that, in all honesty, sir."

"Good. And lastly, I'm anticipating trouble from the boy's real father. He made a scene at the desk last night and I doubt we've seen the last of him. Seems he was a big shot cop in London a few years ago."

The captain threw Nick's business card onto the table.

"He left that with the desk sergeant. Told him he was still a cop. Well, he's not. Not anymore. Left under a cloud, from what I gather. Just keep your eyes on the bugger, Leo. We don't need him interfering."

*

After leaving the captain's office, Leo found Thaní at his desk and sat down opposite him.

"Any doubts, Thaní?"

"What – about Buckingham, sir?"

"How sure are you that he's our man?"

"I think it's a very high probability."

"That's not what I asked."

"If not him, then who, sir? There is no-one."

"That's not what I asked either, Thaní. Come on."

"In my gut, sir?"

"Yes."

"Frankly, sir? I'm disappointed that he hasn't confessed yet and that's beginning to concern me. We've put him under a lot of pressure. He's not a professional criminal or anything. In my experience, most regular people would either have confessed by now or shot their own story full of holes. He's done neither."

"Yes. He's irritating the shit out of me, Thaní. So, let's give it one last shot. We've got the rest of today before his lawyer shows up, I reckon. Let's go in harder this time. The bad cop, worse cop routine. You know the drill."

Thaní grimaced. "Sir."

*

At ten o'clock on Thursday, Stephen and Jen were still finishing break-fast when Jen took the call.

"Mrs Bucking-ham? Is Eléni. They let us see Jason today."

"Oh, that's great news!"

"Yes. You must go to the police station in Irákliou."

Her heart sank.

"Iráklio? But that's *miles* away, isn't it? I thought you said he was here."

"No, the *street* is Irákliou. Here in Chaniá."

Jen apologised and they arranged to meet in reception at eleven thirty.

*

The police station was a large, pale yellow, concrete building. It was functional rather than attractive, set in a street of large, Venetian-style houses with plane and palm trees, pleasant enough were it not choked with traffic. In the end, they were obliged to leave the taxi and walk the remaining hundred and fifty metres. They escaped the traffic fumes as they went through the glass entrance doors, only to be confronted by body odour and tobacco smoke in the air-conditioned reception area. Perhaps forty people were waiting, some queueing at the reception desk, some seated on rows of plastic chairs. Almost everyone seemed to be arguing in Greek, a baby was crying, and two men were smoking despite the *No Smoking* signs. Eléni looked out of place in her smart, dark red suit.

"We must wait," she said.

"Surprise, surprise," said Stephen.

Twenty minutes later, they were escorted to a large, bare room on the third floor and, five minutes after that, Jason was brought in by two men. The older man nodded and withdrew, leaving a young, uniformed policeman who stood in the corner. There were tearful hugs and then they all sat around a pair of Formica-topped tables with an overflowing ashtray and a half-empty bottle of water. Eléni introduced herself and shook his hand. Jason looked exhausted. He was still tanned, of course, but it was not a healthy-looking tan anymore. His face looked jaundiced almost, his eyes were bloodshot and fearful, and his mouth was turned down. He looked thin and wary. He looked like he did not know who to trust. Jen just wanted to hug him and hug him until everything was all right again. If only it were that simple.

"How has it been?" asked Stephen.

"What do *you* think, Stephen? The girl I was about to marry dumps me, out of the blue, then someone kills her, then I get charged with her murder and put in here. It's really not that great, is it?"

The bitter sarcasm shocked Jen. Stephen went on:

"No, it's not, but I meant *in here*, Jason. How are they treating you?"

"It's been rough."

"Have they hurt you?"

"No physical violence, not quite. Just endless questions, aggression, intimidation, you know. Sleep interrupted, possessions withheld. I've only just got my phone back. But the worst thing is not being believed. I don't know what more I can say to them. I've told them everything I know – I don't know how many times – and it's the truth. I don't know who did this to Sam, but it wasn't me."

"We know that," said Stephen.

"You're not on your own anymore, Jace," added Jen. "You've got us, of course, that nice Mr Beeson at the Vice Consulate, Eléni here and we've also tracked down your father. We're all working hard to get you out of this."

"Dad?"

"Who is this please?" asked Eléni.

"My ex-husband, Nick Fisher. Tough as old boots. He was a senior policeman in England. He's retired now but he's living here in Crete. He's agreed to help us."

"How will he help?" asked Eléni.

"He's going to investigate. He's gone to Síva this morning. He's going to try to prove that Jason is innocent."

"How will he do this?"

"I guess he'll have to find out who really killed poor Sam."

"The police here will not like this."

"No, I don't suppose they would, if they knew, but we don't plan to tell them. Anyway, what choice do we have? We must do something. I'm sure Nick will try to be discreet."

"We will say nothing about this, then." Eléni was looking at the policeman in the corner but guessed that he understood little English.

"No, Eléni. We won't." Jen was reaching into her bag for some hand-written notes. "Now, Nick needs some information to get him started. Let's go through this now, Jason. I think you'll find this helpful too, Eléni."

*

It was a long, sad few days for Helen and Michael Martin. They spent their time in the hotel or on a bench in the nearby park. They held hands a lot and talked about their little girl, but often it was just too much to bear and they talked less and less for fear of upsetting one another. Hour by hour, it became a bleaker existence. At last, on Thursday afternoon, Beeson called:

"Hello, Helen. I'm sorry to have taken so long to get back to you. I don't have any good news for you on the embalming, I'm afraid. As

I suspected, the Greeks are not prepared to budge. They're pointing out that it's the law and that you'd have to have this done in England, anyway, and that they'll do a good job here for less money."

"Three thousand eight hundred euros is less?"

"That price includes the coffin, which is expensive due to the lead-lining."

"So, we'll have to forget about any second post-mortem, then."

"Once again, Michael, the Greeks point out that they have very skilled people here who do a thorough, professional job. They don't understand why you'd need to have it done again. Doctor Pánagou trained in London, they tell me."

"Hmmm."

"I do have *some* good news, however. We've managed to move things along a little quicker than expected. The embalming will be completed tomorrow. You could see her later on Saturday and then take her home with you on Monday, if you can organise payment by then."

"I'm sure we can do that."

"Flights are not included in the price quoted, but I think I can organise a flight via Athens for you all with a hearse for Sam, both here and at the London end. You left a car at Gatwick Airport, I think you said?"

They nodded.

"Just the hearse, then, and a taxi for you two and your luggage from the hotel here. Let me get that sorted out and I'll let you know the cost later today."

They thanked Beeson and he rang off.

"There go the savings, then," said Michael.

"It's for our daughter, Mike." Her tone was icy. "Nothing else matters now."

CHAPTER 15
MAKING A START

Nick drew a blank with all the tavernas and cafés between the ferry dock and the town. Some recognised the picture, but they just knew Sam as the girl who drowned or recalled her face from the newspaper. None remembered seeing her or meeting her and the picture of Jason just produced shrugs and shakes of the head.

At the end of the row of tavernas was Café Sorókos, a smarter-looking bar with a touch of modern style. Soft jazz was playing. Nick went up to the bar, which was almost empty, and ordered an iced coffee.

"Nice," he said, spreading his arms and nodding his head.

"You like jazz?"

"I do, but I meant everything. Your place looks cool."

"Thank you. I am Stélios," he said, extending a hand.

"Nick Fisher."

"You want the frappé skétos?"

"I'm sorry?"

"You want milk in the iced coffee or no."

"Just a little."

"Lígo. Entáxei."

"It's Wayne Shorter, isn't it?"

"He's on sax, yes. It's a Weather Report album, Night Passage."

"Love it."

"Me too."

"Maybe I'll take one of those pastries too, Stélio."

They chatted a little while longer and then Nick asked his usual questions. This time he got lucky.

"Yes, I remember them," said Stélios. "They come here three, maybe four times for breakfast. They sit just across the road there, near the beach. They have special yoghurt with fruits always. She has tea and he has coffee. I was sorry to hear what happened to her. She seemed like a nice girl. Why you ask? Are you police?"

"No, I'm not. Don't worry. Just trying to find out a bit more for the family. Do you remember seeing them separately at any time?"

"You mean one but not the other? No, I don't think so. They just come, they eat breakfast, they go. Like everyone."

"There must be many people. You did well to remember."

"There are many for breakfast, but not so many English here. We have mostly Germans now. Also, many ask about her, so I remember again."

"What do you mean, Stélio?"

"Every time someone asks, I am reminded (is that the word?) So, I don't forget."

"You mean the police?"

"Yes. Konstantópoulos from Chaniá was here a couple of times but also before."

"Who was that?"

"Older guy, maybe fifty, long hair. Spoke to me in Greek with an English accent. Looked like a hippy. We used to have many hippies here. Still a few hanging around."

"Was he with the police?"

"No, I don't think so. Like I say, this was before. She's alive and he's looking for her."

"Did he say why?"

"He said he was supposed to meet her here. He didn't have a photo. Just said he was looking for a pretty, blonde, English girl called Sam, twenty years maybe with a tattoo here," and Stélios reached around to touch his shoulder blade.

"So, what did you do?"

"I just shook my head. The guy seemed a little crazy to me. If she comes for breakfast, I tell her about him, but she never does. I guess she's already dead."

"So, this was the day before she died?"

"Yes. Quite late. We close at two and I was getting ready to close when he showed up."

"So, it was the night she died." Nick was now on full alert.

"I guess so."

"Can you be sure?"

Stélios thought for a minute.

"I never work Fridays, and on Sunday we close at midnight. I'm sure it was later than that, so it must have been Saturday night, or rather, very early Sunday morning."

"And did you tell the police this?"

"I don't tell the police anything they don't ask. That way is trouble for me. And, after the girl drowns, none of this matters."

"Anything more you can remember about this guy? Did you see him again?"

"He wore gold earrings – or maybe just one, I'm not sure – and he was carrying a black leather jacket. He drank a small beer. I was playing one of those Ibiza feelgood albums and he said he liked it. And no, I didn't see him after that."

"Too warm for a jacket, surely?"

"Yes, but this was for a motorcycle, I think."

*

Nick did not find anyone else who remembered the ageing hippy that afternoon but, when he switched to the campsite, he found a group where a few people remembered Sam and Jason:

"We knew who they were, man, said 'Hi' and that, but you need to speak to Kristine and Spíros. They were in the tent next-door and got more friendly."

"They sure did."

A few people sniggered.

"What do you mean?" asked Nick.

"The girl and Spíros had some fun, let's say."

"And you can't do that in a tent without someone working out what's going on."

"Did their partners realise?"

"Well, *we* didn't tell them."

"I reckon it was just a quickie," said another. "Maybe they got away with it."

"Or maybe it was cool."

"With Kristine? You got to be kidding. She'd have his balls if she knew, that one."

Nick found their tent about thirty metres further inland. There was a vacated patch next to it and he realised that was where Jason and Sam's tent had been. He assumed the police had taken it and made a mental note to get it back. A woman was outside, sitting cross-legged, threading tiny, pebble beads on a necklace. She stopped for a moment, picked up her joint and stared at him. Nick caught a musky scent mixing with the dope.

"You a cop?"

"What makes you think that?"

"Can smell 'em, as a rule."

"I'm not here to cause you trouble, Kristine."

"So, you *are* a cop."

"No, I'm not. My name's Nick Fisher. I'm just trying to find out a bit more about Sam and Jason, for the families."

"So, you used to be a cop."

"Might have been."

"Thought so."

Olfactory receptors validated, she seemed satisfied. She raised her eyebrows and leaned forward, waiting for him to speak. Nick glimpsed the small, brown breasts under the loose-fitting top. She glanced at him slyly and closed the top button, with some difficulty. He noticed that her hands were shaking a little.

"What do you remember about them?" he asked.

"I remember that she was my friend, or so I thought, and then she goes and fucks my man."

"How did you find out about that?"

"Spíros told me. After she died, he just went to pieces. But the four of us were just casual mates. It made no sense. Then I twigged. The little bitch is on heat and he's the nearest guy. Tells him she's crazy for him and he can't believe his luck. Pretty soon they're shagging in *my* bloody tent!"

"So, you didn't know about this until after she died."

"Not a clue."

"Is Spíros here? I'd like to talk to him if I may."

"Told him to sling his hook. It wasn't the first time he'd screwed around, and I'd had enough of the bastard. Think he took the boat to Palaióchora."

"Did you tell the police any of this?"

"They did take a statement, early on, but I didn't know about Sam and Spíros then. The little shit hadn't confessed. And they never even talked to him."

Nick was not sure she was telling the truth. It all sounded very natural and plausible, but she was a wily, fearless character. It would be important to locate this Spíros in due course and check that he corroborated her story.

*

It was after seven now and the sun was going down. Nick took a break for some dinner and the phone rang just as his grilled dorada arrived. Typical. It was Jen:

"Hi Nick. I've some better news for you."

"Great. Go on." He held the mobile in his left hand and forked some tzatzíki into his mouth with his right.

"We got to see Jason today. He looked awful but he's okay, deep down, I think. It was great to tell him you're on the case with us."

"Be careful not to get his hopes up, Jen. This could be a long haul."

"I know, but right now he needs people on his side and he's always admired your work. You know that. Despite everything. Been in awe of you, to be honest."

"He has? I wish he'd tell me that himself, one of these days. Or at least speak to me. That'd be a start."

"Give it time."

"I've given it three bloody years."

"Anyway … we got him to go through your questions."

"Great … and?"

"I've got a list of the people they met in Síva. There are twelve, but one of them is just a question mark."

"How come?" Hoping this would be a long answer, he risked a piece of fish.

"He says that, when she was breaking off the engagement, she told him there was someone else. Now Jason doesn't know if that was true or not. He can't see that she had many opportunities. Thought she could have said that to get rid of him. That's why it's a question mark. We just don't know, do we?"

"We'll find out, Jen. What else have you got?"

"I've got the itinerary and I've got Jason's mobile for you. The police have had it, of course, so I'm *assuming* all the information is still on it. And we got the lawyer to ask the police about *Sam's* phone and they're saying that there wasn't one. But there *was*, according to Jace: an iPhone 6 in a pink case. He says she kept a diary, too, more like a private journal, but no sign of that either, they say."

"She kept a journal? That must be a rare thing these days. Doesn't sound like the sort of thing a young girl like Sam would do."

"There was more to Sam than meets the eye, Nick. She had an introspective side, wanted to be a writer one day. She wasn't just some bimbo, otherwise Jason would never have fallen for her."

"Fair enough. But things like that don't just disappear. If Jason didn't take them and the cops aren't playing games, then someone else did. If it were the killer, perhaps they took them because they would reveal their identity – phone records, texts, photographs, secret journal entries …"

"Hmmm. So, they could be important."

"Chances are … and these things point to the killer being *known* to Sam and not some random nutter."

"And there was another thing. You asked if they'd *been* photographed at all, to their knowledge?"

"Had they?"

She went through three places while Nick made inroads into his dinner but only the last one was of any interest.

"… and the guy at the beach bar in Síva has dance parties every Saturday. He takes photos and pins them on a board."

"And they were at the dance party last week?"

"Yes."

"What's the name of the bar?"

"He's not sure. Sunset or Moonrise or some such, but it's at the back of the beach between the town and the big rock and the owner is Manólis."

"It's Moondance. I've seen it. I'll talk to the guy."

"Okay, Nick. Great. Let's see if we can get our boy out of this mess and bring him home."

"We'll do our damnedest, Jen. Don't you worry about that. Now, can you email me the list and the itinerary? On second thoughts, don't bother. I'll have to come and get his phone anyway, so I'll drive up to your hotel in the morning."

"Or we could drive it to you?"

In the end, they compromised on meeting halfway, in a village called Prasés, at ten thirty on Friday morning.

After the call, Nick finished off his fish, washed it down with the rest of the wine and then checked his watch. It was eight twenty-five. Could be a good time to catch the beach bar owner.

*

Nick's visit was well-timed; the beach crowd had dispersed and the night-clubbers were yet to arrive. Apart from one couple, the beach bar was deserted. A tubby, breathless guy in his forties was restocking glass shelves with soft drinks and Bacardi Breezers. Nick lowered himself onto a stool. Without turning around, the man called out:

"Just one minute, sir. Don't worry."

Nick was wondering if he looked that desperate for a drink when a round and rather greasy face popped up from the other side of the counter.

"Welcome! I am Manólis. What can I get you, sir?"

"Beer, please."

"You want Mythos, Alpha, Amstel, Fix?"

"Any on draught?"

"The Alpha. Is good."

"I'll try a large one of those then, thanks."

Alongside the beer, Manólis placed a mixture of crisps and peanuts in a dish and a small, pewter cylinder with the bill in it. Nick sneaked a look: three and a half euros. Not too bad.

"You get Happy Hour price, from seven till ten," said Manólis, who clearly had eyes in the back of his head. "After ten, is five euros."

"Good deal," said Nick, thinking *one could get very happy indeed in three hours,* and took his beer for a stroll.

There was a wall of photographs behind glass to the side of the bar. Most were young people making spectacular fools of themselves while looking *happy*, but some were more touching, maybe family pictures. In one, two girls of maybe seventeen or eighteen were looking at the camera with real fondness in their eyes.

"My regulars, over the years," said Manólis with pride.

"Someone said you have a big dance night here."

"Saturday. Every Saturday."

He reached behind the counter and brought out more photographs, this time pinned to a corkboard with the name Moondance on a wooden plaque at the top and *SEP 15* printed on white paper in the corner.

"I just took this down. Every week I take photos. People come back to look at them. They buy a drink or two. Others see them and think: *That looks fun* and they come the next Saturday. Is good marketing for me."

Nick took the board and scanned the photos. They were not very good. There were one or two that might have been Sam, but he could not be sure.

"Do you have any more?"

"Why you ask?" Manólis looked suspicious so Nick explained.

"But the girl drown, no? Why you do this?"

"The family asked me to help. They want to understand how it happened."

Nick was not sure Manólis was convinced. He stared at Nick with his eyes narrowed for three or four seconds but then seemed grudgingly to accept the story.

"These are the best. There are more on my camera that I haven't deleted yet."

"Could I see?"

"Why not? Wait one minute."

He came back with a Canon DSLR and placed it on the bar.

"You can call up the file like this and then scroll through like this."

"Can I zoom in somehow?"

"Sure, like so."

"Great, Manóli. I'm Nick. And thank you; I appreciate your help. Can you get me another beer and something for yourself?"

"Okay. I take a rakí with you, my friend."

"Do you remember this girl?" Nick showed him a photo of Sam dancing with three men and a girl.

"This the girl who drown. I know."

"Do you remember her that night?"

"Sure I do. She flirt, she drink a lot. I wonder if she gonna cause a fight or maybe throw up. This is typical English girl. No offence, Nick."

"No offence taken," lied Nick, "but she came from a good family so I think she may have been acting up a bit on holiday."

"I dunno what is *acting up.*"

"I mean, I don't think she was like that. Not deep down."

Nick was halfway through the photos. He spotted his son here and there. No beard.

"I tell you what, Manóli, I'd like to get prints of all these photos and then go through them with you, see how many people we can identify. Could we do that tomorrow, maybe? I'll pay you for the prints and for your time."

"Three euros per print and thirty euros each hour for me. Is good deal."

"I can offer two per print and twenty an hour. But I'll need prints I can see, postcard size, at least."

Nick shaped his hands into a frame about eight inches by six inches.

"Two-fifty and twenty-five an hour – in cash. The prints will be twenty by fifteen centimetres."

"All right. Deal." Stephen was paying anyway but Nick knew he had to haggle or Manólis would feel he should have asked for more.

They shook hands firmly across the bar.

"Tomorrow at one pm?"

"No, man. No way. I work here till after two in the morning, then I got to sleep and then I got to get your prints ready."

"Three pm, then."

"Okay. Come here at three tomorrow. I can get Spíros to cover the bar."

"Is that the Latvian woman's partner?"

"Kristīne, yes. She is older. He is her tallboy."

"Toy boy, perhaps?"

"Yes, this is what I say. You know Kristīne then?"

"We had a quick chat."

"She a nice woman. Could do better than Spíros."

"Why do you say that?"

"The boy is trouble. He make her cry."

"Did she tell you that?"

"I see this, a few days ago."

"What did you see?"

"She walk past on the way back from the ferry. I ask her in for a drink but she don't want to know. I think she crying."

"Which day was that?"

"I think Monday? Around six? Something like that."

"Where had she been?"

"Agía Rouméli maybe? Loutró? She goes up and down the coast with her jewellery."

"And Spíros works here?"

"He comes here, I pay him but he don't work much. He is the son of my cousin. I say I will help the boy but he don't help me. I can't rely on him."

"How so?"

"Sometimes he is here, then he disappears. I turn around and he is gone. And always he is talking with the customers. Blah, blah, blah. Drugs and politics."

"Politics? That's a surprise."

"In Greece? Everybody talk politics, man, but not like him. Spíros calls himself a Marxist."

"So why do you keep him, if he's so useless?"

"He has big drug problem in Athína. My cousin think new place, new job, help him get clean. Nick – what can I say? I have a soft and foolish heart."

CHAPTER 16
DIGGING DEEPER

The road twisted through rocky gorges, then mountain villages, some pretty, some forgotten. Black or orange nets lay under silver-green trees, waiting to catch olives. Wild chestnuts in their thousands looked like tiny hedgehogs rolled into balls, clinging for dear life to branches tossed by the strong breeze. Crumbling hillsides were supported by blocks of rough-hewn sandstone, encased in wire netting, and stacked to form walls. In the villages, great bushes of bougainvillea burst forth, their papery leaves of crimson, lilac or deep purple transforming the plain, whitewashed houses into palaces of colour.

Ahead loomed the Omalós Plateau and, to the right, The White Mountains topped two thousand five hundred metres. In the higher parts of the journey, there was a good, tarmac road now, but some of the bends were still alarming and Nick found himself frowning in concentration. At the highest point, a row of giant wind turbines faced north to the sea, a glittering horizon of silver and gold beyond a plain scattered with vineyards and orange groves.

Prasés was one of the larger and higher villages. Nick spotted a taverna on the right that boasted a terrace with a glorious view of tree-covered mountains. He parked the Jeep outside. He was ten minutes early, which was fine. He ordered himself a *Ness* – an English-style instant coffee – with iced water on the side, and chose a table shaded by a vine trellis. It would be a hot day. The sound of cicadas built to near-deafening levels and then stopped, only to start building again a few moments later. Nick wondered how many insects were involved and concluded that it must be fewer than it seemed. Otherwise, how on earth could they stop in such perfect unison? Was there a conductor? Nick imagined the insect: its thorax and abdomen encased in evening wear, its large, gossamer wings shimmering behind, bug eyes scanning an orchestra of its peers, now rapping its baton on a lectern …

"You're looking very smart," said Jen.

"Shaved and showered, anyway."

He and Stephen nodded at each other. No hands were offered.

"Can I get you guys coffee or something?"

They all sat around the table and Nick signalled to the taverna owner, who looked like an ageing partisan with his bristling, yellow-white moustache. The cicadas were building to a crescendo again.

"How did it go yesterday, Nick?" asked Stephen, raising his voice.

"Quite well, I think. I've already discovered a couple of things that the police don't seem to have found."

"Such as?"

"Sam had a fling with the bloke in the next tent, according to his girlfriend – now ex-girlfriend."

"The little trollop," said Jen. "Does Jason know?"

"I'd assume not, Jen – and now would not be a good time to tell him. Never might be better still."

"The little trollop!" she said again, with venom.

"Could that be the *someone else* then?" asked Stephen.

"It could …"

"But you're not convinced."

"I'm keeping an open mind. It seems there was another guy around that night, looking for Sam. A much older guy who looked like a hippy. I don't know where he fits in, but I need to find out."

"What about this girlfriend?" asked Jen. "Could *she* have done something?"

"She didn't know about the fling until after Sam died, apparently."

"But she would say that, wouldn't she?"

"I need to check that out. Both she and Spíros are on my suspect list."

"But not on the police's?"

"No, I very much doubt it."

"That's good work, Nick," said Stephen, attempting a smile of encouragement.

You patronising prat, thought Nick.

"What can you do to find the ageing hippy?"

"Well, I'm hoping the stuff you've brought me will throw up some clues, Jen. I've also arranged to go through some photos with the owner of Moondance. Sam and Jason were there that last night. I want to see who else was. That might lead somewhere. I'm having to pay the man for his trouble, I'm afraid. Could get close to two hundred euros."

Stephen raised his eyebrows. "I've brought you five hundred euros advance against expenses, anyway. You can take it out of that."

"Okay. Good."

Jen was delving into a carrier bag.

"This is Jason's phone, and I brought the charger, too."

"Well done."

"And this pad has everything we wrote down together yesterday – the lists you asked for. And the cash is in this envelope."

"Excellent. Thank you. Did you look at the photos on the phone?"

"Not yet. We'll leave that to you, for now."

"Okay. How are you coping, you two?"

"Well, we're feeling better than before, when there seemed to be no hope, and I think we'll get to see Jason again tomorrow morning, so we'll do our best to keep him cheerful … without raising any false hopes," she added when she saw concern crossing Nick's face.

"Good. Look, I'll let you know if I need more from Jason when I've been through this lot and seen the beach bar guy."

"Okay."

"Now, if you don't mind, I'll head straight back and work through this lot. No, don't get up. Finish your coffees. Enjoy the cicadas!"

"Is that what they are?" said Jen.

"You can spot them on the tree bark. They're one or two inches long with big, translucent wings and bug eyes that point in different directions. The males are vibrating their tymbals – tiny skin drums on the abdomen. That's what makes the racket."

"I thought they rubbed their legs together," said Stephen.

"No, I think that's crickets."

"Is it a mating call, then?"

"Yes, it can be, but also, when they get together like this, the mass vibrating session scares away the birds, so they don't get eaten. I guess that's why there are so many of them."

"How interesting," said Jen, kindly.

Nick grinned, then gathered up the A5 pad and the phone and charger and pocketed the envelope. He climbed into the Jeep and swung it through a hundred and eighty degrees before roaring south in a cloud of dust, beeping twice and waving.

"I think he's rather enjoying himself," said Jen.

"Yes. Maybe he'll be okay after all."

"He'll be just fine. He's in his element."

Jen stood and wandered over to a nearby fir tree.

"Come and look at these bugs, Stephen."

*

The drive back took forty-five minutes. Nick was gunning the Jeep because he was keen to get into this material. He was excited now. Maybe he was on to something. And he would have a couple of hours before he needed to be at Moondance. He decided to go back to his rooms to be without distractions. Also, he could be cool there and give his brain a chance. It did not work too well, simmering in the heat. On the way through the town, he stopped for a moment to pick up a pad of A3 paper, some Blu Tack and some coloured pens and, as an afterthought, a large bottle of mixed juice, mostly pomegranate by the colour of it, and some sesame and honey bars.

Back in his room, he shut the doors to his tiny balcony and turned on the air-conditioning while he took a cold shower. Then he poured some of the juice into a large glass, drank some and took a large bite from one of the sesame bars which almost glued his teeth together. Now he was ready.

He wrote headings on three of the sheets of paper and tacked them to the wall. Then, on the first sheet, he transcribed the names Jen had scribbled on the paper pad and read through Jason's comments:

PEOPLE WE MET

Shaun and Chevaune (sp?) – Irish couple met on the first night in Síva. They were at the next table in the restaurant. Got together over rakí after dinner. Good chat. Didn't see them again but think they were leaving anyway. They told us a lot about the town, so I assume they'd been there a while already.

Spíros and Christina – Friendly, older couple (early thirties?) in the tent next to ours. She and Sam got on well and chatted quite a bit. Think she was from one of the Baltic States. He was Greek. I didn't have much in common with them.

Matthias, Ullrick and another guy (Rick?) – three young Germans. Nice guys. Well-educated and thoughtful, philosophical. Big dope smokers. Sam saw more of them than I did. Not into dope, myself.

An American girl – don't know who she was – Sam was dancing and fooling around with her and the German guys on our last night. They all went swimming together after the beach bar closed, up by the big rock. I went up there too, to try and talk Sam out of breaking us up. Didn't work, so I left.

We also chatted with the waiter at Polifímos Taverna (where we met the Irish couple) – I think his name was Babis (?) and with the guy at Sorókos where we ate breakfast (Stélios) and with the guy who runs the beach bar (Sunrise? – he was Manólis).

Sam may have met someone else (male, I assume). She said that as she was breaking up with me, but we were together most of the time, in Síva. We chatted with a few other campers, but I don't know their names.

Nick stood back from the eleven names and a question mark listed on the paper.

Sean/Shaun

Siobhan

Spíros

Kristine/Christina

Matthias

Ulrich

Rick?

American Girl

Babis?

Stélios

Manólis

? (The Someone Else)

Maybe only Kristīne and the three locals (Babis, Stélios and Manólis) were still here, or maybe they were all still here. He would have to find out. Thank God it was a brief list of names. *They must have been a self-contained couple – or maybe it's just the sort of place where people keep to themselves*, Nick thought.

He moved on to the itinerary, went to his second sheet of paper and chose a different-coloured pen, just for the hell of it. He wrote:

ITINERARY

Arrived: Friday, 24th August on Easyjet 22.40 (on time). Took ages to get luggage, took a cab into Iráklio city, stayed at Irini Hotel (Dad's treat) for two nights.

Saturday, 25th – Day in Iráklio. Visited the Archaeological Museum and lots of other sights.

Sunday, 26th - Took the bus to Knossós and visited Minoan Palace site then bus to Réthymno. Stayed in an apartment behind the beach for three nights (Airbnb: can dig out detail if needed).

Monday & Tuesday 27-28th - Réthymno town and beach. Tuesday afternoon I went to visit the fort on my own. Sam preferred to stay on the beach.

Wednesday & Thursday 29th-30th - hitched inland to Anógia, stayed in Airbnb place (host: Maria). Walking in the foothills of Psilorítis together.

Friday 31st - hitched back to the coast at Pánormos. Stayed with Bill and Sandy (grandparents of my friend Chris).

Saturday 1st - bus from Pánormos to Réthymno and then bus to Spíli. Stayed in Héracles rooms.

Sunday 2nd - hitched/walked from Spíli to Séllia. Stayed with Airbnb hosts Peter and Linda Weston for six nights. Explored coastline around Plakiás. Lots of beach time for Sam. Hired a motorbike for three days. On Tuesday Peter took us to a special beach he knew (near Rodákino?) and then I went off to climb Psilorítis Wednesday night/Thursday morning (5th/6th).

Saturday 8thth - Coach trip to Samariá Gorge (at dawn). Did Gorge walk. Took ferry from Agía Rouméli to Síva.

Saturday 8th - Saturday 15th - Camping in Síva. Tuesday (11th) we took the ferry to Palaióchora for the day. I walked to Lissus in the afternoon of Thursday (13th).

I'd planned for us to go on to Elafónissi and Gramvoúsa before flying back on Tuesday, 25th.

Nick drew three columns on his third A3 sheet: date/time, location, Sam alone? He was searching for any opportunities for her to meet someone while Jason wasn't there. He took his marker pen and put red rings around the four dates with a YES in the final column:

Tuesday, 28ᵗʰ August – afternoon – Réthymno Beach – YES

Wednesday, 5ᵗʰ September – evening – Séllia – YES

Thursday, 6ᵗʰ September – morning – Séllia – YES

Thursday, 13ᵗʰ September – afternoon – Síva – YES

Next, Nick turned his attention to the mobile phone and went straight to the *photos* icon. Jason seemed to have filed all the holiday photos in a folder marked *Crete* and even added a brief caption to each one. *Good lad,* thought Nick.

There were thirty-eight photos in all.

There were three typical tourist shots taken in Iráklio and another three at the Minoan palace of Knossós, after which most were landscapes or seascapes or beach scenes, many featuring only Sam. He skipped through those and focused on the remaining seven.

The first of these was a *selfie*, taken with their hosts at Pánormos. As they were Chris's grandparents, it would have been one to send to him, in all likelihood. Bill and Sandy looked to be in their early seventies.

The second one was also a selfie, this time just Sam and Jason in front of the Lion's Head fountains in the square at Spíli. *They look relaxed and happy together then*, Nick thought.

The third one was captioned *at Peter's beach* and it showed Sam and an older man coming out of the water. They were wearing swimming costumes, but Sam's was topless. Both held snorkelling masks and breathing tubes. They looked exhilarated. The man was perhaps fifty or so and looked fit and tanned. His grey-blond hair was swept back and there was a joyful intensity about that face. *He looked like someone who'd just won an Olympic medal and was about to mount the rostrum*, thought Nick.

The fourth and fifth were both taken from the top of Psilorítis as the

104

sun was coming up. Nick knew these climbing trips were organised in small groups by tavernas near the base of the mountain. They began with an early evening get together over dinner, followed by a short sleep. The ascent started at midnight, to arrive at the summit at dawn. Jason must have been away from Séllia from six in the evening till eleven the next morning.

The sixth was captioned *Peter and Linda* and was a posed shot of the hosts in front of their restored stone villa, taken as Sam and Jason were leaving. Peter was staring straight at the camera, head tilted to one side, eyes crinkling as he smiled. His hair, dry this time, was again swept back, although there was a slightly odd look to it. His wife was almost as tall as he was and quite sturdy. Her hair was pale ginger with touches of grey, the crinkles pulled back into a grip of some sort. She wore sunglasses and was smiling a little. Nick thought she looked ten years older than her husband.

The final shot was of a young couple, perhaps still in their late teens. The backdrop was a small, rocky cove with a shingle beach. Nick did not know who they were. The caption said simply: *at Lissus*.

Nick looked at his watch. It was one forty-five. He needed to be at Moondance at three. There was just time to check the phone for calls, texts and Facebook messages.

There were very few phone calls. Nick recognised Jen and Stephen's number, so Jason must have called home twice and then made just three local calls. One was an Iráklio area number – probably the hotel – and two were Réthymno area codes. Nick called them and found restaurants local to the Séllia or Spíli areas. There were a few text messages, but only to three destinations: Jen and Stephen, Sam and friend Chris. Some had photos attached but there was nothing remarkable at all. There was an email with the Lissus photo attached sent to gina.moretti25@gmail.com. Jason had written simply: *Nice to meet you both – have a great holiday.* Jason must have been asked to take a photo of strangers Gina and her boyfriend while at Lissus.

Jason had posted photos on Facebook twice. The first posting, on the second of September, covered the Iráklio, Knossós, Anógia,

Réthymno and Spíli part of the holiday, and the second, on the twelfth of September, covered Séllia, Plakiás, Síva and Palaióchora. There were no photos that Nick had not already seen on the phone. The photos were *liked* or *loved* by various friends and family. The first album attracted sixteen comments and the second twelve. But it was all the usual, tiresome stuff. Nothing caught Nick's eye as different or unusual. Anyway, it was now time to pick up Manólis's photos.

*

"Sorry, sorry, I sorry …" Manólis looked sweaty and flustered. "Many customers from the beach today. There was a coach from Chaniá. And Spíros has buggered off somewhere. The boy cannot be relied upon. Sorry."

"Are you almost there?"

"Nearly, man, give me twenty minutes?"

"I'll give you half an hour. Until three thirty, but don't let me down then, Manóli."

*

Nick used the time to go back to the campsite where he found a few of the same crowd he had spoken to before.

"Yeah, man, it happened in the afternoon, that's for sure. I'd say around this sort of time."

"A few of us have siestas, get out of the sun for a bit," explained another.

"For a bit of what?" joked a third.

"Haha. Not what *she* wanted, man – just to rest up, you know?"

"So, around three – would that be on the Thursday afternoon, two and a half days or so before she died?" asked Nick.

"Sounds right but, like, every day's the same here, pal. Know what I mean? Couldn't swear it was Thursday."

"Anybody else?"

"Well it wasn't Friday if that's any help, 'cos I wasn't here then. Took the guitar over to Palaióchora to earn a few pennies. A *very* few, as it turned out."

106

"Okay. That does help, thanks. Now, last question, does anyone remember seeing Spíros after that Thursday?"

"Sure, he was behind the bar at Moondance, Saturday night."

"And after that?"

Silence. Puzzled faces.

"Come on, guys. Someone must have seen him since then."

"He left, I think someone said."

"Did anyone see him go?"

But no-one volunteered anything more. Spíros seemed to have gone, so maybe Kristíne was telling the truth about that. As to the timing of his affair with Sam, it was good enough. Nobody was saying that it *was not* Thursday and that was, after all, the only day a clear opportunity would have presented itself. Jason was walking to Lissus in blissful ignorance while his wife-to-be was shagging the guy from the next-door tent, much to the amusement of half the bloody campsite. Nick shook his head in anger as he strode back to Moondance.

*

"Hi Manóli. All set?"

"Yes, yes. We sit here, my friend. You want beer?"

"Why not?"

Nick sat and Manólis handed him a pack of prints in a cellophane envelope.

"You have thirty-two prints so is eighty euros so far – okay?"

"Okay."

"Plus my time, of course."

"Right."

"You look. I bring beer."

Nick went through the prints with care, separating them into two piles. The ones where he could spot Sam or Jason, he left face up, the others he put face down. After going through once, there were ten in the face-up pile and twenty-two rejects. What was very disappointing was that none of the thirty-two featured anyone who looked like an ageing hippy. *Bugger*, thought Nick, *I suppose that was too much to hope for.* He went back through them all again. He moved one print from the rejects pile when he spotted the blue butterfly and realised that he was looking at Sam from behind.

"One beer," said Manólis and placed it in front of Nick before slumping beside him with a frappé in his hand. He mopped at his brow with kitchen towel and then wiped the sweat off his hands. "It should be quiet now until six or so, and Rudi is here anyway, so I will help you now if I can, my friend."

"Still no Spíros?"

"No. Useless piece of shit. Buggered off somewhere again. Rudi is good guy though. Swiss. Reliable, like a watch."

"Okay, Manóli. Thanks for these. This pile is the eleven which feature Sam or Jason, mostly Sam. Let's start with them."

They worked through the prints, identifying the people one by one. Manólis knew the names of most of them and, where he did not, he was often able to give Nick some useful pointers.

"These guys are the three Germans. This is Matt. Nice guy. And here is Erik."

"Matt being Matthias?"

"I know him as Matt but maybe, yes. Oh, and this is the other one. He's a pain in the backside, that one, name of Ulrich."

"I have a Rick."

"No Rick – Ulrich or Erik."

"Okay, Jason wasn't sure about that one. Must be Erik, then."

"Yes – Matt, Erik and Ulrich, for sure."

"And this one?"

"The one facing away. I know this big bottom. That is American girl, Andie."

Nick wrote down all the names. It took them forty minutes but, by the end, Nick was recognising people and they were getting quicker. When they went through the second pile, they identified only three new people, giving a final list of just thirteen names.

"Of course, maybe I didn't photograph everyone who was there," said Manólis. "I am running the bar and the music, so I can't be sure

I get everybody."

"Do you *remember* anyone else being here that night?"

"You joke with me?"

"Not at all."

"My friend, I take the photos *so* I can remember people who come. And I try to get them all. But no photo, then no memory for me."

It was a quarter to six. Nick was feeling disappointed and irritated. Had this been a complete, bloody waste of time – and Stephen's money? He paid Manólis the hundred and forty euros he was due and thanked him. Manólis went back to work, then returned with another beer.

"This from me," he said.

"Cheers, mate," said Nick, attempting a smile. Then he stared forlornly at the list of names:

SAM

JASON

GERMAN HIPPIES: Matt/Matthias, Rick, Ulrich

ANDIE – American girl

BETH – Canadian musician. Plays guitar sometimes at the bar.

KENNY – Irish philosopher type. Redhead.

MIKEY – young Greek guy from Thessaloníki. In Síva quite a while.

STEFAN – Swedish guy, blue & green coloured hair. Dopehead. Gay?

VASSILY – Russian in his thirties. Big guy. Shaved head.

French girl with Vassily (name?) – Attractive brunette. Much smaller.

Polish girl (Magda?) – Short blonde hair. Drunk, not happy. Break-up?

There were eight guys and five girls. From that ratio, and the small total, Nick reckoned this was more a drinkers' bar than a dancers' bar; more Moon*shine* than Moondance, perhaps.

Where was all this getting him? Manólis thought it likely that Mikey and Andie were still in town, but he did not know about the others. Nick thought Beth might be, too, but he wondered if there was much point in trying to trace the others anyway. His gut was telling him it would be a waste of time. No ageing hippy had been unearthed and Manólis had not come up with anyone matching that description, when asked.

In the absence of a better idea, he decided to go and eat at Polifímos Taverna which seemed to be a popular place. At least he should get a decent meal. He finished his beer, gathered up his papers, waved thanks to Manólis and once again scrunched over the shingle to the town.

A large plate of moussaká with a Greek salad and half a litre of a good, local red wine and Nick was feeling much more cheerful. There was a band with a lyra, a kind of small violin played vertically, and two laoutos or lutes. They were playing and singing in a corner of the open-air restaurant. Nick enjoyed this uniquely Cretan music for half an hour, but then it became repetitive. He asked his waiter which of the catering team was Babis and, when the after-dinner rakí arrived and the band finally took a break, he called him over.

"O Babí? I am Nick Fisher. Will you take a rakí with me?"

"I will, Kýrie Fisher, but I cannot stay long. We are still busy, as you see."

"I'll come straight to the point, then. The girl who drowned – Sam Martin – I believe she ate here and met you?"

He pulled out one of the photos from his cellophane envelope and showed it to Babis.

"Are you police?"

"No. Don't worry. Just a friend of the family."

"She was here, yes, maybe two weeks ago. I only saw her once. I already told the police. She was with her boyfriend and the Irish pair, Sean and Siobhan."

110

"You knew them already?"

"Sure. The Irish guys ate here most nights. They love the music and the wine."

"Do you know where they were staying?"

"Rent rooms somewhere near, I think. There are many."

"Not camping?"

"Not those two. Plenty money."

"Do you know when they were leaving Síva?"

"Not for sure, but maybe this was their last night. They drink special bottles of wine. Bottles with labels, not carafes. I don't think they came here again."

"At least, not while you were working."

"I work always. All summer. In winter, no work. And now ..."

"Just one last thing. Did you notice anything *between* Sam and Sean?"

"How you mean?"

"Were they attracted to each other, would you say?"

"I'm a busy waiter, Mr Fisher, but no, I don't think so. Sean and Siobhan very close, always laughing together. He don't notice nobody else."

The band were threatening to start again, so he summoned the bill. The cops could ask around in the rent rooms places and find out who these two were, when and where they went. It sounded like a chance, after-dinner meeting between two couples that led to a fun evening with music, wine and rakí and the Irish couple probably left soon after, almost a week before Sam's death. Nick decided to cross them off his list.

All in all, a rather frustrating day but the beauty of the evening, still warm but with a gentle onshore breeze, was soothing him now. The sky was crystal clear with the Milky Way visible. The Libyan Sea was rippling the shingle. He would sleep well tonight, put all this out of his head for now.

CHAPTER 17
KNUCKLES RAPPED

Thaní took the call at seven thirty am Saturday. As he picked up, the baby stopped screaming, stared at him wide-eyed, then puked on the kitchen table. Everywhere there was dirty laundry. The house felt like an out-of-control nursery. He was wondering, aghast, at how little Ioánna was dominating their lives. They were so tired, all the time. He took the phone to the living room as his wife threw up her hands in angry disbelief.

"Thaní. Good morning. It's Leo. That chat we had on Wednesday, and then the hard-ass session with the Buckingham boy that got us nowhere, left me thinking."

"Yes, boss. Me too."

"Just suppose, for a moment, that he didn't do it. We could find ourselves in a tricky position if Athína gets involved and he turns out not to be our guy."

"Hmmm."

"We've assumed that all that circumstantial evidence can lead to only one conclusion. I still think we're right, but he hasn't confessed and, if we're honest, we haven't done a lot to explore the possibility that someone else might have done it."

"What do you want me to do, boss?"

"Get your arse down to Síva again. Take Demétrios, he's a bright lad. Ask some more questions. See if anyone else showed interest in this girl. Think about motive. Who, other than Jason, might have wanted her dead?"

"The press might catch on, boss."

"Yes, I know, but that's too bad. The Department of Tourism will just have to live with it. I can't see that one murder's going to bring the world crashing down."

"Okay."

"And while you're doing that, I'll explore the *someone else* idea with Buckingham and see where that gets us. If I come up with anything, you'll be the first to know."

"Right, boss."

"And Thaní?"

"Boss?"

"That bar owner, Alexandrákis?"

"You mean the Moondance guy?"

"Yes, him. Slimy bugger. Some would say his readiness to serve alcohol to drunks and turn a blind eye to drug abuse contributed to this girl's death. So now he's trying to stay in with us, keep us sweet, hold on to his licence. He called me."

"Did he, now?"

"Someone's been snooping around, he says. Asking questions. An English guy. Says he's acting for the family but who knows? Could be a private investigator, could be the press smelling a rat in the *drowning* story."

"Didn't he get a name?"

"He says not."

"It could be the father. Remember what the Spíli cops told us."

"Could be, but it's all the same to me."

"What do you want me to do, boss?"

"Find out who it is and what he knows and then warn him off. Don't take any shit from him. This is our turf. We don't want him getting in the bloody way."

"Or finding stuff we should have found."

"Quite."

"Couldn't we ask the families if they hired someone?"

"Let's just find a few things out first, Thaní. Then we'll be in a better position to figure out our next move. On your way now. Call me later."

*

Nick knew that, when he slept, his brain kept working. Like a computer, sorting, scanning, filing, looking for anomalies. By the morning, it was not unusual for it to present him with issues thrown up by this process, as if by magic. This Saturday morning, three items were flashing red in his brain's out-tray:

Firstly, it dawned on him that, although Sam's iPhone was missing, she too might have posted photos on Facebook and, if Jason was a Facebook friend, which surely he must be, then his phone would have received a copy. Nick was surprised not to have spotted anything on the first run-through but then there was so much rubbish; heaps of postings from all manner of idiots, not to mention the marketing trash. He could well have missed something. He needed to double-check.

Secondly, it occurred to him that he had made an assumption – never a good idea in police work. He had assumed that the thirty-two prints Manólis had given him were *all* the shots he took that night. Perhaps they were, but he had not made certain. He needed to do that.

Thirdly, he remembered that the itinerary contained nothing about Jason's movements after the final row on the beach. It worried him a little that Jason had failed to provide that, and he needed to follow that up.

Breakfast was a large cappuccino with a chocolate croissant in his left hand while he scanned Jason's Facebook pages again with his right. He soon found the posting on the second of September and then trawled through the dross with great care after that. By the time he reached Jason's twelfth of September posting, his coffee was getting cold and he had found nothing. So much for that idea. He skipped forward listlessly and then something caught his eye. It was Sam's face and it came from a posting dated the fourteenth of September. Just a week ago. Yes, this was it! A posting from Sam, copied to her Facebook friends, including Jason. He could see why he had missed it. It was so late. It was the Friday before the dance. The penultimate day of her life, as it turned out. It was an album of forty-five photos. He scanned through in mounting excitement but couldn't see any ageing hippies. The photos covered many of the same events as Jason's, but nothing from Psilorítis or Lissus, confirming that Jason was alone then. There were three photos taken on their first night in Síva: one of Sean and Siobhan, presumably, a shot of the band and then one of all four of them which didn't look like a selfie, so perhaps Babis took it for them. There were few captions, but when he came to the trip to Peter's special beach, on the Tuesday, he found a long note:

This is our Airbnb host in Séllia, Peter. Nice guy. Took us to this fabulous, secret beach. So cool. Hard to believe he's almost fifty, isn't it? He's into music and politics and gets The Guardian Weekly *delivered out here in the middle of nowhere! He's so well-informed – a clever guy.*

Three things struck Nick there and then. Firstly, she seemed to admire Peter a great deal. For his mind, yes, but perhaps for his body too, judging by the comment about his age. Secondly, there was no mention of Linda, and thirdly, she must have known Jason would read this. In Nick's experience, people that are besotted do not notice that they are hurting people or acting irrationally. Was she besotted with Peter? If she were, Jason seems to have been oblivious. Or perhaps he dismissed such thoughts because Peter was old enough to be Sam's father and had been married to Linda for thirty years. Or that the relationship between host and guest was quasi-professional, ruling out anything more intimate. Or perhaps he was just a sweet boy who thought his fiancée loved him and would always be faithful to him. Nick blinked back a tear.

Four shots had been taken at the beach. Nick rolled them round into landscape and studied each one, using his sticky fingers to zoom in where it helped. Three were taken looking towards the sea. One was just a standard pose of Sam and Jason and one was a sideways view of the whole cove. But it was the third and fourth photos that excited Nick. The third was a shot of Peter, wet from the sea, with Jason behind him, still in the sea. Peter is half-turning, looking back at Jason. His bedraggled ponytail is clearly visible. *So that's why his hair looked odd in the earlier photo,* thought Nick, *it wasn't swept back, it was being pulled back. And any man with hair long enough to wear in a ponytail could look like a hippy if he were to let it down.* Then he looked at the fourth photo.

"Yes!" he shouted and thumped the table.

This was a shot looking inland. In the foreground were Peter and Jason, arm in arm like best buddies, but it was the background that interested Nick. In the shade of the tamarisk trees at the back of the beach, he could see two motorbikes. One was a modest, safe-looking bike, maybe one hundred and twenty-five cc or so, and the other was a wild-looking track bike with a much more powerful engine, perhaps five hundred cc. He wondered which one Sam went back on and thought he knew the answer. One was hired by Jason and the other was owned by Peter, reckoned Nick, and that would be the bike that Peter rode to Síva on the night of Sam's murder, and for which he needed that leather jacket. Then Nick remembered the earrings that Stélios had mentioned and he went through the photos of Peter once again. No earrings. *Nevertheless,* he thought, *looks like you're going on a little trip, my son – and you're going to need bed and breakfast.*

He threw the dishes into the sink, then called Jen.

"Oh yes, I'm sorry Nick. My fault. He *did* tell us what happened. I just forgot to pass it on. He hitched a ride out of Síva late that night with a couple of Cretan boys and ended up staying at their place."

"Yes, I know that, but what time did he leave?"

"Between three and four am was all he could say. He reckoned that was thirty to forty minutes after he left Sam near the big rock. The next morning, he was driven to a place called Kándanos and took buses to Chaniá and then out to Gramvoúsa."

"That's it?"

"I'm afraid so. He was in a sorry state, Nick."

"Why Gramvoúsa, though? Why not go straight to the airport?"

"He says he needed to think things through. To decide whether or not to go back and talk some more with Sam; to give himself some breathing space before doing something as final as leaving the country."

"So, he didn't know she was dead at that point."

"No, of course, he didn't. How could he have?"

If he'd killed her, thought Nick but he just thanked Jen and ended the call.

116

*

Next, he walked over to Moondance. It was only just noon, so he was pleased to see Manólis already behind the bar.

"Hello again, Nick. You want a beer?"

"Not just now, thanks, Manóli. I want to ask you something."

"Sure thing."

"The thirty-two prints you gave me – were they *all* the photos you took that night?"

"I print for you all the ones that were okay. Taking shots in the dark, you know, sometimes they don't work."

"So, there *were* more?"

"There were four others, but they are very poor. I don't want to take your money for these. One was very blurred, and the others are just very dark. You can't see nothing."

"Can you show me, on the camera?"

"I deleted them already. Sorry, Nick."

"Isn't there a way to recover deleted files?"

"Could be, man, but I don't know how."

"Could you find out? Try to get them back for me?"

"You're wasting your time, man."

"Look, I've got a gut feeling about this, Manóli. You get them back and make prints for me, I'll have fifty more euros for you."

"One hundred."

"Come on! It might take you half an hour. Fifty is very generous."

"Seventy-five. These things take a lot of time."

"Sixty-five. Final offer. And only if you get them to me tonight."

"You're a hard man, Nick Fisher, but okay, I try. Now we have one rakí to close the deal."

He called out to Rudi. He called again, then jerked his head around.

"Where's that boy got to now? These guys drive me crazy, Nick."

"Don't worry. We have a deal, even without the rakí."

"Okay. You come for nightcap instead, at eleven tonight?"

"I'll be here. Do your best, eh?"

He turned to go and found his path blocked by a tall, young Greek.

117

"Mr Fisher?"

"Yes, I'm Nick Fisher."

"I would like to talk with you please. My name is Konstantópoulos. I'm an investigations sergeant with the Chaniá police. May we sit over here and perhaps have a coffee?"

He signalled to Manólis and they sat down at a table, well away from the bar.

"What can I do for you?" asked Nick in as bright and open a manner as he could muster.

"You can tell me what you're doing here."

"In Crete? I live here."

"You live *here*?"

"Yes, not in Síva. I have a place in Saktoúria, the other side of Plakiás."

"So why are you in Síva, Mr Fisher?"

"I love it here. It's one of the places I come to, from time to time. Just for a few days."

"You're not being straight with me, Mr Fisher. You are not here for a holiday. I know that. You've been asking questions, talking to people. What are you doing?"

Nick raised his hands in submission.

"You're right, Sergeant. I was asked to come here by Jason Buckingham's mother and stepfather. I'm Jason's real father and I used to be a policeman in England, so they asked me to help."

"Help how?"

"Our son is accused of murder. You know that. You're on the damned case, aren't you? They want me to help prove his innocence to you."

"And how will you do this?"

"Well, the best way to prove someone innocent is to prove someone else guilty. I want to find out who really did this and help you put them away."

"This is police business, Mr Fisher, and this is not your country."

"I accept that. But you can't expect me to sit back and do nothing when you charge my son with murder."

"You should have come to the police."

"First thing I did. You wouldn't even let me see him."

"No. So you tried to bribe your way in, I hear."

"That was a little clumsy, I grant you, but I was rather upset."

"You should have spoken to the team – me or my boss."

"So you could tell me not to interfere?"

"At least you would not have broken the law."

"Since when is asking a few questions breaking the law?"

"Interfering with police business is an offence in Greece, Mr Fisher."

"All right, Sergeant, let's cool off, shall we? You're not going to arrest me."

"You will tell me everything that you have found and then you must go back to Saktoúria and leave this case to the police. If you do this, I will not arrest you. No policeman wants to arrest another – even an ex-policeman from another country."

"Well thank you for that, at least."

While they were talking, Nick realised he would have to give up some information to keep the police off his back. He decided to give him everything that related to Síva but keep him away from the itinerary or any thoughts about Peter Weston. He told the sergeant about Sam's fling with Spíros and how he had since left – perhaps for Palaióchora.

"You need to find this guy," said Nick.

"You suspect him?"

"He has sex with the girl. Two days later she is murdered and he has gone. That has to be enough to make him a suspect until you find him and rule him out."

Nick watched him note down all the details of Spíros and Kristíne and the location of their tent. He told him about the photos from Manólis and showed him the thirty-two prints and the list of people that Sam and Jason met in Síva.

"We have interviewed many of these already," said the sergeant.

"But not all."

"No, not all."

Let *him* spend the hours and manpower needed to track down Sean and Siobhan and the disparate rabble at the beach bar that night. Nick did not think it would get him anywhere, other than ruling them out, in the end.

"All right, Mr Fisher, thank you for that, we will follow up these leads over the next few days."

"If I can be any more help, Sergeant, I'd be delighted to assist."

Nick wrote his mobile phone number on the back of another of his old business cards and handed it to Thaní.

"Please feel free to call me. Anytime."

"What is this?" Thaní was pointing at the acronym on the card.

"Oh," said Nick, casually, "DCI is Detective Chief Inspector, Sergeant. The Metropolitan Police Force is the police force in London."

"Yes. I have heard of this. I will tell my boss, Lieutenant Christodoulákis, but I am sure he will want you to stay out of it, Mr Fisher. You will leave Síva now?"

"I will be on the ferry in the morning, Sergeant. You have my word on that."

They shook hands and Nick walked away, smiling to himself. *That's what we call a win-win situation*, he thought, smugly. *Konstantópoulos is happy – he has plenty of information to check out, potential suspects to track down and others to locate and interview. He's done his duty and warned me off, or so he thinks. His boss should be pleased with him. I, meanwhile, have broken the ice with the Cretan Police, not been arrested, and provided some apparently useful clues. I'm confident that, when I get back in touch, I'll find a receptive ear. And, of course, I was taking that ferry anyway, on my way to Séllia.* Nick was feeling so pleased with himself, that he promised himself a late afternoon swim and a good evening meal, on Stephen, but first he needed to book some accommodation.

*

As soon as Nick moved out of sight, Thaní went back to the bar.

"So, Alexandráki, you will tell me about your conversation with this man Fisher. What did he want from you?"

"I make prints for him, Sergeant. Photos I took here in the bar. He tries to identify everyone who was here."

"But he already did that. He showed me the prints, gave me a list."

"Yes, but then he wants prints of the four images I didn't give him."

"Why didn't you give him those, to begin with?"

"Because they were rubbish. I delete, but then he asks me to recover the file."

"I see. Well, you must give me a copy of all the prints, including those four. I will call again to collect them."

"They are two euros fifty each, Sergeant."

"Let's pretend you didn't say that, Alexandráki. It would be a serious mistake to piss me off."

"That's what *he* paid me."

"This is police business. I could seize your camera if you prefer, or request a review of your operating licence?"

Manólis raised his hands in self-defence.

"I thought not. Get them ready for me, please."

*

Once Nick found the correct Séllia on Airbnb, Villa Erató was easy to spot. It was a pleasant looking, restored, stone house, enlivened by intertwined lilac and white bougainvillea. There was a lovely infinity pool, set in attractive gardens that overlooked the sea, with a glorious view down to Soúda Bay. A rather pretentious alabaster statue of the muse of love poetry herself gazed blank-eyed over the pool.

There were three letting rooms, all doubles: one in the house and two in a separate, purpose-built unit. The one in the house was available at sixty-five euros. He booked two nights.

He spent an hour or so sorting out papers, paying the very reasonable bill for his room and buying himself and the Jeep some ferry tickets. There was a nine am boat to Agía Rouméli and then a second boat late afternoon from Agía Rouméli via Loutró to Chóra Sfakíon. It would take a large part of the day to get there, due to the long wait between the ferries, but that was okay. It would be good to relax and prepare.

*

At eleven pm, the beach bar was livelier, and the music was throbbing louder. Manólis looked shifty. He had snitched to Konstantópoulos, Nick reckoned, but, rather than saying anything, he opted for a show of bonhomie:

"Yeiá sou, Manóli. Pós eísai?" He threw him a warm smile.

"Eímai kourasménos. I am tired, Mr Fisher. Many hours I work for you."

"Did you recover them?"

"In the end, yes, but I don't know why I bother."

"What do you mean?"

"They are rubbish, like I say. Sorry, my friend, but you waste my time and your money."

"Well, let me have a look, at least."

"I make big for you, forty by thirty centimetres, so you see better. Same price."

"Thank you, Manóli. Good of you."

Nick took the four larger prints from him and ordered a Metaxá. Manólis poured one the size of a small wine with a separate carafe of water. Nick moved under the light, but it was still difficult to see. And it was difficult to think with the bass beat pounding his brain and churning his gut. In the end, he downed the Metaxá, gave Manóli his sixty-five euros plus five for the brandy and took the prints back to his room.

He moved the bedside light to the small table and spread the prints out on it. He scanned them, snorted and shook his head. It looked like he had wasted sixty-five euros of Stephen's money. One was well-lit but all blurred, as if someone knocked Manólis's elbow as he took the shot. Two of the others were very dark. Only the blurred, dance floor lights were visible in one of them; the other was just black. In the final one, the foreground was dark and somewhat blurred with two or three people in silhouette, but the background was just about visible. It showed the remains of the earlier campfire, now reduced to embers with three people gathered around it. He recognised Andie from the other photographs. She was talking with a girl that might be Beth. Then he spotted a guitar lying on its back nearby. Two North Americans getting to know each other made sense.

To the right of the fire was a young man sitting alone, hugging his knees. At first, Nick thought it was Jason, but then he realised that the hair was too light, perhaps blond or redhead, it was hard to tell. Maybe it was Kenny the Irishman or one of the Germans. He put the print down and then snatched it up again. He squinted. Yes, over to the right of the picture and away from the fire, a faint glow reached the side of a fourth face. It was hard to tell if the person was male or female. Shortish hair was crowned by a hat of some sort with a tiny light on it. It was too dark to see what else they were wearing. Whoever it was seemed to be staring at the dance floor.

Nick rubbed his stubble, stood up, gathered the prints, and put them with his investigation papers. There were a few question marks there, but he was not going to find answers tonight. His eyes were beginning to droop after the Metaxá, and it was twenty minutes to midnight. He got himself to bed and switched his brain back to how good that swim felt, sliding through the crystal, clear water. In three minutes, he was asleep.

CHAPTER 18
VILLA ERATÓ

On Sunday morning, Helen and Michael were finishing a silent, miserable breakfast when Beeson appeared.

"Good morning to you both," he said.

"Good morning," they chorused, though neither could see any good in it.

"How did it go yesterday?"

Helen dabbed her eyes with a tissue. Michael said:

"It was pretty dire to be honest, Mr Beeson. We struggled to recognise her."

"She looked, I don't know, *Germanic* somehow. Hard-faced. Not our pretty Samantha at all," added Helen.

"Embalming can make people look different, I'm afraid."

"Bad embalming can," said Michael, sourly.

"And her skin was so cold and hard. It was like touching marble."

"Yes, it would be, Helen. I'm sorry."

"It just brought it home to us that Samantha is dead. She couldn't be more dead. There's nothing there anymore. We should never have gone."

"Don't say that, Helen, we *had* to go – for her."

"She's beyond caring, Mike. We have to look after ourselves now."

"Yes, I rather think you do," said Beeson, "and the best thing now is to get yourselves home. You'll have the comfort of family and friends and familiar surroundings there, at least. I have the tickets with me – and the final bill for everything. Are you set up to transfer funds in the morning?"

"Yes," said Michael.

"Good. So, here's the final statement."

Michael went straight to the total: four thousand nine hundred and ten euros.

"We've managed to come in the right side of five thousand euros, thanks to the generosity of the Greek airline, whose staff send their condolences. They'll transport the coffin for free."

"That's a nice gesture," said Helen.

"Given that they're charging us two hundred and seventy-five euros each for a one-way flight, I should think so too," said Michael.

"It is two flights, via Athens, Michael, so that's not unreasonable. I think they meant to be kind."

"I'm sorry, Mr Beeson. I expect you're right. I'm just in a poor state of mind."

"Of course, you are. Don't worry. Your flight is at three ten pm, so we'll need to leave for the airport at twelve thirty, tomorrow."

"What about Sam?"

"That's all taken care of. She'll be on the same flight and the undertakers will meet you at Arrivals. You'll have the option of following the hearse in your car, should you wish to do so."

"You've been very kind and helpful, Mr Beeson."

"That's what I'm here for, Helen."

*

The ferry arrived from Palaióchora and there were no more than fifty people on board. Almost half of these got off at Síva while Nick and a dozen others got on. The Samariá was quite a large vessel with room for several hundred passengers and thirty or forty vehicles, Nick guessed, so it was quite empty on this Sunday morning in late September. Nick went upstairs and leaned against the railings on the port side, watching the coastline slide by while Síva faded in the wake. This was an area of towering cliffs, deep gorges and echoing sea-caves. The water was clear and deep blue. There were no other boats, just the ferry grinding on as the blinding sun rose higher.

At Agía Rouméli, the ferry docked at a jetty which extended from the shingle beach. That was as far as this ferry went. Meanwhile, a similar, larger ferry, the Daskalogiánnis, was making its way from Chóra Sfakíon. Both ferries would dock in Agía Rouméli and then go back the way they had come. On the return trip, they would be crowded with exhausted walkers, as this was where the seventeen-kilometre Samariá Gorge walk ended. Nick would have a peaceful couple of hours in Agía Rouméli and then, from twelve thirty or so, the fittest of the walkers would start to arrive, tear off their backpacks and run into the sea to float, exhausted, just as Jason and Sam would have done only two weeks ago, Nick reflected.

Agía Rouméli felt like a Wild West town to Nick. It seemed unnatural to have any kind of town in this wild, inaccessible place. The buildings were a ramshackle collection of wood and concrete, linked by dusty tracks with very few cars. That there were *any* cars was a little surprising, given that there were no roads out, but then he supposed that some residents kept cars so they could take them on the ferry to places where there *were* roads. *A strange way to live,* he thought.

Nick spent the next couple of hours on the beach. At lunchtime, he wandered back to the town and found a taverna selling the freshest kalamária, squid flash-fried in a light batter, which he ordered with a Greek salad and a bottle of retsína, the light, uniquely Greek wine infused with pine resin. The taverna was deserted at first but soon it started to fill up with walkers in various conditions from exhilarated to exhausted, with a handful of walking-wounded amongst them. After lunch, the waiter delivered a rakí and some watermelon chunks and Nick decided to call Lauren:

"Hi hun. It's Dad. How're you doing?"

"Trying to carry on as best I can. It's not easy, with what's going on over there."

"No, I bet."

"Mum called me after they got to see Jason."

"Ah. That's good."

"Sounds like he's sort of coping, for now."

"I think so. He's quite strong, inside."

"Hmmm. Maybe. Where are you now, Dad?"

"I'm on the south coast, looking back at the Samaría Gorge."

"Where we did that mammoth walk?"

"That's right. But I'm just passing by, following up a hunch."

"Daddy to the rescue?"

"In my dreams, but at least I have a suspect."

"Yay. Brilliant!"

Nick went on to tell her that he would be out of contact for a couple of days and not to worry. Then he just went on sitting there, absorbing the sights and sounds of the people, the beach and the boats. After a while, he took out his pad and started making notes.

The Daskalogiánnis sounded its foghorn late afternoon and swimmers dried themselves hurriedly as almost everyone gathered up their belongings and shuffled in the direction of the ferry. Nick retrieved the Jeep from a side street and nudged his way through the crowds to get aboard.

*

Villa Erató was hard to find. It was not in Séllia itself; it was along a newish, concreted lane, an offshoot from the steep, asphalt road that snaked in hairpins down to Soúda Bay. It was about a quarter of the way down. Nick drove past the house and stopped a hundred metres beyond. No-one in the world knew he was here and that was not such a great idea, given that he might be entering the house of a murderer.

He called Jen and explained that he was following up a hunch, nothing more. He asked her to keep it from Jason. If it led anywhere, she would be the first to know. He told her where he was staying.

"Wasn't that where Jason and Sam stayed?" she asked.

"It was, and that's why I need you to keep it quiet. If I'm wrong, I don't want the police blundering in. Okay?"

"No, it's not okay, Nick. What if you're *right*? You could be in terrible danger. I don't see why you need to put yourself at risk like this. It's unacceptable."

"I have to confirm my suspicions before I go to the Greek police and I can't think of any other way of doing it."

"Why not go to the police now? It's their job to take risks, not yours."

"Because they wouldn't listen to me. I'd be told to stop interfering again or they might even put me in jail. That wouldn't help Jason."

127

There was a pause. Nick sensed her fear and frustration ebbing a little.

"Listen, Jen. I promise to be careful and I'll give you the green light in a couple of days, just as soon as I'm out of here."

"You'd bloody well better."

"You still care a bit then?"

"We were married for eighteen years, Nick. What do *you* think?"

"You married someone else since."

"Yes, and I love Stephen, now. But it was a pragmatic compromise, Nick. You know that."

"I don't understand compromise, Jen."

"No. You never did."

*

Nick was apprehensive. All his knowledge, all his years of experience told him he was going out on a limb. He would be playing the part of a humble tourist. Being disingenuous was alien to him but it was necessary. He wanted to catch Peter unawares, watch him close up, observe what could be observed and, most of all, find evidence to support his hypothesis.

He rang the doorbell. A woman who looked about sixty opened the door. She was sturdily built and must have been at least five foot nine inches tall. Her face was quite lined and drawn under a frizz of pale ginger and grey hair, but there were traces of a former prettiness when she smiled, as she did now, and her pale blue eyes lit up.

"Well hello! Is it Mr Fisher?"

"It is, but Nick, please."

"Hello, Nick! I'm Linda Weston. Come on in. Gosh, is that all you've got?"

She was looking at Nick's bag.

"Oh, it's just a few nights. A whistle-stop tour, you might say."

They were standing in the hallway. A door was open to a light-filled living room which gave out onto a paved veranda. An acoustic guitar leaned against a wall.

"You're through here, Nick. You have your own entrance to the

128

side, but we may as well go through this way, now that we're here."

At the end of the hall were three doors.

"Yours is the one on the right," she said, opening the door and going through as Nick followed, "and you can lock it from inside for privacy, thus."

She turned the key and raised her eyebrows as she twirled around.

"The pillows are made of duck down. Let me know if that's a problem. Extra blanket in here if you get cold and there's air-conditioning if you get hot." She picked up a remote control from the bedside table and waggled it at a white box near the ceiling before putting it back.

"You may not need it now the nights are getting cooler. There's a shower room and loo in here. I assume you know what to do with the loo paper?" Nick nodded. "And a tiny living room through here with a fridge, microwave and tea-making facilities. The best thing about this room is the door. It gives out onto a private terrace facing west, to The White Mountains and the sunset.

"You're welcome to use the pool at any time from nine am to sunset. We clean it every day before nine. You can reach it through the garden to your left here. Let me know if you need a towel.

"Your room rate includes a small breakfast of coffee or tea, yoghurt with honey and fruit or cereal and a pastry or some toast. Breakfast is between eight and ten and we bring it to the table on your terrace. I think that's everything."

"Broadband?"

"Ah, yes. There should be a card somewhere with the password and such."

"I see it. And the other guests?"

"Yes. Both outside rooms are occupied. You can just see the rooms through the walnut tree to your right here. There's a young German couple who are always out exploring and an older gentleman from Athens. We don't get many Greeks but it's nice when we do. We feel vindicated or validated, somehow. I'm not sure of the right word."

"I know what you mean. Like a chef choosing to eat at *your* restaurant."

"Ha! That's it exactly! Now, I'll leave you to settle in. Peter and I have a drink before dinner on our terrace, if you'd care to join us for half an hour. Would eight thirty be too soon?"

Nick glanced at his watch. It was already just after eight.

"No. That'd be very welcome, thank you."

"Just a little icebreaker, so to speak. We try to do it with all our guests."

She gave him a professional, practised smile and unlocked the door adjoining the main house.

"Remember to lock me out now." *She almost winked*, he thought.

*

A tall man with a boyish smile stood up as Nick approached the table. His greying, blond hair was swept back in a ponytail, tied with an elastic band. His eyes were a darker blue than his wife's. The colour of deep sea.

"Hello, Nick. I'm Peter Weston. All settled in?"

Nick gave a reassuring smile.

"Doesn't take me long. All seems very nice, thank you."

"Great. Have a seat. We're drinking Bellinis – care for one?"

"What's that: peach juice and champagne?"

"We start with a tiny dash of Metaxá and cheat on the champagne – it's just cava – but the peach juice is real enough."

"Sounds good to me."

"And Linda's made some cheese straws. Do help yourself."

"They're not my best. Can't get the gruyère out here so I use graviéra."

"Well, they look delightful, thank you."

Peter positioned the over-full cocktail glass in front of Nick and sat down.

"Cheers. Welcome. Yeiá mas!"

They clinked glasses.

"So, what brings you to our out of the way spot, Nick?"

"I'm just taking a few days to explore the south coast, along from Palaióchora to Agía Galíni."

"Best bit of Crete, in our opinion. Well, that's why we're *here*, isn't it?"

"I love it, too."

"You know Crete, then?"

"I was here before, many years ago, and then I came back early last year and found somewhere to rent for a year or two. Thought I'd see if I liked living here and then maybe buy somewhere later, if I did."

"And you're still here."

"Indeed. Winter was a bit of a surprise, mind you."

"Oh, you mean that there *is* one. Yes, a lot of people think winter doesn't exist in the Mediterranean and they get a shock when they come here, especially if they're living high up. At least it doesn't last too long. So, this is a house-hunting trip, Nick?"

"I'm just trying to nail down the area, at the moment."

"It depends what you want, of course, but it's lovely right here."

"I know it is, Peter. The area behind Soúda Bay would be wonderful, but it's out of my league. With my budget, we're talking about doing up an old stone house, maybe inland a bit."

"Well, there are quite a few of those in Séllia. The Greeks don't seem to be interested. They'd rather slap up a new concrete one. It's a shame."

"Is it just for you, Nick – the house?" asked Linda.

"Well, I hope my children will come and visit, once in a while, so I'll need at least one spare bedroom."

"What have you got?"

"One of each. Jason's twenty-one and Lauren's nineteen."

"Nice names."

There was a pause as Linda wondered whether he was divorced or widowed and decided it would not be right to ask.

Peter leaned across. "Here, let me top you up."

"So, what brought you two to Crete?" Nick turned the conversation around. He didn't want to reveal too much about himself if he could avoid it.

"We first came in the mid-eighties, soon after we met. It was so beautiful, Nick, so unspoilt. Everything was so relaxed – *laid-back* I think we said then – we just adored it."

131

"We spent most of the time on the beach, did a huge amount of swimming and snorkelling and, in the evenings, a few of us would gather at the taverna or around a fire on the beach and eat, drink, make music. I played the guitar a little. Still do. I suppose we thought of ourselves as latter-day hippies."

"But you didn't move out here *then*, did you?"

"Lord, no. Didn't have any money and I don't think you could buy here then. It wasn't until Greece joined the EU that things opened up and foreigners started buying."

"Anyway, we both had careers, for nigh on twenty years," said Peter. "I was an art director in an advertising agency ..." "... and I was an orthodontist," finished Linda.

"That's some kind of dentist, isn't it?"

"Yes; the kind that straightens teeth."

"Very different jobs. Unusual."

"Yes, I suppose it is, but then Linda's a meticulous person as well as being rather brainy, whereas I am more of a layabout with a creative mind. We are the two halves of a rather well-rounded person."

Nick chuckled at the self-deprecation as he was supposed to.

"Anyway, we kept coming back. Crete gets to you, somehow. We've met so many people that return, year after year."

"Something gets under your skin: the scent of wild thyme on the hillsides; the mountains turning pink in the sunset; the crystal, clear water; the lyra music; the warmth and fierce independence of the people. Whatever. It got to us, too. In 2004, we chucked it all in and came here. Opened for guests two years later."

"Well, you picked a wonderful spot."

"Wait till you see the view in the morning."

The sun had set but an afterglow lingered over the sea to their right. The new moon was rising to their left and stars were beginning to appear in the darkening sky.

These two are an accomplished double act, thought Nick. *They have a set of well-worn stories that they tell – by rote, almost. They finish each other's sentences, as if they had practised, rehearsed over the years*

132

to produce a faultless presentation. The immaculate couple. The perfect hosts. And yet something was not right. It was too glib, too slick, too professional. There was no self-expression. There was no personal warmth between them. There was no love. Not anymore. He was observing a professionally presented marriage of convenience, and he knew it.

"I'll take that as my cue to leave you to your supper," he said. "Thank you for the drink. That made a nice change."

"What time would you like breakfast?"

"Would eight forty-five be all right, Linda?"

"Perfect."

CHAPTER 19
TAKING A LOOK

The door to the hallway creaked faintly and Nick froze. He had been around the side of the house already and spotted Peter pulling a giant paddle across the surface of the pool. After a breezy night, walnut-tree leaves were clogging up the water, so that would keep him busy for quite a while, Nick reckoned. He hoped Linda was in the kitchen which must be the left-hand door. He reckoned the middle door must lead to their large bedroom, which he had seen from outside. There was a radio playing in the kitchen, so it was difficult for him to hear her movements, but then a kettle whistled as it came to the boil before fading as someone turned off the gas. That was all the proof he needed, so he softly closed his door and padded down the hall into the large living room. He could see the pool from here. Peter was facing the other way, but he would need to be careful. Also, there were sliding doors which must lead to the kitchen. They were closed now but Linda could open them at any time. He crouched behind the sofa on a large, Aztec-style, multi-coloured rug and looked around him.

There was a low-backed, thick-cushioned three-piece suite in corn-flower blue with a scattering of dark blue and yellow cushions. The sofa looked out on the terrace and, beyond that, the pool. In front of it was a large, low coffee table with a few magazines and a copy of the Chaniá Post newspaper. There was a large television screen on a glass stand in the corner. To one side of the room was an octagonal walnut table with an old, leather armchair next to it under a standard lamp. Nick flipped the newspaper over and saw that it was dated yesterday. Sam no longer featured on the front page but, as readers of the Post and television watchers, they must be aware of her death. There was nothing in this room that gave anything away about their characters. There was a touch of Greek in the paintings of Mediterranean scenes but, in all other re-spects, it was a showroom; something from the Ideal Home Exhibition.

Keeping low, he ran across to a side-door. It was unlocked, so he went through and found himself in another passageway. There was a door off to a downstairs toilet and a second door which led to the garage. It was quite dark in here. He could not be seen from the pool now and felt more able to breathe.

The garage was a modern, breeze-block affair housing a red Volkswagen Golf with a few scrapes and dents, like all the cars here. A mess of tools and paints, gardening and pool equipment was scattered over wooden workbenches. As he moved around the car, Nick spotted what he was looking for. It was against the wall, towards the front of the garage. There was a rubberised, grey cover over it, but he knew what it was. He pulled the phone from his trouser pocket. That was when the backdoor to the garage opened.

From the shape of the silhouette, Nick thought it must be Peter. He ducked down behind the Golf's hatchback. Had he been seen? There was no shout of rage, no yelp of indignation, just a long moment's silence and then the reassuring sound of someone pottering around at the back of the garage. Maybe the switch from bright sunlight to the dark of the garage made Nick invisible for a moment. He could think of no excuse for being here, if discovered. He would be viewed as a direct threat to this household, this idyllic existence, this glorious freedom; a threat to someone who had killed already and would not hesitate to kill again to avoid discovery.

After an agonising half-minute, Peter seemed to find what he was looking for and went out again. Nick lifted his head a fraction. In the bright light, Peter was walking away, carrying a large plastic container of chemicals for the pool.

Nick's phone beeped, loud in the silence. He had forgotten to switch it off. Peter seemed not to have heard, thank God. Five seconds earlier and that oft-repeated message from his network provider could have been a death sentence. Nick's mouth dried and his heart lurched arrhythmically. He swallowed hard and then wasted no time. He wiped his sweaty palms on his trousers and then pulled back the cover to reveal the motorbike. It looked like the one in the photo. It was a Ducati

Scrambler, four hundred cc, finished in flame-red paint on the tank and mudguards. It was coated with dust. He took two photographs with his phone, then replaced the cover. He checked that Peter was still working on the pool and then took some wooden stairs to a *his and hers* office above.

There were two Velux windows in the roof and a smaller window facing the rear, and the pool. The end and right-hand walls of the room were fitted with long, home-made worktops on angle support brackets. Three office chairs, three filing cabinets and a cupboard were positioned below. There were two desktop computers, one to the right of the small window and one along the back wall with a large pinboard next to it and a bookshelf with half a dozen red ring binders above it. There was a pile of papers in a plastic tray and Nick riffled through them, but it was just invoicing, bills and accounts for the bed and breakfast business. The filing cabinets were not locked, and Nick flipped through the crammed, hanging files but found only domestic bills, local service providers, sources of decorative materials and a large file labelled VE Refurb. The cupboard, however, was locked and he could not find a key. The opposite end of the room, to the right of the stairs, was dominated by a framed poster of Che Guevara. It was the iconic head and shoulders image of the visionary young Che; a pen and ink drawing on a blood-red background. The hair is long, and he has a wispy moustache. The eyes seem world-weary, yet they burn with hope and pride. He looks to the horizon and an idealist's future: justice, equality and a classless society. He wears a beret with a star badge, centrally positioned.

Near the computer by the window were several framed photographs. Linda's medical qualifications amongst them, together with a certificate from a religious study and meditation course three years before. There were photographs of them when they were younger, perhaps in their mid-thirties. Peter's hair is shorter and blonder. There is a gold earring in his left ear lobe but not the right. Linda is attractive if a touch overweight. She looks wholesome, fulfilled. There is a light in her eyes. Not the professional twinkle of the flirtatious host he saw earlier, but some deep, inner glow. She is wearing a large wooden cross on a chain.

Nick took more photos and then glanced at his watch. It was eight forty-one. He checked that Peter was still at the pool, then retraced his steps down the stairs, through the garage and into the corridor. He peered through the keyhole of the door to the living room and cursed under his breath. The sliding door to the kitchen was now open but Linda was not in the kitchen. Then he heard her call: "Are you done?" and caught a glimpse of her from the back, disappearing around the side of the house.

"Yep. I'll just put the stuff away," Peter called, as he started walking back to the garage.

Oh, God. She must be delivering my breakfast already, thought Nick.

He waited until the moment Peter entered the garage and then sprinted soundlessly across the living room and into the hallway. As he was about to enter his room, he felt the handle turn from the other side. Then Linda was facing him.

"Ah. I was wondering where you'd got to."

Nick whipped his phone out of his pocket and waved it.

"Left it in the Jeep, yet again."

"You can get around the side from your terrace you know, past the trees."

"Ah, yes. You did tell me that. Sorry."

"I've just delivered your breakfast. That's why I was looking for you. I assumed coffee and toast, but would you prefer tea or a pastry?"

"Coffee's good, thanks, but a pastry would be nice."

"I have pains-aux-raisins or chocolate croissants. Not home-made, I'm afraid, but they are rather nice."

"A chocolate croissant would be a treat. And I could eat the toast as well."

She smiled indulgently and twirled past him and through the door to the kitchen. Nick would need his nerves to settle before he could eat. That was a close shave. Gold dust, though; now he could show that Peter owned a motorbike that matched the one in the photo and that he had worn a gold earring in the past. There would also be a leather jacket here somewhere, but he could not look just yet. And then there was something else he could try, just to get a reaction. It was risky, but it was important to test the man. That would have to wait until this evening.

*

There is an unwritten code, in the world of bed-and-breakfasts, especially British-owned ones. Guests are not welcome on the premises much after breakfast and are not expected to return before late afternoon. The notes to Villa Erató made no mention of this, unsurprisingly, but Nick was very much aware of it. During, or just after breakfast, the host enquires as to one's plans for the day under the pretext of offering local knowledge and advice, but both sides know there is a subtext. It reads: *Just wanted to confirm that you're getting out of my house soon and that you're going a nice long way and won't be back before five or six. That way, in your absence, I can enjoy the pitiful remains of my private life for a while.* Nick knew he would not be able to hang around all day waiting for opportunities to look around further or talk. Lingering would break the code and raise questions.

He was just finishing his croissant when Linda reappeared, right on cue.

"Lovely day, Nick, if a little windy. What are your plans?"

Nick resisted the urge to say *mind your own business* and, instead, invented a cover story.

"There are a couple of estate agents in Plakiás and Agía Galíni I want to have a chat with, so we'll see where that leads. I'd like to explore the villages between the two."

"I'm sure you can still pick up an old stone house that needs work for not very much, even less without a sea view."

"Yes, I think so too. And I'd just as soon be looking at an olive grove with some mountains in the distance. Still beautiful – and not so exposed."

"Very pragmatic. Well, good luck with that. If you're around this evening, join us for a drink again. We normally start a little earlier, between seven and eight, so we can watch the sun go down."

"Sounds wonderful. Thanks. I'll just wander round then, shall I?"

"Yes, do that. I'll just grab these things. Have a great day."

Nick recognised the hosts' code for *you have thirty minutes to vacate the premises* and stood up.

*

He did drive down the hairpins and along the beach road to Plakiás, but with no plans to see estate agents. Instead, he went to the Ostráco Bar on the front and ordered more coffee. He searched the Internet and found a number for the Sorókos Café.

"Kaliméra. O kýrios Stélios, eínai ethó?"

"Éna leptó."

Nick waited.

"Né?"

"Kýrie Stélio – is that you?"

"Yes."

"It's Nick Fisher. Do you remember me?"

"Sure I do, Nick. I thought I was the only person in the world who liked Weather Report and then you showed up."

"Of all the bars in all the world … huh? I think there might be a few fans scattered around, mind you, and I'd love to listen to some more of that with you one day but I'm not in Síva right now and I need your help."

"What can I do for you?"

"I have some photos that *might* be the guy you mentioned – the one who was looking for the girl who drowned? He has a ponytail in the photos and there is no earring, so I need you to imagine the hair down and the earring in place. Can you do that for me? If I email them to you, could you let me know if you recognise him?"

"What is ponytail?"

"Ah sorry, long hair tied back with a band, so it looks like the tail of a horse?"

"Ah yes, I know. Sure thing, Nick."

"And Stélio? I need you to be sure, for there to be no doubt in your mind."

"That's a *big ask*, as you say, but I'll try."

"And Stélio? Can we keep this to ourselves, for now?"

"I must tell the police, but only if they ask the right question."

"That's fair enough. Good man."

Nick took Jason's phone out of his bag, selected two of the photos of Peter and forwarded them to the private email address that Stélios provided.

It was just coming up to eleven am. A string of boats was moored against the harbour wall to his right. To his left, the beach stretched for perhaps two kilometres around the bay. Shops and restaurants pursued it for the first half-kilometre, after which it broke free of the town and became wider and sandier. Further round there were now some low-rise apartment blocks behind the beach, the mountains soaring behind them. *But it was still a view to take one's breath away,* thought Nick; *nothing will ever spoil the natural beauty of this bay.*

He had come to Greece island-hopping in the late eighties, soon after Peter and Linda. He and his university mates visited several islands, but it was the final stop, Crete, that left a lasting impression on Nick. Just the name seemed to ring with mythology, history and romance – and the wildness and rugged beauty of the island stunned him.

He remembered, years later when he needed a bolthole, a haven. And Crete did not let him down.

A string of events had left Nick devastated. Firstly, his father died. Paul had been a prisoner-of-war in Burma towards the end of WWII and was damaged by that. He was prone to bouts of depression, anger and moodiness. Nick was never close to him as a kid. Dad was distant, confused, sometimes frightening. It was not until Nick dropped out of his law degree at Manchester and came to work in Paul's electrical shop that they found each other, and Nick discovered how much his father cared, in his quiet way. He was not pushy like

Mum Shirley, he just wanted Nick to find the peace and happiness that had eluded him – or been stolen from him by the war.

When Nick decided to become a copper, Shirley pretty much washed her hands of him. She had imagined him moving up a class, mixing with the gentry, earning huge fees, perhaps making it to QC or even a judge, someday. Now her dreams of Nick the barrister lay in ruins. But Dad was supportive from the outset and worked on Shirley. Paul said Nick would be better at catching criminals than performing in courtroom dramas or mending toasters. Even if it was not the Inns of Temple, it was still the law, when all was said and done, and the Met had plenty of prospects for bright minds, not to mention fair salaries and excellent pensions. In the end, he won her round. After that, Nick and Paul were solid.

Nick had not expected him to die. Not yet. Not before they had shared the great stretches of time he thought the years would find for them, someday. The illness was short and brutal. Paul was dead in four weeks. Only then did it dawn on Nick just how little time he had found for his Dad since those days in the shop. How many things remained unsaid. How little Nick ever gave back to him. And it tore him up.

Nick was considered a high-flier in those days. He had made it to Detective Inspector at thirty-three and was respected for his hard work, diligence and intuition. Now, at thirty-eight, he was the star performer, the leading criminal detective at his rank. When Paul died, Nick was working round the clock on a big case. His young family did not get much of a look-in, let alone his Dad. It was a nasty, seedy case. Two young rent-boys had been murdered and Nick knew for a fact that Jon Kitchen was the nasty bastard behind it, only there was no real proof. Just lots of circumstantial stuff. More than enough to confirm Nick's gut feel but not enough to stand up in court. He interviewed another rent-boy who he was sure was at the crime scene but, not only did the kid deny that he had been there, he also claimed that he had spent that evening with Kitchen elsewhere. If that were true, Kitchen could not be guilty.

Nick was convinced that the boy had been paid off. He was furious. He could see the case collapsing, all the team's hard work being in vain and that bastard Kitchen walking free. Laughing in his face. He could not bear it and ripped into the vulnerable boy. He did not question him. He intimidated him. He bullied him. After three hours, the boy was shaking in confusion and sobbing. Nick let him clean-up for half an hour but then he was back. When, at last, he suggested rather forcefully that the boy might want to withdraw his statement, the boy stared at him with dead eyes for a long moment and then nodded, just once. Nick had his man. The boy was released later that day but the next morning a body was found floating in the Thames. He had overdosed on methadone and jumped off Westminster Bridge.

The incident was never referred to the anti-corruption unit and Nick was never investigated or disciplined, but he was disturbed by it deep-down and started to question his own judgment. His reputation with some of his closest colleagues took a dive. In the end, Kitchen was put away for twelve years, but some questioned the means to this end.

While he was grieving over Paul and battling with the Kitchen case, Nick was under enormous stress. He was working too hard and drinking too much. He was difficult to be with and he knew it.

Jen had gone back to work the previous year, after retraining as a Legal Executive. She was in her early thirties then, looking great and enjoying her new career. What she was not enjoying was coming home after a full day's work, sorting out the kids and Zoë, their part-time nanny, then organising an evening meal, only to find that Nick was working late or stressed out and unpleasant to be with or even drunk and abusive. It was all getting too much. She had spoken to him about it, but nothing changed. If anything, he grew more abusive, started seeing Jen as a block to whatever he was trying to achieve at work, not the support that she most certainly was.

One night, Nick came home early and sober, for once. Jen was not there. Zoë was looking after the kids and, when Nick asked her where Jen was, she was evasive. Nick got angry, started drinking spirits in front of the kids, demanded to know where she was. Eventually, Zoë said:

"I'm sorry, Nick. She's been seeing someone. Someone she met at work. That's all I know."

Nick felt like a cartoon character running off a cliff. A yawning gulf had opened up below him even as he kept on running blind. Now he had failed his dying Dad, his reputation at The Met was trashed, Jen was having an affair and his family was in jeopardy. If things went on like this, he had a long, long way to fall.

Jen came in an hour and a half later and Zoë was dispatched. By then, ice had formed a wall around Nick's anger, leaving only sadness and a kind of robotic pragmatism.

"How serious is it?" was all he asked.

"Oh, Nicky. Couldn't you see? This was bound to happen, the way we were going. It's someone I've been working with. He's been kind to me. He makes me laugh. He's been there for me. I like him a lot."

Nick saw a light in her eyes that had not been there for quite a few years.

"You've slept together?"

She nodded once.

"You love him?"

"I don't know yet. Maybe."

"I'll move out. Sort myself out. Let me know if you want me back."

The next day Nick's boss ordered him to take two months' stress leave.

"Learn to forgive yourself, Nick," he said. "You're a great copper and I'm quite sure you've been a great son, a great father and a great husband, too. Go somewhere, find some perspective. Take a little time. I want you back to your old self and back in this job in October, firing on all cylinders. Right?"

Crete was the natural choice and he flew out two days later. After three weeks staring at the sea, he found a ruined stone house in Saktoúria and bought it for sixteen thousand euros. It was a stake in the ground. A declaration of independence. One day he would come back and restore it, with or without Jen and the kids.

Now he looked across the bay to the mountains beyond. *Ever since that day*, he thought, *it has always been a comfort and a source of secret excitement to know that I own a tiny piece of this extraordinary island.*

143

The phone started ringing and shook him from his reverie.

"Hello Nick. It's Stélios – from Síva."

"Hi Stélio. Thanks for getting back to me."

"So, I've looked at the pictures. Nick, and I think he's our guy."

"You think?"

"I can't say one hundred per cent. Remember, it was dark, it was late, he looked a little different with the hair and it's a couple of weeks ago."

"What *can* you give me?"

"Maybe ninety per cent?"

Nick made a fist and shook it, in triumph.

"That's good enough. I'll take it. Thanks, Stélio. Good job. Listen, if the police want you to identify him at some stage, could you do that?"

"If it helps *you*, Nick, sure."

"Terrific. Thanks a lot, mate. I'll buy you drink when I make it back to Síva."

"I'll look forward to that."

Nick was pacing up and down in front of the café. Now he flopped back in his chair. He had a witness who would identify Peter in the early hours close to the murder scene. He had a photo of the motorbike Peter used to get there. He had a photo of him wearing the earring.

So, Peter was there, no question. But what was the motive? There must have been an affair, despite the huge age difference. Nick remembered the photo on the beach, that expression on Peter's face. He had not won an Olympic medal, but he might have learned that a beautiful girl of twenty wanted him. That would do it. He could have lost all perspective, all common sense. Maybe she threatened to tell Linda afterwards, and so destroy his idyllic, carefree life. Or, if she later rejected him, it could have all been too much. Did he ride to Síva to meet her and resume their affair, maybe even to run away with her, or did he ride there to kill her and bury their secret?

*

There was not much that Nick could do for the rest of the day. He looked in at a couple of estate agents in Plakiás, just to come up with some properties he might have gone to see, then he spent the afternoon at Soúda Bay, three kilometres west of Plakiás. He ate kolokíthokeftédes – fried balls of zucchini, mashed with a little feta – with some fresh bread and tzatzíki, washed down with a beer, then hired a beach umbrella with a sun lounger and took a nap. Later, he swam right across the bay and back. At six, he checked in with Jen and Stephen.

"We went to see Jason again today," said Jen. "He was irritable and snappy. I think he's getting very down."

"I'm not surprised, are you?"

"No, I suppose not."

"I still don't want to get his hopes up too much, but I think I'm making progress. I have one more night here and then I'll go back to Síva. I hope I'll have enough by then to persuade the police to switch their investigation to Peter Weston."

"Might they let Jason go?"

"In due course, yes they might. That's the hope. But they won't do that before they have someone else in custody. Someone they're convinced is guilty."

*

He was back at Villa Erató just before seven, showered off the beach and changed into a pair of stone-coloured chinos. Shortly afterwards, he saw Peter and Linda settling down with drinks on the terrace. He gave it a couple of minutes, checked again, and then went straight to their bedroom. It was a large, airy room. French doors and windows with net curtains gave out onto gardens, with the terrace and pool just visible to the left. There were separate beds, each with a bedside table. In the en-suite bathroom were his and hers sinks. He moved to the wardrobe. That, too, was divided. He was not surprised. He searched through Peter's clothes but there was no sign of a leather jacket. He glanced at the drinks table outside. Nothing had changed. He moved to the bedside tables. The one near the window was a bit of a mess. A stack of dog-eared thrillers, a crossword book, a plug-in mosquito repeller, a bottle of water and a clock all jostled for space on the dusty top. Inside, a Greek language course and a booklet for the air-conditioning gathered more dust. Nothing else. Nick moved to the table between the beds. This was quite different. Everything was clean and neat. There was a box of tissues, a jar of face cream and a crucifix on the top – not the large, wooden one in the photo, but a finer, silver one on a chain. Inside was a bible, a Jane Austen novel and a couple of self-improvement books. On top of these, Nick spotted an A5 leaflet and pulled it out. On the front cover was a picture of a large stone house with a distant sea view. Below the picture was printed:

TEMPLE OF AKESÓ HEALING CENTRE
KAMBÁNI
AKROTÍRI PENINSULA
CRETE

Inside were details of a treatment course – a mix of a healthy and nutritious diet, spa, sauna, massage and meditation. There was also a piece of paper. It was a copy of an email dated the tenth of September:

Thank you for reserving a place on our Detox and Healing Programme, Linda. I can confirm that there is a Catholic church in Chaniá which offers a Sunday service at ten fifteen am. This is less than twenty minutes' drive from here. You will find it on a street called Halidon. I look forward to welcoming you on Saturday evening.

Nick turned back to the leaflet. The course was for Saturday, Sunday and Monday, the fifteenth to seventeenth of September. That was the weekend of Sam's murder. If Linda were away, Peter could have made it to Síva and back without being discovered. He took out his phone and photographed the leaflet. Someone was knocking.

"Nick? Are you there?"

It was Linda, knocking on the door from the garden to his bedroom. She must have walked past the window. Nick cursed himself for being so careless and hoped to God she had not spotted him through the net curtains. He rushed to the bedroom door, then turned and ran back. He had forgotten to put the leaflet back in the bedside cupboard. He took a deep breath before leaving their bedroom and then slipped into his own bedroom. Linda was standing outside but looking over towards Peter. It took Nick a split second to realise that she could not see his bed because of a half-drawn curtain. He threw himself to the floor and then padded around the side of the bed, ruffled his hair, and messed up the bedclothes.

"Hello-oh! Anybody home?" called Linda again, tapping on the door.

Nick drew back the curtain and tried to look rueful. He opened the door, rubbing his eyes.

"Sorry, Linda. Must have nodded off."

"Happens a lot here. Don't worry. Just didn't want you to miss the sunset. It's going to be quite spectacular tonight. We're having mint juleps if you'd like to join us – or perhaps you'd prefer a beer?"

"A beer would go down very well if you don't mind."

"No problem. See you in a minute, then."

Nick was observing her keenly. Had he got away with it? Either that or she was a very cool customer indeed. He checked his phone to make sure those last photos came out right. They had, thank God.

*

"Ah. Here he comes," said Peter as Nick finally wandered round to join them.

"Sorry, guys. Must be the sea air."

"That'll do it every time – at our age. I'm forever dropping off on the beach, aren't I, darling?"

"And I must confess to another failing. I have no idea what a mint julep is."

"It's pretty easy," said Linda. "Just crushed ice, mint leaves, a little sugar syrup and lots of lovely Bourbon. It should be served in a special pewter cup, apparently, but we don't have any of those."

"I'll stick with the beer."

"So, how was your day? Chosen somewhere yet?"

"There are four contenders." Nick ticked them off on his fingers:

"Saktoúria and Mélambes, where I went today, the hinterland of Plakiás, then Rodákino or Síva."

Nick was studying Peter's face as he said the last name and was sure he saw a shadow of alarm flit across it.

"Síva?" he blurted. "You were there?"

Nick did his best to sound mundane:

"That was my first stop. I like it there but buying is difficult. There are Roman ruins. It can be tough to get the archaeological permit."

"When were you there?"

"Ah. Let me see. About ten or twelve days ago?"

"So, were you there when the English girl drowned?" asked Linda.

"I was. Tragic. Such a pretty girl. And so young."

Peter looked desperately uncomfortable. He slurped his cocktail and coughed.

"She was here, you know, with her fiancé Jason," he managed to say.

"What? They stayed *here*?"

"They were here for almost a week. Linda suggested that they went on to Síva."

Nick glanced at Linda and saw her face take on an expression of pained regret. He turned up the heat:

"Bit of a coincidence – them going from here to Síva and me coming back from there to here, albeit via Rodákino."

"It certainly was," said Linda. She was not smiling.

"I guess everyone uses the same websites these days," said Peter.

"Do you know Síva?" asked Nick.

"We know it well. It's only small, as you know. It was one of our favourite haunts when we first came here."

"But not these days?"

"When did we last go there, darling?" She turned to Peter.

"It's been a while – several years I should think," he murmured, but he was looking at the ground.

"Excuse me," he said a moment later and went inside.

"It must have been a shock to you both, the drowning."

"It's a shock to everyone, that sort of thing, isn't it?"

"I suppose so. Did Peter get close to them while they were here?"

Her response was acerbic:

"What do you mean?"

"Just that. A week is a long time. And he seems upset."

"He's just soft. He's always been soft. Everything upsets poor Peter, but he'll get over it."

Peter did not return and conversation with Linda was becoming monosyllabic. Nick finished his beer and made his excuses.

"Breakfast at the same time?" The professional in her resurfaced as if by magic.

"Perhaps a little earlier? Can you do eight o'clock?"

"The earlier the better for me. Eight it is."

"Thanks for the beer."

"See you in the morning."

CHAPTER 20
THE TEMPLE OF AKESÓ

The following morning, Leo and Thaní were heading to Moondance. Leo had driven down that morning to review the investigation and interview Kristíne. Spíros had not yet been found; the search for him at Palaióchora yielded nothing.

"Good morning, Kýrie Alexandráki, this is my boss, Lieutenant Christodoulákis."

Manólis looked shiny and seedy. He was shielding his eyes.

"Morning. Sorry, it's early for me, gents."

"Do you have the prints?"

"I do."

He reached under the counter and brought out a plastic wallet.

"All thirty-six prints for you, gentlemen. The recovered ones are on the top. Now, can I get you a coffee, on the house?"

They accepted and went to a table.

"You must have put the shits up him," said Leo.

But Thaní just raised an eyebrow. The hint of a smile played around his lips.

"Okay. Let's have a look."

They started with the four on top. The coffee arrived and Leo lit a cigarette. Then he picked up the fourth print and leaned back, squinting at it, then held it at arm's length and exhaled.

"Ha!" He turned to Thaní.

"What have you got, boss?"

Leo was pointing over to the right of the photo.

"Do you know this person?"

"Hard to tell from that, but no, I don't think so."

"What about the hat?"

"The hat with the light?"

"It's not a light, Thaní. Whoever heard of a hat with a light? It's a bounced flash; a reflection."

"Of course, it is!"

"And I think I know what caused that."

"You do?"

"Remember that hat we found on the beach?"

"The maroon beret – yes."

"What was attached to it, just here?" Leo touched the centre of his forehead.

"A metal badge of Che Guevara's face?"

Leo tilted his head in confirmation.

Thaní grabbed the photo.

"Yes, that could be a beret. It's hard to tell. It looks rather bulky."

"If that *is* the beret, it would place this person at the scene of the crime."

"But we've no idea who it is. I can't even tell if it's male or female from this photo."

"No. But I'd guess it's not Andie or Jason or any of the three Germans."

"A new suspect, then?"

Leo's phone rang.

"Né. Ah. Yeiá sou, Demí."

He listened for a few seconds.

"Yes, okay. Good. I'll be there in fifteen."

He turned back to Thaní.

"Demétrios has this Kristīne in a room at the hotel. I'll make a start with her and let Demí sit in. Join us when you can, but first, I want you to get Alexandrákis to enlarge that part of the photo and tell us what time it was taken.

"Go through the other photos with him, identify all the players from the list that Fisher gave you and see if you can spot this person in any of the other shots. If you're not sure, get *them* enlarged too, and check the timings."

"Okay, boss."

*

Nick decided to drive back to Síva rather than taking the ferries. It was a long drive, but it would be quicker and, if the Jeep were there, he could leave at a moment's notice and that might become important. He could also check something out on the way.

After an hour of heading north, and then west down the National Road, he turned right and cut through towards Chaniá Airport. The road snaked up and away from the city. To the right were spectacular views of the bay and the harbour. A navy minesweeper was at anchor in the bay and a large ferry from Piraeus was at the dockside. After a further ten kilometres, he ignored the airport turn and instead went straight on for another three kilometres to a T junction and turned left. This was an elevated area, dusty and windswept. Doubling back towards the city, after six kilometres he came to the village of Kambáni. He crawled through the village, but it was not until he was leaving it that he saw the sign to the right, pointing up a smart, tarmac drive bordered by pink, white and yellow oleander bushes. As he approached the house, he saw that it was bigger than he had expected from the leaflet. There was a modern building to the left-hand side and a car park for, perhaps, twenty cars. Behind the house and the west-facing gardens, Nick saw that the land fell away to give a view of the sea, five or six kilometres away.

Reception was in the hallway of the old house. He pressed the white button on the empty desk and a woman in a white coat appeared. She was Nick's age or older, slim to the point of anorexia, tanned and wrinkled. When she spoke, it was in English, but there were traces of an accent. German?

"Good morning. May I help you?"

Nick read the name stitched onto the breast pocket of her coat and extended his hand.

"Hello, Martina. Nick Fisher."

"What can I do for you, Mr Fisher?"

"Would you have been here for the detox programme a few days ago – the one that started on the evening of the fifteenth?"

"Yes, for sure. There are only four of us. When we have a residential course, it is a big thing for us. We were all here. Why do you ask?"

"Do you keep records of who attends the courses?"

"Of course. It's all on the computer."

"I'm a British policeman, Martina. I've been assigned to work with the Greek police on a murder investigation as the victim was British."

He passed her one of his old business cards.

"A murder – here in Crete?"

"Yes, I'm afraid so. I need you to tell me whether a certain person attended that course or not."

"This is private information."

"Yes, it is, and we will treat it as confidential."

"One moment."

Martina went back through the door. Nick hoped she was not going to ask for more formal ID. In two minutes, she was back, looking relieved.

"We are happy to work with the police, in confidence, Detective Chief Inspector. What was the name of the client?"

"It's a Linda Weston."

"Oh, I remember Linda. Quite a tall lady. About our age or a little older? A lot of ginger hair, rather frizzy?"

Nick held up Jason's phone.

"Would this be her?"

"Yes, for sure – and this is her husband? Hmmm."

Martina seemed to approve of Peter.

"Can you tell me when she arrived?"

She started tapping the keys of her computer.

"Linda Weston checked in at six minutes before eight on the Saturday evening. She would have been one of the first."

"And then she would have been here the whole time – until late Monday afternoon?"

"Actually, no. She went out on Sunday morning. She's a religious lady. She wanted to go to the mass in Chaniá, so she had to miss the *Why Detox?* lecture."

No great loss, thought Nick, but he was looking through his phone for the course programme.

"What about the Welcome Supper on the Saturday night?"

"That's very informal. We just lay out some simple food. People help themselves, say hello. Sometimes they sit and chat for a while."

"I mean, was she there?"

"I don't remember seeing her there, but I might have missed her."

"But she was there the rest of the time apart from a couple of hours on Sunday morning?"

"I'm sure she was. Hold on."

She rummaged under the desk and came up with a large photograph.

"At the end of the course we take a group photograph, and everybody gets a certificate. There she is."

And there she was, indeed, in the centre of the back row, wearing that professional smile.

"That's helpful, Martina. Thank you. Could I ask you to check with your colleagues about the Welcome Supper? I'd like to know if any of them remember seeing her there."

"Yes, I can do that. Is Linda in some kind of trouble?"

"No, no, not at all. It's just police procedure. The boring stuff. We need to confirm the details so that we can rule her out of our investigation, as I'm sure we will."

"Okay."

"So, you'll call me?"

"I will."

Nick thought about visiting the church to try and confirm Linda's attendance at the mass, but he didn't see much point. Instead, he skirted Chaniá and headed west on the National Road until he picked up the Síva Road at Galatás. After forty minutes' driving, he stopped for a break in Prasés, at the taverna where he met Jen and Stephen. While he was waiting for his snack to arrive, he called Lauren.

"Hi, Dad."

"Hello, sweet pea."

"Still alive, then?"

"As the man said as he fell past the twenty-fifth floor ..."

"What?"

"... so far, so good."

"Oh, that's very reassuring!"

"Don't worry. I've escaped the villa and I'm making for the Swiss border."

"You'll get wet!"

"Ah. Didn't think of that."

"You are a very silly man, Daddy."

CHAPTER 21
TRUCE

Thaní was frustrated. Alexandrákis had taken a hell of a long time to come back with the enlargements and he was itching to be part of the interrogation of Kristīne. In the end, he lost patience and left a message saying he would come back later. When he made it to Síva's only hotel, it was already eleven twenty. The receptionist showed him to a room at the back. Thaní opened the door and found Leo with his feet on the table. At the far end, Demétrios was looking out of the window. The room was filled with cigarette smoke.

"You've missed all the fun," said Leo.

"Already? What's the story?"

"Kristīne says Spíros and Sam had an affair, but she didn't know about it at the time."

"Very convenient; seems like she was the only person who *didn't* know then, from what Nick Fisher was telling me."

"Really? Still, I don't think she was lying to us. She only found out because Spíros seemed unnaturally upset after hearing the news of Sam's death and she put two and two together. When he finally confessed, he got his marching orders."

"And he was allowed to leave with his balls intact?"

"So it seems. She says it wasn't the first time he'd been unfaithful. Far from it. But this was the last straw. She just washed her hands of him, there and then. No big deal, by the sound of it."

"And does she know where he is now?"

"No. He told her he was taking the ferry to Palaióchora, but she hasn't heard from him since. I told her we didn't find him there and she wasn't surprised. Said he could be travelling again or maybe he'd gone back to Athína."

"Does she have an alibi for the night of the murder?"

"She was playing cards with a couple from a nearby tent until after midnight and then she went to bed. Spíros was working at the beach bar until after two. She was fast asleep by then. She didn't hear him come in."

"Hmmm. Maybe. But where was Spíros after the beach bar closed? Did he go straight back to the tent or not? Also, either one could have sneaked out, later in the night."

"It's possible, sure. But what motive did Spíros have for killing Sam? He was onto a good thing with her."

"Maybe he wanted a repeat performance and she rejected him? He has to be a suspect. After all, he seems to have done a runner."

"Yes, but there could be other reasons for that. We know he's had money problems and a history of drug abuse. I think he was the supplier at Moondance."

"And you think he fell out with *his* suppliers?"

"It happens – and they're ruthless bastards, those guys."

"Hmmm. Going back to Sam, have we checked out this other couple?"

Demétrios responded.

"I found them, Sergeant. They're still here – and they back up her story."

Thaní turned back to Leo:

"So, you let Kristíne go, boss?"

"I did. But she's not going anywhere. Her jewellery business is here."

"We need to find this Spíros."

"We do. But it might not be easy. We can alert Athína and the other Prefectures, check flights out of Crete."

"And meanwhile, we're left with Buckingham," said Thaní.

"Yes, Sergeant." Leo took his feet off the table and leaned forward, suddenly deadly serious. "We are holding a suspect that neither of us is convinced is the killer and, right now, we have no-one else in the frame.

"Athína is breathing down our necks. We're just a day or two from being relieved of this case. That will be a huge, black mark for Chaniá and for us, Thaní. You and me, buddy. You can forget about that promotion. We'll be lucky to keep our jobs."

*

Nick drove straight to the rent rooms place and found that he was able to get the same room. He booked another couple of nights with the option of more after that. After sorting out his things, he wandered into the town for some lunch. He did not want much after the snack in Prasés, so he settled for a panini with chicken and roasted vegetables and a peach juice at a newish, orange and white café he hadn't tried before. He was starting on his lunch and shading his eyes to read a string of follow-on text messages from Lauren when suddenly he found himself in shadow.

"Mr Fisher. You will come with us, please."

It was Sergeant Konstantópoulos with two other men. Nick shrugged and started wrapping the remains of his panini in a serviette.

"Leave that. You will come now, please."

Nick made a show of reluctance and resignation but then pulled himself to his feet and trudged with them in silence for about eighty metres to an empty taverna. Nick was told to sit at a corner table, and they all gathered round, rather too close for comfort. The oldest man spoke first.

"My sergeant warned you about interfering in police business several days ago Mr Fisher and yet you are still here in Síva. Tell me why I shouldn't arrest you."

"I always like to know who's threatening to arrest me. You are?"

"Christodoulákis, lieutenant, Chaniá prefecture."

"I am not *still here* as you put it, Lieutenant. I went away, as I told your sergeant I would, but then I came back, just an hour ago."

"Why are you not at home in Saktoúria, tending your garden like a good, retired person? Why are you here if it is not to interfere again?"

"You know perfectly well why I'm here. I can't rest – tending my garden or whatever else – while an innocent son of mine is rotting in your jail. Before you clap *me* in irons as well, you might want me to help you with your investigation."

"He thinks he can help, now." Christodoulákis looked askance at his colleagues. He lit a cigarette and blew smoke into Nick's face.

"The last time you *helped*, we wasted three days of police time pursuing dead ends," said Konstantópoulos.

"Not dead ends, Sergeant, *loose* ends that needed to be tidied up, and I imagine that you've done that by now. You've established that Sean and Siobhan were not involved in the murder and, as far as possible, you've eliminated the other people who were at Moondance that night. Am I right?"

The sergeant and the constable deferred to the lieutenant. He looked like he was chewing a lemon.

"We're still following up on a couple of things and trying to locate Spíros Tavouláris so that we can rule him and Kristīne out, but yes, you're largely correct."

"If I may make one important observation?"

"If you must."

"Your investigation has been focused entirely on Síva, I think."

"That is where the murder took place, after all."

"Yes, it is, but it may not be where the murderer came from."

"We have found nothing to suggest that."

"Well, I have."

There was a stunned silence, a dawning. The policemen stirred in their seats. Nick had their attention now. He went on:

"Suppose Sam and Jason met someone *before* they came here? Someone that followed them here and killed Sam?"

"You have someone in mind, I think."

"I do, Lieutenant. And I've spent the last two nights in his house."

"Who is this?"

"His name is Peter Weston. He and his wife run a guest house in Séllia: Villa Erató. Sam and Jason stayed there before they came to Síva."

"And what makes you so sure it was him?"

"Oh, I'm not. Not yet. But he matches the description of a man who was seen here, trying to find Sam just before two in the morning on the night of her murder. I have a witness who can identify him. There may be others.

"He was carrying a leather jacket on a warm night, so the witness assumed he was using a motorbike. I found one in his garage and a motorbike of the same make, model and colour appears in one of the photos that Sam posted on Facebook before her phone disappeared."

The lieutenant threw a look at the sergeant.

"How you know this?"

"Her Facebook posting was copied to Jason, so it was on *his* phone. It was easy to miss because it was later than Jason's own postings and buried amongst lots of other rubbish. There's a montage of photos pinned to that post, including some of a visit to a beach Sam and Jason made with Peter. I'm wondering if that started some intimacy between Sam and Peter."

"What are you saying?"

"I think she may have seduced him, like she seduced Spíros."

"We've seen this guy. There's a photo that Jason posted. He's not young."

"He's not, but he's in good shape; quite an attractive man."

"And he is married."

"Yes, but from what I've seen, their marriage is in name only now."

"They are not sleeping together?"

"They have separate beds, separate sinks. She has a separate life now, focused on self-improvement and God."

"The menopause does strange things to women."

"Or maybe she just gave up on him? Who knows? But I'd say that Peter is a bit lost."

"And then along comes a dream girl ..."

"So why kill her? What's his motive?" asked the sergeant.

"I'm thinking that, for Sam, it was the same as Spíros. She was hot for it, he was there, she seduced him. End of story. But for Peter it was different. He thought there was more. *Much* more. That it was love. He became obsessed. Either she lured him to Síva for more sex or he pursued her out of love. Maybe he even thought they could have a future, run away together."

"He must be thirty years older!"

"Thirty-two."

"Silly sod."

"A naïf, I would say."

"What is that?"

"An innocent, a gullible person."

"How do get to be fifty-two and an innocent?"

"You're a dreamer, an idealist …"

"You never joined the police force, that's for sure."

Everyone laughed. Nick felt he was establishing some rapport with these guys. Encouraged, he went on:

"So, when Sam later rejects him, it's too much to bear. If he can't have her, no-one else will."

"But why leave Jason if this guy is just a casual fling for her?" Demétrios asked.

"I'm sorry, I don't know your name."

"I am Demétrios."

"Our brightest constable," added the lieutenant, and the boy tilted his head in gratitude and respect.

"That's a good question, Demétrio and I can only guess at the answer. Maybe she was getting bored with Jason anyway and Peter became a catalyst for change? I don't know yet."

"And this is your only theory?" asked Leo.

"No. There is also the possibility of blackmail. Unlike Spíros, Peter *does* have some money. After their affair, Sam could have threatened to tell Linda unless he paid up."

"But what does he care about Linda now?" asked Demétrios.

"Oh, he cares. They might not be having sex, they might not even love each other anymore but, without Linda, his idyllic life here could not continue. And he loves Crete, their house, their little business. In many ways, it's a paradise for him."

"A loveless paradise."

"Exactly, and in a wild, obsessed moment, a dreamer like Peter could put all that at risk for the chance of true love. But then, if he's blackmailed, he knows he *hasn't* found love at all, he's found some bitch who could destroy his idyllic life. She has to be stopped."

"An appealing but fanciful theory, Mr Fisher. How many twenty-year-old girls will try to blackmail someone? It's a rare crime."

"It may not have been about money. If we take the first scenario and then add something like: *and now leave me alone, Peter, or I'll tell Linda everything,* that might have been enough to turn deep hurt and resentment into a killing fury."

"All right, Mr Fisher, you have a good imagination but let's stick to the facts, shall we? It seems that we have some circumstantial evidence concerning this Peter Weston – rather *less* circumstantial evidence than we *already* have against your son – and you've added quite a lot of conjecture to that. I don't think that's enough for us to change our focus."

"I agree we need more, but you've interviewed Jason I don't know how many times. It must be worth questioning Peter, surely?"

"Let's go through it all again and examine the case against him and the evidence that we have. Demí – get some coffees and water and maybe we can get a snack here? We didn't let Mr Fisher finish his panini."

"Yes, boss," said Demí and went to find the taverna owner. Nick sensed the moment and turned to Leo.

"Please, call me Nick."

There was a pause, a tipping point in their relationship. The lieutenant looked at him without expression.

"I prefer *not* to use the first names of people I'm about to arrest."

"That's easy, then. Don't arrest me. Just call me Nick, let me work with you. I can help."

The lieutenant continued to look at him for several seconds.

"With your son being our prime suspect, it goes against all the rules. Can you be objective? Impartial? Of course, you can't. So, let me be clear. I am the boss, DCI Fisher, not you. You will *not* act independently, but only as part of the team which I direct. You will not be paid, although we will refund any essential expenses, and, if I say so at *any* time and for *any* reason, you will leave the team and that will be that. No discussion. And if you interfere in *any* way after that, you will be arrested on the spot and put in jail for as long as I can keep you there. Is that clear?"

"Crystal. And fair enough. My first goal is to get Jason released but I'd like to help you guys nail this bastard if that's all right with you."

"We all want that. So, let's try to work together now. I am Leo. This is Thaní."

They shook hands with Nick, in turn.

"Demí," called the lieutenant, "Get him to bring a carafe of rakí as well."

It was going to be a long lunch.

CHAPTER 22
PETER AND LINDA

The next afternoon, Thaní was able to collect the enlargements from Alexandrákis. They were no help; just larger, grainier versions of the same murk. It had been a waste of time. Frustrated, he tucked them into the growing evidence folder.

At five pm, Leo and Thaní jumped into the Skoda Octavia for another smoke-filled, hair-raising ride back to Chaniá. Nick did his best to follow them in the Jeep, but he knew where he was going anyhow. Leo dropped off a disgruntled Thaní at Chaniá, insisting that he did not want to appear mob-handed for the first meeting.

Two hours later, the police car rolled forward onto the gravel behind the red Golf. Nick tucked the Jeep away in the lane and entered the drive on foot.

"So, chats over drinks will be a little different tonight, my friend," said Leo.

"I'm sure they will."

Leo got out and they rang the doorbell. Linda came to the door. She glanced at Nick, recognising him, and was about to speak when Leo cut in:

"Mrs Weston? I am Lieutenant Christodoulákis. I think you have already met Mr Fisher. May we come in?"

"I…I don't understand."

"Mr Fisher is helping the police with our current investigation."

Linda threw a confused and hostile glare at Nick but stood back from the door. They pushed through, brushing past the coat rack.

"Thank you," said Leo. "Now, is your husband at home?"

"Peter? Yes, he is. We were just sitting down for a drink. Come through."

Peter stood up from the terrace table, looking wary.

"Darling, this is Lieutenant … I'm sorry, I'm not sure I can …"

"Christodoulákis. Hello, Mr Weston. I apologise for the intrusion, but we would like to ask you a few questions."

"What are *you* doing here, Nick?"

"I'm working with the Cretan police, Peter. I used to be a policeman in England."

Peter looked hurt, more than angry.

"So before, you came here as a policeman?"

There was an awkward pause, then it was Leo who spoke:

"Before today, Mr Fisher was acting as a private citizen."

"Jason's my son. I'm sorry for any deception," added Nick.

"So, this is about Jason and Sam?" asked Linda. "We were very sorry to hear that the poor girl drowned, but I don't understand how ..."

"Where can we talk with you, Mr Weston?" asked Leo.

Linda looked furious, suddenly, and spat out the words:

"Whatever you have to say, you say to *both* of us."

"We must speak with Mr Weston alone, and then, later, with you alone, Mrs Weston. It is standard procedure."

"It's all right, darling, we must do as they ask," said Peter firmly. "I'll take them to the office."

They followed Peter into the garage and up the wooden staircase. He erected a wooden, folding table in the middle of the room and wheeled over three office chairs.

"Please," he said, extending his hand, and Leo and Nick sat. "Can I get you something? Tea, coffee, water, a drink?"

"That won't be necessary, thank you," said Leo. "Please sit."

Peter did as he was told, moved his chair closer and put his arms on the table.

"I hope you won't mind if we use this," said Leo as Nick took a recording device out of the police bag and set it up on the table.

Peter shrugged, Leo nodded and Nick pressed a button.

"First interview with Mr Peter Weston, commencing at seven twenty-five pm on Wednesday, the twenty-sixth of September. Also in the room are Lieutenant Leonídas Christodoulákis and Mr Nick Fisher."

165

Peter confirmed his full name, address and passport number for the recording. Then Leo led the questioning:

"I understand that you and your wife offer accommodation under the name *Villa Erató*?"

"Yes, that's correct."

"And did you receive a booking from Jason Buckingham and Samantha Martin covering the period of six nights commencing Sunday, the second of September?"

"That sounds right, I'd have to check."

"Please do so, then."

Peter went to the computer at the far end of the room and tapped a few keys.

"Yes. They arrived late afternoon on Sunday, the second and left very early on Saturday, the eighth." He returned to the table.

"How would you describe your relationship with Samantha Martin?"

Peter was floored for a moment by the directness of Leo's question. His face coloured and he avoided eye contact:

"I am a host; she was a guest. She seemed like a nice girl."

"Were you attracted to her, Mr Weston?"

"She was less than half my age, Lieutenant. An attractive girl, for sure, but ..."

Nick cut in:

"Tell us about the beach trip, Peter. Your secret beach."

"Oh, it's no secret. Just a place that's less well known. It's near Rodákino. There's a string of five beaches. I like the fourth one along. I took them both."

"How did you get there?"

"We went on motorbikes. Jason rented one and I own one. Linda needed the car that day anyway, as I recall. It's not that far."

"Do you make a habit of taking your guests to the beaches?"

"No."

"Then why, this time?"

"It just came up in conversation. They were interested in finding

166

more remote beaches. They seemed like a nice couple and I had nothing else to do, so why not?"

Peter seemed relaxed, blasé almost. Nick went in hard.

"Let's cut the bullshit, shall we Peter? You took them because you were powerfully attracted to Sam. Isn't that the truth?"

"No, and look, I don't like where this is going. Am I supposed to have done something wrong?"

"Sam didn't drown, Mr Weston, she was murdered. And you're a suspect."

"Murdered? Jesus! No!"

Peter's face paled and he started walking around the room.

"Sit down please, Mr Weston," said Leo.

"You are in serious trouble, Peter. You need to tell us the whole truth, right now."

He sat, but was squirming in his seat and wringing his hands.

"How was she killed?"

"We're not at liberty to say."

"But there's no doubt?"

"It was murder. The Medical Examiner has no doubt."

"Oh, my *God*."

Peter put his head in his hands and rocked back and forth in his chair, moaning under his breath. After perhaps twenty seconds, his hands slid down and he turned his face to the ceiling. He blinked several times. Finally, he levelled his head and spoke:

"Is this interview confidential?"

"Of course."

"Only there are things Linda must not find out."

"We can't vouch for what may come out in court, should there be a trial, Mr Weston, but *we* will not tell your wife anything you tell us here today."

"All right. Thank you."

There was another prolonged pause as Peter studied his hands. Nick and Leo exchanged glances, but both knew to say nothing. At last, he started to speak again, in a raspy, toneless voice as if all life and hope had been sucked from his body:

"Yes, I was attracted to Sam. More than that, I fell for her, body and soul. She was a wild girl, a free spirit. She was tantalising beyond belief but then so passionate, so loving. And I hadn't felt love for so long. So long …"

Tears streaked down his face and he went across to the bench for a box of tissues. Nick made big eyes and tilted his head. Leo smirked.

"My wife, Linda. She's cold and barren – and so distant, these days. We seldom touch, let alone make love. She treats me like an irritant, for Christ's sake, a nuisance. She makes me feel old, clumsy, vulgar – grubby, even. But Sam made me feel young again, desirable."

"Talk us through what happened, Peter. Let's go back to that beach."

"It's a relaxed beach. There's some naturism, so it was natural for Sam to go topless. She must have done it before because her breasts were tanned. Then she asked me to show her how to snorkel. Jason didn't seem to mind, so I showed her how to wear the mask and how to use the breathing tube.

"She practised a little and then we went around the rocks together. There are more fish to see there although the whole of this area's pretty much fished out. We were out of sight of the beach when she said her mask was letting in water and would I help her tighten the straps. While I was trying to do it, her nipples were brushing my chest.

"Then she sat on a rock to make it easier for me to get at the mask and hooked her legs around my leg to stop the waves from pulling her off. She did it in such a pragmatic way that, at first, I wasn't sure she meant anything by it but then her legs started moving and touching me.

"I still wasn't sure it was deliberate, maybe it was the swell, but I was getting hard. Then I looked at her and the desire was unmistakable. I'll never forget what she said: 'You're a gorgeous man, Peter. Linda doesn't know what she's got, does she?'

"And then she kissed me; a long, hard kiss, pushed her tongue right into my mouth. By this time, I'm bursting out of my trunks. She sees this and slides down my body and starts going down on me."

"What is that?" asked Leo.

"Fellatio," said Peter.

Nick turned to Leo. "She was sucking his dick."

Leo blinked several times. "Ah."

Peter went on:

"Yes, just like that. If anyone had swum around the point, they'd have seen. And she's bloody good at it. Got one of those studs in her tongue. My dick was hard as a rock, like I was eighteen again and, when I came, she sucked it all out of me, every last drop and swallowed it.

"And then she slid up my body like a naughty mermaid and said 'Mmmm' in my ear, like she'd savoured some exotic delight and then kissed me again, but gently this time, more loving. I tasted myself on her lips.

"Then she said: 'Next time, you can have me if you like' and, before I knew it, she's swimming away and looking back at me with that teasing face, like it was all just a silly prank. Yes, gentlemen, you could say that I was attracted to Sam. Every man's dream."

"And then what happened?"

"We get back to the beach and she kisses Jason like nothing's happened and I'm hoping he can't taste me and then we just spend the rest of the afternoon together like normal people.

"She takes a few photos. We have a drink at the beach café. She and Jason play beach tennis and then, when we come to go back, she asks if she can ride pillion on *my* bike as it's bigger and more exciting and she gives me a wink, but Jason doesn't seem to notice, and he says: 'If Peter doesn't mind!'

"All the way back she's hugging me tight, but not in a sexual way this time. It's like I'm saving her, protecting her, like she needs me. And, when we get back, we're way ahead of Jason but she just strokes my face and kisses me on the cheek and says: 'Thank you.' Then I see that the car's in the garage, so Linda's back anyway."

"Does she notice anything?"

"Linda? I don't think so but, in a way, I don't care, you know?"

"So, did you take Sam up on her suggestion?"

"It happened like this. Linda and Jason are around most of the next day, Wednesday, until Jason rides over to the Amári Valley for the overnight climb of Psilorítis. I know he's going to be away until at least eleven the next morning. But Linda's there all that evening.

"Sam joins us for our early evening drink, and she sits sideways – opposite Linda, but on the same side of the table as me. She's wearing this little summer dress and she keeps crossing and uncrossing her legs. Just enough for me to glimpse that she's not wearing any knickers.

"And all the time she's keeping up this banal conversation with Linda about her and Jason's plans. The little minx. It was torture. She wanted me that night, but I couldn't leave our bedroom to go to her. I just couldn't do that to Linda."

"How very honourable, Mr Weston. Or could it be that you are frightened of your wife?"

"I didn't want to hurt her."

"Hmmm."

"Anyway, the next morning, Linda went off to do the weekly shop in Réthymno at about eight thirty. I knew she'd be at least two hours.

"I'd just finished cleaning the pool and saying goodbye to our other guests when Sam came over. She was wearing a robe and carrying a beach towel and asked if she could swim now. When I said it was okay, she slipped off the robe and dived in.

"She was stark naked. I couldn't take my eyes off her. I sat on one of the poolside chairs and just watched. And then, when she came out, she just stood over me, dripping. I could see everything. She said: 'Could you dry me please, Peter.'

"So, I dried her, starting with her hair, her shoulders, her back, then her arms, her legs, her bottom, her breasts and then gently between her legs. By this time, she was panting and rubbing herself on the towel. She begged me to lick her and I did.

"Then she pushed me back on the grass, tore off my shorts and pants, sat facing me on my chest, played with herself for a few moments while I watched and then lowered herself onto my dick. God, that felt wonderful.

"I came far too soon, of course, but she stayed with me, holding me, kissing me as we lay naked together by the pool and then, after perhaps half an hour, she started fondling me and soon I was rock hard again and taking her from behind.

"I'm fifty-two years old. I'd no idea I could still get that excited, or so soon after. Later, we showered together. Ten minutes after we dressed, Linda came back and then Jason, fifteen minutes after Linda. It was that close."

"Did you get another chance with Sam?" asked Leo.

"No. Either Jason or Linda was around until they left, Saturday morning."

"And did you ever see Sam again?"

"No. I didn't."

"Where were you on the night she died, Saturday the fifteenth?"

"Right here."

"With Linda?"

"Er … no. Not after seven or so. She left for one of her wellness courses."

"So, is there someone else who can confirm you were here?"

"No, I don't think so, unless the neighbours spotted me."

"We'll check that," said Leo.

"But it's not very likely, is it, Peter?" said Nick.

"Why do you say that?"

"Because you *weren't* here, *were* you? You waited for Linda to leave and then you jumped on your motorbike and headed off to Síva in search of Sam."

There was a pause. Peter examined his hands, found a nail to pick at.

"What makes you think that?"

"We have a witness who will place you in Síva late that night, looking for Sam. You'd let your hair down and you'd put on the single earring you used to wear, but it was you, Peter. The witness is certain. And you were carrying the leather jacket that I've just seen hanging in the hall. You needed that for the motorbike; the one in the garage that's covered in dust from a long ride."

Leo cut in:

"Be in no doubt, Mr Weston. You are in serious trouble. You are a suspect in a murder inquiry. And yet you lied to us just now. I strongly advise you to tell us the whole truth about what happened and to do it now."

"Perhaps I should call my lawyer."

"That is your right, Mr Weston."

There was another, longer pause. Peter stood and looked out of the window. The first patter of raindrops for many weeks could be heard on the roof.

"I apologise for the lie. I was just trying to keep out of it. I *did* go to Síva that night, but I didn't kill Sam. I could never have done that. As it was, I didn't even find her."

"Had you arranged to meet?"

"Well, yes. Kind of. I texted her to say I thought Linda was going on this course and that I could come over at the weekend, if that would work."

"When did you text her?"

"Thursday afternoon, I think. I can check."

He brought out his mobile phone and started scanning back through his messages and then stopped.

"I'm sorry. I can't do that. I forgot. I deleted the string of messages in case Linda found them. I'm pretty sure it was Thursday, though."

"And what reaction did you get from Sam?"

"She seemed very laid-back; if you can make it, that'd be great, sort of thing. So, I texted: 'What about Jason?' and she came back with: 'Let me worry about him, just get here if and when you can.'"

"So, tell us about Saturday, the fifteenth."

"I was on tenterhooks. Linda seemed uncertain about going. Said she wasn't feeling all that great and it was a long way and so on. This humming and harring went on all afternoon. It was driving me crazy. I started to think she was doing it on purpose, but then I put that down to paranoia.

"At last, around seven, she appears, dressed up and with a small suitcase, and says she's decided to go after all. She reminds me about feeding the chickens and getting things ready for the guests that are coming on Monday and then, at last, she's out the door."

"You keep chickens?"

"Do I look like a chicken farmer to you?"

"My job has taught me that people are not what they seem, Mr Weston."

"Yes, well. Linda had agreed to feed our neighbours' chickens while *they* were away, so I was lumbered. She was going to be away for two nights. I thought of just piling up a heap of feed and clearing off, but I know nothing about chickens. Perhaps they'd eat themselves to death? Perhaps they'd only eat if it were fresh, and then starve? I had no idea. I didn't want to kill the bloody things.

"In the end, I decided to ask someone else in the village. There's a woman who rescues animals, Carla. I told her I needed to rush over to Chaniá because a good friend had been taken into hospital. She agreed to feed them for me, and I gave her twenty euros for her animal charity."

"Wasn't there a risk that she would talk to Linda – that your story would be exposed?"

"Yes, but I just wanted to go. I was desperate to get away. Perhaps I'd think of something to say to Carla when I got back."

"So, you'd sorted out the chickens. What next?"

"The rooms needed to be prepped, or else I'd have to come back early. They wanted both the garden rooms from Monday afternoon. I had to make up the beds. Linda hadn't bothered to iron the sheets and pillowcases, so I had to do that first. Then clean the showers, sweep and mop the rooms, make sure all the little touches were just right. Took bloody ages. Then I left them a note with keys in an envelope. If I didn't get back, I could send a message and they'd be able to sort themselves out.

"By the time everything was ready, it was almost ten. And I still needed to pack. For a moment, I wondered if it was worth it. Why not just have a good night's sleep and go in the morning? But then

I thought about what it felt like, being with her, and I knew I wanted to get there now."

"Why did you think you might not get back for your guests?"

"I don't know. I was confused, besotted. Half of me wanted her like crazy and was desperate for her body, but the other half thought this might be real love. That she might leave Jason and I might leave Linda and we could be together. Have a future together. If I was right about that, maybe I was *never* coming back."

Leo took out a cigarette and lit it. The chair creaked as he leaned back and blew a stream of blue smoke at the ceiling, then he extended both his arms sideways.

"You would leave all this for some young chick who gives you a hard-on?"

"It was so much more than that, Lieutenant."

"Was it, Mr Weston? Was it really?"

"Please go on, Peter," said Nick.

"So, I decide to go, and I rush around putting a few things together. Síva's a cool place. It still has a hippy feel to it. So, you're right, I let my hair down, dug out a headband, put the old gipsy earring in and took out some cool, old clothes."

You sad bastard, thought Nick, but it was Leo who spoke:

"Describe the headband, please."

"Um ... Paisley design, blue and purple. Made of cotton, I suppose. Elasticated."

"And you still have it?"

"It'll be in the bedroom. Why do you ask?"

"Never mind."

"I think I'm entitled to know why you ask."

"You're a murder suspect, Mr Weston," Leo snapped. "We ask the questions, you answer. That's how it works. You're not entitled to know anything."

"Please go on, Peter," Nick said again.

"So, I'm packed and ready, at last. It's about ten thirty. It's quite a warm night but it's never warm on a motorbike, so I take the leather jacket."

"Did you take a hat of any kind?"

"Just the crash helmet."

"Nothing else to wear on your head? Something you'd packed? Something for the beach?"

"Nothing else, Lieutenant."

Peter looked from Leo to Nick and back and, seeing there were no more questions, he carried on:

"I finally got away, but it's a long trip, via Réthymno and Chaniá and then over the mountains. By the time I got there, it was well after one am, but I know Sam's a bit of a night owl, so I started looking for her right away."

"Do you recall where you went?"

"I started at the ferry end. Most of the tavernas were closed, but not all. Some bars were open. There was a modern-looking bar on the left but that was almost empty. Further up, on the right, things were still humming and there was some good blues guitar music coming from a bar with a tree growing up through it. All wood and palm fronds.

"I stopped for a quick beer and talked to a German woman called Bridget or Birgit or something. She seemed to be running the place, but she told me it was owned by her Greek ex-husband. She didn't recognise Sam from my description. I didn't have a photo, believe it or not.

"I remember worrying about whether or not to send Sam a text. I didn't want to embarrass her with Jason. So, I held off. I tried the Sorókos Café and then the Rakí Bar up the main street. The woman in there suggested I try the beach bar but, by the time I got there, it was closed.

"It was frustrating but, in a way, I felt relieved. I was feeling very tired and I wasn't going to be much use to Sam in this state. I'd also lost some confidence. I wasn't certain that I'd done the right thing by coming. Would she be glad to see me or was I an old fool on a dream mission? Maybe the looks I'd been given by Birgit and that guy at Sorókos put doubts in my head.

"Anyway, I figured that, by now, she'd be with Jason, tucked into a sleeping bag in one of the tents – and there were dozens of them – so

I decided to leave it until the morning. If I couldn't find her then, I could send a text and it would be less suspicious at that time of day. She'd be able to make up a cover story.

"So, feeling a bit more reassured, I went back to the bar with the tree, ordered a Metaxá and chatted to a woman on the next barstool. She was Kirsten from Heidelberg, I remember, and she came to Síva every year. After half an hour or so, it was getting late, so I went back to the bike, took down the bedroll and curled up on the beach."

"Which part of the beach?"

"Just to the right of the sun loungers."

Nick remembered that the only sun loungers were near the town, a fair way from the beach bar and even further from the big rock.

"Why there?"

"Why not? It was near the bike and at that time it was quiet."

"And you slept?"

"Oh yes. I was knackered, and then the Metaxá just finished me off."

"And you were alone?"

"Yes, of course, I was alone. I don't try to sleep with every woman who talks to me, Lieutenant."

"So, what happened in the morning, Peter?"

"I woke soon after seven, I think. I was getting hot and a dog was barking somewhere. It had been quite a windy night, but it was a very still morning and the sun was already up. I swam and showered on the beach, then went in search of coffee and something to eat.

"I remember seeing the ferry come and go, so it must have been around nine by then. I was wondering if it was too early to text Sam when I noticed that something was going on.

"Small groups of people were gathering, there were hushed conversations, people were pointing over towards the big rock, looking apprehensive, shocked even.

"Some people started making their way over there. I fell in with the crowd and asked a Dutch guy what was going on. He said: 'I dunno man, they're saying someone drowned.'

"Right away I knew, somehow. A pit formed in my stomach. My

heart began to race. I started asking people: 'Is it a man or a woman?' No-one seemed to know anything, but then an older, Greek man said: 'They say to me it is a girl.' 'A girl how old? A girl from where?' I asked. But he just shrugged and shook his head and we kept on trudging through the shingle. Was it shared humanity or morbid curiosity driving them? I don't know. But for me now, it's rising panic.

"I push my way to the front and then I start running. But, on the shingle, it's a nightmare; the harder you run, the more the shingle holds you back. Then people are stopping to undress because you have to wade around rocks to get to the second beach, but I just splash on.

"I see a young policeman and he's trying to keep the people back and then there she is. Face-down on the shingle, half out of the water. I'm horrified. I didn't expect that I would see her just like that. It's a real shock. And I know it's her. It's her hair, her body. I recognise the bikini bottoms. Then I see the tattoo – the blue butterfly – and I know for sure. It's Sam."

Peter clamped his lips together and his eyes looked bloodshot and wet. He accepted a paper tissue from Nick.

"Did you say anything to anyone?"

"I don't think I did. People were asking if she was dead and others were nodding and saying she'd drowned."

"Did you find that surprising?"

"That she drowned? You know, I didn't even think about it. You see a bedraggled-looking corpse on the beach in a swimming costume and drowning? Well, it fits with your expectations, doesn't it? It never occurred to me that something else could have happened; that she could have been murdered."

"Just give us a minute, Peter," said Nick, and raised his eyebrows at Leo who then followed him out of the room, downstairs and into the garden. Linda called from the living room door:

"Are you carrying on? Shall I bring coffee and water?"

"Thank you. That would be kind, Mrs Weston."

"Is Peter all right?"

"He's okay."

She disappeared inside.

"So, what do you think?" asked Nick.

Leo fumbled for his cigarettes, then remembered that they were still inside on the table and cursed to himself.

"If he's lying, he's doing it very well."

"Yes. He makes a convincing besotted, old fool, doesn't he? And all that oversharing; he must be deep-down lonely, poor bugger."

"A naïf, I think you called him."

"Yes. I'd stick with that."

"Perhaps. Or a clever man playing the part of a naïf rather well?"

"It has to be tested."

"I agree," said Leo. "When we go back in, I'll go in hard, like I don't believe a word of it. You can pick up the pieces."

He gave Nick a fierce look.

"We need to get angry, Nick. It might not be like he says at all. This bastard – a married man of fifty-two – may have seduced, or even raped, a young girl thirty-two years his junior, when, as their host, he was in a position of trust. Then he pursues her and kills her when he's done with her, so he can carry on his idyllic life as though nothing happened."

"Yes, except that we know Sam seduced Spíros two days earlier and we know she'd just ended the engagement to Jason for some reason."

"Yes, okay. We know she's no angel, but this guy has to be put to the sword."

"Agreed."

They went back to the room.

"Are you okay, Peter? Happy to carry on?" asked Nick.

He nodded.

"Please just confirm that for the recording, would you?"

"Sorry, yes, I'm okay to carry on."

"Linda is bringing coffee."

"Great."

"So, going back to that morning, seeing her body on the beach, how did you feel? What did you do?"

There was a pause. Peter rubbed the index finger of his left hand with his right thumb. When he looked up, there was an enormous sadness in those eyes.

"I was devastated. All my hopes for the future died with Sam. And her life was over, at twenty. It was crushing. I just wanted to throw myself onto her body and weep. But I was also acutely aware of my situation.

"I had to keep myself under control. Jason might be in the crowd, somewhere. If he saw me there, he'd know. I could think of no excuse for being there. It would be hard enough for him to learn that his fiancée was dead. I didn't want him to discover that she'd been cheating on him, as well."

"A bit late for caring about Jason's feelings, wasn't it, Mr Weston?"

"I'm a human being, Lieutenant. Why hurt the guy more than necessary?"

"Necessary. Interesting choice of word. Was it *necessary* to hurt him at all?"

"I fell in love with his girl. You don't *choose* to fall in love. It just happens. He was going to be hurt, as a result, and I was sorry about that."

"You fell in love? Do you even know what love is, Mr Weston?"

"Well, I'm not sure I *did*, but I think I do now. You see, for me, love and sex never worked together. All my relationships had been one thing or the other. I'd love and respect them, put them on a pedestal, I suppose.

"I'd want to take care of them, but the sex was disappointing, or it just didn't work. Bad chemistry, perhaps. Others I'd have great sex with, but it was like that prevented me from truly loving them; as if the intimacy took away the respect.

"With Sam, it was quite different. Sex with her was so natural. It was delicious fun. It was so much a part of her. She was so uninhibited, and she had such a fantastic sense of humour. I found that I loved her *through* sex, not despite it. We found a true passion."

"Listen to yourself, Mr Weston. You're a dreamer. An ageing hippy. You meet a girl. Perhaps fundamentally a nice girl, but she's looking for a fling or two. She seduces you without difficulty and then she moves on. She seduced another guy in Síva, by the way."

Nick thought he saw a dark shadow cross Peter's face like an aircraft passing in front of the sun. Leo went on:

"But you? You don't move on, do you? You don't give thanks that she chose you, pat yourself on the back for your performance – not bad for an old guy – and then creep back to Linda like a good adulterer. No.

"You think she wants *more*. That she lusts after you, too. You. A washed-up, fifty-two-year-old with bags under his eyes and thinning hair. Like the rest of us. Every gorgeous twenty-year-old's dream? I don't think so.

"But you think she loves you, maybe even wants to spend her life with you. You take your motorbike on a three-hour ride to Síva on a wild impulse. You find her late at night, you confess your love to her, but she is shocked and tries to set you straight." And here Leo attempts a girl's voice: "What are you doing here, Peter? What we had was just a fling, just a bit of fun."

"Please don't do that. Don't imitate her like that."

Leo ignores him and continues in the same high-pitched whine:

"I thought you knew that. I don't want to break up your marriage, I don't want to run away with you. It's not like I'm in love with you or anything, Peter. Maybe she even says: Anyway, you're old and the sex wasn't so great, if you want to know."

"Stop this. For God's sake. It wasn't like that. I didn't find her. And I didn't want to hurt her. I told you the truth."

There was a knock at the door and Linda came in carrying a tray. She did a double-take when she saw Peter, looking frightened and red-eyed, but she quietly moved the tissue box and the ashtray to one side and laid her tray on the table.

"I brought a few slices of pizza, too, and some biscuits."

"You're very kind."

"Will you be much longer, do you think? Only, I try to be in bed by ten."

Nick checked his watch. It was five past nine.

"We'll get to you as soon as we can, Mrs Weston."

"Thank you."

She closed the door gently as she left. Leo drove on right away, ignoring Peter's last response:

"Being rejected was too much for you, wasn't it? How dare she destroy your dream? And what hurts most is that she deflates you. You were nothing to her. How could you have been so stupid? And she does it so casually: 'What were you *thinking*, Peter?' But still you don't leave, do you, Mr Weston?"

Leo was staring venomously at Peter.

"She asks you to leave but you don't. So, she has to hurt you some more or threaten you to try to get you to leave. She's getting frightened now. She's all alone on a deserted beach with you in the middle of the night and you're starting to act strangely.

"Maybe she gets out her phone and threatens to call 112? Maybe she threatens to call Linda and tell her about your affair? She has to be stopped. *You* have to stop her. You reach for a rock, she starts to run and you bring it down with all your might on the back of her head."

Leo banged the table hard as he finished speaking. Some coffee spilt but he seemed not to notice. Nick was watching. Peter was looking down, shaking his head, tears dripping. He reached for another handful of tissues. After a few more seconds, he spoke in a small, shaky voice:

"So that's how she died? I didn't know. What more can I say? I didn't find her. I didn't kill her. I could never do that to her, anyway. I loved her. After I saw her body on the beach, I just wandered back to the town. I was in a daze. I remember sitting, staring at the sea for quite a while. And then I came home."

"You lied to us before, Peter," said Nick. "Why should we believe you this time?"

"Because it's the truth. Put me through a lie detector. Inject me with sodium pentothal. Whatever. It's the truth."

He spread both hands on the table and looked up at them, like there was nothing left inside him, nothing more to say. Then it was Leo who spoke:

"Drink your coffee, Mr Weston. I'm not going to arrest you today, but you remain a suspect and you must stay here for the time being, in your local area. You will please give me your passport and then we would like to talk with your wife."

Nick spoke to the recorder: "Interview terminated at twenty-one thirty."

Leo lit a cigarette and stood up. Nick stood, stretched and opened the small window. Peter left his passport on the table as he left, while Che continued to draw inspiration from a brighter horizon.

*

Five minutes later, Linda appeared. Without speaking, she cleared the detritus of coffee cups and half-eaten food from the table, emptied and returned the ashtray. Then she sat down and Leo spoke:

"Thank you for seeing us, Mrs Weston. I'm sorry about the time but we'll try to keep this short. If you don't mind, we'll record the interview."

Leo was not interested if she minded or not. He nodded to Nick, who spoke to the machine:

"Interview with Linda Weston commenced at twenty-one forty-six. Also in the room are Lieutenant Christodoulákis and Mr Nick Fisher."

Linda cut in straight away:

"Perhaps you could start by telling me what on earth is going on? A girl drowns. She and her fiancé happen to have stayed here more than a week earlier. A retired British policeman stays in our house under false pretences and now you interview my husband for over two hours?"

"As we explained to your husband, the Medical Examiner has concluded that Sam didn't drown; she was murdered."

Linda took it in her stride.

"Well, I'm sorry to hear that, but what has it to do with us?"

She is not sorry at all, thought Nick.

"You were the last people to host them before they went to Síva. We need to eliminate you from our inquiries," said Leo.

182

"So, we're suspects?"

"As I said, with your help, we need to eliminate you both."

"From your list of suspects."

"If you like, yes."

"I don't much like, as it happens. And what the hell was *he* doing in our house?" She pointed at Nick.

"Mr Fisher was not working with the police then."

She turned her anger on Nick.

"All right, I'll ask *you*. What were you *doing* in our house? Snooping around? Searching without a warrant? Trying to entrap us?"

Leo cut in:

"Entrapment is about causing someone to commit a crime they would not otherwise have committed. That doesn't apply here, Mrs Weston. The crime had already *been* committed. Now, if you will let *me* ask the questions, we will get through this and you'll be able to go to bed."

Linda gave Nick a filthy look but said nothing more.

"We understand that Samantha Martin and Jason Buckingham stayed with you for six nights in early September."

"Sounds right."

"How was that? Did you all get on?"

"We run a business, Lieutenant. We provide services to our customers. We don't need to *get on*."

"Are you saying you didn't, then?"

"No, not at all. I'm saying it's not like that. It's a professional relationship. They were a nice enough, young couple. Said all the right things, ate their breakfasts, left the room tidy."

"Did you invite them for drinks, as you did with me?" asked Nick.

"Just on the first evening, as we usually do. Oh, and we invited Sam when Jason went off to climb the mountain, just because she was on her own."

"And did you notice anything odd about either of those occasions?"

"Odd? I don't think so. Just the usual banal chit-chat. We English are good at that," she added for Leo's benefit. He looked sceptical and reached for a cigarette.

"I'd rather you didn't smoke," Linda snapped, and he let the pack fall back onto the table with a thwack.

"Were you aware that your husband took them to a beach, Mrs Weston?"

"Yes, I was."

"And you didn't have a problem with that?"

"Why would I?"

"It's not quite the professional relationship you described, is it?"

"I suppose not, but that's Peter for you. He likes to help people. They wanted a remote beach, so he took them to one. And why ever not?"

Linda, the consummate professional, was playing it bright and breezy. Both men were curious about how she would react to learning about Peter and Sam, but that would have to wait. Instead, Leo probed a little:

"How would you describe your relationship with your husband, Mrs Weston?"

"Private."

"Would you tell us a little more, in confidence?"

"Peter and I have a solid marriage."

"Do you sleep together?"

"We share a bedroom."

"But not a bed."

"We've been married almost thirty years, Lieutenant. When we moved here, we both decided that we'd sleep better in separate beds. Peter stays up later than me."

"And do you have sex?"

"Mind your own business."

"We're trying to establish whether Peter has a sexually fulfilling relationship with you," said Nick.

"Why?" She glanced from one to the other, then snorted with forced laughter. "You're not suggesting Peter tried it on with Sam? Sorry, guys, but that's laughable. If you didn't notice, Sam was a gorgeous, fit little thing, twenty years old and engaged to a good-looking lad.

"Peter? Well, you know Peter. He's a nice man but he's a waste of space. He might *think* he's God's gift, but the rest of us know different.

And he's got the sex drive of a giant panda, if you must know. We have sex whenever *he* wants it – which is once in a blue moon."

Leo looked sheepish, but Nick was sceptical. He said nothing.

"Can we move to the evening of Saturday, the fifteenth of September then, Mrs Weston?"

"Oh yes, let's … *please.*"

"Tell us what was happening."

"I was getting ready for a three-day wellness programme near Chaniá. I left around seven."

"This would be at the Temple of Akesó?"

She blinked in surprise but managed to keep her cool.

"Yes, that's right."

"And you went straight there?"

"Yes, I did. Got there about eight."

"And were you there the whole three days?"

"Not quite. I left them on Sunday morning for a couple of hours so that I could attend mass in Chaniá."

"But you were there from eight pm Saturday until what, nine am Sunday?"

"It was a ten fifteen service, so I'd have left at about nine thirty-five on Sunday morning and been back before noon. After that, I was there till Monday, late afternoon. Got back here around six thirty Monday evening, I think. In time for our usual drink, anyway. There were new guests to meet and greet."

"And what was Peter up to, while you were away?"

"You need to ask him. I don't monitor his every move."

"We're asking you."

"Well, not much, I should think, as usual. He had the rooms to prepare, neighbours' chickens to feed. He said he'd spent some time on a beach somewhere."

"You were in contact."

"I think I texted him once or twice, just to make sure he was okay."

"And did you notice anything unusual about Peter's behaviour, either just before you left or just after you came back?"

"Nope. Same old Peter."

"All right. Thank you, Mrs Weston. We can let you go to bed now. Thank you for your time."

"Interview terminated at twenty-two nineteen," said Nick.

*

Leo lit a cigarette as soon as they were outside and exhaled with obvious relief.

"I notice you didn't take *her* passport," said Nick.

"She's not a suspect," he said through the smoke, "and she's not going to leave the island without her husband."

"So, where are we now, do you think?" asked Nick.

"I think we come back with a search warrant and, if we find anything, we take him to Chaniá for more questioning."

"Well, we can expect to find a motorbike, a leather jacket, an earring and maybe a bandana. He hasn't denied owning any of those things. What else would we be looking for? There won't be a murder weapon. That's one of the stones in the sea, I should imagine."

"True. We could get your witness to identify him."

"But Peter has admitted to being there now. There's no point."

"Also true."

"We are in the same situation as we are with Jason. There's circumstantial evidence, but the suspect denies the crime. We need something more."

"Okay. It's getting late now. Let's think it through and catch up in the morning."

"While you're thinking, Leo, you might ask yourself why you're holding Jason. Why not just take *his* passport and release him for now, treat him the same as Peter?"

"Because he's been *charged*. Goodnight, Nick."

The Skoda sprayed gravel as Leo gunned it down the lane. Nick was tired now and grateful for the shortish drive back to Saktoúria and a sleep in his own bed.

CHAPTER 23
LINDA REACTS

As soon as Linda heard the Jeep follow the police Skoda down the lane, she slapped Peter hard across the face. So hard that his head twisted forty-five degrees on his neck.

"Ow! What the hell was that for?"

She did it again, only harder.

"Jesus, Linda. What is *wrong* with you?"

"How dare you?"

"What?"

"How dare you screw that little slut! How dare you trash everything we've built together? Thirty years of loving each other, caring for each other, this beautiful place we've made our own and you'd throw it all away? For what? Lust? For that little tart? For some grubby teenager?"

"What the hell are you talking about?"

"All right then, explain to me why the police would interview you for over two hours about the murder of a young girl who stayed in our house if you didn't have some kind of relationship with her? Did you rape her or did the little bitch seduce you?"

"What *is* this. Have you lost your mind?"

"Answer the fucking question, Peter!" She pounded him on the chest with both fists. Peter managed to grab her wrists.

"They asked me about the relationship between Sam and Jason. They asked me a lot about the day at the beach, other places they went. We talked about Síva, how we used to go there."

"Two and a quarter hours you were in there. You looked terrible. You'd had one of your little weepies, you pathetic man. So don't give me this bullshit, Peter. If you're in trouble, I need to know. I'm your wife, remember?"

"I'm a suspect, for some reason, but I think I've convinced them it wasn't me."

"For some reason! There's only one reason I can think of."

Linda swung back for blow number three, but Peter moved forward and caught her arm.

"Stop this! Don't hit me again. For God's sake, Linda, calm down! Look, some guy in Síva said he saw someone who looked like me, that's all. They found photos of us on Jason's phone and walked them around the town. I explained that I was here all the time but that took a while because I was on my own, if you remember. I couldn't come up with an alibi. Just the bloody chickens. And I cried because they described how Sam died. It was such a terrible thing. Such a total, bloody waste."

She looked at him straight in the eyes, unblinking.

"Tell me that you didn't have sex with her."

"Of course, I didn't. Why would she be interested in me? I'm old enough to be her father."

"But *you* were interested in *her*. I saw that. Did you force yourself on her?"

"No way, Linda. What kind of man do you think I am?"

"A weak man, like all the rest. Only weaker."

"Thanks a lot."

"If I *ever* find out that you lied to me today, Peter, I will *feed* you to those fucking chickens and I'll start with these bits." Before he could stop her, she grabbed his testicles in a vice-like grip. She squeezed hard and kept on squeezing. "And then I'll leave you. And make no mistake, I'll find the best divorce lawyer known to man. For all practical purposes, your life will be over."

She stormed out of the room and Peter heard the front door slam. A few moments later the Golf roared off into the night in a shower of gravel. Peter sank to his knees, clutching himself and moaning softly.

CHAPTER 24
THE TEMPLE REVISITED

The next morning, Nick found that he was out of groceries again. He walked down to the kafenío for breakfast.

"Yeiá sou, Níko! Pós eísai?"

"Eímai lígo kouresménos, Kostí. A bit knackered, mate."

"But you doing okay?"

"Yes, I'm enjoying myself, to be honest."

"And you getting somewhere, helping your family?"

"I reckon I'm making progress, thanks."

Kóstas looked at him in curiosity for a moment.

"You look different, my friend, your eyes are brighter, more alive."

"That's what a few days away from your rakí will do."

"Ha! But it is more than that. You have found a woman!"

"Oh, not that old chestnut again!"

"What is chestnut?"

"Kástano, I think."

"Kástano?"

"Never mind. Just bring me some breakfast, Kostí."

"You want toast?"

"Just coffee, yoghurt and honey with some fruit, if you have it?"

"I have cherries, from the winter."

"Perfect."

It was already nine fifteen and another beautiful morning. The air was crisp and clear, the sky cloudless and there was an autumnal freshness that the sun would burn off in an hour or two. It felt good to be back in his home village.

As Nick waited for his breakfast, the phone rang.

"Mr Fisher?"

"Yes."

"It's Martina. From the Temple of Akesó?"

Nick had forgotten about her.

"I'm sorry it took so long to get back to you but one of our team was on leave and it took me a while to get hold of her."

"But you spoke to her in the end?"

"Yes, I have spoken to all three and no-one remembers seeing Linda at the Welcome Supper."

"Can I take it that she wasn't there, then?"

"No, for sure *not*. There would be times when no-one from the team was in attendance."

"Is that so?"

"Like I said, it's very relaxed. She might have been there with other guests but no team member present, she might have taken some food and gone back to her room, she might have just stayed in her room and forgotten all about the Welcome Supper."

"Would there have been someone on reception all evening?"

"Most of the time, for sure, but not all. We have the bell, as you saw. And now I must go, Mr Fisher. I have a guest waiting. I'm sorry I couldn't be more help."

"Might I pop round again, later today?"

"If you wish. It's quiet now. Only two of us are here."

"Great. Thanks. I'll see you around midday."

Nick could feel that tingling sensation. He recognised it from long ago. There was something there. Like a word on the tip of one's tongue or the faintest whiff of a half-remembered scent. It was pure impulse to return to The Temple of Akesó, but he felt there was unfinished business there, somehow, even if he couldn't quite nail down what it was. He still believed in his intuition, but he also knew it to be fallible. He would need to proceed with caution.

At that moment, young Xará appeared with a tray. As she laid out his breakfast, she said, under her breath:

"The police were here, Mister Níko. They look for you."

"Oh really? Police from where, Xará?"

"Just the Spíli guys, I think."

"Right. Thanks for letting me know." He patted her hand. "But everything's okay now, I think. All sorted."

Her little face radiated relief and she beamed.

"Is good, I worry for you."

Nick grinned and settled down to his breakfast. But the phone would not leave him in peace. This time it was Jen:

"Hello, Nick. You didn't call. Just wanted to make sure you were okay."

"Sorry, Jen. We were in transit."

"We?"

"Yes. I'm working with the Greek police now."

"Oh, great! That's good news."

"Yes. Should make things a lot easier, all round."

"Any chance of Jason getting out anytime soon? He's been held for ten days now, you know."

"I've started to push for that, Jen, but it won't be just yet. Tell him there's a good team on the case and we *are* moving forward. I'd hope to have him out of there in a few days, all being well, but let's keep that to ourselves for now."

"Yes, of course."

"Great … and now …"

"Do you know what today is?"

"What do you mean?"

"It's Sam's funeral. I spoke to Helen two days ago and she told me it was today. She sounded depressed, poor thing, which I suppose is only to be expected. We sent a wreath – from us and Jason."

"You told him, then?"

"He kept asking when it would be. We couldn't lie to him." She paused for a moment. "Helen also said that she and Michael are splitting up. 'Isn't this a time to be staying together, helping each other through it?' I said."

"Major family trauma often leads to a break-up. I've seen it a number of times."

"It makes no sense."

"It's about self-preservation. When they look at each other, they see only their dead daughter. They drag each other down. To start any kind of healing process, they have to break free."

"So, there's some logic to it then, in a weird way. It's incredibly sad, nonetheless."

When Nick had finished his breakfast, he called Leo.

"Ah, hello Nick. I was about to call you. Listen, I have an update meeting with my boss this morning, but then I want to review the case with the whole team, and I'd like you to join us here in Chaniá. Can you make it for two pm?"

*

"Hello again, Martina."

"Mr Fisher." She extended her skeletal, brown hand. "Can I get you some tea or coffee?"

"A coffee would be nice. Thank you."

"Do have a seat. I'll be with you in a minute."

There was some Scandinavian-style seating in the air-conditioned foyer; teal-coloured cushions on pale, wooden benches framed two sides of a smoked glass corner table with a light scattering of health magazines on it. A large, potted plant shielded the right-hand bench from the windows' glare. Nick lowered himself onto the seat and took out his large notepad.

The door opened again but it was not Martina.

"Mr Fisher?"

Nick got to his feet, nodding. Another hand was extended.

"Karl Schröder, General Manager here."

"Ah, hello."

They sat, one either side of the corner table.

"Martina will be with us shortly. It's a quiet day and I'm a little curious, so I thought I'd join you."

"No problem."

Schröder placed a business card on the table and Nick reached for it only to discover it was one of his own.

"You left this with Martina last time you came, Mr Fisher but, since you were here, we have checked with the London Metropolitan Police's online service and there is no Nick or Nicholas Fisher among their current list of employees. Perhaps you could explain that to me."

"That's easy. I retired not long ago."

"Since you were last here?"

"No, of course not. Within the last two years."

"Don't you think they'd take a dim view of you representing yourself as a *current* senior officer? Isn't impersonating a police officer a crime?"

Martina backed into the room with a tray of hot drinks and a plate of thick, chocolate biscuits. She put the tray on the magazines and Karl made room for her on the bench so that she could pour. Her arrival gave Nick a little thinking time. He tried to be as straightforward as possible:

"I wasn't trying to misrepresent myself, Karl. I was in the Met for almost thirty years. It was just the easiest way of telling Martina who I was."

"Who you *used* to be."

"Strictly speaking, yes, but I also said I was working with the local police and that's true."

"You will please give me a contact name that I can call before we talk further so that I can verify what you say. We treat client confidentiality very seriously here, Mr Fisher."

"Well, I'm glad to hear that," said Nick, and extracted Leo's card from his breast pocket. "The most senior policeman I've worked with so far is Leonídas Christodoulákis. He's a lieutenant in Chaniá."

"Thank you – and excuse me. I will call him now."

Karl went back through the door and Martina handed Nick a coffee.

"Help yourself to milk and sugar."

Nick hoped Karl did not ask when his secondment had started but, even if he did, there was a chance that Leo would be supportive. Otherwise this was going to get very awkward indeed.

Karl breezed back through the door just a couple of minutes later and handed the card back.

"He was in a meeting, but a Sergeant Konstantópoulos was able to confirm what you say," he said, slapping his hands on his thighs. "Now, what can we do for you, Mr Fisher?"

Nick decided to ride his luck.

"I'd like full names and contact details for all the staff members and clients who attended the September fifteenth to seventeenth detox programme."

"Staff members, no problem. Why clients?"

"Same reason, I need to establish whether or not Linda Weston was at the Welcome Supper on the Saturday evening. If we can *prove* that she was here, it will help me remove her from my list of possible suspects. It's just police procedure."

"There's no obligation to attend the supper. She might have preferred to stay in her room."

"I realise that, Karl, but if someone *does* remember seeing her, it will save everyone a lot of time – and spare Linda from further questioning."

"I see. Well we can run that off the computer for you, can't we Martina?"

"Sure. We have all that."

Nick turned to Martina.

"And you said she went to church on the Sunday morning. Do you have the name and address of the church she attended? Oh, and the photograph you showed me before – the one taken at the end of the course – could I have a copy of that please?"

Martina went over to the reception desk and reached down for another print of the photograph. She handed it to Nick.

"This one?"

"Yes. Thanks. Can you confirm that the picture includes *everyone* that was on the course?"

"I can tell you if the number of people is the same. I may not recognise all of them."

"That's fine."

"You will excuse me for a few minutes?"

Nick nodded and smiled as she left.

"So, we have a murder on Crete?" said Karl.

"It does happen from time to time. Greece has between eighty and a hundred murders in a typical year, I believe."

"But not many here in Crete, surely?"

"I don't know about that, Karl. Most villages have unlicensed rakí stills and secret caches of WWII weapons. I wouldn't be surprised if Crete were above average."

"It's a passionate place. That's for sure. My grandfather was here in the war. He was one of the guys that came with a parachute, in 1941."

"Brave man."

"He didn't have a choice. Fortunately for him, he was in the *second* wave, dropping onto the mutilated bodies from the first wave. Many were hacked or bludgeoned to death by the local civilians, I believe. He was a leader in the group that eventually secured the airport. He was put forward for the Iron Cross."

"That would have been a huge honour."

"Would have is right. He was killed by partisans before they could present it to him."

"I'm sorry to hear that."

"Yes. Thank you. I never met him, sadly."

"No, of course you didn't. It's a long time ago now. But there's still some bitterness here; just the oldest people in the mountain villages, these days."

"Yes, I know. I encounter it from time to time. It's upsetting but it also makes me a little angry, to tell the truth. We live in a different world now. Germany is a different nation. We will not go to war again. And we do a lot for Greece these days. It's time to move on from a war that ended so long ago."

Nick was saved from responding by Martina's return.

"I think I have everything you want: the staff contacts, the list of attendees and the details of the church. Also, there were seventeen clients on the course and there are seventeen in the picture, so I guess that's all of them."

Nick got to his feet.

"Well, that's *very* kind of you. I'll be on my way, then. But first …"

He reached down and grabbed a chocolate biscuit.

"These look too good to resist and, coming from you guys, I'm sure they'll be good for me, too."

"Even we are not without vices, Mr Fisher," said Schröder with a twinkle.

*

Outside, the day was heating up. A tanned young man was standing back from a newly-clipped hedge, inspecting his work. He glanced in Nick's direction.

"Good morning," said Nick.

"G'day," said the young man.

"Good job."

"Maybe need a little more off the top?"

Nick cast his eyes around the beautiful gardens.

"You look after all this?"

"The company does. I'm just a hired hand – for the summer?"

Nick noticed that every sentence ended with an uplift, like it was a question.

"You sound like you're a long way from home."

"Couldn't get much further, to be honest; I'm a Kiwi."

He put down the hedge trimmer, walked over and extended a powerful hand.

"Hi. Connor McHugh."

"Nick Fisher."

"You don't look like the average visitor, Nick. Mostly mature ladies here, if you know what I mean?"

"Well I'm not a customer, Connor, I'm a cop. Tell me, do you work here every day?"

"The contract is for three days a week. It's usually me they send."

"Which days would those be?"

"We seem to have settled on Friday, Saturday and Sunday now."

"You work Sundays?"

"One of our busiest days, mate. And it suits me. I get my time off when the beaches are quieter, mid-week. And with the days all bunched together now, they feed me and put me up here, Friday and Saturday nights."

"Sounds like a good deal."

"It's terrific. They get a little extra gardening and I don't have to faff about getting to and from the city. I like it here. And there's a good beach at Kaláthas, just six kilometres away."

"Tell me, Connor, were you working here on Sunday, the sixteenth of September?"

"Reckon so."

"It was the weekend of the detox and healing programme."

"Yeah, I remember. The car park was pretty much full. They asked me not to operate any machines before nine."

"What time do you start then?"

"Around seven thirty? It's cooler then and I can knock off at two or so and get to the beach."

"Early start, then."

"I'm from a farming community, back in New Zealand, so it's normal for me. I'm up around six, as a rule. Try to get a run in before work, most days."

"Cast your mind back to the weekend of the course for me, if you would."

"No problem."

"Did you work both days?"

"All three: Friday through Sunday."

"Were you here when the guests arrived, Saturday evening?"

"I'd been to the beach. Couple of beers after. I'd have been back here by eight or so, but I'd be in my room then. I don't pay any attention to the guests. Mr Schröder likes me to keep out of the way, anyhow."

"Okay. Then, on Sunday, did you follow your usual routine?"

"Yep. Went for a run, then started work at seven thirty, doing the quiet stuff."

"Notice anything unusual?"

"Like what?"

"You tell me."

There was a pause and Nick could almost hear Connor's brain calling on memory, shuffling information, filtering.

"Not really, Nick."

"Nothing at all?"

"Well, maybe one small thing."

"Go on."

"Like I said, the car park was *almost* full. But it wasn't completely full. Nevertheless, one car was parked along the drive here. A little red one. It was tucked away under that tree."

"Perhaps the car park had been full earlier?"

"Yes, that's possible, I suppose. But there was something else. As it happened to be there, I was a bit cheeky. I put my foot on the front bumper, just to tie my laces and do my stretching, and I noticed something."

"What?"

"It felt warm. I put my hand on the bonnet then and, sure enough, it *was* warm. The windscreen was clear too, but the cars in the car park had morning dew on them."

"What time was this?"

"Early. It'd have been about six fifteen."

"So, what did you make of that?"

"Well, I figured that one of the guests must have only just arrived, but I couldn't see why they didn't use the car park. Anyway, I just got on with my day. The car was still there when I started gardening, but, when I came round with the mower at around ten, I noticed it was gone."

"You didn't see it go?"

"No, I was fixing up the paths around the back garden most of the morning."

"And you don't remember the make or number?"

"Sorry, mate. I'm going to sound like a woman now. It was a red car. It was small. I'm pretty sure it was a hatchback."

198

"Well, Connor, it was a pleasure to meet you. You've been very helpful."

"No worries, Nick. Good luck with the sleuthing."

*

Nick went straight back to reception.

"Did you forget something?" said Martina.

"No, I need to ask you a couple more things."

"That's okay."

"The seventeen guests that came to the course, did any arrive very late, like five or six am on the Sunday morning?"

"Oh no, I'd remember that. I think all of them were here well before ten pm on the Saturday."

"I thought you'd say that. And do you keep details of the cars they drive?"

"No, we don't bother with that. If there's a problem with a car, we're small enough that we can just ask around."

"That makes sense. And, lastly, how many spaces are there in the car park?"

"I think twenty-four, but it would be better to go and count them if you want to be sure."

"And how many of them are used by staff?"

"We have four marked out for the four of us and two for gardeners, workmen and so on."

"So, there would always be at least eighteen spaces for guests?"

"Yes, that's right, unless people park very badly, I suppose."

Nick went straight to the car park and counted out twenty-four spaces. They were generously sized, so you would have to park like a complete idiot to reduce the number available. He got back into the Jeep and tooted at Connor as he drove past. Connor waved and saw Nick beaming with delight.

CHAPTER 25
CHURCH

Even this late in the season, the centre of Chaniá was teeming with tourists. Nick found a car park for the Jeep down a side street and continued on foot. It would have been madness to do anything else. The Catholic church was a substantial and impressive, pale stone building with a campanile to the left. It dominated a paved square fringed with palm trees. Nick went through the massive, wooden door to the right. Inside, it was cooler. An aisle led across a chequerboard, stone floor between rows of wooden pews flanked by arches. At the end was the altar with a lectern to the left and the crucified Jesus on a tall cross to the right. Nick paused for a moment, partly from a childlike reverence, but also to take in the beauty of the scene lit, as it was, by sunbeams streaming colours from the stained-glass window, high above the altar. As he edged forward, he noticed a church official laying out Order of Service leaflets.

"Signómi. Excuse me?"

The young priest looked up.

"May I talk with you for a moment?"

He inclined his head, placed the pile of leaflets on the pew, and whispered:

"Come with me."

When they reached the side of the church, he stopped and smiled.

"It is forbidden to talk in front of the altar, but here is okay. How may I help you?"

"My name is Nick Fisher. I'm working with the Greek police on a murder inquiry."

The priest blinked several times and crossed himself.

"I'm interested to know if a certain person attended the ten fifteen mass here on Sunday, the sixteenth of September."

"This is a church, Mr Fisher. We are open to all. We don't take down the names of the congregation."

"No, of course you don't. Look, I realise it's a long shot, father, but I thought the celebrant might just remember this person?"

"You will follow me again, please."

On the way to the office, he explained that Father Michális would have led the mass that day. A large man with a white beard was sitting behind an ancient desk as they entered the office.

The young man held Nick back and went forward himself to whisper to the priest, who looked up sharply, then nodded.

"Please have a seat, Mr Fisher. I will try to help you."

Nick extracted a mobile phone from his bag while the priest watched, fiddling with his crucifix as if it were a set of worry beads.

"Thanks for your time, Father Michális. I understand that you officiated at the morning service on Sunday, the sixteenth of this month?"

"Yes. I do most of the Sunday masses."

Nick placed the phone in the priest's hand.

"Do you by any chance recall seeing this woman in the congregation?"

He looked, and Nick thought he spotted a flash of recognition. Then the priest put his hands on the desk and leaned forward.

"This mass is well attended but I always try to spot new faces. This one I *do* remember. The red hair is quite distinctive, but also, I remember her because she asked if I would take her confession and then changed her mind for some reason. Afterwards, I saw that her eyes were closed during my sermon.

"Now, it's not unusual for people to fall asleep, I'm sorry to say, but for the *whole* sermon, at the *morning* service? This is not usual. And then, when it was time for the Eucharist, I saw that she was awake, but she didn't come forward."

"Why do you think that was?"

"It's not so unusual for people to attend mass but decline communion. There could be many reasons."

"This is a devout woman, Father, a convert to your faith."

"Then I could only speculate as to why, Detective, and that's all it would be: speculation."

"Would you do that for me, Father? Would you speculate a little?"

201

Father Michális stared at him for a few moments. The bell in the campanile sounded the half-hour and a faint waft of incense drifted through the room.

"Well, if she felt herself *unworthy* to take the Eucharist for some reason, she would have held back. It is said that to take the Eucharist when one is unworthy is damaging to the soul and that one will have to answer for it on the Last Day."

"Judgment Day?"

"Indeed."

"So that would be a *no-no* for a fervent Catholic, if you'll excuse the vernacular."

"Most certainly."

"And what makes one unworthy, Father?"

"That's an easy one: sin. We're all sinners, Mr Fisher. Some more than others, of course."

"So how does a sinner get to be worthy again, so to speak?"

"Contrition and confession. Then one must expiate the sins through penance."

"But, in the end, she decided against confession."

"She did."

"Do you have any idea why?"

"I do not, and that's *not* something on which I'm prepared to speculate."

"Thank you again for your time, Father. You've been very helpful."

It was good to be out in the sun again. Nick took a table at one of the cafés at the side of the square. It was now ten minutes to one. He would just have time for a light lunch.

CHAPTER 26
LINDA

Leo was banging his coffee mug on the desk.

"All right. Listen up, everyone."

The hubbub died down and those standing now took their seats. There were about fifteen people in the room. Leo waited a few moments until he had their full attention.

"Is everyone here? Right. I need to speak in English today. I think you can all cope with that but let me know afterwards if there's anything you didn't understand. For those of you who don't know, we now have a senior British police officer assisting us on this case. Please give him your full support. His name is Nick Fisher."

Leo held out a hand in Nick's direction and Nick half stood, half saluted and sat down again.

"That's the good news. The bad news is that we now have only forty-eight hours to solve this case before a team from Athína flies in to take over."

There was a collective groan.

"None of us wants that to happen, so we need to give it our best shot, use our brains and work hard over the next two days to get a result. Agreed?"

There were desultory murmurs of assent.

"AGREED?" shouted Leo.

"Yes, sir," they chorused, as one voice.

"Good. Now Sergeant Konstantópoulos has prepared these two boards which summarise our main suspects, Buckingham and Weston. Familiarise yourselves with them and then we'll split you into two groups, one to look at each suspect. Choose a leader for your group. Look at your suspect with fresh eyes. Consider the case against him, the pluses, the minuses, anything we've forgotten, what actions we should take next. I'm looking for your considered judgment and your action plans. Now get to it."

Chairs slid back, people stood and then started to group around the boards. Nick saw his moment.

"Leo. Might I have a word? In private?"

"Sure, Nick. Thaní can run this for a while. Let's go down the corridor."

They grabbed a coffee on the way and then settled around a Formica-topped table in a room two doors down. Leo opened a window, pulled a glass ashtray from a cupboard, and lit a cigarette.

"Was it true about Athens?" asked Nick.

"Worse. They wanted to come right away, but I persuaded the captain to hold them off. If, in the next forty-eight hours, we arrest someone we believe to be guilty, then I think we can keep them away. Otherwise, they will come, and we will have failed. For now, we have two suspects but we're not sure about either of them; hence this morning's exercise."

"I think we have a third suspect."

"I'm listening."

"*Linda* Weston."

"What have you got, Nick?"

"If Linda found out about the affair and feared that Peter would leave her for Sam, we have a strong motive."

"Do we? You said it was a loveless marriage now."

"Linda's whole way of life would be under threat if Peter left her, to say nothing of the social stigma for a woman with strong Christian values, the loss of financial security, the threat of loneliness – and all because of some young girl who would drop him in a year or two anyway. She might even still love the old fool, in her strange way."

"So, you think she *did* find out?"

"I don't *know* that she did, but Peter was hardly discreet, was he? Linda might well have seen him arrive back from the beach with Sam on the back of the bike and seen her kiss him."

"But that was just a peck on the cheek."

"So Peter says, but it might have been enough to sow the first seeds of doubt. After all, what was he doing going to a semi-naturist beach with his young guests, anyway?"

"True. But if Linda already suspected something, why go off to Réthymno for the groceries and give him his opportunity with Sam?"

"You can't run out of groceries when you are running a bed and breakfast. And remember, there were other guests still there. She may have thought she'd get back before they left."

Leo put his elbows on the desk and steepled his fingers.

"That sounds a bit weak, Nick. But suppose it was a test?"

"Of his fidelity? God, that's a bit extreme."

"Remember, they *thought* she arrived only ten minutes after they showered and dressed. Was that their remarkable good luck or was she there earlier, watching him fail her fidelity test in spectacular style?"

"Banging away beside the pool was hardly discreet."

"No, and maybe she saw it. Or maybe a neighbour saw it or overheard something and told Linda?"

"Okay, as a working hypothesis, let's assume she knew. It was also *her* that proposed Síva to Sam and Jason for their next stop; a place Linda knew well."

"At the same time, setting up a *second* test for Peter. Would it be all over with Sam after she left, or would he follow her to Síva?"

"Right – could the fling with Sam be forgotten or was she an ongoing threat that would have to be dealt with?"

"I like the theory, Nick. But she was on this detox programme the whole time, wasn't she? You've been checking that out, I gather, without my knowledge. We agreed that you would act as part of the team, Nick, and not independently."

"You're quite right, we did. Sorry."

"You crossed the line. Do it again and you're off the case. I'm serious."

"I understand."

"This had better be good."

"I think it is, and I must thank Thaní for backing up my credentials."

"He told them you were seconded as soon as we knew the body was a foreigner; that it was our normal practice."

"He's a sharp one."

"He is, but don't you push your luck with us, Nick Fisher."

Nick inclined his head to show due contrition, then went on:

"So, Linda arrived at the centre just before eight pm. There was a Welcome Supper but none of the staff remembers seeing her there. I don't know about her fellow attendees, but I do have a contact list for them. You might get one of your constables to check with them as well, because there were times when no staff were at the supper."

"So, you're saying she could have checked in and then left again soon after?"

"Yes. Reception wasn't always manned either. People were coming and going. It wouldn't have been hard to sneak out. And then, early the next morning, I have the young gardener going for a run and seeing a little red car parked on the drive, not in the car park, with a warm bonnet and no dew on the screen."

"Her car – the Golf?"

"He couldn't give me the make or number, but your constable could check the attendees for car colours and makes while he's at it."

"Was the car park full?"

"No. There are twenty-four generous spaces. Eighteen are always available for guests. Even if every single attendee arrived in a separate car, it can't have been."

"So, she parks there at five or six in the morning to avoid being heard."

"I assume so."

"Anything else?"

"She left the centre again the next morning to attend mass. This won't be disputed – she'd arranged it with reception earlier. But I visited the church and the priest told me she asked for confession but then changed her mind. She attended the mass but seemed to be asleep most of the time and then she didn't take communion."

"She wouldn't feel able to take communion if she had sinned and not confessed. She would be unworthy."

"Yes, so I understand. And maybe the enormity of what she needed to confess made her hesitate. Or she didn't like the look of Father Michális. Could she put that much trust in the confidentiality of the confessional?"

"It would be a huge test of her faith, no question. And, by the sound of it, she was exhausted, maybe confused, so she plays safe, says nothing."

Nick could sense him warming to the idea as Leo went on:

"Okay, so *if* she left the centre overnight, how does the timing work, Nick?"

"If she skipped the Welcome Supper, she could have left between eight thirty and nine. The warm bonnet was discovered at about six fifteen the next morning, so I'm guessing the car arrived no earlier than five – otherwise it wouldn't have been both warm and dew-free. From there it would take less than two hours to get to Síva."

"So that would give her at least four hours in Síva."

"Between eleven pm and three or four am. Yes."

"This is good stuff, Nick." He gripped Nick's upper arm and grinned. "Can we *prove* where she went? Is there anything that places her in Síva?"

"Not yet, but then we haven't been looking for *her* there, have we?"

"No, we haven't. Wait a moment, Nick."

Leo left the room and returned with Thaní and then brought him up to speed, checking details with Nick as he went.

"So, are we wasting our time with this meeting, boss?"

"Maybe, but it might throw up something. And our hypothesis could be wrong. Give it another hour, perhaps, but then we need a team in Síva, seeing if anyone spotted Linda Weston. They can start with that slimeball at the beach bar."

Something appeared to dawn on Thaní, and he excused himself for a minute and came back with the case file. He rummaged for a moment and then produced an enlarged photo.

"Your mentioning the beach bar got me wondering. I know you've seen this before, but this is the enlarged version."

He placed the photo on the table in front of the others and pointed to the shadowy figure on the right, away from the embers of a fire where three others were more visible. "Could that be her? Could that be Linda Weston?"

"Where's all that ginger hair?" asked Leo.

"It's all tucked up in that hat, I bet," said Nick, "look how it's bulging."

"Get the evidence bag, Thaní."

Thaní knew what Leo wanted and rushed out of the room. When he came back, he was carrying a large plastic bag. He pulled out a smaller plastic bag and put it on the table. Nick picked it up and rotated it in his hand.

"Where did you find this?"

"It was in the water, in line with Sam's body but a few metres out."

"So, this little beauty places that person," he was tapping the photo, "right at the murder scene. This is gold dust, gentlemen."

"Except that we can't see enough to identify that person as Linda Weston," said Thaní, "and Alexandrákis said he didn't know who it was."

"What about the kids around the fire. Have you interviewed them?"

"Of course, Nick. They are Andie, Beth and the Irish kid, Kenny. None of them took much notice of the shadowy figure and none of them was able to identify the person. You know what it's like when you're around a fire; everything's extra dark outside the ring of light."

"Hmmm. Even so, that doesn't mean it wasn't Linda, keeping a low profile." Nick was fingering the badge through the polythene. "Do you remember when we were interviewing Peter and Linda at their house, Leo?"

"Sure."

"Do you recall the poster on the wall by the stairs?"

"Vaguely."

"It was the revolutionary leader, Che Guevara." Nick held up the beret with the badge facing the others. "Snap."

There was a moment's silence and then Leo sprang to his feet.

"Okay, we're moving on this. Thaní: break things up next door. Send Demí and another couple of guys down to Síva to see if they can find witnesses to Linda's presence. Get two of the other constables ringing round Nick's list of seminar attendees. Get them to tell us if they saw her at the Welcome Supper, if they saw her leaving at any time after eight pm, and what make and colour of car they used themselves that day."

"And me?"

"You're with us. I'll try to get a search warrant for Villa Erató. We'll be looking for something that can link Linda to that beret and anything else that might confirm her guilt or Peter's innocence. After that, we'll interview them again."

"And Jason?" asked Nick.

"We'll review his continued detention tomorrow. If we have a clear case against Linda or Peter, I'll suggest to the captain that we let him go."

"Brilliant."

*

The momentum from the morning soon slowed to frustration as Leo became embroiled, first with the captain, then with the investigating judge and the public prosecutor. All needed to be brought up to speed before a search warrant could be issued. It was not until almost seven pm that Nick took the call:

"Nick, it's Leo. We have the warrant."

"That took a while."

"Believe me, this is quick. Often the investigating judge wants to get more involved. Some even take over the investigation. But, with the cutbacks, that's happening less and less. They just don't have the time. Anyway, we're clear to take things to the next stage, at least."

"Great. Well done."

"Thank you. It's getting late now so I suggest we meet at Villa Erató at eight in the morning. I will bring Thaní and two constables to help with the search. Okay?"

"That's fine, Leo. Have you checked with Thaní on the ring-rounds?"

"Do you want to do that? He can update me on the way tomorrow."

"Early night for once?"

"I might reintroduce myself to my wife."

"Good plan."

*

Nick found Thaní working with his constables:

"Hi, guys. How are you doing?"

"There are still two we haven't reached, but we should be able to get them later this evening."

"What news from the first fifteen, then?"

"Interesting. We have someone who says she *did* see Linda at the Welcome Supper. The two of them chatted for a couple of minutes and then Linda took a plate to her room."

"There was no-one else there?"

"No, it was early."

"Did you get a time?"

"She was hungry, this woman. Says she went down soon after it opened, maybe eight thirty-five?"

"Linda was establishing an alibi but still leaving enough time to dash to Síva."

"Yes. Or she was just hungry, too. It was going to be a long night, after all."

"True."

"I don't suppose anyone saw her leave?"

"No, not as such, but I think you'll like this."

"Go on."

"A man was arriving around nine and parked. He noticed a woman rummaging in the boot of her hatchback. 'Quite a tall woman with a lot of frizzy hair,' he put it."

"Make, colour of car?"

"He wasn't sure, in the dark, but he spoke to her."

"Why?"

"He was just being sociable. Thought she was arriving too, that they might walk in together."

"And?"

"She didn't look up, which he thought was rather rude, and just said: 'You go on in. I could be a while. I've lost my bloody phone.'"

"Got caught on her way out and ad-libbed, do you think?"

"Would fit, wouldn't it?"

"Did he see her again, this man?"

"Not until lunchtime on the Sunday, he says."

"Because Linda missed the Why Detox? morning session to go to church. Might be worth checking if any other women on the course also missed that session. If not, it *must* have been her that he spoke to."

Thaní was nodding enthusiastically.

"Well done, Thaní. That's very helpful. Any joy on the cars?"

"Two other red ones, but one's a Mercedes 220 so I'm guessing the gardener wouldn't call that a small car."

"And the other?"

Thaní made a face: "a Nissan Micra."

"Ah. That doesn't help. You might get one of the constables to contact Connor, see if he can choose between a Golf and a Micra."

"But he said he didn't know."

"He did, but choosing between two pictures may just jog a memory. It's worth a shot."

"Okay, will do."

"Great. I'll see you at Séllia in the morning. Let me know if anything comes from those last two calls."

"Sure thing, Nick. Goodnight."

The light was fading as he left the office and birds were fighting over roosting spots in the tree by the Jeep. As he climbed the National Road past Kalíves, the sun was a red ball of fire sinking into the darkening sea behind him.

It would be eight fifty by the time he reached Saktoúria. Remembering the empty larder, he decided to call Lena. She might like to join him at a nearby taverna. As he drove, he remembered the last time they met. It was just a couple of weeks ago, but the world had changed since then ...

211

She had called up from the lane when he was working on the roof terrace wall:

"Hello, Nick. May I come up for a minute?"

"Sure. It's a mess and not very safe but come up if you're careful."

She made her way gingerly up the crumbling stone steps.

"I've been collecting apricots. The villagers let them rot and I hate waste. So, I made jelly and jam. I brought you a pot of each. If you like them, there's plenty more."

"That's very kind. I'm sure I will."

"Your wall is looking good."

They stood back and admired it together.

"Thanks. I have to finish the blocks today, then, tomorrow, the base plaster."

She was ogling his bare chest.

"I must get you down to my studio. I need a model for Apollo."

"Ha! I don't think so."

"What are you? Fifty years old?"

"Fifty-three."

"You're looking pretty good, Mr Fisher."

And she pulled her blonde hair away from her eyes and gave him that intense, sideways look of hers.

"Hmmm. I have a piece of Carrara marble you might be hiding in. I could dig you out with my hammer and chisel, set you free."

"I'm not sure I want to be one of your cold, stone statues."

"No. So we leave all Nick Fisher's cold, stone bits in the statue. Then you are free to be warm and human again."

The abstract idea of liberation through sculpture was not unappealing but Nick was not going for that just yet.

"A bit intense for me, Lena," he said, and she got the message.

Lena was at least Nick's age, maybe a few years older. He did not find her pretty; the strong jawline and a face wrinkled by too much sun precluded that. But she was in good shape; slim and elegant. He might not always be safe from those dark blue eyes and that firm, tanned body. When she went to the beach, she swam naked, she told him once, and that had tantalised him quite unreasonably.

"Anyway, well done, you," she went on. "Is the place getting to feel more like home?"

"Yes, but every time someone goes past, I don't have the faintest idea what they're saying or how to respond. I need to learn Greek."

"Yes, you do. And I could teach you, if you like."

"That could work."

"Nothing too *intense*. Maybe we start with an hour twice a week and at the end of each lesson you get a beer, if you're good?"

"No homework?"

"No homework."

"Sounds like a plan."

"You can start next Tuesday at six, if you like."

"It's a date."

…Well, he'd missed that date, but he called her now and suggested the taverna.

"Not another souvláki, Nick! Why don't you come round *here*? I was about to sit down to rabbit and celery casserole with rice and there's far too much for just me. You can have the portion that was heading for the freezer. Oh, and there's plum crumble if you want that, with a little yoghurt, maybe?"

"Mmmm. You said the right thing there, Lena. I'll bring the wine, but I have to be good. Big day tomorrow."

"You invite yourself to dinner, then tell me you have to be good? What a spoilsport you are, Nick."

*

Next morning the phone rang just as Nick was backing the Jeep out of the alleyway he used as a parking space.

"Kaliméra, Nick. It's Thaní."

"Hi Thaní. I'm just leaving Saktoúria."

"Yes, we are on our way also. Leo says we'll be there in half an hour."

213

"Well, take it easy guys. I can wait. Any news on the outstanding issues?"

"Yes. This is why I call. We reached the last two attendees last night but nothing new. Neither saw Linda at the supper or on her way out and neither has a red car."

"Okay."

"But we did have one lucky break."

"We did?"

"Yes – your idea, Nick. Connor, the gardener. He says he would have recognised a Micra because he hired one not long ago. Seems there's a distinctive badge on the bonnet that reminded him of a London Underground sign."

"So, he's sure it wasn't the Micra?"

"Yes. He said the car was small, but more stylish than a Micra. The constable showed him a picture of a red Golf, but he still wasn't sure."

"He must know Golfs and Polos, they're everywhere."

"You'd think so, wouldn't you? And guys from that part of the world are quite into their cars, as a rule. It was early, though; I guess he just wasn't that alert."

"Anyway, it doesn't matter, does it? If he's certain that it wasn't a Micra or a Mercedes, and he's certain it was red, then it must have been the Golf."

"Exactly."

"Good work, Thani. Thanks for letting me know."

"Wait please …"

"Nick? It's Leo. There are four of us here, as I said. As soon as we get there, we'll get the search going but you and I can break off and spend a few minutes planning the interrogation, okay? We don't want to miss a trick on this one."

"That makes sense."

"Okay. See you near the house. Don't get too near till we get there, will you?"

"I won't scare them away if that's what you mean. Thirty years in The Met did teach me a thing or two."

"The famous British understatement, ha!"

"I could have said: 'Don't teach your grandmother to suck eggs.'"

"What the hell are you talking about, Nick?"

"I'll explain one day."

"I can't wait."

CHAPTER 27
SEARCH

This time the drive was empty. Nick imagined the Westons' hearts sinking as the blue and white Skoda with its flashing blue light rolled onto the drive, crushing gravel. He tucked the Jeep in behind. Leo got out and signalled to the others to stay put, for the moment. He rang the bell.

"Back again, Lieutenant," said Peter. It was not a question.

"Good morning, Mr Weston." Leo was holding up a piece of paper. "This is a warrant to search these premises issued by the investigating judge appointed to this case and authorised by the public prosecutor. Is Mrs Weston here?"

"Er … yes. I think she just nipped up to the office." He turned into the house. "Linda!"

A few moments later, she appeared behind him. They were doing a loving husband and wife act, thought Leo, but there was an atmosphere of fear and distrust that no amount of practised smiles could dispel.

"Hello again," said Linda without a trace of warmth.

"They want to search the house," said Peter.

"I thought Nick Fisher already did that," Linda snapped.

"Here, your Greek's better than mine," said Peter, handing the warrant to her.

"It's not *that* good," she said, looking at the dense, small print.

"I can assure you that all is in order, Mrs Weston. May I come in?"

They opened the door a little wider and Leo strode through into the living room.

"We are not going to ransack your house. We will treat your belongings with respect, but it will be a thorough search."

"What are you looking for?" asked Peter.

Leo just looked at him, raised an eyebrow and carried on:

"You will both please remain in here. There are five of us, including Mr Fisher. We will be as quick as we can."

Peter looked bewildered, Linda looked belligerent, but it was a fait accompli. Both sat on the large blue sofa and said nothing.

"Thank you," said Leo and went out to summon the troops and pass out the forensic gloves. He told one of the constables to go straight to the living room to see that Peter and Linda remained where they were.

"I don't want them going anywhere without my express permission, Pandelí," he added. Then he called Nick over and leaned into the window of the Skoda so that all could hear.

"Remember, our main aim is to place Linda in Síva at the time of the murder. Links to the town and to that beret are vital, so pay particular attention to her clothing, photographs, old invoices and receipts.

"We need to be alert to anything that might incriminate her or give us an insight into a different side of her character. But we also need to check out Peter's story: the motorbike, the leather jacket, the headband, the earring.

"Thaní? I want you on Linda. Start with their bedroom, then the office. Vangéli? You're on Peter. Start in the garage, then the office, then move to their bedroom. Nick – let's make our plan in the office, then we can do the kitchen, living room and guest bedrooms. Two hours, gentlemen, and then we review what we have."

They all got out of the car and Thaní and Vangélis went inside to their appointed locations. Nick grabbed Leo's arm outside.

"Why don't we just ask Peter about the beret? He'll remember if Linda owned something like that, surely?"

"We may have to, Nick, but I'd prefer some other way. I don't want Peter knowing that we suspect his wife. He might lie to protect her. He might think *he* is off the hook.

"Also, I don't want Linda to know that we're interested in the beret. If it *is* hers, she must realise that she lost it at Síva. She might know she lost it at the murder scene.

"It's hot property for both her and us. But she doesn't know that we have it. That gives us an advantage and I like that."

"Okay, I see where you're coming from. Good thinking."

They went on up to the office.

*

By late morning, Demétrios was disheartened. He and the other two constables called at the beach bar, all the other bars and tavernas, every shop and every rent rooms place in Síva. For the last hour, they had been asking people at random at the campsite and on the beach. Not a single person recognised the photo of Linda or could place her in the area that weekend. And, as if that were not bad enough, one of the constables then managed to unearth a journalist. Instead of shaking her head like all the others, she said:

"Why do you ask?"

"I can't say, madam."

"Three constables from a police force that keeps saying its resources are stretched to breaking point come all the way from Chaniá to look for a witness to a drowning? This smells more like a murder enquiry, Constable. Is that what we're talking about now?"

"I'm not at liberty to say, madam."

"But you're not denying it."

"What I'm saying – and *all* I'm saying – is that I'm unable to answer your question, madam."

"We both know that's code for *Yes*, Constable, so don't you think the people have a right to know if there's a murderer in their midst?"

"Just answer *my* question, please."

"No, I don't recognise her. Now tell me who is leading this investigation."

"I can't do that, madam."

"What? You don't know?"

"No, I'm …"

"Not at liberty to say? Well, don't worry, I can find out."

The constable concerned informed Demétrios right away. He decided to call in and update the boss. They were wasting their time here, anyway.

*

Thaní came up the stairs to the office.

"Hi boss. Demí just called. He's got nothing. No bites whatsoever and he thinks they've alerted the press now."

"Bugger. Still, that was a risk we took, wasn't it? I suppose it's about time. We had a good run. I'll talk to the captain. We should put a statement out now rather than have the press suggest we've been hiding something. Are you bringing the boys back?"

"They're on their way."

"Well done."

"Can I search in here now, boss?"

"Yes, Thaní. We're done here so we'll get on to our part of the search. You might want to swap the constables, at some point. I'm sure Pandelís would like to be part of the search rather than just a dumb guard."

Five minutes later, Thaní was in the living-room.

"Pandelí? Go swap with Vangélis. He's in the main bedroom. Get him to brief you on what he's found so far. Mrs Weston, there's a locked cupboard in the office, may I have a key?"

She took a set of keys from her handbag and handed them over.

"It's the little, shiny one."

Thaní waited for Vangélis to come in, grasped his shoulder by way of thanks, then went back upstairs.

When Thaní unlocked the cupboard, he found it was empty. *Why lock an empty cupboard?* he asked himself.

At ten thirty-five, the four of them assembled in the office, leaving Vangélis with the Westons.

"All right let's start with Peter. Pandelí?"

"No big surprises, boss. The motorbike is in the garage and matches the photo at Peter's beach, although the picture is not clear enough to confirm the number plate. There's a man's leather jacket hanging in the hall that Mr Weston admits is his and we found both the earring and a bandana in the bedroom along with loads of old hippy shit: beads, incense, a device for rolling large cigarettes with some fag papers. There's even a kaftan and an Afghan coat hanging in the closet."

"No dope?"

"They must have cleared that out."

"There's a lot of music from the late sixties and early seventies in the living room, too," said Nick, "psychedelia, prog rock, Velvet Underground, Pink Floyd – all that sort of stuff. Linda's tastes seem to have moved on, but Peter's stuck in his youth."

"But he's not old enough for that, is he?" said Leo. "I don't know about you, but all my favourite music was from when I was about fourteen. Peter might have been *born* in the Summer of Love, but he was fourteen in the early eighties."

"True. A born-again hippy, then."

"Something like that. Let's move on to Linda. Thaní?"

"I went through her clothes, boss. No berets. No hats at all apart from a couple of straw sun hats. Nothing flamboyant, very little dressy. Reserved, frugal. The total opposite of my wife, in fact."

That drew a chuckle from around the table.

"I went through the compartments in the wardrobe and the en-suite – just what you'd expect: underwear, accessories, cosmetics, perfumes and so on. And the bedside table? Self-help books and some religious stuff. Nothing steamy."

Poor Peter, thought Nick.

"Then I went to the office. I found some boxes of old photos, but there hasn't been time to go through them yet. There are hundreds, so I thought maybe we could do that as a team after this? I found papers to do with the bed and breakfast business: invoices, bills, agreements, guarantees. Everything you'd expect. The only odd thing? There was a cupboard to the right of the window that was locked. I got a key from Mrs Weston but found it was empty."

"Did you ask her about it?"

"No, boss, not yet."

"Anything else?"

"No."

"I think we might need to take another look in this room, Thaní," said Leo.

Everyone turned to him in surprise.

"When we arrived, Peter said Linda had *just nipped up to the office.* Maybe that was to take out whatever was in the cupboard and put it elsewhere. If so, she must have hidden it somewhere in this room; if she brought it downstairs, we would see it."

"But why lock the cupboard again afterwards?"

"Force of habit, perhaps? In too much of a rush to think? Let's all give it ten more minutes in here."

"What are we looking for, sir?" asked Pandelís.

"You'll know when you find it," said Nick.

They each took part of the room and searched minutely. They looked through all the cabinets again and under and behind them. They scanned the floorboards for secret hiding places. They even took Che off the wall for a moment to check behind the poster. After a few minutes, Nick called out:

"Who checked in here?"

He was looking at a drawer, stuffed full of heavy hanging files, in a cabinet on Peter's side of the office.

"Me. I've been through all those, Nick," said Thaní.

"Did you look underneath?"

Thaní looked confused.

"You see, if you squash them together, like this ..." He compressed the files with his left hand. "... you can slip something behind like this." He used his right hand to demonstrate the gap of perhaps five centimetres that he had created. "If you can get whatever it is to lie flat, *under* the hanging files, you'd never know it was there unless you took them all out. Did you do that?"

Thaní was looking embarrassed and shaking his head.

"No? Okay, give me a hand here."

Nick started lifting out the heavy files two at a time and passing them to Thaní who stacked them against the side of the desk. After four lots he murmured: "Eureka," reached in and pulled out a small book bound in mauve leather. It was a little larger than a mobile phone.

"Any betting men here? I've got ten euros that says this was in that locked cupboard until eight this morning and another ten that says it's Sam Martin's journal."

221

He chucked it at Thaní who riffled through the pages.

"How did you do that?" he said, after a few moments. Then he looked up at everyone, eyes shining. "He's only bloody right!"

"My Dad's electrical shop used a filing system like that, years ago. I used to hide my cigarette packets underneath when I was a kid. He never found them."

"Brilliant stuff, Nick. Thank you," said Leo. "I think you've earned first look at the journal. Thaní – bring out those boxes of photos for the rest of us to go through. Any of you who need a smoke can join me in the garden for ten minutes."

While he was smoking, Leo made one call: "Kaliméra, Captain. We have a breakthrough in the Martin case, I believe. We found the dead girl's journal hidden in the Westons' house. I want to bring them both in for questioning. I'll need another car."

"All right, Leo. Will this lead to an arrest?"

"I'd hope so, sir."

"We have twenty-seven hours left."

"I'm very much aware of that, Captain. Also, we need to pull together an urgent press release. A journalist in Síva seems to have worked out that it's murder."

"Damn. Okay, we'll have to come clean. You focus on The Westons. I'll brief Athína, then sort out the press release and any flak that comes from that."

"Thank you, sir."

*

It made Nick feel both sad and angry, reading the journal of a dead girl; a girl who was only a year older than Lauren. All the simple, fresh hopes, the optimism for the future rang out loud and clear. But it was also a private journal. She was explicit about her feelings and her sexual encounters. There were expressions of frustration about Jason. It was clear that she cared about him, but she also used words like *uptight, boring, careful, sexless,* and *immature.* Her frustration with him appeared to have been growing as the holiday went on and the planned marriage grew nearer.

Soon after arriving at Séllia, entries were mentioning Peter as *fanciable, interesting, caring, knowing such a lot,* and *having a crazy streak, like me.* There was no mention of love, but little doubt that she was attracted to Peter, despite the age difference. And she was not disappointed with the sex, either. She thought he had a great body. She also thought he was *wasted on that sour-faced bitch, poor sod.*

No vision of a future with Peter was mentioned, but she seemed happy to have a physical relationship in the present. She would have welcomed him in Síva for another bout of physicality but not anticipated much beyond that. Poor Spíros did not get a mention, Nick noticed, or maybe she just got herself killed before she'd finished the entries for Thursday onwards. Nick passed the journal to Leo and it went on around the group.

Meanwhile, the rest of the team had been going through about two thousand photos. It was almost midday when Thaní announced:

"Not a beret to be seen, I'm sorry to say."

"It's a bugger. We still have nothing that places Linda in Síva," said Leo.

"But, if we question her, she has a hell of a lot of explaining to do about her absence from the centre, her behaviour in the church," said Nick.

"But if she's unfazed and comes up with some plausible explanation?"

"Then we'll need to speak to Peter about the beret."

"Maybe we could get that photo near the fire *enhanced,* rather than just enlarged?" said Thaní, almost to himself.

"Tell us about the journal," Leo said, and Nick gave the group a précis of what he had read, then summarised what it meant to the enquiry:

"The journal confirms a few things that we suspected. She was frustrated with Jason long before Peter came along. I'd say she was planning to end the engagement anyway. She may have brought that plan forward when Jason was standing in the way of some more enjoyable sex with Peter.

"She was attracted to Peter, but it doesn't seem to have been love. I doubt she was ready to run away with him. But it's not the *content* of the journal that's so interesting, to me. It's more, why is it here? Which of them took it, when and why?"

"Well it must be Linda if your theory about her moving it as we arrived is correct."

"Of course, Leo, but that's still an *if.*"

"Fingerprints on the journal might give us a clue, sir."

"You don't have to call me sir, Pandelí, but yes, good point. We can get forensics to explore that."

Thaní was scanning his notes. Then he stopped and read something.

"I thought so," he said. "Do you remember when we questioned Sylvie, the French girl at the campsite? She said that she thought Sam came back, late that night?"

Nick was holding his hands out, palm up, looking from one to the other.

"Sorry, Nick. This was before you got involved."

"I do, Thaní," said Leo, "but she said she was half-asleep and there was nothing to support the idea that Sam could have returned to the tent after the late-night swim."

"That's right, boss. So, we dismissed it, rather. But supposing it wasn't Sam she heard – or saw – but Linda."

"They don't look much alike," Nick pointed out.

"No, they don't. But it was late, she was half-asleep, maybe a little drunk or a little high. She hears crunching shingle, she opens one bleary eye and sees a female form going past her tent. She *assumes* it's Sam."

"We need to talk to her again."

"We do, Leo, but let's pursue the theory for a minute. Why did Linda go to the tent?"

"To take Sam's things."

"Not all her things. Remember, we found the backpack and the passport."

"Just those things that could link Sam to her or Peter: Sam's phone and this journal."

"Quite so, Thaní," said Nick. "She couldn't do anything about *Jason's* phone or the Airbnb records, so she couldn't eliminate the fact that they stayed here, at Villa Erató. But what she *could* do was eliminate any suggestion of impropriety between Peter and Sam there might be in Sam's phone or the journal. Of course, she couldn't do anything about what Sam had already posted on Facebook or what she said to others."

"No ... So, where *is* Sam's phone?"

"Who knows, Leo? Probably in The Wilds of Wanney by now."

"We don't have time for your word games, Nick. Where is this, please?"

"Sorry – that just means somewhere remote, somewhere it wouldn't be found."

"Okay. So, why lose the phone but keep the journal?"

"This is where it gets interesting. We've found it in Peter's part of the office but maybe Linda planted it there this morning. It's just believable that Peter would be stupid enough to *take* it, if only to read what Sam wrote about him or to bask in his sexual prowess – whatever. But if he took it, why the hell would *he* keep it? There was a huge risk that Linda would find it and he would be dead meat if that happened."

"People do foolish things. Maybe it was a dangerous memento, but it was something from the girl he loved."

"But do you think Peter has *read* this, Leo? It's clear from her writing – he was an interesting bloke and a fair shag but there's no mention of love. No hint that she wanted any future together. Peter's dreams of that were just castles in the air. No, I don't think he'd have said half the things he said to us if he'd ever read this."

Leo was nodding in agreement.

"Linda, on the other hand, once *she* has taken it, perhaps she lies on her bed back at the Temple of Akesó reading it. She gets angry, she gets bitter and then she gets cold and determined. She'll keep this as her insurance policy. If she decides to divorce Peter, it'll help her get a generous settlement. If she decides to face him with his lies, she has the evidence right here." Nick waved the journal in his hand. "In the meantime, she has control. She gets to decide whether to continue their life in the same vein or to bring it to a shuddering halt. Anytime. People like Linda are control freaks. This is a control freak's dream."

He slapped the journal on the table.

"All right, everyone," said Leo. "Thanks for your good work this morning. We're going to take them both back to Chaniá for further questioning."

*

"Are you arresting us?" asked Linda.

"No. Not unless I have to."

"We will come if we can have a lawyer present at the meeting."

"That is your right, of course."

"Give me ten minutes to arrange that then, please."

*

Pandelís was dispatched to the newly arrived, second police car along with the suspects. Vangélis travelled with Leo and Thaní so that they could bring him up to speed.

Nick knew the Jeep would struggle to keep up with the police cars, so he set off ahead of them. Soon after he left Réthymno, they streaked past him, sirens blaring and lights flashing. The speed limit was ninety kilometres per hour. He reckoned they were touching a hundred and fifty. Thaní gave him a nervous wave. Nick felt a little out of it, pottering along in his windblown Jeep, doing ninety-five. He hoped they would wait for him before starting the interrogation.

*

As they were passing Kalíves, the phone rang in the leading police car. In a rare display of prudence, Leo handed it to Thaní.

"Hi Demí, where are you?"

"We're in Langós, boss."

"Are you? Thought you'd be back by now."

"We've been stopping at all the petrol stations."

"Have you now?"

"Using my initiative, Sergeant."

"Good lad – any joy?"

226

"That's why I'm calling." Thaní switched the phone to the in-car speakers and raised his eyebrows at Leo. "This garage closes at nine every day, including Saturdays, but it has one pump which operates on a twenty-four-hour credit card basis. The owner, Stávros, reckons he does pretty well out of it, says his is the only fuel for miles around, late at night."

"Go on."

"I got him to go back through the machine's records for September, and guess what?"

"You're kidding me!"

"I'm not. At twenty-one forty-eight on the fifteenth of September, forty euros of unleaded was sold to one L. A. Weston."

Thaní and Vangélis were whooping, Leo was hitting the steering wheel and shouting "Yes!"

Leo grabbed the phone.

"You carry on like this lad, you might land yourself a promotion. Well done, Demí. I could kiss you! Explain that, Mrs Weston!" He was beaming as he handed the phone back to Thaní.

"Yes, great work, Demí. Now listen, we need one of you to go back to Síva. When we get to Chaniá, I'll send one of these cars to Langós to collect you and one of the other constables. The *other* constable needs to get back to Síva now and question Sylvie some more. He must ask her if the person that went past her tent late that night could have been Linda, not Sam. Have him get a statement from her."

"Okay, Sergeant."

"And Demí? It'll be at least an hour before we can pick you up so find a nice taverna and have some lunch – on me. You've earned it."

"Thanks a lot, boss."

Thaní disconnected and turned to Leo:

"How could she have been so stupid?"

"It must have been that or run out of petrol. She must have had no choice."

"Bad planning."

"She'd have hoped to find a place to pay cash, I guess."

"Most places out there you *have* to pay cash, boss."

"Yes. But at that time of night, it's a different story."

"Good old Demí!"

"Yes. But remind me to berate him for unauthorised use of police resources."

"That might just slip my mind, boss."

They grinned at each other and Thaní looked over his shoulder where Vangélis was grinning too and looking like an excited sixteen-year-old.

CHAPTER 28

INTERROGATION

At the police station, they booked out two interview rooms and put Peter in one and Linda in the other, each guarded by a constable. Now they needed to wait for the lawyer and, ideally, for Nick as well.

"You're going to interview them separately, then?" asked Thaní.

"At least to start with," said Leo. "The usual thing. Look for any inconsistencies in their stories. Later, though, I'm not sure. Might add pressure to have them together. We'll see. Now what about that photo enhancement idea of yours?"

"Yes. Good point. Maybe I can get someone on that while we're on the interrogation."

"There must be a technical team in Athína that could help."

"It's not all that technical, boss. Anyone who knows their way around an image editor could have a go. They have an *auto-enhance* feature or, if that doesn't do it, there's a multi-stage process you can go through to change the colour vibrance and saturation level, contrast, hue, luminosity and so on."

"Sounds like we need more luminosity. Then we might be able to see something! Anyway, just get on it, Thaní. When that's in motion, come and join us."

"Okay, boss."

Thaní did not want to miss a moment of the interrogation, so he raced out of the room in search of the expertise they needed, cursing himself for not having organised it from the car.

Nick and the lawyer arrived at the same time, but in contrasting styles. Nick leapt out of the Jeep, hair blown to hell, in his chinos with the lumberjack shirt. Antónis Staréniou swept into the car park in a BMW 540i that matched his silver hair. He was immaculate in a beautifully cut, lightweight Italian suit in charcoal cloth, with a cream shirt, open at the neck, and a pale blue silk handkerchief

229

sprouting from his breast pocket. He looked fresh for any challenge. Nick held the door open for him and half expected a tip, but Staréniou appeared not to notice him. *He's only interested in the principal players,* thought Nick, *in particular, himself.*

"If I might have ten minutes with each of my clients before we begin, Lieutenant?" he said to Leo when they arrived. They seemed to know each other. He glanced back, bewildered to see the lackey still there.

"This is Mr Nick Fisher, former DCI with the Metropolitan Police Force in London, Kýrie Staréniou. He will be joining the interrogation."

"In an official capacity?"

"Yes, he's been seconded to the Greek Police for this case."

Staréniou went through an instant oil change and held out a manicured hand.

"Delighted, Mr Fisher."

His dark eyes drilled into Nick's for a second longer than was necessary.

*

After briefing Nick about Langós, it was two forty pm when they began with Peter. Leo and Nick faced Peter and Staréniou. Just as they started, Thaní crept in and stood at the back. Nick went through the recording routine and pressed the button. Right away Leo produced the mauve leather journal and laid it on the table.

"Do you recognise this, Mr Weston?"

Peter glanced at Staréniou who inclined his head.

"Yes, I do."

"Then perhaps you could tell us what it is?"

"It was Sam's. It's a journal. I took it from her tent."

"And her mobile phone?"

"That too." He raised his hands off the table as if to say *mea culpa.*

"Why didn't you tell us this before?"

"With respect, you didn't ask." He paused, but his hands were indicating that they should wait a moment. "When I saw her body on the beach, it occurred to me that those investigating her drowning could discover our affair. Linda might find out. She'd already accused me of it, and I denied it. I couldn't risk her finding out that I'd lied.

"And here was a one-time opportunity to remove any connection to me. So, I went looking for their tent around noon. I remembered it from Sam's photos – an unusual tent – so it wasn't too hard to find. And there was no-one there. I soon discovered the journal, then found the phone. And decided to take both."

"What did you do with the phone?"

"I stopped on the ride back, took out the SIM card and the battery and threw everything into the Irini Gorge."

"The Wilds of Wanney," mumbled Leo.

"I'm sorry, Lieutenant?" said Peter.

"So, why keep the journal?" Leo asked.

"Curiosity, vanity, stupidity? I don't know. I haven't even read the thing. I suppose I was afraid of what I might find there, in the end."

Leo returned the journal to the table drawer.

"Are you familiar with your wife's clothing, Mr Weston?"

"As much as any husband, I suppose."

"Does she wear hats?"

"Weddings and funerals, sun hats in hot sun, not much else these days."

"These days?"

"Well, we all go through phases of wearing different things, don't we?"

"So, there are hats she used to wear but doesn't anymore?"

"Where is this going, Lieutenant?" asked Staréniou in a bored voice.

Leo opened the drawer and took out the beret in its plastic evidence bag.

"Would this be something she used to wear?"

Staréniou place his hand on Peter's arm and whispered something in his ear.

"I couldn't say."

"Would she have worn something *like* that?"

"My client declines to speculate," cut in the lawyer.

"And the badge, as you can see, is an image of Che Guevara. There is a poster of him in your office, too. Is he something of a hero of hers?"

"You'd have to ask her, but I doubt she knows much about him. He was just a symbol, wasn't he, in those days? Freedom, rebellion, courage in the face of adversity, we all bought into that. He was cool."

"I'm not sure my client's views on some Argentine revolutionary from fifty years ago have a great deal of relevance, Lieutenant. Can we *please* move on?"

Leo returned the beret to the drawer.

"I have nothing more for Mr Weston right now. We'd like to move on to *Mrs* Weston." Leo nodded at Thani.

Peter looked startled. Thani led him out of the room and the lawyer followed. In a couple of minutes, they returned with Linda. When they were seated, Leo leaned back in his chair and lit a cigarette.

"My client would prefer you not to smoke," said the lawyer.

"I am aware of Mrs Weston's preferences, thank you," said Leo. "But there are no restrictions on smoking in this building, I'm happy to say."

Nick heard Linda mutter something that sounded like "Vengeful, little shit" while Leo blew a smoke ring and grinned like the Cheshire Cat.

Nick went through the recording routine again and then started the questioning, as agreed:

"I'd like to start with the wellness programme at the so-called Temple of Akesó."

He was shuffling back through his notes.

"Now you told us that you were there from around eight pm on the Saturday night until about nine thirty-five on the Sunday morning, when you went to church. Is that correct?"

"Yes," she said, without reference to the lawyer.

"Could you explain why your car was not in the car park all the time?"

"The car park was full, to begin with. I had to park along the drive."

"We know that the car park was *not* full."

"Well, it looked full to me. I'm not good at squeezing into small places so I didn't try."

"And yet you were one of the first to arrive, according to the staff."

"I can only tell you what I saw."

"But you started in the car park, didn't you? You were seen rummaging around in your boot by a gentleman attending the course. He spoke to you."

"Not me," she said, breezily.

"Strange. He remembers you clearly," said Nick, "and he remembers that you weren't at the Why Detox? session on Sunday morning."

"Well I wasn't, was I? I was in church."

"So, let me get this straight. It *wasn't* you in the car park, but it *was* you that was absent from the morning session. Are you saying he's remembering two different people?"

"Must be."

"And yet you were the only person who did not attend that session. We've checked."

"So what? It wasn't me in the car park."

Nick took the group photograph from his folder.

"Do you see anyone in this photograph that he could have confused with you? You have, after all, a rather distinctive appearance."

"It's not for my client to speculate on how a stranger's confusion came about, Mr Fisher."

"My point is that none of the other women looks at all like Mrs Weston. They are smaller or slighter or older. None has the mass of frizzy hair that the witness recalls."

"She says it wasn't her. Let's move on."

"All right. Let's jump to the next morning, early. Your car is now parked in the drive. We have a witness who will say that the engine was warm and the windscreen clear at six fifteen am. Yet all the cars in the car park had cold engines and misty screens. How do you explain that?"

"Maybe it doesn't get misty under the tree? Maybe I have a different type of glass? How would I know? As to the warm engine, he or she must be mistaken. I have the only keys and I was fast asleep in my room."

233

"Yes, you were. But you'd only been there for about an hour, hadn't you?"

"Where are you going with this, Mr Fisher?" asked the lawyer.

"*We* say that Mrs Weston arrived just before eight pm, parked in the car park, checked into the course and attended the Welcome Supper, but only briefly. This was to establish an alibi.

"She left the building covertly before nine but encountered a gentleman arriving in the car park. She then pretended to have lost her phone and rummaged in her boot until he went away. Then she drove off.

"At twenty-one forty-eight that evening, she used her credit card to buy forty litres of fuel at Langós, just off the Chaniá-Síva road. Plenty for a trip to Síva and back.

"She did not return to the Temple of Akesó until five or six am, when she parked in the drive. She did this *not* because the car park was full, which it could not have been, but because she didn't want to be heard by the other guests as that would destroy her alibi.

"When our witness encountered the car, the engine was still warm and the windscreen clear *because she had only recently returned in it.*"

There was a whispered consultation between Linda and Staréniou which went on for some time. Leo drummed on the desk with his fingers.

"I need five minutes with my client in private," said Staréniou, at last.

Leo made a sour face, but the two policemen and Nick left the room. They found some coffee and Leo lit a cigarette.

"I think you nailed her on the car, Nick," he said. "I can't imagine what they're going to come back with now."

"She's a bright woman, Leo. Let's not congratulate ourselves just yet."

Two minutes later, Staréniou put his head around the door and said simply: "Gentlemen?"

When they reassembled, the lawyer said:

"My client wishes to apologise to you. She felt unable to reveal the full truth as it would threaten both her marriage and the privacy of an old friend. Now, if you can assure her that this conversation is confidential – and I mean watertight, even with respect to Peter

Weston – she is ready to be open with you."

Leo and Nick exchanged a glance of irritation and worry.

"Well, that's good of her," said Leo, before raising his voice. "Telling the police the truth is not a matter for negotiation, Mrs Weston. It's a legal and moral obligation. You can go to prison for perverting the course of justice or be fined for wasting police time. You'd do well to remember that.

"However, I will say that whatever is said in this room is confidential and we won't intentionally reveal it to Mr Weston. Should this case go to court, however, I'm unable to give you assurances about what may be said there."

Staréniou glanced at his client with an eyebrow raised and she nodded slightly.

"What do you have to tell us, Mrs Weston?" asked Leo.

She sighed and stared at the ashtray for several moments.

"Twenty-eight years ago, I was a dental student at Queen's – in Belfast. That's Northern Ireland, Lieutenant. I met someone. He was a fellow student, Martin McConnell. We worked together on a project and we fell in love. But I was already married to Peter and Martin was married as well, to Aileen. And she was pregnant with their second child.

"I think he was ready to walk away from all that for me, but I wouldn't let him, and I didn't want to hurt Peter. We'd only been married a couple of years and I was quite happy with him, on the whole. He was different then; more alive, somehow. So, Martin and I went our separate ways when the course ended."

When she looked up there were tears in her eyes.

"It was the most difficult thing I've ever done. Over the years, we stayed in touch. Good, old-fashioned letters – remember them? We sent them to each other's practice addresses. He joined a dental practice in Dungannon, I switched to orthodontics. They had a third child. We were both superficially happy, I suppose, but that yearning was still there – the wondering what might have been.

"Then he lost his first child, killed in a car crash at seventeen and he was devastated. I *so* wanted to be with him. He rang me and we

235

had this long, sad conversation for an hour and a half. It must have been fifteen years since we'd spoken, but the feeling was just as strong. I remember my heart was racing and I was talking too much and getting all jumbled up, to begin with. We both knew that calling was too dangerous though, so, after that, we went back to the letters.

"Soon after Peter and I moved here, Aileen was diagnosed with ALS. It's a type of motor neurone disease, just awful. Everyone felt a kind of guilty relief when she finally died three years ago. By then, the two remaining kids had left home, and Martin was on his own. He wanted to see me, so he came out here for a holiday and I made excuses to Peter and saw him three times while he was here. We made love again then and it was wonderful. So gentle, so romantic.

"The next year, he retired and then told me he'd bought himself a house here, near Néa Roúmata. We started seeing each other when we could. I made it clear from the outset that I wasn't going to leave Peter, but I think he hoped to change my mind. Still does, perhaps."

She looked up again and straight into Leo's eyes.

"So yes, I'm sorry. I did leave the centre at about nine that night. I drove to Néa Roúmata and got there about ten, ate a late supper with Martin and then we talked for ages. Around two, I think, we went to bed together. I got up very early to be back before I was missed."

There was a pause as Linda looked at her fingers and rotated her wedding ring.

"I'm not proud of myself, Lieutenant. To be a religious woman and an adulteress is not easy for me. I love Martin and he loves me but when I said those words *till death us do part* to Peter, I meant them. I meant them to Peter, and I meant them to God."

"So, what *did* happen with the man in the car park?" asked Nick.

"Like I told him, I *was* looking for my phone. I wanted to text Martin to say I was on my way. I'd left the phone in the wrong bag."

"And, at church, you changed your mind about confession."

Linda blinked a few times. Perhaps she had not expected them to talk to the priest or for a priest to be so forthcoming.

"I was tired. In the end, I couldn't face it. That's all. He didn't look a very sympathetic priest, either. Too much the macho Greek for me."

"We'll need to speak to Mr McConnell," said Leo.

"I understand, and that's fine, as long as Peter remains unaware. I don't want him to be hurt. Not now. Not after all this."

She wrote down contact details for McConnell and handed them to Leo.

Leo took the beret out of the drawer.

"Now, Mrs Weston, could you tell me if you recognise this?"

"No, I don't. It's not mine."

"You're quite sure?"

"I'm certain. It looks like something a much younger person might wear."

"Or you, when you were younger?"

"No. I don't think I've ever worn a beret."

"But you are a fan of Che Guevara, are you not?"

"I own a generic poster. So do millions of others. That's not my beret and it's not my badge."

"I think my client has been crystal clear about this, gentlemen."

"Let's take a quick break," said Leo.

*

"Jesus! What a total, bloody hypocrite that woman is," said Nick.

"Where's that map?" said Leo, and then a few moments later, "Shit!"

"Where is it?"

"Néa Roúmata is just a few kilometres past the petrol station at Langós. Demí's fuel bill only confirms Linda's new alibi, as I'm sure will Mr McConnell."

"What about the church – do we believe her?"

"Why not? This affair's been going on for years, Nick. She's been *unworthy* for a long time. Why confess now if she didn't feel comfortable with the guy?"

"So, unexpiated sin kept her from taking communion, but it was the sin of adultery, not murder."

"Exactly."

"And neither of them recognised that sodding beret."

"No, and I don't think they were lying about that."

Leo lit a cigarette and kicked a chair.

"Shit. Less than twenty-four hours to go and we're fucking nowhere."

Leo had not sworn before, Nick noticed. He went to the window and opened it. It was cloudy now and the air was clammy. Car horns were blaring as the traffic built up again after the afternoon lull. People were scurrying back to work. Yellow leaves were falling from plane trees.

Demí appeared at the office door.

"Sorry to bother you, Lieutenant, but I just took a call from Valádis, the constable that went back to question Sylvie Deschamps."

"And?"

"She couldn't be *certain* it was Sam."

"But she's sure it was a woman?"

"It was the *perfume* she recognised, more than the woman."

"I suppose a French woman would tend to pick up on that."

"Yes, sir. *Dégueulasse* she called it."

"That's not a brand of perfume, Demí. It's French for *disgusting*."

"So I've learned, sir. And she pulled a face when she said it, apparently. Called it *that musky shit*. Said Sam wore it all the time – far too much of it."

"But we know it wasn't Sam," said Nick. "She never made it back from the swim, and it wasn't Linda – she was in Néa bloody Roúmata. So, who the hell was it?"

"Someone who wears musky shit. Now we need a goddamned bloodhound.

"All right. Thank you, Constable."

Leo was joking but he looked a little defeated, Nick thought.

"Anyway, Leo, now we know Peter took the phone and the journal. Why on earth did he keep the journal?"

"I guess he'd have destroyed it in due course."

"Just got caught out by our search?"

"Hmmm."

"One could argue that keeping it *at all* implies that he's innocent.

It would be incredibly stupid to keep something so incriminating otherwise."

"So, if it wasn't Linda who took it, what was she doing *nipping up to the office* when we arrived?"

"We can ask her, Leo."

*

Linda responded to their question. Now that she had unburdened herself, she seemed quite relaxed, almost friendly:

"I just popped up there to file a couple of invoices. I sold some home-made jams to that young German couple. I was up there when I heard the police car arrive."

"And the cupboard in the office? There was an empty cupboard on your side of the office which was locked for some reason."

"Oh, I keep it locked because the door swings open otherwise. The latch is out of alignment or something. Been on Peter's DIY list for years, of course."

After she left the room, Nick observed:

"So, with Linda up there, fiddling with invoices, Peter couldn't move the journal when we arrived with the warrant."

"Maybe he thought it was pretty safe where it was, like you and your cigarettes."

"You think so? I think he was shitting bricks."

*

Thaní reappeared a few moments later. He spread an A4 glossy paper on the desk. It was that photo from Moondance.

"The enhancements have made a difference, boss."

Leo and Nick crowded round.

"That's got to be the beret, hasn't it?"

"No question."

"But who is it?"

"It's hard to tell with the grainy picture and the hair stuffed up into the beret, but the face is quite long, and the eyes are dark."

"Male or female?"

"I'd say female but that would be a guess."

"And it's not Linda, it seems."

They sat down again.

"Do you think Linda knew about Peter and Sam?" asked Leo.

"Not knew, no. Not for sure."

"But she suspected?"

"Peter said that, didn't he? But then she'd been unfaithful to him for years, anyway, so maybe it wasn't such a big deal for her."

"Meaning she wouldn't care? I'm not sure she thinks that way, Nick. She denied herself Martin's love for decades to be faithful to her vows to Peter. Okay, there's been some fun with Martin in recent times, but I don't think that counts for much in her eyes. She sees herself as having stood by Peter, stayed with him."

"I think *bloody hypocrite* about sums her up, then. She's done neither of them any favours by perpetuating a loveless marriage."

"Ah, but you're forgetting about God."

"*My* God believes in letting people find happiness, Leo."

Demí was at the door again.

"Sorry to interrupt again, Lieutenant, but I've taken a couple more calls. The captain is asking to see you urgently and a journalist from the Chaniá Post is holding for you."

"Tell the journalist to speak to the captain but after I've seen him. Okay?"

He turned to Nick, looking anxious:

"You British have a saying, I think: *It never rains but it pours.*"

"Yes – and then it pisses down from a great height," said Nick, helpfully.

CHAPTER 29
BACK TO THE BEACH

Leo entered the captain's office.

"Sit down, Leo. There's been a development."

"Sir."

"More one of Zeus's thunderbolts, to tell the truth."

"Sir?"

"Another body's been found at Síva."

Leo clamped his eyes shut and winced.

"Oh, God. Who is it, sir?"

"We don't know yet. It's male, been in the water for some time."

"Where was it found?"

"Beyond the second beach. There's a channel that runs through a cave to a tiny beach. The body's wedged in that channel."

"You mean it's still there?"

"It's not going anywhere, Leo. Get hold of Pánagou and those forensics boys at the FSD. Get down there, soon as you can. I'll deal with the press and the investigating judge."

"Yes, sir. Thank you, sir."

*

The FSD said they would send a two-person team, but only if the ME felt it was necessary. The officer did not relish a three-hour trip to the south coast of Crete for a case that was being handled locally. Pánagou could not make it until the following morning, so Leo agreed to meet her in Síva at nine am. In the meantime, he arranged for two constables from Palaióchora to get over there in a boat, cordon off the scene, set up lighting in the cave and then take alternate shifts to guard the scene. One of them was to bring the boat to the jetty at nine. He brought Nick and Thaní up to speed then and they agreed to meet back at the police station the next morning and drive down together.

*

Pánagou looked even more cadaverous, thought Leo, as he spotted her gripping her raincoat with one hand and puffing on a cigarette with the other. The strong wind was whipping the smoke away as she exhaled.

"Still giving up then, Doctor?"

"It's a work-in-progress, Christodouláki. I've stopped buying them, at least; my driver gave me this one."

"Progress indeed."

"I think I'll have to change jobs before I can stop completely."

"I can understand that. You remember Investigations Sergeant Konstantópoulos?"

"I do." She extended a bony hand and proffered a rather grotesque smile.

"And this is Mr Nick Fisher, who is working with us."

"You are from England, Mr Fisher?"

"Originally, yes. I was with the London police."

"I studied at UCL about a hundred years ago. London is a wonderful city."

Its underbelly isn't quite so delightful, thought Nick, but he smiled, anyway.

"So, gentlemen, this must be a very important body to merit all three of you in such straitened times." She was smirking.

"We are hoping it will be," said Leo. "Shall we take a look?"

The constable started up the outboard motor and idled while all four squeezed in, then they swung around and buffeted their way along the shore through cresting waves.

"I'll drop you as close as I can to the little beach," yelled the constable, "then you can make your way through the cave opening. That's where the body is." He looked around at their footwear and pulled a rueful face. "I'm afraid you'll get rather wet."

A few minutes later, he ran the boat onto the shingle in front of a natural archway in the rock and Nick was first over the bow, dragging the boat in and helping the others out in the lulls between the small waves. They stood on the beach for a minute. It was no more than six metres wide and there was only a two-metre strip between the sea and the archway opening. To use it as a beach, one would have to sit in the cave, under that colossal weight of limestone. As they hesitated, the other constable appeared from a passageway to the right, inside the cave. He was an older man of perhaps fifty.

"Kalimérasas. Good morning, everyone. It's not as bad as it looks. Don't worry."

"Is it stable?" asked Pánagou.

"Well it hasn't changed since I came here as a boy, ma'am, so I think we'll be all right. There's plenty of headroom. It's just dark and wet underfoot and the water's up to a metre deep in the channel."

"Who found the body?" asked Thaní.

"Kids, I'm sorry to say. Because it's not a pretty sight. Two lads from Thessaloníki, here on holiday with their parents, just eight and ten years old. They were exploring, poor little buggers."

"Are they being looked after?"

"They're just with their parents in the town right now, ma'am. They didn't seem too damaged when I spoke to them. Kids are pretty resilient, on the whole."

"All right, Constable. Let's get on with it," said Leo. "Take us to the body."

"Sir."

There was indeed plenty of headroom, but the pitch dark and the monstrous weight above their heads made for a tense and claustrophobic couple of minutes as they squelched their way along the echoing chamber. The water in the channel grew deeper as the cavern floor sloped downwards to the sea. Soon, though, it grew brighter as they neared the arc lights that the constables had rigged up and then some natural light also filtered through as the sea cave opening came into view.

"Why not just bring us in through that opening, Constable?" asked Thaní.

"There's no shelter and no beach there, sir. And there are rocks. It's easy enough to swim in from there, but it's not the place for a boat, not when the wind's up."

The constable came to a stop as he was talking and waited for the others to gather around.

"The body's wedged at the end of this channel, near the cave opening. Just over there. The water's about eighty centimetres deep there."

"All right, Constable, thank you," said Pánagou. "I will take a quick look here but then I'll want to move him back to that little beach or maybe to the main beach. We're going to need your help with that."

"Yes, ma'am."

The constable moved back to get himself out of the way and then they all negotiated the slippery rocks towards the cavern mouth. The body was face-down in the channel, largely submerged, wearing only swimming shorts. The skin looked bluish and dark.

"It can't be him. This is a much bigger guy." Leo sounded irritated.

"Who did you think it might be, Lieutenant?"

"A man we've been looking for elsewhere: Spíros Tavouláris."

"If he's been in the water for several days or more, it'd be normal for the body to bloat a great deal. Bacteria in the gut and chest cavity multiply and produce gases: methane, carbon dioxide, hydrogen sulphide. He's full of gas, Lieutenant. He may seem much bigger than he was."

Pánagou was examining the head. Splintered white bone was visible through the hair.

"You see this, gentlemen? The occipital bone, here at the base of the skull, has been shattered. This is a strong bone that protects the lower part of the brain. It takes a lot to break it like this. This is a penetrating skull fracture; a major trauma that would cause intracerebral haemorrhage."

"What's that?"

"Bleeding *inside* the brain; most often fatal."

"What could cause that kind of wound, Doctor?"

"Oh, I'm not going to speculate just yet. But there are other impact wounds here, to the back and the buttocks."

She was feeling the skin on the man's back and legs and checking a measuring device of some sort.

"The skin is loose, you see? You could almost pull it off. And it's discoloured. There will be putrefaction already."

She lifted one of the feet, which looked half-eaten, and then jumped back as some small crabs scuttled away over the rocks.

"Nature is at work, gentlemen. Another month or two and they'd have picked him clean. I'd guess he's been in the water for a couple of weeks, so the scavengers have made a start, as I'd have expected."

She seemed oddly pleased, thought Nick, *that nature had started its ghastly recycling work. As if all was right with the world. As if everything she had studied in books was now, to her childlike delight, being confirmed by reality.*

She went to examine the hands and then held one up.

"If you were hoping for fingerprints, that's going to be a challenge," she said with a smirk.

The hands looked to have rotted away or perhaps been eaten. The puffy blue-white fingers were torn and stubby with fleshy ends.

"If he still has some teeth, we can check dental records."

"Yes, or maybe DNA?"

"If he's on a database or we can find some of his DNA elsewhere." Pánagou stood.

"I'll need to examine this head wound in natural light, so I don't want to turn him over here. I need you strong men to carry him, face-down as he is, through to the little beach."

"What about the FSD?" asked Leo.

"I think they'd be wasting their time, Lieutenant. This is not where he died, just where he washed up. I don't think there'll be any clues for them here. So, let's get him moved."

The apprehension was palpable. No-one relished handling a swollen, rotting corpse. But Pánagou was brisk and no-nonsense:

"We'll need your colleague, too," she said to the older constable who nodded and went back down the cave to call him in from the boat. When all five men were assembled, she said:

"I want one of you under each thigh and one under each armpit with the remaining one holding his head. We don't want anything falling off now, do we?"

She chuckled in delight at their sickly faces. Nick found himself at the head-end, trying hard to remind himself that this disgusting, bloated mess was a human being that should be treated with respect and not revulsion. He shuddered as he cradled the cold, leathery face in his hands.

"All in place? Good – so one-two-three and *lift*."

They staggered as they took the weight and more crabs and some other shrimp-like creatures swam for the dark. One bigger crab clung on, waving a pincer angrily until the young constable swept it off its breakfast. It landed on the rock with a clatter. And then they were squelching and scrunching up the channel, away from the light, with Pánagou walking backwards in front of the macabre procession, holding a torch and croaking out instructions and growls of admonishment.

Finally, they laid the body on the tiny beach and stepped away, soaked and queasy but relieved. Leo lit a cigarette and offered one to the doctor.

"Thank you, Christodouláki, but no. A body that's been immersed for a long time putrefies rapidly when exposed to light and air – you can almost see it change – so I must go to work now."

The men moved away, leaving her to it. The constables lounged in the boat and smoked while Nick, Leo and Thaní sat on the smooth rocks at the back of the shingle beach, conscious of the weight of rock above them and gazing out through the arch.

"He's not going to be a pretty sight when we turn him over," said Nick.

"No. I was going to get Kristīne or Manólis to confirm that it's Spíros but that might not be possible. He might be unrecognisable."

"We have the yellow swimming shorts. With those red stripes at the side, they're quite distinctive. If we get lucky, there might be jewellery or tattoos."

"If the worst comes to the worst, we take a photo of the swimming shorts and check it with Kristīne, then go for DNA or dental records for the formal ID."

Pánagou had been taking photographs. Now she was taking swabs from the deep head wound.

Nick turned to Leo: "Are we looking at another murder, do you think?"

"It's hard to say, but, if the doctor's timing is right, Spíros could have died the night Sam was killed."

"Which would mean Kristīne has been lying to us."

"Indeed."

Pánagou was calling them.

"Okay. We turn him over now. Will you help me, please?"

Nick shuddered. The body had no face. The parts that had escaped being eaten were swollen and dark blue. The thing was not recognisable as any particular person. It was barely recognisable as human.

"We're looking for anything distinctive, Doctor: rings, other jewellery, tattoos, scars?"

"Of course, you are, Christodouláki. But rings require fingers. If there were any, they will be in the sea or some fish's gut, I imagine. I can see no other jewellery, can you? I will look for tattoos or scars but, with this discolouration, it will be difficult."

Leo went over to the boat and spoke to the older constable:

"I want you to go back to where the body was found, Constable. Move your lights close and scour the sea cave entrance and that channel. You are looking for anything that might have come *from* the body that could help with identification: a ring, for example. It's a long shot but I need you to give it your full attention."

"Sir."

"And you," turning to the younger constable, "in a minute, I want you to ferry these guys round to the main beach."

"Yes, Lieutenant."

Leo came back to Nick and Thaní:

"Let's assume the shorts are all we're going to get. Take a photo to show Kristīne but start by talking to Alexandrákis."

"He'll be asleep at this time of day."

"Well, get him up, Thaní. We need to know Spíros's movements. Has he seen him since the night of Sam's death? If so, where and when exactly? And have him tell us everything he knows about Spíros."

"Okay, boss."

"Then go to Kristīne. See if she can confirm that these swimming shorts belonged to Spíros. See if there's anything in their tent which might have his DNA on it. If so, bag it up. Then detain her."

"On what grounds, boss?"

"Tell her we need her to identify the body."

"She might lie about the shorts to throw us off the scent," said Nick.

"Yes, she might, so start by asking some others at the campsite – or even Alexandrákis. I'll stay with the doctor for now. Call me when you've finished."

CHAPTER 30

MANÓLIS

It was ten thirty-five when Nick and Thaní arrived at Manólis's scruffy little apartment to the side of the beach bar and started hammering on the door. When he appeared, he was not happy.

"What you do, guys? This when I sleep. You know this."

Nick caught the stench of sweat and stale beer and saw the puffy, unshaven face as Manólis blinked in the piercing morning light. Thaní spoke:

"This is urgent police business, Alexandráki. We need to ask more questions."

He waved them to a table, sat down like a sack of potatoes and sighed.

"When I spoke to you before," said Nick, "you told me that Spíros had 'buggered off somewhere.' How did you know that?"

"I called his cell phone to get him to come in but it just ring and ring. Nobody answer. So, I remember I have number for his woman."

"For Kristíne? Why did you have that?"

"He gave it to me before. I must have next of kin in case of accident. She was the nearest thing he could come up with. He don't get on with his family. Believe me, I know."

"So, you called Kristíne."

"Yeah. And she say he gone. Took the ferry to Palaióchora and then who knows?"

"When did she tell you that?"

"That day – just two or three hours before you come."

"And, before that, when did you last see him?"

"On the Saturday night – well, Sunday morning by the time we close. Maybe two thirty am?"

"The night Sam died."

"Yes, I suppose it was."

"And have you seen him at all since then?"

"No, but that's not so unusual. The boy is unreliable."

"It's been two weeks, Manóli."

Manólis spread his hands on the table and looked back hard at them.

"What can I do? The boy is almost thirty. I take him in out of the goodness of my stupid heart, give him good job, straighten him out, but I must watch him all the time. Then, just as I think he might be doing a bit better, he lets me down big time. Clears off and leaves me in the shit. Back to his drug buddies in Athína, I expect."

"And your cousin?"

"I call him. Tell him I do my best but I can do no more for Spíros. He wasn't surprised. He's been there himself many, many times. He passed the problem to me and he don't want it back."

"Going back to the last night you saw him, was there anything different or unusual about him?"

He rubbed his chin and searched the sky for a minute.

"Yes. He did *good* work for once. And then his lady comes to surprise him. But he don't know. She falls asleep waiting and he already gone." He waved his arm.

"What did Kristīne do?"

"She go after him, down the beach."

Nick and Thaní exchanged glances and got to their feet.

"We need to talk to her," said Nick.

"Then you got a problem, man," said Manólis, "she gone."

"What? When?"

"The day before yesterday. I'm up early and she's here already. She tell me she go find Spíros, talk things over. I say: 'Forget this boy. He is wastrel. You can do better.' We chat for a while, have some coffee, then she goes to use the toilet and I hear her throwing up.

"When she comes out, I say: 'You okay?' and she nods but she don't look okay. And then I get it, though it don't show or nothing. 'You having a baby,' I say and she starts to cry and comes over to me and I give her a big, Greek hug and I say: 'Don't cry, because that's a wonderful thing, Krissie.'

"But then she looks at me all sad, pats her tummy and says: 'My baby will need his daddy too, Manóli; that's why I have to find him.' And then she go. She a nice woman but she screw up badly with this boy."

"Did she say where she was going?"

"I guess she taking the boat to Palaióchora like Spíros."

Nick and Thaní exchanged a look of frustration, then Nick said:

"Did you ever see Spíros in his swimming shorts, by any chance, Manóli?"

"Why you ask that?"

"Just answer the question, please."

"Many time. He often take a swim in the afternoon after we work lunchtime."

"Do you recall the shorts?"

"Yes. Always the same. Yellow with red stripes on the sides, here."

He drew his middle fingers down his hips.

"I remember because I take photograph. Come." He led them across to his display board.

"Hmmm. It's here somewhere. Ah yes – here. My nieces and Spíros. He was good with them. They play in the water together."

Spíros is wet from the sea and grinning. Two little girls aged eight or nine are standing in front of him, looking coy. One of them is holding a green and yellow Lilo in the shape of a crocodile. His swimming shorts are a very bright, mimosa yellow with pillar-box red stripes down the sides.

Thaní fiddled with his phone for a few seconds, stared at it and then nodded in confirmation to Nick.

"What is it, guys? Has something happened?"

"Another body has been found, Manóli. We have not yet formally identified it but it's a male wearing swimming shorts like these."

"My God. You mean it's Spíros?"

"It looks that way."

"Somebody kill him, too?"

"We don't know yet."

"And you find him here, in Síva?"

"Yes. He never took that ferry, Manóli. I'm sorry."

Manólis looked out over the sea and pursed his lips.

"She never going to find him, then. No daddy for her baby. And I'm sorry now for all the bad things I say about the boy. He had big problems, but he didn't deserve to die so young. And now I must find a way to tell my cousin."

"Not yet, Manóli. You must wait for formal identification before you do that."

"You want me to identify him for you?"

"It's not as simple as that, I'm afraid, but you can help by letting us have something of his that we can check for DNA."

"Like what?"

"A hairbrush? A toothbrush? Something he wore?"

"I have his apron. Will that do?"

"Anything else?"

"I think there may be a sun hat he wore sometimes, out the back."

"Okay we'll take both – and that photograph, please."

*

They left Manólis and walked over to the campsite. As expected, there was no trace of Kristīne's tent and a nearby couple confirmed that it was indeed two days before that she had left, quite early in the morning. Thaní took out his phone and put it on speaker as he brought Leo up to speed.

"Damn. She shouldn't have left without informing us first."

"I doubt she just forgot," said Nick.

"Alexandrákis reckoned she was following Spíros to Palaióchora."

"Only there are two things wrong with that idea," cut in Nick. "First thing? We know now that Spíros never left Síva."

"But *she* didn't know that, Nick."

"I'm not so sure about that, Leo, given that she was seen following him away from the beach bar on the night of Sam's death."

"Was she now? You think she killed him?"

"I don't know, but my gut's telling me she was involved in his death,

252

somehow. Maybe even Sam's as well. He'd been unfaithful with Sam, remember, just two days earlier. Maybe she found out.

"And Palaióchora as a destination? I don't think so. She left quite early in the morning, according to the campers. The ferry to Palaióchora doesn't leave till five in the afternoon."

"Maybe she hitched a ride there, instead?"

"Maybe. Or she hitched a ride somewhere else, or she took the morning ferry that goes east."

"All right, Nick. There are enough questions there, and she's failed to keep us informed, so I'll alert the exit points."

"She might have left the island already."

"We'll check all the flights out of Crete."

"You might want to check all the flights out of Greece in case she took a ferry first to cover her tracks. That's what I'd do if I were her. And check flights to Latvia first. She's a pregnant, single mother-to-be now and she's in distress; I'd guess she's headed home."

"I don't appreciate you telling me how to do my job, DCI Fisher."

"Sorry, Leo. Just trying to help."

"Anyway, the doctor has finished here so we'll meet you two at the jetty in ten minutes. Bring your evidence bag."

CHAPTER 31

FRUSTRATION

The body was in a bag now, thank goodness, but the constables needed help to get it out of the boat, up the stone steps to the jetty and into the waiting ambulance car.

"Thank you, gentlemen," said Pánagou to all of them, then the younger constable departed in the boat.

"Aren't you going with him?" Nick asked the older constable.

"Er … no, sir. Thought I'd just check on those boys again. Make sure they're okay."

"That's good of you. I don't suppose you found any rings or what have you in that cave, did you?"

The constable didn't speak but deferred to Leo.

"No, he didn't, Nick. There was nothing there," said Leo and the constable went on his way.

The doctor had removed her protective gear and was looking slightly more human:

"I'll take that cigarette now, if I may, Christodouláki?"

Leo raised an eyebrow and offered Pánagou the packet. They each took one and lit up in a huddle against the wind. As she exhaled, she looked relieved and a little wicked.

"Thank you. That is *so* good. Now, you have some clothes for me, Sergeant?"

Thaní removed the photograph from the bag and handed the rest over. "An apron and a sun hat, Doctor. That's all there was."

"Well, with luck there will be sweat on the apron and hairs in the hat. I'll ask the FSD to run a test when I get back."

"Can you confirm that he too was murdered, Doctor?"

"No, Mr Fisher. At this stage, I cannot tell. When I get back to the laboratory, I will check for any residue in the wound that has not been washed out and that may help. Also, I am interested in the other wounds to the back and the buttocks. To me, these suggest a fall onto rocks but, of course, it doesn't tell us if he fell or if he was pushed.

"Or, he could have been attacked with a jagged instrument of some sort and the other markings could have resulted from colliding with rocks whilst in the water. Any attacker must have been a powerful man to do this much damage with a single blow."

"Not a woman, then."

"I very much doubt it."

*

The next two days were intensive for Thaní, who was managing the team trying to trace Kristīne. Leo, meanwhile, was swallowed up by politics. He had to keep the captain and the investigating judge up to speed and fight the constant threat from Athens, who were pushing still harder to take over the case. Also, there was pressure now from Staréniou to get his clients released.

Once McConnell had given a sworn statement, confirming Linda's story, Leo agreed to her release, but he remained intransigent regarding both Peter and Jason.

"We still cannot be certain of their innocence, gentlemen," he said when Nick and Staréniou tackled him together. "They were both in Síva at the time of Sam's murder, both had opportunity and motive and neither has an alibi for the time of the murder. I'm sorry, but I won't release either of them for the time being."

"You must release Weston or charge him, as you know, Lieutenant."

"I have three more days, Kýrie Staréniou."

*

Nick wandered round to Thaní's team and asked him how they were getting on.

"She wasn't on any flight out of Crete since the murder. We've checked all three airports."

"There are three?"

"With Sitía, yes."

255

"So, she took a ferry?"

"We are assuming that, probably an overnight ferry to Piraeus. Buying a last-minute ticket as a foot passenger, she'd have been anonymous."

"No passport checks?"

"No. It's all within Greece, isn't it?"

"So, you're checking flights from Athens now?"

"We are, but it won't be straightforward. We know she didn't fly Athína-Riga."

"I'm not surprised, are you?"

"What do you mean, Nick?"

"Well, if she takes an eight-hour ferry ride to avoid using the Cretan airports, she might fly somewhere else rather than heading directly into Latvia, don't you think?"

"So, she could have flown anywhere or nowhere, in fact. Christ!"

Thaní threw his biro against the pinboard with a thwack. It was a rare moment of petulance. Nick saw that he was tired and frustrated. He grasped his shoulder:

"Think it through, Thaní. Work it back. Check which departure airports offer flights into Latvian airports, then which of those also receive flights from Athens or any other Greek airports she could have reached by ferry from here. That way you'll narrow it down. You'll get there."

*

It was a frustrating time for Nick, too. He did not think he could add much value to the work that Thaní and his team were doing or the politics that were absorbing Leo. He did not want to get in the way but, at the same time, he did not want to miss out on interviewing Kristíne when the time came, so he spent the afternoon in a borrowed office at the police station. He called Jen and Stephen to update them on Jason's position but also to get Jen to ask him one more question. Then he caught up with Lauren, but most of the time he stood with his hands in his pockets looking out of the window, thinking.

Why did Kristīne go to the beach bar to meet Spíros? Why not just wait for him to come back to the tent? And where did she wait? Was it near the fire, perhaps? Why did she follow him down the beach? They would each have passed Jason and then Andie and the Germans, you would think, but there was nothing in any of the statements about that. If they had, nevertheless – perhaps without being spotted – they would have reached the end of the main beach at about the time that Sam was there alone, swimming around the rock. Did Sam have a secret assignation with Spíros, a follow-up to their coupling two days earlier? Did she shed her companions with that in mind? Did Kristīne know of, or suspect, their involvement? Was she following Spíros out of curiosity or jealousy or fear? And, if all three ended up at the big rock at the same time, that would be an interesting dynamic, to say the least. And yet Kristīne seemed so unruffled at that first meeting, so unfazed by his questions, so calmly insolent. Could she have killed one – or even two – people just a few days before?

*

It was not until the next day that the breakthrough came. Leo called Nick into his office and Thaní was already there, looking pleased with himself.

"Tell Nick what you told me, Thaní."

"We've got her, Nick. You must have been right about the ferry to Piraeus. She took an Aegean flight from Athína to St Petersburg on Thursday, the twenty-seventh and then an Air Baltic flight from St Petersburg to Rīga the next morning."

"Via Russia, then. Could she have flown direct to Rīga?"

"There are direct flights."

"So, it was another attempt to throw us off the scent, like the ferry trip. Good job, Thaní."

He beamed as Nick slapped his shoulder. Leo took up the reins:

"I think we need more before we can get an arrest warrant, so we've informed the Latvian police and they've agreed to us questioning her there. They've identified her parents' address, close to Rīga. It seems likely they'll find her there and bring her in."

"Will there be extradition issues if we want to bring her back to Greece?"

"Both Greece and Latvia are in the EU, Nick, so there's an agreed procedure. There shouldn't be any major issues, but we'll have to organise an EAW – that's a European Arrest Warrant – and then it takes a couple of weeks or so. First, though, we have to find out what the hell happened. Her behaviour implies that she's guilty of something, but we need to find out exactly what."

*

Later that evening, Jen called Nick back:

"You were right, Nick. He remembers it very well."

"Is he sure?"

"Oh, more than that; he's quite certain."

Nick downed his Metaxá in one and slapped the table.

"Clever lad. Fanbloodytastic, Jen. That might just do it."

*

The next morning, Leo was looking glum when Nick got in.

"She wasn't at her parents' place, Nick. They thought she was still in Crete and say she hasn't been in touch."

"Oh, bugger."

"The Latvian cops are checking out all known friends and relatives, favourite haunts, and they're putting her picture on television for us. We know she's somewhere in Latvia and there are only two million people there, so it's just a matter of time."

"What about Jason and Peter, meanwhile?"

"I'll have to talk with the investigating judge. Jason's been charged and is being held in pre-trial detention, but Peter hasn't been charged. We'll have no choice but to release him tomorrow."

"There must be scope for at least granting Jason bail now, surely?"

"If his lawyer petitions for bail, it'll be reviewed, but this is a very serious crime and a foreigner will be regarded as a flight risk. I wouldn't expect bail to be granted."

"I'll suggest the Buckinghams talk to their lawyer."

"It might be worth a try, Nick but, in my position, I'd have to oppose bail."

"I understand. Do we have anything more from the good doctor?"

"She thinks Spíros fell, back first, onto jagged rocks. The impacts suggest he fell ten to twenty metres. Death was probably instantaneous."

"Fell or was pushed?"

"She won't be drawn on that one."

"So, there's nothing to suggest he was pushed."

"No. But then what would you expect? Red handprints on his chest?"

Nick walked over to the window. Large drops of rain had started to fall.

"If only we could see what Spíros saw."

"We'll know what Kristīne saw, in due course. Or at least what she tells us she saw. I'll let you have a copy of Pánagou's report as soon as it comes in, but I've a feeling it won't be so enlightening this time."

"No, but thanks anyway, Leo."

"And now, Nick, you might as well take a break. There's not much more we can do until the Latvians find Kristīne. Both Thaní and I are moving on to other things, for now."

CHAPTER 32

TRACED

The month of October started with strong winds and torrential rain. There were violent thunderstorms in the mountains. Dry gorges hosted rivers again; rivers that would become raging torrents in January and February. The beaches emptied earlier than usual and the seaside resorts were already turning into ghost towns.

Early in the month, Nick received his copy of Pánagou's report but there was nothing new on the body, only on the identification of it. There was an MtDNA match with a single hair found caught in the straw sun hat. Also, dental records traced to Athens confirmed that the body was that of Spíros Tavouláris. Nick called Alexandrákis and broke the news.

"My cousin will be relieved," he said.

"But sad too, surely?"

"He sad all his life for this boy. Now, I think he relieved."

"That *is* sad, Manóli."

Nick tried to get back to renovating his house, but the weather was too bad to work outside so the wall made no progress and he focused on trying to plaster what would become his guest bathroom. But his heart was not in it and his plastering skills were limited. It looked a bloody mess, he decided, and called a plasterer.

Eléni told Stephen and Jen that, in her opinion, there was nothing to be gained by a petition for bail, so the boy's incarceration went on and they started taking it in turns to go back to England, leaving the other to try and deal with Jason's increasing frustration and depression.

Nick thought long and hard about trying to see Jason himself but, after a long chat with Jen, he made the painful decision to hold off, for now. Any reconciliation was going to be difficult for both of them and the best time for that would be if and when Nick could obtain his release, rather than now, with all the uncertainties that lay ahead.

Peter was released, much to Leo's frustration, but they retained his passport and required him to check in at his local police station every week until further notice, despite Staréniou's objections.

At last, over three weeks later, when Nick had almost given up hope, the telephone rang. It was the twenty-seventh of October.

"Nick? It's Leo. They've found her, at last. They got a bite from the second television screening. She was sighted in a town called Kuldīga, some way west of Rīga, and the cops were able to trace her to the home of a former partner there. It seems her sister knew and was lying to the police."

"So, they have her in custody?"

"Yes, but get this: she says she wasn't hiding or running away."

"Yeah, right."

"Listen, Nick. I have a problem. The captain's got me embroiled in another case now. It's sensitive. Corruption. A senior politician seems to be involved. He insists on me remaining focused on that. I don't suppose …"

"You want me to go to Latvia?"

"With Thaní, of course. Would you? Only it needs one of us with him, I think."

"If you're paying my expenses, I'd be happy to."

"Good man. It's just for the questioning. You won't be able to bring her back with you at this stage, whatever happens. Get yourself over here for nine tomorrow morning and we'll talk it through and get you on your way."

*

As the Airbus 321 dropped below the cloud and banked, the Latvian countryside appeared for the first time. It seemed almost miraculously flat after Crete and all the mountains of central Europe they had seen on the way; a grassy, quiet country interlaced by rivers and dotted with small towns, nudging up against the grey Baltic.

They were met at the airport by two local policemen in uniform who rushed them in sleek silence to the large, new police station, a stylish and expensive-looking building in the Āgenskalns district of Rīga, not far from the Daugava River. Nick saw narrow, red-brick columns fronting rows of recessed windows, each one crisscrossed with security mesh in diamond patterns. The overall effect was that of a rather elegant prison.

They were asked to wait in a comfortable, light-filled side room and offered coffee. After a few minutes, a blond-haired man in his mid-thirties wearing plain clothes came in.

"Good afternoon, gentlemen. I am Sergeant Jansons. Welcome to Latvia." They shook hands and, at his invitation, sat down at the table. "We have a room set up for your interview with Kristīne Ozola. She is entitled to have a lawyer and an interpreter present and we will also require a Latvian police presence at all times, although the officer's role will be to observe, rather than participate. In which language will you conduct the interview?"

"In English," said Thaní, to Nick's relief.

"In that case, the defendant has said that an interpreter will not be necessary, so we can avoid a delay. Her lawyer is already present but has requested a few more minutes with her client, so ..." he looked up at the clock on the wall, "might I suggest a three thirty start?"

"That'll be fine," nodded Thaní, glancing at Nick.

"And if we need to continue tomorrow?" asked Nick.

"The room is blocked out for you, so you may continue throughout tomorrow as long as we are satisfied with the defendant's ability to withstand further questioning. There'll be meal and comfort breaks, naturally. There's a subsidised restaurant here that you gentlemen are welcome to use. We will take care of Ms Ozola's needs."

"And we may use our recording device?"

"Yes, of course."

The sergeant got to his feet.

"Help yourselves to more coffee. Someone will direct you to the interview room in a few minutes. Do you need me to find you a hotel for tonight?"

"We're already booked, thanks; The Vecrīga?"

"Sure. That's nice. Just across the river in the old part of the city. Parking is a problem around there but, if you don't have a car, it's a great spot. Make sure you leave yourselves some time to look around while you're here."

"We'll try."

"He thinks we're tourists," said Thaní after the sergeant left the room.

"He's proud of his city, and why not?" said Nick, looking out through the meshed window. "There's a lot of history here."

*

Kristīne looked quite different, Nick thought. The hippy clothes were gone, replaced by a brown leather jacket over a pale, green cotton top that sparkled and designer jeans. She looked cleaner, fresher and fuller in the face and her hair was dyed a little darker.

Her lawyer was young, perhaps not even thirty, but she looked sharp. Her blonde hair was pulled back into a clip and her make-up was immaculate. The dark blue frames of her glasses enhanced her blue-grey eyes. The crisp, white blouse contrasted with the dove grey suit. The chunky, silver and pewter jewellery and the man's chronometer belied her femininity.

She introduced herself as Inga Petersone. A uniformed Latvian policeman closed the door and took up his position, standing between the windows.

"For the avoidance of doubt," the lawyer began, "my client has not been charged with any crime and is here of her own free will. This interview may be terminated at any time she wishes. She is entitled to refuse to answer any question or, indeed, to remain silent. Is that understood?" she said.

Nick and Thaní nodded, reluctantly.

"Very well, you may begin."

Thaní opened proceedings:

"We are here in Latvia to pursue our enquiries into the deaths of Samantha Martin and Spíros Tavouláris in Síva, Crete on or about the sixteenth of September this year."

Kristīne's face registered plausible shock: "Spíros is dead?"

"A body later identified as Mr Tavouláris was found near Síva on the thirtieth of September."

"No, no … God, no." She reached for a tissue and seemed to be crying.

Nick spoke for the first time:

"We'd like you to start by taking us through your movements on the night of Saturday the fifteenth and Sunday the sixteenth of September this year. As you will recall, this was the night that Sam died."

She dabbed her eyes and screwed the tissue into a ball in her right hand.

"Spíros was working at Moondance that night – the beach bar – so, I think I already told you, I was with a couple from a nearby tent, drinking and playing cards until after midnight."

"And then you went to bed?"

"I did, but I couldn't sleep. In the end, I got up and wandered down to the beach bar."

Nick was looking back through his notes.

"You didn't mention that when I interviewed you on the twentieth of September."

"No – perhaps because it proved to be a waste of time?"

"So why did you go there?"

"I thought I'd meet up with Spíros when he finished his shift."

"Why did you want to do that?"

"There was something I needed to tell him."

"Was this about your pregnancy?"

She took up the tissue again, sniffed and nodded.

"Answer for the recording, please."

"Yes. I wanted to tell him he was going to be a father."

"And did you?"

"No," she said in a very small voice.

"How come?"

"I was too early, so I waited for him to finish. It was cosy near the fire and I was really tired. I just fell asleep. The bar owner woke me but, by then, Spíros had left."

"So, what did you do?"

"I tried to follow him along the beach, but I couldn't see him so, after a while, I gave up and went back to the tent."

"What time would that have been?"

"Two forty, two forty-five, I guess."

"And did you find Spíros in the tent?"

"No. He didn't come back till later. I don't know what time, but he was there in the morning."

"And did you tell him then – about the baby?"

"No. We slept a bit late and then everything was going crazy because Sam's body had been discovered."

"And did you wonder then where he'd been and if he was somehow involved in her death?"

"No. Of course, not. We were told that she drowned."

"But you must have asked him where he'd been?"

"No, because he was very upset. He was sobbing uncontrollably. I thought he was having a breakdown. This went on for ages, then finally I twigged. Sam meant far more to him than she should have."

"Or he was responsible for her death?"

"I didn't think of that."

"You didn't think of that. Really?" Nick stood up and started pacing around the room. "Your partner disappears in the middle of the night for God knows how long and, in the morning, an attractive young girl from the tent next to yours is found dead, not six hundred metres away. He is then distraught, inconsolable for hours, but it never crosses your mind that he might have been involved in her death, somehow?"

"No. As I said, we thought she'd drowned. Why would I think someone else was involved? What *actually* crossed my mind was that the little bitch might have seduced my boy and he'd fallen for her. That would explain why he was grieving so hard. So, later that day, I asked him straight out: 'Did you and Sam have an affair?'

"In the end, he admitted it. As I told Mr Fisher, they'd done it in my tent while Jason was out walking, and I was swimming with friends.

I was livid with anger and embarrassment. It was a horrid, deceitful thing to do. And half the bloody campsite must have known. As you know, in the end, I told him to just go. He pleaded with me, but I was adamant. He'd broken what was left of our trust and I was finished with him. He told me he'd take the ferry to Palaióchora. I think he told me that in case I should change my mind."

"And did he?"

"Go to Palaióchora? I assumed so."

"And then what happened?"

"Life went on, as it always does. The police interviewed me at the campsite. You questioned me, Mr Fisher. The police questioned me again at the hotel. It turned out Sam had been murdered.

"But, towards the end of the second week, things seemed to be dying down and I'm softening a bit on Spíros. He's been a real shit to me but, to be honest, I miss him and he's the father of my baby, after all, so in the end I decide to go looking for him."

"Where did you go?"

"To Palaióchora, of course."

"On the ferry?"

"Yes."

"But you didn't find him."

"No. I went to all our usual haunts. I asked a lot of people, but he wasn't there. It didn't seem like he'd ever been there."

"Where did you stay?"

"I used my tent. Just set it up on the beach. Later the next day, I was wondering what to try next, when I get a call from my sister about Uldis."

"Uldis?"

"This is the guy I've been staying with, in Kuldīga. We used to be partners, years ago, and now we're still good friends but he's ill, poor guy. He's been fighting bowel cancer for several years and Alise, that's my sister, tells me that it has spread to his liver now and it's terminal. They told him he had between two and six months to live. He's only forty-four." She took out the tissue again, dabbed her eyes and wiped her nose. "So, I go to Uldis to be with him before it is too late."

"Your loyalty is touching but you agreed to keep us informed of your whereabouts," said Thaní.

"That's true. I should have let you know. But, to be honest, the enquiries seemed to have died down and I couldn't see what more I could tell you, anyway."

"You committed to keep us informed. It was not for you to decide that it was no longer necessary."

"My client has apologised, Sergeant. There is no need to labour the point."

"So, you've been in the country for a month now," Nick continued. "Have you spoken to your parents in that time?"

"No. I guess that might sound a little strange, but you know what families are. They'd expect me to be with them, to stay with them. I'm here to be with Uldis so it's better they don't know. I was planning to see them for a few days before I went back."

"I see." Nick nodded, stroking his chin. "But your sister – Alise? – she does know you are here. She arranged it with you."

"She told me about Uldis. I arranged the trip."

"But she knows you're here."

"Yes."

"Did you ask her to lie to the police?"

"No. Not at all. She just panicked when she heard it was the *Greek* police who wanted to talk to me and lied; said she'd never heard from me. She even told my parents the same lie, after the police spoke to *them*. Very protective, my sister."

"So, she would have called you after that, to tell you what she'd done and to warn you?"

"My client declines to answer," said the lawyer.

"I'll take that as a *yes*, then. So why didn't you contact the Latvian police when you heard they were looking for you?"

"My client declines to answer."

"All right. Let's take a short break," said Thaní, turning to the Latvian officer who nodded and then opened the door to the corridor where there were restrooms and a coffee machine.

Nick went to a far corner right away and made a phone call. As he walked back, he was signing off:

"Yes, send it now and get both images to my phone please, soon as you can."

"What do you think?" Thaní asked Nick when the women were out of sight.

"I think it's all lies, Thaní, other than the unfortunate Uldis, perhaps. You can't fake terminal cancer, but her decision to go to him was more about hiding herself than being at his side for his final weeks on the planet. The poor guy may not even know he's being used. I expect he was touched by the generosity of her gesture; hadn't realised how much she still cared for him." Nick raised his eyebrows and twisted his mouth to show deep scepticism.

"Or maybe he agreed to hide her. He doesn't have much to lose, after all."

"Yep. That's possible too. Either way, I'm sure she *has* been hiding from us. Why else would the sister lie to the police? I don't buy the idea that she did that *just in case*. People don't lie to the police *just in case* their sibling might prefer that. They do it, against their better judgment, because they've been begged to do so by someone they care about. No, that part was all nonsense, and now we're going to pull the rest of her story apart, bit by bit."

"I'm not so sure," said Thaní. "She seems quite convincing to me. I was toying with the idea that perhaps Spíros killed Sam and then, instead of going to Palaióchora, he went back to the murder scene the next evening and somehow ended up dead."

"Well, we know that both Jason and Peter were gone by then so I'm not sure who else would want to kill Spíros. Or are you suggesting suicide? By jumping backwards onto the rocks? There must be easier ways, Thaní."

"There could have been an accident, couldn't there? It would explain why Kristīne thought he'd left when he hadn't."

"But what about his belongings? If she thought he'd left, he must have taken all his stuff. He'd have had a bag, clothes, money, passport with him and he'd have been wearing something other than just swimming shorts. Why wasn't any of that found on the beach or in the water?"

"Where is all that stuff, anyway?"

"She destroyed it, Thaní. After his death, she destroyed it all to support her story that he had left."

At that point, the women emerged from the restrooms, grabbed a drink from the machine and went back to the interview room. The men followed them back in. Nick's phone beeped and he took a few seconds to check it. Then, when everyone was settled, he resumed:

"I'd like to take us back to the beach bar that night. While you were waiting for Spíros to finish his shift, you told us you were near the fire. Could you describe that in more detail for us?"

"How do you mean?"

"Where were you, in relation to the fire?"

"It was to my right, I guess six or seven metres away."

"And was anyone else there?"

"Yes, there were three or four kids around the fire, much closer to it than me."

"Kids?"

"Well, students perhaps, that sort of age. One had a guitar, I remember."

"And you said you were early. What time of night was it?"

"I was early, relative to the end of Spíros's shift, but it was quite late; around one thirty am, I think."

Nick located the enhanced photo on his phone and placed the phone on the table, facing them.

"This photograph was taken by Manólis Alexandrákis, the owner of the Moondance beach bar at one thirty-six am. From the description you gave, this has to be you then, doesn't it?"

"That could be almost anyone, Mr Fisher," said Inga Petersone.

"It's not a perfect shot by any means, but this person is about six metres from the fire, there are three youngsters around the fire, there's the guitar you mentioned and it's just after half-past one. It *has* to be you, Kristīne."

269

"We cannot be sure," said the lawyer.

"I think we can," said Nick, "and I'll tell you why. You'd agree that this person is wearing a hat of some kind?"

They shrugged.

"Well they are. And can you see a flash of light coming from the hat?"

"Or a fault in the print."

"No. That's the camera flash bouncing off the metal badge. The Che Guevara badge attached to *your* maroon beret, Kristīne. That's what you were wearing and that's what we're looking at."

"It's very hard to tell what we are looking at, Mr Fisher."

"But you can confirm that you own such a beret, Kristīne?"

"My client will not confirm or deny any such thing until we see where this line of questioning is leading."

Nick took back his phone, brought up a second image and turned the phone around again.

"This is a photograph of the same beret. It's now with the Greek police and forms part of the evidence collected at the scene of the crime. It was found in the water by police officers on the day Samantha Martin's body was discovered. It was only fifteen metres from the body."

"My client has not admitted to owning such a beret."

"Nevertheless, Ms Petersone, we have a witness who will testify to having seen Kristīne wearing *exactly* such a beret many times in the recent past and, by her own precise description of her whereabouts, that must be her, wearing it in the previous photograph. The presence of the beret at the crime scene places your client there that night, between two thirty and nine fifteen am when the Palaióchora police secured the crime scene."

"We will dispute that."

"No doubt, but I think the court will find our evidence compelling. I've also requested an examination of the beret for traces of your client's DNA."

Nick glanced at Thaní, who nodded in encouragement. Then he watched Kristīne's face over the lip of the cup as he took a sip of coffee. She looked bewildered, rattled even.

270

"Now I'd like us to reflect on the lies you told us this afternoon, Kristīne. Firstly, you told us you gave up on following Spíros along the beach that night, but you didn't, did you? I think you followed him right to the end of the beach. And when you got there, you found both Spíros and Sam.

"We have several witnesses who can place Sam there at that time and, as you know, that's where her body was found the next morning. We have a witness who saw Spíros walking in that direction at around two thirty am and we found Spíros's body nearby two weeks later. And now the beret places you there, Kristīne. So, it was the three of you, late at night on a remote beach, was it not?"

"My client will not comment on conjecture."

"Secondly, you lied about Spíros returning to the tent. He never made it back, did he? Because he died that night, near where Sam died. You were the sole survivor of that encounter. Thirdly, you lied about him admitting his affair with Sam the next day. Not only was he already dead and so not in a condition to admit anything, but also, he didn't need to tell you something you already knew. It was the talk of the campsite, wasn't it, how Sam and Spíros had *got it on* in your tent when Jason and you were not there?"

"No, that's not true," said Kristīne. "I didn't know and neither did Jason."

"Oh, come on, Kristīne! You're not stupid. You must have seen him lusting after that gorgeous, little blonde over twenty years younger than you and you must have overheard the campsite gossip after what happened on the Thursday afternoon."

"All right. I admit I was a bit worried. People seemed to be avoiding my eyes. I thought something may have happened."

"A bit worried? Yes, just a bit." Nick consulted his notes for a second. "Your fourth lie was about dispatching the unfaithful Spíros the next day and him saying he would take the ferry to Palaióchora. And yet we found no-one who remembers seeing Spíros after he left the beach bar early that Sunday morning. No-one at all. No-one in Síva. No-one in Palaióchora. A nice bit of local colour that story, but all utter nonsense. He was lying dead in that bay and you knew it."

Kristīne found another tissue and the tears seemed real enough this time.

"The next few days, you're quite clever. You dispose of all Spíros's belongings to support the story of his departure. He won't need them anymore, that's for sure. You must be deeply upset by the events of early Sunday, but you manage to file it away somewhere deep inside and assume your normal persona. When you're interviewed by me and then by Christodoulákis, you give bravura performances as the nonchalant, insolent, hippy chick whose casual relationship has gone awry. No big deal.

"But it *was* a big deal. The reality was that your feelings were anything but casual. You loved this man, body and soul. You wanted a future with him, and you wanted a child with him. You didn't mention your pregnancy to us at the time because it didn't fit well with the role you were playing. A baby is too serious a thing for the easy come, easy go attitude you were trying to convey.

"But, despite these skilled performances, over the next week or so you are haunted by guilt and doubt and fear of discovery. You're like Lady Macbeth and her damned spot of blood. It seems as if the police are pursuing other leads, but will they come back for you? How long will the lie about Spíros going to Palaióchora hold up? The police are out there looking for him. And what about Spíros's body? My guess is that you don't know where it is. Will it just wash up on the beach one day soon?

"You can't decide whether to stay and try to bluff things out or run. After a while, you can't stand it anymore and you run. You've sworn to keep the Greek police informed of your whereabouts but that slips your mind. You tell Alexandrákis that you are following Spíros to Palaióchora, but you don't, of course. Instead, you make your way to one of the ferry ports, probably Chaniá, and you take the overnight ferry to Piraeus so you can fly from Athens rather than Crete.

"You're trying to keep below the radar – avoid detection – and that's why you fly Athens-St Petersburg and then double-back rather than direct to Rīga and why, when you get to Latvia, you don't stay with your family but with an old friend from years ago that the police don't know about, in a town that *no-one* knows about. These are not the actions of an innocent person, Kristīne. Why did you hide? Why did you get your sister to lie for you?"

When Nick stopped, there was a silence punctuated only by sniffs from Kristīne. He finished the rest of his cold coffee. Then the lawyer spoke.

"You've thrown a lot at us, gentlemen. I'd like to suggest a fifteen-minute break so that I can consult with my client."

The Latvian officer must have understood because he came over and said, "There is another room, gentlemen, if you'd care to follow me."

*

Fifteen minutes later, on the dot, they were back.

"My client prefers to remain silent at this stage, gentlemen, as is her right. Her silence does not imply that she accepts any of the points you made."

"Very well," said Thaní.

Nick stood up and went to the window and the Latvian officer moved across to give him some space. He went on:

"So, there you are, the three of you coming together somehow at the end of the beach. It's three in the morning and everyone else has gone back. You followed Spíros to tell him about the baby but you're also being eaten up inside, worrying about him and Sam. Did they have sex? Was it more than that, even? Could it be love? Would Spíros have been unfaithful if he'd known you were carrying his child?

"That's eating you up, too. You should have told him before, but you were scared, weren't you? Scared of how he'd react to the news. And now you're desperate for him to know and to keep him with you, to have a father for your baby. And you're desperate to keep *them* apart lest a physical attraction should become something more; something that takes him away from you. You can't allow that to happen, can you Kristīne?

"He's twelve years younger; just twenty-nine years old, with a history as a serious drug user and a reputation for unreliability. Why would a man like that tie himself to a forty-one-year-old having a baby, with all the commitment and responsibility that goes with that? Of course, you were worried about how he'd react.

"And then along comes Sam. She's pretty and sexy and she's twenty years old. Less than half your age. And one day she seduces him, just because she feels like it. 'The little bitch,' I think you called her.

"Now the baby you longed for is coming but you're not sure *he* wants it. You're not even sure he wants *you*. You're so vulnerable, aren't you Kristīne? You're vulnerable and you're scared. This is what you're thinking as you follow Spíros along that beach, isn't it? And then you get to the end of the beach and you see something. Tell us what you see."

There was a choking, spluttering sound and Kristīne seemed to be about to speak but the lawyer placed a hand on her forearm and all that happened was that another tissue joined the growing ball pressed to her face.

"I'll tell you what *I* think. I think you saw the worst thing you could imagine. Your worst nightmare. They are together. Maybe they're even having sex. Making love. Lost in each other's bodies. Laughing together. Laughing at you.

"Because you're *out*, aren't you, Kristīne? Excluded Kristīne. Forgotten Kristīne. Pregnant Kristīne. Old, abandoned Kristīne."

A suppressed wail broke forth from behind the tissues, but Nick drove on, not pausing for a second.

"Something inside you snaps. How dare she? How dare she, *the little bitch*?"

Nick had been standing in front of the table, right in front of Kristīne, staring at her as he spoke, but now he backed off a little and adopted a softer tone.

"The Greeks see us Northern Europeans as a self-controlled lot; inhibited, aloof, cool even. But most of us are not like that at all, are we Kristīne? Not underneath. The control hides passions that run deep. All of us here can understand how a passionate woman carrying a longed-for child would be horrified and enraged to see a careless, young girl stealing away the father of that child. The man she loves.

"We could understand a violent reaction, even violence that could lead to the death of that girl, whether accidental or intentional. We might not be able to *forgive* murder, but we could understand it, see the circumstances that led to it. Our judgment of the killer would be less harsh as a result."

He paused and drew closer again. His voice grew deeper, almost sorrowful:

"But to kill Spíros? To murder the man she loves? To deprive her unborn child of its father? To push him savagely off the cliff to fall back through the air and dash his brains on the rocks far below ..."

"NAOOoo!" Kristīne's scream of anguish sounded like a wounded animal, the jaws of a trap tearing into its flesh. She was fighting to shrug off the cautioning arm of her lawyer. "No, no, no! It was Sam! Sam pushed him."

"Why on earth would she do that?"

"I can see now that maybe she didn't mean to, but she was crazy reckless. Sam and I were fighting. We were getting too near the edge. I loosened my grip on her for a moment and she went to head-butt me. Spíros got himself in the way somehow. He saved me. And then ..."

The room was silent apart from the soft patter of raindrops on the window and the muffled sobs from Kristīne. Nick waited a full minute before speaking again. Then his voice was soft and clear, almost gentle:

"We have a report from the Medical Examiner on the death of Samantha Martin. It's conclusive: she was murdered; a single blow to the head caused by a blunt instrument, probably a smooth rock. Just three people were at the scene of the crime after about two fifty am that night: Sam, Spíros and you, Kristīne.

"If, as you say, Sam was responsible for Spíros's death, then you, Kristīne, *must* have been responsible for Sam's murder. There was no-one else. You've borne the weight of this for a long time now. All alone. That must have been tough. Now, it's time to free yourself from that burden. When you're ready, take your time and tell us exactly what happened."

"It's ten minutes to seven, Mr Fisher. My client is distressed, and we

275

are all tired. I suggest we break for the evening. I can discuss things further with Kristīne and then we can meet again in the morning."

"All right, Ms Petersone. We can live with that. Shall we say back here at nine thirty am?"

After the others left, Nick and Thaní spent twenty minutes updating Leo, after which Sergeant Jansons appeared.

"It's been a long day, gentlemen. I am guessing that you're ready for a beer?"

"That," said Nick, "is music to my ears, Sergeant."

*

They walked across the spectacular, single-strut, suspension bridge over the Daugava into the old part of the city. Narrow, cobbled streets led to fine, open squares. Many of the buildings were painted bold colours: deep reds, pastel oranges or blues, yellows and pinks. Straight lines were softened by curves and arches, campanile featured magnificent spires. The bells of Saint Peter's pealed in celebration as if announcing the return of Christ.

"It's a beautiful city," said Thaní. "I didn't know."

"Thank you," said Jansons, eyes shining. "We have quite a few tourists now, so I think the word is beginning to get around."

He was holding a door open for them and they found themselves facing a long bar in pale wood with a row of matching stools.

"The craft beer in Rīga is good," said Jansons.

He stayed with them for two beers but finished his second in a hurry.

"And so, gentlemen, I will take my leave. I am sure you want to relax now, maybe talk about the case. So, you can eat here if you like. It's okay, but I've taken the precaution of booking a table for you at one of my favourite restaurants. It's just around the corner on Skārņu Street, right by the church. It's a small place, so you have to book. They have tasty food, well presented. It's very friendly and not expensive. How does that sound?"

Nick and Thaní were nodding and grinning. He handed Nick a note with the name and address of the restaurant and a little map.

"The table is booked for eight thirty in the name of Fisher, so you still have twenty minutes to enjoy your beers."

*

The restaurant was down a cobbled street between two enormous churches. There was some outdoor seating bordered by plants in wooden boxes. Inside, it was small, modern and comfortable. They ordered mussels followed by oven-roasted Arctic fillet with green peas and a butter sauce. Maybe they would stretch to the cherry cheesecake later. Nick found the wine list printed on a bottle. They had done well today. It was time to ratchet up some expenses.

CHAPTER 33

COMPROMISE

Over breakfast the next morning, Nick took a call from Leo.

"I have good news, DCI Fisher."

"What have you got, Leo?"

"We sent the beret for DNA testing as you suggested and, even after twelve hours underwater, they were able to find some hairs, but without the ends – the follicles I think you call them – so they were only able to do a *mitochondrial* DNA test. You understand this?"

"Yes, I think so."

"Well the MtDNA confirms that the hat was worn by someone from the same maternal line as Kristīne."

"Meaning it's her hat."

"Meaning she or a sibling must have worn it."

"Her only sibling is her sister Alise who lives in Latvia, so it's got to be hers."

"Yes, Nick, there's an excellent chance that it is. Go get her."

*

At nine thirty prompt, Inga Petersone appeared, but without her client.

"Where is Ms Ozola?" asked Thanī.

"She is waiting at the hotel. Don't worry. I want to speak with you gentlemen alone, to begin with. I'd like to explore something with you, off the record."

"Okay," said Thanī, warily.

"If you were to charge Kristīne ..."

"As we will," cut in Nick. "We now have a DNA match on the beret in addition to our witness. That proves beyond any reasonable doubt that it was worn by Kristīne."

"As I was saying, if you were to charge her, what would you charge her with?"

"Murder – no question," said Thaní. "It might be difficult to prove premeditation, so we'd go for second-degree murder."

"And *we* would argue that the circumstances in which she found herself led to the balance of her mind being disturbed. That, if she did hit Sam, it amounted to a crime of passion. There'd be a serious risk for you that the judges and jurors would empathise with her predicament and find her not guilty of murder."

"My understanding of a crime of passion is that it only applies if the defendant lashes out as an *immediate* response to a situation; an almost involuntary, primeval, violent response. Given that Spíros fell from the back of the big rock and Sam was found on the edge of the beach, one hundred and seventy metres away, how could you justify that?

"Even if it were an immediate pursuit, it would have taken *several minutes* for them to cover that distance over and down the rock and across the shallows to the beach. Several minutes for that blinding passion to dissipate. Several minutes for common sense to resurface and a more moderate response to prevail."

"I think your timing is adrift, Mr Fisher. Something between one and two minutes seems more plausible. In any event, we would argue that this wild, young woman crushed my client's hopes before her very eyes.

"She had already seduced Spíros on the Thursday afternoon, my client believes. She has sex with him again late on the night of the murder – an act my client is obliged to observe – and then, whilst attempting to murder my client, through unforgivable recklessness she kills Spíro Tavoulári instead, and in the most horrible of ways.

"Kristīne watches him fall and she sees him hit the rocks. This was the man she loved, the man who was the father of her unborn child. Of course, there was a blinding, passionate fury that would have carried her through whatever brief period there was before she could stop Sam in her tracks."

"You're careful to avoid the word *kill*, I notice, but there's no doubt she intended to kill Sam. Whoever found that rock and then hit her as hard as they could – and *then* sat on her shoulders and pushed her face into the shingle was doing more than *stopping her in her tracks.* They wanted her dead. No question about it."

"But is there such a thing as *intention* when you are blinded by passion, Mr Fisher? My point is that any prosecution for second-degree murder carries a high risk of failure for you. The judges and jurors will see how deeply my client was wronged. They will feel her horror, her rage. They will likely conclude that a passionate fury blinded her to her actions; she didn't know *what* she was doing. They would be unwilling to convict a pregnant woman in such circumstances."

"I feel that you have an alternative proposal, Ms Petersone," said Thaní, "but you must be aware that the Greek system has no provision for plea bargaining."

"I'm aware of that, Sergeant, and I'm not offering *nolo contendere* as such. But I am here to offer your public prosecutor a choice. Either continue to push for murder two, in which case I must advise my client to remain silent in further interrogations and to plead not guilty at trial or elect to pursue the lesser charge of voluntary manslaughter.

"If you choose the latter course, I will encourage my client to be open with you now, and to plead guilty to such a charge at trial while at the same time filing a request for the application of mitigating circumstances."

"Are we talking about a confession?"

"We'll have to see what she says, but yes, I think it could amount to that."

"We'll need to consult with my superior, the investigating judge and perhaps the public prosecutor on this, Ms Petersone. Might I suggest you return to the hotel and wait for me to call?"

"I will. Thank you, Sergeant."

"I'm going to ask Sergeant Jansons to send a constable with you to guard Ms Ozola. I don't want to elevate these issues only to find that she's absconded again."

"If you feel you must."

*

Later, when they called in, Leo was upbeat:

"You've found Sam's killer, gentlemen. Fantastic. Well done!"

"So it seems, but manslaughter?"

"It's not ideal. She might get a sentence of a few years, but her lawyer will push for that to be a *suspended* sentence. And there's a precedent for that, here in Crete."

"Couldn't we go for more, stick with murder two?"

"We could, but we have quite a thin case, Nick. We have no murder weapon and no witnesses. The only thing that puts her on the scene is that damned beret. We can prove it's hers now, but we can't prove *when* she lost it. Suppose the defence comes up with the idea that she lost it a day or two earlier? Sure, her behaviour after Spíros's death supports the idea that she's guilty, but we don't have a witness who saw her burn his clothes, for example.

"She might be able to convince them that she truly thought Spíros went to Palaióchora and that she did follow him there. And suppose she took the Piraeus ferry because there were no seats on direct flights from Crete? Perhaps the Athína-Rīga flight was full and that's why it made sense to go via Russia? Suppose she can *prove* that her sister made that call about Uldis and that he *does* have terminal cancer?

"The defence could introduce enough doubt to undermine our position. And with her sitting there looking sad, lonely and pregnant …There has to be a risk that our case would be dismissed for insufficient evidence.

"Also, ask yourselves what is a fair outcome here? What would be gained by jailing this hapless woman with no history of violence for fifteen years, for example? The kid would go into care, get a chip on his or her shoulder, come out and maybe kill someone! Listen, guys. You've done a great job. You've found the killer. We can arrange for Jason to be released now. Don't get hung up on the legal aspects. Okay?"

"Yes, okay boss," said Thaní.

"And Nick?"

"I don't see how this differs from a plea bargain, Leo, and I think plea bargains stink. Innocent people are persuaded to plead guilty to lesser crimes *that they didn't even commit* because the risk of being found guilty of something more serious is so frightening. Or, as we have here, perpetrators can face lesser crimes if they plead guilty – and for what? So the system can score an easy victory, clear the backlog. But then they're getting away with a much lighter sentence – often too light to bring any kind of justice for the victims' families. I don't know how we got here, frankly."

"I hear you, Nick. And it often stinks, I agree. But, in this case, I think it's a reasonable outcome for all parties."

"Including Helen and Michael Martin?"

"Yes, truly I think so. We've found who killed their daughter. If Kristīne is found guilty of manslaughter, then we'll have brought them some kind of closure; a chance to move on. Anyway, gentlemen, it's my decision and I intend to recommend Ms Petersone's suggestion. I will speak to the investigating judge and get back to you."

The line went dead.

*

It took only two hours for the call to come through. Both the investigating judge and the public prosecutor accepted Leo's recommendation and a short document was prepared and sent to Inga Petersone. Nick and Thaní were to wrap things up today with a final interview that, with luck, would amount to a confession to manslaughter. In the meantime, Leo was in touch with senior police in Latvia and would be applying for a European Arrest Warrant to bring Kristīne back to Crete for trial.

"It's not everything we wanted, but it's clear, at least," said Nick.

"It's okay," responded Thaní. "We did our job, Nick. They did theirs. And it's quite a fair result, I think, depending on what happens in court."

*

The interview recommenced at one thirty pm in the same room as before. Kristīne was looking a little more composed.

"I want us to go through it one more time, Kristīne. And this time,

282

we leave nothing out. Understood? Can we start from when you decided to meet Spíros at the end of his shift at Moondance, please?"

There was a long pause. Across the river, cathedral bells belatedly chimed the half-hour. Pigeons flapped over scraps outside the mesh-covered window. Kristíne seemed to be examining her fingernails. Nick was on the point of intervening when she finally lifted her head and started to speak:

"Sometimes, I thought his face would light up at the news of the baby and he'd hug me close and tell me he couldn't be happier, that he loved me and wanted to stay with me forever. All Greeks seem to adore kids, after all.

"But then, at other times, I imagined him being shocked, feeling trapped and looking for a way out. Maybe he'd even think I'd set out to trap him, like some desperate, old spinster.

"At the worst times, I imagined him telling me he was sorry, but he was in love with Sam now. They'd slept together and now they wanted to be together always, baby or no baby.

"This stuff was all going round my head, driving me crazy. I hadn't slept properly for weeks and I wasn't sleeping that night, so I checked my watch. It was one fifteen am. Spíros's shift at the beach bar would end soon after two. I decided to wander down there to meet him as he finished work for the night.

"I'd walk him to our favourite spot on the beach. We'd sit down, maybe share a joint, and then I'd hold his hands and look into his eyes and tell him, gently, that he was going to be a father. He'd be happy – of course he would – and everything would be cool and then I could stop worrying and we could start planning for the baby.

"I remember, I dressed in my Turkish silk trousers and a dark green top and wrapped a shawl around my shoulders. Then I checked my face in the mirror and put on my favourite earrings and the beret that Spíros gave me, tucking my hair under it.

"I knew that made me look younger, more vulnerable, somehow. Then I made sure that the badge was in the middle, as it should be.

"I used a little dark red lipstick to match the beret and smiled at myself. I was looking good. Maybe it was the bloom of motherhood. In that light, I didn't look much over thirty.

"To avoid waking anyone, I carried my flip-flops until I was well away from the tent. When I arrived at the beach bar, it was just coming up to one thirty, so I sat quietly, not far from the fire. I couldn't see Spíros, but he'd be around somewhere. I'd wait.

"I felt a great calm now and it was cosy. I could hear some people murmuring around the fire, music throbbing gently from the bar, the sea toying with the shingle. I felt part of things but on the outside, you know? That's just where I like to be; anonymous but not lost. Everything felt good. It was going to be all right. After a few minutes, I put a hand on my womb and laid my head on the shingle.

"It was Manólis who woke me up. I heard him coughing up phlegm in that disgusting way of his and then he poured water on the fire and it hissed and smoked. He was surprised to find me there. Everyone else had gone, including Spíros. I remember him saying something like: 'Your boy was shit-hot tonight. He finish already.' Then he told me Spíros had gone off, up the beach, about five minutes before. 'Wasn't he heading back to the tent, then?' I asked.

"He said: 'It's not the route he takes most days, but who knows?' But there was something about the way he said it. I thought he was either covering for Spíros or trying to protect me. I didn't know which.

"Then he started encouraging me to go back to my tent and that just made me more suspicious. I decided to follow Spíros down the beach. I'd gone there to tell him about the baby and I still hoped to. I'd waited far too long and now I was desperate for him to know.

"I couldn't see him ahead, but something told me he was there. There were blasts of wind now and the sea was dragging the pebbles but, in between, I thought I could just catch the crunch of his shoes on the shingle. I didn't try to catch up. I was struggling in the flip-flops anyway, but also, as I walked, I could feel this strange, fascinating neurosis forming in my mind.

"What the hell was he doing? Why was he here? Was he doing something secret, something criminal maybe? I knew he dabbled in dealing soft drugs so maybe this was something to do with that. Or was he cheating on me, meeting someone else? Whatever it was, I felt a weird thrill but also a deep sense of foreboding, dread almost."

"Did you see anyone else as you walked down the beach?"

"Yes. I remember a group of three or four people coming towards me. I was going to ask them if they'd passed Spíros but then they veered off to the campsite before I got close enough."

"Did you see anyone else, before you saw them?"

"No, I don't think so."

"Okay. Please go on, Kristīne."

"Near the end of the first beach, where it narrows before the rocks, something caught my feet. It was Spíros's shorts and top, weighed down by his espadrilles and a small rock. I realised he must be in the water. Then I heard someone cry out.

"The moon came out from behind a cloud and I could see someone in the water, but it wasn't Spíros. The swimmer was just about to go round the back of the big rock. That was where the cry had come from, I thought. And then I saw him.

"He was right on the top of the big rock and moving swiftly across the flat bit, away from me. I thought about calling out, but something stopped me. He soon disappeared from view, as did the swimmer. I decided to wait and watch.

"I remembered Spíros warning me that it could be dangerous out there when the wind blows from the south. The rocks on that side are jagged and razor-sharp and there's also a hidden current, below the surface.

"He used to play there as a kid, he told me once. A bunch of them would dare each other to leap off a ledge, about eight metres above the water. It had to be a good, strong leap to make sure you got clear of these lethal rocks. And he must have been bullied, I think. These macho, bloody Greeks. He was only about ten, poor little sod.

"Anyway, this one time, he was petrified, hesitated and made a poor leap, more of a back-sliding jump. He missed the rocks by a whisker and then went deep without taking a proper breath. And then the current took him. He was halfway across the bay before he made it back to the surface. One of the other boys helped him then, but he very nearly drowned.

"If it *was* Spíros and he was climbing down the other side of that rock, in the dark, to try and help someone, I knew he'd have to pass that ledge. His nemesis. He'd remember and be terrified again. My heart went out to him. And, even without that fear, it was just such a dangerous thing to do, at night. I was scared.

"With the wind now, it's difficult, but I think I hear the swimmer cry out twice more and then I hear a man's voice, calling out to her. But all this is happening on the other side of the rock. I wait several minutes. The wind's making my eyes weary but I'm hard-wired to the view.

"And then, at last, I see him again. He must have climbed the back of the rock and now I see him reach down and lift someone up. It's a woman and I see that she's limping. I run forward a few steps and stare. I'm horrified and fascinated at the same time. Her hair's dark but then it must be wet.

"The woman's wearing no top and her breasts reflect the moonlight for a second before she sits down abruptly and lies on her back. It's Sam, I'm sure it is. And that's Spíros. Something in the way he kneels is unmistakable. He's cradling her foot in his hands. Now she's propped on one elbow, saying something to him. Her hand is tracing down her body to her bikini bottoms. And then suddenly he's on top of her.

"'No, no, NO,' I cry, and I start sprinting towards them, water splashing as I run through the shallows. My heart's heaving with fear and frustration. I'm thinking: *This can't happen. I can't let this happen.* I reach the big rock. I've never climbed it before, but desperation drives me up it without thinking. I cut my hands, I slip, I graze my knee, but I scramble on and, within two or three minutes, I'm hauling myself up onto the flat top.

"And then I see them, and I stop dead. Sam's facing away from me, the blue butterfly on her moonlit skin is rising and falling, rising and falling, as she eases herself up and down, up and down on his glistening cock. His knees are a little off the ground, brushing the sides of her bottom. His head must be between her breasts.

"For a moment, I stand there aghast. I'm too late and, for a few moments, I feel excluded: the lonely voyeur. Guilty, even, of intruding on their intimacy. But then the rumour-mongers crowd back into my head, cackling behind their hands and pointing. I feel the angry shame of the cuckold, the hot bitterness from being so callously deceived and, above all, I remember the baby. The blood's rushing in my ears now. How dare she? How dare this bitch try to steal my baby's father? And suddenly I'm running towards them, arms wide like some crazed, avenging angel.

"'NO! You get *off* him, you bitch. You *fucking* bitch!'

"I see Sam turn her head in alarm before crudely extricating herself and struggling to her feet. But I'm on her. I catch her hair and then go straight for her neck with the other hand. Sam's trying to push me off, batting her arms. I see Spíros getting to his feet, slipping on his swimming shorts. I'm stronger than Sam and catch her unawares. We're locked in wrestlers' grips now, stumbling across the rock.

"'Stop!' yells Spíros. 'You're too near the edge.'

"'Get her off me!' screams Sam and then starts choking as my grip tightens. We're perilously close to the edge now. Spíros tries to intervene, tries to force us apart, push us away from the edge. He yells: 'For God's sake, stop. This is far too dangerous!'

"I stop to look behind me and loosen my grip for a second. Sam sees an opportunity and the treacherous bitch goes to ram me with her head but Spíros sees the risk and pushes me to the left, away from the edge. But that just brings Sam's remaining momentum into him.

"Her head hits his stomach, hard. She stops then, but it's already too late. Spíros is slipping on the scree, arms flailing. For a second, he stares at us as if struggling to recall something, then a wave of confusion and horror sweeps his face as he topples backwards ...

"And there's this hollow silence as he falls, still staring up at us, wide-eyed in disbelief. Two or three seconds of ghastly, suspended animation before the sickening crunch as his head hits the rock pinnacles below. There's something dreadfully final about that sound. Like a pick-axe through a coconut.

"We lean over, and I scream his name and then we both scream his name together, but the sea just washes against his broken body, lifting it slightly, as the wind whips around the rock. He's staring at the moon but he isn't blinking."

"And then what happened?"

"I said, 'Oh God, have we killed him?' or something like that, and I remember Sam looking over the cliff and saying: 'Oh, he's dead all right.'

"I think that's all she said but I looked at her then. It sounded so heartless, somehow. She'd been making love to him five minutes before, making love to *my* man and now his brains were spattered over the rocks fifteen metres below and yet she seemed to have no feeling for what had happened. No remorse. And, worst of all, no sense of guilt.

"She must have seen something in my eyes because she turns and starts running. I feel the rage boil up in me. This bitch has stolen my man's love, my baby's daddy and now she's taken his life, too, and she doesn't seem to care about any of it.

"I run after her and then we're clambering down the front of the rock. I jump the last three metres into the water, right behind her, and she turns to look at me in horror and then we're splashing our way across the shallows. She's limping and shrieking: 'Get away from me, you evil old witch.'

"I don't even remember picking up the rock but then I feel it in my hand, round and smooth and heavy. Just before she reaches the beach, I grab her left hand and bring the rock down on the back of her head, as hard as I can. She slumps forward and I jump on her shoulders, force her face down into the shingle but she's not resisting.

"I sit there for a long while. I know she's dead. I realise what I've done, and I'm shocked at myself and afraid of what's to come but I'm not regretting it. I was out of control, but it still felt right. Like I'd been God's instrument, almost. To atone for Spíros, to punish her for everything she destroyed. She was so casual. So thoughtless. It was alien to me. Inhuman."

She looked up at them, searching their eyes for understanding.

"Go on, Kristīne," said Nick gently. She took a sip of water and continued:

"After a few minutes, I got up and threw the rock way out to sea, as far as I could. I thought about moving her body, but I didn't think I was strong enough and I didn't know what to do with it anyway. She looked like she'd drowned, lying there, so I just left her.

"I went back to the big rock but Spíros was gone. For a moment, my heart leapt and I thought maybe he'd swum away, somehow, but then I saw him again, staring back, falling, heard that terrible sound again and I knew he must be dead, as Sam said, and that the sea had taken him.

"I sat there crying for ages until the first streaks appeared in the sky. It was the first day of my new life as a murderer. And it was only then that I realised I wasn't wearing the beret.

"My heart sank because it was a special thing for us. Spíros called me a brave, little rebel when he gave it to me three years ago. It was old, he said – an antique almost – and showed me a photo of his grandfather wearing it in 1968 when the Colonels stamped on the student riots in Athens. It was precious to me. Wearing it made me feel proud. And loved.

"In the grey light of dawn, I looked over the rocks for it. I looked everywhere. And then I looked over the sea for it and for Spíros. Nothing. The beret must have been in the water somewhere, but Spíros? I had no idea what would happen. Would he sink or float? Would he be carried out to sea or into the shore?

"Meanwhile, Sam was still lying there, and it was getting light. I decided it was time to leave if I were to get back without being seen. I picked up Spíros's clothes on the way. By the time I crept back into the tent, it was just after six in the morning."

"So, what happened then?"

"I knew Sam's body would be discovered soon, so I knew I had to get moving. I emptied my rucksack and put all Spíros's stuff into it, along with the clothes I'd just been wearing. I took my jewellery box with me but left the rest of my stuff in the tent, zipped it up and made my way around the back of the campsite and behind the town.

"It was still early. I don't think anyone saw me. I knew the ferry came at nine and I waited for over an hour nearby. I sneaked on at the last minute. There was hardly anyone on board. As soon as we were well clear of Síva, I started dropping clothes into the water, bit by bit. Then his phone, then his passport and wallet. By the time we got to Agía Rouméli, the rucksack was empty."

"But you came back. Why would you do that?"

"Oh, I knew I had to, Mr Fisher. People must have seen me that night. Manólis always had a soft spot for me but I didn't expect him to lie to the police – and then there were the people on the beach, the people by the fire at the beach bar ...

"I knew the police were likely to work out that she hadn't drowned, and if they heard that Sam and Spíros had got together, I would become a suspect. If I disappeared, that would make it worse and they'd come after me. And I didn't want to spend the rest of my life running.

"So, I set up my jewellery display near the tavernas at Agía Rouméli. Tried to pretend everything was normal though my heart kept juddering with fear and grief. Sold a few bits and pieces to the gorge walkers and then I found a cheap room for the night, but all the time I was thinking things through. The next day, Monday, I took the afternoon ferry and I'm back in Síva late afternoon. By the time you came on the Wednesday, Mr Fisher, I had my story worked out.

"I *so* wanted to tell you the truth, but I was afraid. I was afraid of the Greek police and their justice system. The police seem so aggressive sometimes. I was afraid that I'd be charged with murder or even double-murder and that would be the end of my life. I might have accepted that for myself, for what I'd done, but I couldn't accept that for my baby. For Spíros's baby.

"So, I decided to try and bluff my way out of the mess. But his death haunted me. It was all I thought about; all I saw in my mind's eye. Still is. Never Sam; only Spíros. I felt guilty because he died saving me. In my nightmares, his body floated in and they came for me. I might have killed myself were it not for the baby. I had to leave as soon as I thought I might get away with it. Come back to Latvia. Hide. You know the rest."

"And Uldis?"

"That was all true. It was the call from my sister that was the final prompt for me to leave and go to him. He knows nothing of my situation."

"Thank you, Kristīne." Nick looked at Thaní and then at Inga Petersone with eyebrows raised and his hand poised over the recording device. "Interview terminated at four twenty-two pm."

The machine clicked off and they all sat back with relief.

"When's the baby due?" asked Nick.

"Oh, not for almost six months yet. It'll be a spring baby."

"Whatever else happens, I wish you all the luck in the world with that."

"Thank you."

"Do you have a name in mind?"

"If it's a girl, I'll call her Gaida. It means *waited for*."

"And if it's a boy?"

"He'll have a Greek name. You know which one."

*

Jansons took Kristīne into custody to await the issue of the European Arrest Warrant and the procedures that would follow that. Leo and Thaní were booked on the eighteen fifty-five flight back to Athens but Nick wanted to make two calls before they left. First up was Leo.

"Hi, Nick. I was expecting your call. Yes, okay. You can call Jason's mother if you wish. Say he'll be released tomorrow morning at ten."

"Why not tonight?"

"Don't push your luck, my friend. There are procedures. And it's been a tough day."

Nick thought about going straight to where Jason was held, but it would be late by the time they got back to Crete and besides, the news shouldn't come from him.

"Jen? It's Nick. I have good news, at last."

There were shouts of joy from Stephen, tears of relief from Jen.

"Does he know?" she managed to ask.

"No. I thought I'd leave that to you."

"How can we thank you, Nick?"

"Jason's freedom is all the thanks I need, Jen."

"At least be there in the morning so he can thank you himself and we can all give you a massive hug."

*

Arriving at the hotel, back in Chaniá, Nick checked his watch. It was ten twenty pm. His phone pinged. The text message read:

I knew you could do it, Nicky. Next to the message was an emoji of a kissing face, with a J and an x. Somewhere inside him, a sputtering candle sprang back to life and ice walls started to drip.

It was a hell of a long drive for a drink, but Nick felt it was important. Seeing the place once more might be cathartic. More importantly, nascent friendships should never be left to wither on the vine.

*

The familiar sight of the dark blue and white café gave him a good feeling and he was pleased to see the owner in situ and the bar quiet.

"Kalispéra. You rent rooms?"

"I do, and I have one for you at fifty-five euros including breakfast, my friend."

"Breakfast will have to be early. I need to be back in Chaniá for ten."

"Breakfast at seven thirty, then. No problem."

"And the bar closes at two?"

"Yes, but with friends, it is sometimes a little later."

"Now you're talking. I think we'll need a bottle of something interesting and some of that jazz of yours. Then I can tell you about my day."

"So, the guy with the pony's tail – it was him?"

"No, it wasn't him."

"I didn't think he looked like a murderer."

"What do they look like, then?"

Stélios was putting on a jazz album.

"I mean he looked like a nice guy."

"He *is* a nice guy in his way. But he's lonely and insecure and he hasn't grown up. He's my age but with the heart of a foolish sixteen-year-old. He meets someone thirty years younger and falls head over heels in love and lust with her. The girl that was going to marry my son, as it happens."

"Your son's girl? My God, Nick."

"Why do you think I got involved, Stélio? Anyway, this girl is not what he thinks she is. She's a wild child. Likes to play dangerous and dirty, no boundaries. She gets away with it with this guy, Peter. She got away with it with my son Jason before that. But she didn't get away with it when she messed with the killer's man."

"But there were two bodies, no?"

"There were."

"Two murders, here in Síva?"

"The police have accepted that one of the deaths was an accident."

"But you have not?"

"And the court may determine that the other was a crime of passion."

"And this means what?"

"If we're right, the man died in an accident, the circumstances of which were so traumatic that it led this woman to lash out and kill the girl whilst blinded by fury. Momentarily out of her mind. A complete one-off. It'd make no sense to lock her up for several years."

"And if you're wrong?"

"Then we've been outsmarted by a devious woman who killed two people in a deliberate act of revenge. And may now walk free, if her sentence is suspended."

"Wow. Let's hope you're right, then."

A melancholy jazz trumpet was floating out over the water. Peace was returning to the world. Nick could almost feel his pulse rate slowing.

"Do you think we're all capable of murder, Nick?"

"I'm quite sure we are, given the right set of circumstances. To me, good and evil are two sides of the same coin. Just a flip away."

"And she flipped."

Stélios placed a bottle of Metaxá on the counter with two glasses.

"I think this might be a seven-star night, Nick."

"You're spoiling me."

"Do you know this album?"

"I'm not sure. Is it Miles Davis?"

"Well done. It is, but it's an early one; it's called *Ballads and Blues*. We can listen to this for a few minutes and then you can tell me the whole story."

The wistful purity of early cool drifted over them, the fiery spirit warmed them, and the Libyan Sea continued to lap the shingle as if nothing had ever happened.

CHAPTER 34

JOB DONE

Perhaps it was the quality of the brandy because Nick's hangover was not too bad, considering. It started to fade over the White Mountains and disappeared altogether by the time he reached the orange groves. He made it to the police station at nine fifty-eight and spotted Jen and Stephen in reception.

"Here's the man of the moment," said Stephen, all bonhomie now.

"Thank you, Stephen, but I rather think it's *Jason's* moment, don't you?"

"Christodoulákis already spoke to us. He told us about your brilliant interrogation."

"Oh, hardly that."

"He also apologised for holding Jason for so long, which we appreciated," said Jen.

"He didn't have to do that, after all," added Stephen.

"No, but he's a decent man. A good cop."

The swing doors opened and there was Leo, nodding and smiling. Nick wasn't sure he'd seen him smile before. Not like that, anyway. It made him look years younger. Tucked in behind was a paler, thinner Jason, looking like a tentative young rabbit emerging from the warren on the first day of spring.

"Can you spare me a few minutes when you're done here?" said Leo. Nick nodded.

"I'll leave you all to it, then," called Leo. Waves and smiles from Jen and Stephen. Sullen silence from Jason. They hugged him, making gleeful noises, but his body was limp, unresponsive. Eventually they backed off and Jason padded warily over.

"Are you okay?" asked Nick.

"I don't know what to say. It was Kristīne, I gather?"

"Yes."

"Why?"

"It doesn't matter now."

"It matters to me, Dad."

"Let's just say she suffered a moment of madness."

"Was Sam with Spíros?"

"It's complicated. He seems to have rescued Sam from drowning but then there was a terrible accident and Spíros died. Kristíne was there, blamed Sam and went for her in a wild rage. She's having his baby, but he never knew."

"Oh, wow. Nor did we. I might go see her. I liked her and I don't understand this. She was Sam's friend."

"That might not be such a great idea, mate. Anyway, it'll be a while before she's extradited. If I were you, I'd go home, spend some time with your Mum, catch up with your friends. If you still want to see Kristīne, you can always come back. You could come and see your old Dad, while you're at it."

Jason chewed his nails and searched Nick's face for a few moments. A trace of warmth had crept into those wounded eyes or was it Nick's wishful thinking?

"Yeah. Maybe I'll do that. I could pay my respects to Sam and her family."

"And get your career sorted out?"

"Hmmm. Anyway, Dad, thanks for everything you've done. I'd have been rotting in a Greek jail for years if you hadn't come to the rescue. I'm not sure I'd have coped with that, especially knowing I was innocent."

"You're my son, you idiot. Did you think I'd sit by and let that happen?"

"I shut you out, though."

"And I probably deserved that."

"I'm not sure you did. Not really."

"*Whatever* you do, son, I can never stop loving you. It's as simple as that. When you get to be a father, it will be the same for you. It's unconditional ... Now come and give your Dad a hug."

Nick felt Jason's bony body shaking as he gripped it tight. Gradually, they became one, the boy feeling the father's strength feeding into him, nourishing his body, calming his mind. Finally, Nick took a half step back but still holding Jason by the shoulders and looking warmly into his eyes, he said:

"Don't let what's happened rule your life, son. It was a terrible thing and you'll need some time to deal with it, to remember Sam, what you both had together. That's only natural. But, after that? Move on. Put this behind you. You're still very young; there's plenty of time to find love, happiness, success – whatever you want."

The temptation to tell Jason more about Sam's behaviour was palpable, but it would not help the boy, Nick concluded. If Jason spent the rest of his life with Sam up there on a pedestal, then so be it; there are times to be economical with the truth.

*

Leo's office was full of blue smoke. He was stubbing out a cigarette as he waved Nick in. Then he threw open the window, letting the smoke out and the sounds of traffic in. He extended his hand.

"Sit down, Nick."

Leo looked at him steadily and that unfamiliar smile was there again.

"Quite a day, yesterday."

"Yes. Sorry you couldn't be with us."

"Me too. Managing up, I think they call it – looking after the bosses."

"Brown nosing, we used to call it," said Nick, but Leo seemed not to hear.

"We Greeks are proud men, Nick, and saying *thank you* doesn't come easy. We resisted your help, to begin with, although we were getting nowhere at that point. We couldn't see beyond our noses in Síva but then you woke us up."

"Only to take you on a wild goose chase after The Westons."

"Wild goose?"

"It means a search that proves to be a waste of time."

"I love your language, Nick Fisher. So many mysteries."

"And then, of course, the Westons proved to be red herrings."

"Now you're teasing me!"

"Not at all. Red herrings are distractions; things that take the pursuit *away* from the main goal."

Leo was clapping and laughing.

"Bravo. That is perfect, my friend. So, you took us on a wild goose chase after some red herrings."

"I did."

"And what was that thing with the grandmother?"

"Don't teach your grandmother to suck eggs – because you don't need to. She already knows how to do it far better than you. In other words: *Don't presume to educate seniors with more experience than yourself.* Something like that, anyway."

Leo grinned. "I stand corrected, although my grandmother never did anything quite so disgusting, I'm happy to say."

He was friendly but serious now.

"So, Nick, despite all these rather odd distractions, you achieved exactly what you set out to do. Your son is free, and you helped us *nail the bastard* even if she wasn't so much of a bastard after all. So, well done and thank you."

Leo handed him an envelope.

"This is a small payment to cover your expenses and a there's a letter from my boss, the captain."

"There's also the small matter of my tent, when you've finished with it."

"It's already been returned to your ex-wife."

"Ah, well. I think my camping days are over, anyway."

Nick started to open the letter. Leo placed his hand on it.

"Open it later. I can tell you that it expresses the gratitude of the Chaniá Prefecture for your help in this case. It also says that we're open to the idea of working with you again, should a suitable case arise. We might even pay you a little next time. Would that be of any interest, Nick?"

"Well, I don't know. I have some gardening to do, a wall to build ..."

"You joke with me!"

"Of course. As I'm sure you know, I'd like that very much, Leo."

"So would I, Nick, and so would Thaní. We've enjoyed working with you."

"It's been fun, hasn't it?"

Leo sneaked a carafe of rakí out of a side cupboard and filled two small glasses. It was not yet eleven am.

"To the next time," said Leo.

"Bottoms up," said Nick and Leo shook his head in despair.

CHAPTER 35
HOME

By mid-afternoon, Nick was back in Saktoúria. He managed to creep back into the village without seeing anyone. At that time of day, most of them were taking a nap. It was always the most peaceful time of day; even the dogs stopped barking for a while. He badly needed some sleep himself, but he noticed a note and a business card on the doormat and the red light on his ancient Ansafone was flashing the unprecedented number two.

The business card was from some local stonemason, asking him to call.

The note was from Lena:

I assumed you needed me to feed the cat, so he has not died! If you want me to feed the man too, call me when you are back. I have pie!

He sat down. The first Ansafone message was from Lauren:

"Hi, Dad. Mum tells me you've saved the day, as usual. Glad you survived, at least. Call me when you get a chance. Lots of love."

He pressed the button again:

"Hi, Dad. It's Jason. I'm taking your advice. They're flying back in the morning and I'm going with them. But I'd like to plan a trip back here in early spring, if that's all right with you. Will you have a spare bedroom sorted by then? I'd like to come and stay for a bit. We have some serious talking to do, I think, so get some rakí in. I might want some career advice, too. I'm looking at the police, believe it or not. Haha. No, really! And thanks so much, Dad, for everything. Speak soon."

But Nick wasn't speaking anytime soon. He was already horizontal, eyes closed. The machine beeped a couple more times, then clicked itself off.

＊

The impending extradition of Kristīne Ozola was all over the Chaniá Post the following morning and a copy was being passed around the tables at the kafenío. When a rumpled Nick rolled up at almost ten, there was spontaneous applause from the scattering of villagers, which included Yiórgos and Kóstas and Xará and a few faces he barely recognised. Kóstas gave him a bear hug.

"Kaló mína, Níko. You big hero, man. Breakfast is for me."

"Gosh, is it November already? Thank you, Kostí. That would be very nice."

Nick waved and gave the crowd a cheesy grin, then sat down at Yiórgos's table.

Yiórgos reached over and pumped his hand.

"Good job, Níko."

"You want eggs?" asked Xará.

"Any bacon?"

"Óchi. We don't have."

"Eggs, tomatoes and toast would be lovely, and lots of my special coffee, please."

"Okay, Níko."

Nick noticed she was still there, looking coy. Then she bent down and pecked him on the cheek before running off with his order.

"How sweet was that?" said Nick.

"Every woman loves a hero."

After Nick had enjoyed his breakfast, Kóstas joined them.

"You will come tonight, Níko?"

"What's happening?"

"We will be at the kazáni to taste the rakí. You will come, yes?"

"This is the first from this year's grapes?"

"Not the first, but it will be the best, for tonight the rakí is from the grapes of Panayiótis." He had raised his voice and now a diminutive old man stood, raised his cloth cap to reveal a nut-brown pate and took a bow.

"I'd love to come, Kostí. Efcharistó!"

Yiórgos cut in:

"But first, you will come out with me this afternoon. We find fish to cook at the kazáni."

"Now why would you want *me* of all people to come fishing with you, Yiórgo?"

"It's okay. I will catch fish. You will tell me about the case. Deal?"

"Well, I guess I could use the fresh air. Why not?"

Yiórgos's bearded face lit up like a beacon.

*

Later that morning, Nick called the stonemason out of curiosity.

"You left your card for some reason?"

"Yes. I am stonemason, general builder. What you want?"

"Well, I don't want anything."

"Wait, please. I come."

Before Nick could put him off, he had ended the call.

Twenty minutes later, just as Nick was leaving a message for Lauren, a motorbike pulled up outside. Nick opened the door to find a man of about forty with a boy of perhaps twelve or thirteen riding pillion. The boy spoke first:

"You call my fadder. He bring me because my English better."

The man beamed and stretched out his hand.

"Well, I'm sorry that you've wasted your time, but I do my own building work."

There was a rapid exchange between father and son. It didn't sound like Greek at all.

"You have wall. You will show us, please."

"The roof terrace wall, you mean? Well, all right, you can look, I suppose."

They followed Nick up the stone steps and the older man started inspecting the wall. He was shaking his head, looking over it and round it.

Any moment there will be a sharp intake of breath, thought Nick.

The man was frowning at the unplanned curvature now. Then he kicked it.

"Oi!" yelled Nick, "what the hell are you doing?"

Another exchange of words. *Perhaps it's Albanian*, thought Nick.

"My fadder say is not safe but don't worry; he can fix. Stone, not block. And he will make beautiful. You will be proud."

"Look, I'm sure he's very good at his work but I can't afford it. No money." Nick pulled the pockets out of his shorts for emphasis.

"Your friends pay," said the boy.

"Now why would they do that?"

"No. They pay. Wait."

He was rummaging in the pockets of his trousers. "Here."

It was a copy of a receipt for three hundred and fifty euros. At the top was written something that approximated to Stephen Buckingham. The boy pointed.

"This man pay. Is to thank you."

"Stephen! Who'd have thought it? Ha! And this will be enough?"

"Yes. My fadder say is two days' work. Monday, Tuesday. Finish. Entáxei."

*

The party at the kazáni started early. The entire village was there, gathered around the wood fire which burned under the still, many staring as if hypnotised at the clear spirit plopping, drop by drop, into a large, metal bowl. Trestle-tables and benches were set up inside, and dishes of olives, tzatzíki, dákos, stuffed courgette flowers, fried aubergine slices, Greek salad, lamb and pork meatballs in tomato sauce and chicken in lemon sauce were being assembled, along with baskets of fresh bread and copper carafes of local wines. A smell of potatoes frying was coming from the kitchen and mixing with the wood and cigarette smoke. Outside, a charcoal barbecue was glowing in readiness.

Nick and Yiórgos were the last to arrive. Yiórgos was still wearing his bobble hat from the boat and each held a basket. At the door to the kazáni, he held Nick back.

"I will go first, Níko."

There was a collective cheer as Yiórgos was spotted. He put up a hand to hush the applause.

"Please, my friends. Thank you, but your cheers are premature. It was not a good day for me; I have only these for you." He showed them the basket with just eight mid-sized fish: three mullet and five bass.

There was a groan of disappointment and mutterings from the crowd. There were over thirty people, so those would not go far.

"I sorry …"

Yiórgos threw up his hands in self-disgust and walked out. The villagers looked at each other in confusion. Outside, Nick was holding the other basket. Yiórgos grabbed his arm and marched straight back in.

"… but happily, my friend Níkos, star of the police service yesterday, has saved us all once again."

He pointed to his basket and Nick took the cue and upended his. A further five silver fish dropped from it and the cheers started.

"No more *Óchi Psári*. Now we can truly call him Fisher-man!" Yiórgos yelled over the din.

The crowd shrieked with delight. Nick raised his arms and grinned. Rakí glasses were thrust into the hands of the new arrivals and Nick downed his in one. To more cheers, Lena stepped out from the crowd and kissed him full on the lips. Then, moving her mouth close to his ear, she spoke in a deep, salacious voice:

"Playing the hero is all very well, Nick Fisher, but now I will have to *slap* you for missing your Greek lessons."

THE END

LEAVING A REVIEW

If you have enjoyed reading my book, it would be wonderful if you could find a minute to complete a short review of *The Unforgiving Stone* on your chosen retailer's website. Thank you!

Alex

THANKS TO EVERYONE

Two people never let me forget that I was supposed to become a writer, one day. They were the burrs under my saddle, the nagging voices of my conscience, and they kept the dream alive through the many years when my head was elsewhere. One was my late brother: artist, musician and songwriter David. The other was my good friend Stevie Brown. For their unswerving faith in me, against all odds, this book is dedicated to them.

One person made a direct and significant contribution to *The Unforgiving Stone*. We devised the plot of the first draft together and came up with the character and back story for *Nick Fisher*. She later put a great deal of work into a review of the book and a substantial edit of the story. She is my very good friend Leonie Carter McMahon and she has my sincere thanks and gratitude for all her help and support. I hope she, too, will become a published writer before too long.

I would also like to thank:

Jericho Writers for introducing me to Gary Gibson, whose insightful, editorial assessment helped me raise the stakes for my protagonist and bring him to the front and centre of the story.

Friend Alexandra ("Sandy") Smithies whose background in journalism helped me through some plot challenges and some detailed copy editing, and all for the price of a carafe of rakí and a plate of meatballs.

Friend Ruth Pedley who found time from her busy schedule to give me detailed feedback on every line of this novel in her supportive and quirky style. It is so encouraging when someone savours your use of words and spots your little jokes. Ruth got it all, and her input was very encouraging at a difficult time. I hope her novel *Blind Chance* makes it into print very soon.

All the members of Eastcott Writers, especially founder Andrew ("Andy") Larter, for their support and feedback over the last three years, and Andy, Judith Hawkins and Helen Parker-Drabble, in particular, who were kind enough to read and review this novel for me. Helen's book *Who Do I Think You Were? – A Victorian's Inheritance* is an engrossing study of Victorian culture and its psychological legacy.

All my other brave beta readers, including my half-brother, Dr David Tune, and good friends George Schrijver, Christine and Bob Hoare, Kathrina Valters, Gina Zagni, Kenrick Ghosh, Catherine Stead, Steve Clark, Peter and Denise Simon.

And lastly, but by no means least, you for buying and reading my novel. I hope you enjoyed it and will look out for more Nick Fisher books.

ABOUT THE AUTHOR

Alex abandoned a career in finance at the age of forty-nine and spent a few years staring at the Mediterranean, contemplating life and loss. Finally, he accepted what his heart had always known. So, he joined a local writing group, Eastcott Writers, then also Jericho Writers in Oxford. And he began to write.

Over the next three years, he completed his debut novel, *The Unforgiving Stone*, the first in a series of crime thrillers set on the island of Crete and featuring British protagonist Nick Fisher. The second in this series is expected in early 2021.

He also wrote a collection of short stories, *The Late Shift Specialist*.

Simultaneously, he has been working on a novel in a different genre, a black comedy set in the world of corporate finance.

Born in Derbyshire, Alex now divides his time between Wiltshire and Crete, where he has an old, stone house in the central south of the island, between the Amari Valley and the Libyan Sea.

CONTACT

If you would like to get in touch with Alex, please visit his website: www.alexdunlevy.com where you can join his mailing list, if you wish, and find out about any special offers, or just drop an email to alexdunlevyauthor@gmail.com

He can also be found on Facebook and Twitter.

Made in the USA
Las Vegas, NV
21 February 2021